THE THIEF KNOT

A GREENGLASS HOUSE STORY

BY

KATE MILFORD

WITH ILLUSTRATIONS BY

JAIME ZOLLARS

CLARION BOOKS, AN IMPRINT OF HARPER COLLINS

HARPERCOLLINS PUBLISHERS

BOSTON NEW YORK

※

Clarion Books
3 Park Avenue
New York, New York 10016

clarionbooks.com

The text was set in HMH Bulmer MT Std.
Interior design by Sharismar Rodriguez

The Library of Congress has cataloged the hardcover edition as follows:
Names: Milford, Kate, author. | Zollars, Jaime, illustrator.
Title: The thief knot : a Greenglass House story / Kate Milford ;
with illustrations by Jaime Zollars.
Description: Boston ; New York : Clarion Books, [2019] |
Summary: When Marzana's parents are recruited to solve an odd crime,
she assembles her own team, including a ghost, to investigate the kidnapping.
Identifiers: LCCN 2019004987 (print) | LCCN 2019012810 (ebook)
Subjects: | CYAC: Mystery and detective stories. | Adventure and
adventurers—Fiction. | Kidnapping—Fiction. | Mothers and
daughters—Fiction. | Ghosts—Fiction. | BISAC: JUVENILE FICTION /
Mysteries & Detective Stories. | JUVENILE FICTION / Action & Adventure /
General. | JUVENILE FICTION / Fantasy & Magic. | JUVENILE FICTION / Fairy
Tales & Folklore / General.
Classification: LCC PZ7.M594845 (ebook) | LCC PZ7.M594845 The 2019 (print) |
DDC [Fic]—dc23
LC record available at https://lccn.loc.gov/2019004987
ISBN: 978-1-328-46689-1 hardcover
ISBN: 978-0-358-34820-7 paperback

Manufactured in the United States of America
22 23 24 25 26 BRR 10 9 8 7 6 5 4 3

*To Gracie and Charlotte,
the newest members of the Knot;
and, as always, to Tess, Griffin, and Nathan,
my favorite adventuring companions*

CONTENTS

one   WHERE NOTHING HAPPENS   1

two   THE DINNER GUEST   20

three   THE KIDNAPPING   29

four   OF TRUFFLES AND BACON   48

five   MARYMEAD   58

six   EMILIA   73

seven   FLETCHWOOD   87

eight   THE MAGICIAN AND THE CAMOUFLEUR   99

nine   STRATEGIES   132

ten   MILO   145

eleven   HOORAY, HOORAY, HOORAY!   160

twelve   NEXT-DAY POST   190

thirteen   DUMBWAITERS   198

fourteen   GENUS *ANHINGA*   217

fifteen   THE THIEF KNOT   230

sixteen   SECRETS AND FINDINGS   247

seventeen   OTTOMY STALLS   264

eighteen   NUMBER 72   282

nineteen	RUM THINGS	296
twenty	THE SNAKEBIRD	304
twenty-one	SHELL GAMES	319
twenty-two	COTGRAVE WALL	339
twenty-three	THE REVERSE OF THE MESSAGE	360
twenty-four	THE SACRIFICE CHAPTER	377
twenty-five	THE BELOWGROUND	386
twenty-six	MERGENTHALER STREET	398
twenty-seven	PAS DE DEUX	412
twenty-eight	THE TREASURE HUNT	421
twenty-nine	LOCKER 152	429
thirty	VERSES	442

one

WHERE NOTHING HAPPENS

HE TWO CONSPIRATORS met as planned at three p.m. at
the corner of Cafender and Thomasine Streets, in front of the
old iron façade of the Ambrose Bank. Yesterday the façade
had been whimsical in design, framing each window and entrance
with wrought vines and flowers and bells in the shape of lilies that
rang periodically for no apparent reason. Today the iron had dialed
down the caprice and reconfigured itself into something more befit-
ting a bank, with big staid columns topped by fussy capitals on either
side of the massive main doors. The perfect backdrop for a heist.

The taller girl, her seal-brown hair done in braids, caught the
glance of her shorter, pinker accomplice in passing. Then, without
a word, she pulled a pair of sparkly green sunglasses down over her
dark, deep-shadowed eyes, pushed herself off from the fluted column
she'd been leaning against, and strode up the street in the wake of a
young man the other had been following. She knew without looking
that her partner would follow at a safe distance.

Just as he had every afternoon for the past week, her quarry walked another dozen yards down Cafender Street, then stopped at the outside counter of a café where he purchased his usual (Americano, cream, two sugars). He sat on a bench and sipped his beverage. As he sipped, he watched — surreptitiously, but to the trained eye, his attention was unmissable — the jeweler's shop across the narrow lane.

The tall girl in the green shades strolled over to the counter and bought a cup of decaf with milk and cinnamon, which she carried to a table under the café's awning, where she could see the man with the Americano as well as the shop he was watching so closely. A moment later her friend appeared with her own cup and a basket of steaming soft breadsticks, which she deposited wordlessly on the table between them. The two sat in silence, watching.

The man finished his coffee. He stood up and tossed his cup into a trash can next to the bench.

So far, so normal.

Then something happened that had not occurred before. The man hesitated. Instead of heading off to the right, as he had done each of the past six days he'd been casing the jeweler, he leaned back on the bench and glanced at his wrist. A moment later, in what was clearly an arranged meeting, a young woman the girls had never seen before walked up and sat next to him.

The two adults on the bench looked at each other.

The pink-cheeked girl peered at them over the rims of her tortoiseshell shades. "He's nervous."

The woman spoke. The girls leaned as far as they dared in the direction of the bench and could just barely make out her words. "You ready for this?"

The taller girl grabbed her friend's arm at the same time Tortoiseshell reached for hers.

"I think so," the man said quietly, glancing back at the jeweler's. "Yeah. Yeah, I'm ready. You know what you're going to say?"

The woman nodded. "I'm your cousin from out of town, and I'm looking at rings so I can bring my soon-to-be-fiancé back to take a look while we're visiting."

"Get her talking."

"Won't be a problem." She grinned at him. "Shall we, *cousin?*"

He nodded resolutely. They stood, and headed for the street. They waited for a break in the passing bicycle and foot traffic, then crossed.

The two girls looked at each other.

"Is this going down?" asked Green Sparkles in a disbelieving undertone. She glanced at her own watch. "At three p.m., in broad stinking daylight?"

"I . . ." Tortoiseshell hesitated. "Oh, wow. I think it might. Mars, what do we —"

"Shhh." Green Sparkles put down her coffee and stared as the man opened the door of the shop for his companion and followed her inside. Both girls scrambled to their feet and nearly fell over their own chairs and several bicyclists in their haste to follow them. All efforts at subtlety gone, they darted to the jeweler's front window, crouched side by side to peer over the bank of red cyclamen flowers in the window box, and watched as the man they'd been tailing and his obviously fake cousin walked up to a pretty redhead who was busy arranging merchandise in a glass case on one counter.

"They're just going to —?" the taller one began.

"I mean, they're trying to look like customers, right?" her companion finished.

The man and the young woman at the counter exchanged a few words; then he introduced the lady he'd come in with. Green

Sparkles frowned. "Looks like they know each other, doesn't it? The guy and the girl who works there?"

Her companion nodded. "Yeah, it does."

"That seems less-than-ideal. If you were going to rob a place, you wouldn't go somewhere they knew you well enough to identify you, right?"

"*I* wouldn't, but then I also wouldn't have been so obvious about casing the joint."

Inside, the redhead and the fake cousin fell into deep conversation. After a moment, the redhead began to take rings from a glass-topped display table and arrange them on a piece of black velvet on the counter. The fake cousin made a show of trying some on, and after a moment she even had the redhead popping rings on and off her own fingers. "She's good," Green Sparkles said, shaking her head. "That sidekick, she's really good. Look, she's got the woman who works there acting like they've known each other all their lives and they're just out shopping together."

A second clerk materialized from a back room and began polishing a nearby, already-spotless counter. He probably thought he was playing it cool, but it was obvious to both girls that he suspected the aimlessly browsing young man might be up to something and thought he'd better keep an eye out.

"That dude knows something's up," Green Sparkles observed.

"No question," Tortoiseshell agreed.

The two women tried on a few more rings each, but they both kept coming back to one particular item. At last, after a final bit of discussion, the redhead wrote a few lines down on a business card and handed it to the supposedly almost-engaged woman. Then the fake cousin pointed across the shop to a different counter, and the two women strolled over that way together.

"She's not going to leave all those rings out, is she?" Tortoise-shell whispered. "That would be ridiculously careless."

But the redhead did, in fact, do exactly that. The polishing co-worker was still there, but he was on the other side of the counter. If the would-be thief was fast, he could sweep up a bunch of diamond rings in a single whisk of his hand and be out the door in a matter of seconds.

"Here it comes," Tortoiseshell said. "Get ready."

"I was born ready," Green Sparkles muttered back. "Game time."

"In three . . . two . . ." The countdown died on her lips. Inside, the unobtrusive coworker plucked up one of the rings from the velvet it lay on — it was the one the two women had lingered over the longest — gave it a fast polish, and popped it in a box, keeping his hands low and almost out of sight the whole time. The "thief" took a credit card from his pocket and passed it clandestinely across the counter. Both men glanced now and then at the two women, but Fake Cousin had managed to position herself and the redhead with their backs to them.

"This might not be what we think," Tortoiseshell said slowly as the polishing coworker handed back the credit card, along with the maroon velvet box that now contained a ring. Not a minute too soon, either. The fake cousin and the redhead finished up with whatever they were looking at on the other side of the shop and returned to the man who now held the box behind his back. Fake Cousin took a camera from her pocket. The young man opened the box and got down on one knee.

The redhead squealed loud enough for it to be audible through the window. The man stood, and she threw her arms around him.

Outside, both girls wilted. They looked at each other for a moment. Then, without discussion, they returned to the café across the street.

The door to the jeweler burst open. "She said yes!" the young man called to the world. Applause broke out from everywhere except the table where the two girls slumped in their chairs.

Marzana Hakelbarend yanked off her glittery green sunglasses, folded them, and dropped them next to the breadsticks. "We should've known."

Nialla Giddis switched out her tortoiseshell shades for a pair of ordinary glasses with cat-eye frames, then leaned back in her chair and laced her fingers behind her head. "Yep. Know why?"

Marzana let out a deep breath and tried to retroactively spot the clues she'd missed — the clues that should have told her there was nothing nefarious to see here. But as hard as it was to spot evidence of something being off, it was even harder to spot evidence pointing to normal, because normal was just . . . well, *normal.*

So the guy had looked a bit shifty. A high percentage of people who lived in the city-within-the-city of Nagspeake called the Liberty of Gammerbund *were* shifty — or had been shifty to one degree or another in a previous life, and hadn't quite managed to shed the sense of having to watch their backs. So that was . . . pretty normal.

"I should've known it was nothing because . . . because . . ." She spotted it just as the guy and his new fiancée came out of the jewelry store, hand in hand, waved goodbye to the fake almost-engaged cousin, and all but skipped up the street together. He was wearing sneakers, but they were loose on his feet. Rather than tying them, he'd knotted the laces separately, the better to be able to slip them on and off quickly. Marzana's neighbor Mr. Waltersson did that with his shoes, and they went flying off the minute he tried to go faster than his usual amiable shuffle. Marzana saw it happen every time Mr. Waltersson's kid, Griffin, took off down the sidewalk and his dad had to sprint to catch him.

"His shoelaces," Marzana finished. "If he were up to something that might involve running, he'd have at least tied them."

Nialla opened her mouth, frowned, and considered their quarry's shoes. "That's a good point. But no." She turned back, shaking her head. "You should've known because we live in the Liberty of Gammerbund, and this is the place where nothing happens. It's where previously exciting people come to live boring lives. If they do anything exciting at all, they do it someplace else." She took a breadstick from the basket and pointed it at Marzana. "A thing you know perfectly well, seeing as how even you had to leave to have an adventure."

"This has a very disappointing ring of truth to it," Marzana grumbled.

Nialla reached across the table and patted her shoulder. "Have a breadstick."

"I don't want breadsticks; I want jewel thieves!"

"Shhh." Nialla put a finger to her lips. "I know, Mars, but breadsticks are all I have to offer right now."

They drained their cups and sopped up the last motes of cinnamon sugar with the last bits of bread. As Marzana shrugged on her backpack, a folded piece of paper dropped onto the table between them. Marzana just had time to glimpse the back of a tall, thin person in an unseasonable trench coat, his or her head covered in a dark beanie, before he or she rounded a bend in the street and went out of view.

Nialla picked up the note and gasped. Marzana glanced down at it: a piece of letter-sized paper, folded four times, with something printed on the inside. Nialla had unfolded it only once, and part of a sentence had been scrawled in blue ballpoint there: *if you're really looking for jewel thieves.*

The girls eyed each other warily. "No way," Marzana whispered. She held her breath as Nialla finished unfolding the paper. For a heartbeat Nialla did nothing, just stared down at the page in her hands, which was angled in such a way that only she could see it. At last she turned the printed face toward Marzana.

Now Appearing Every Friday
at the Hadley Park Bandshell
Gammerbund's Premier Cover Band

THE JEWEL THIEVES

Playing All Your Favorite Gems
from 6 P.M. to 11 P.M.

(Picnic Dinners Available from Raegan's on the lake)

Marzana dropped her head into her hands.

"Know why you should've known this would turn out to be nothing?" Nialla inquired.

"Because no actual jewel thief would be stupid enough to actually write 'If you're really looking for jewel thieves' on anything?"

"No." Nialla folded up the flyer again. "Because *this is the town where nothing happens.*" She tapped Marzana on the forehead with the paper to emphasize each word, then tucked it gently into her clenched fingers. "Not even, apparently, original music."

They left the café and headed out into Cafender Street. "Want to go by Lucky's?" Marzana asked.

Nialla brightened. "Sure. The new Quester is supposed to be in this week, I think."

Competition for the title of Crookedest Street in Town was steep in the Liberty of Gammerbund, where a very limited amount of space, centuries of random building on the bones of what came before, and a total lack of planning, even when planning might have been done, had combined to create a labyrinth. Still, Hellbent Street, the location of their friend Lucky's shop, Surroyal Books, was one of the prime contenders. Marzana and Nialla edged between the masses of bicycles overflowing the stands where Hellbent met Wilkens (bikes weren't allowed on Hellbent because of all the blind turns) and strolled up to a door below a faded gold awning decorated with pairs of antlers silhouetted in dark gray.

A familiar cluster of mismatched bells rang as they stepped inside. The store was lit by sconces that peeked out from between the tall, book-stuffed shelves, their old, chipped, and painted glass shades casting warm watercolor light in pools and puddles. The main room also had a register counter, a very tiny coffee counter, a fireplace, and half a dozen chairs scattered about. The fireplace was always hidden behind a pair of iron doors and whatever seasonal decorations trimmed the hearth. Since it was June, there was an elaborate beach scene wherein waves cut from blue construction paper lapped on crinkly brown tissue-paper sand.

The owner, a young blond woman busily shelving from midway up a rolling ladder, glanced over her shoulder and waved. "Hey, you two. Nialla, before you ask: Yes, and it's there." Lucky shifted her armful of books onto one of the wide rungs of the ladder and pointed to another stack on the desk by the register. "Two copies. Knock yourselves out."

"Thanks, Lucky." Nialla made a reasonable effort to merely elbow past Marzana rather than flinging her bodily out of the way as she darted for the pile, where two gold-upon-green book spines peeked out from between Harry Potter #5 and *The Oracular Records Department: Codifier Z,* the latter of which was presently tearing through the local lower schools like a rampant flu bug. Nialla, however, went straight for the green-and-gold books.

She—and, to an only slightly lesser degree, Marzana—was all about Quester's Crossroads, a series of Choose-Your-Own-Adventure–style tales in which some choices were available only if you solved puzzles, accomplished certain tasks, or discovered certain objects in the story along the way. One book, *Quester's Crossroads: The Carry-Witchet,* had actually required readers to sacrifice an entire chapter if they wanted to follow a particular plot thread: you could successfully read the hidden, alternate Chapter Six only by cutting out the correct series of words on the even-numbered pages of Chapter Nine, putting those pages with their holes over the odd-numbered pages of Chapter Three, and reading the words that were revealed. Readers who did this wouldn't be able to follow any threads that required any part of Chapter Nine.

But a handful of savvy fans (including Nialla) had discovered that if you reassembled all the words cut from Nine in reverse order, you got a short story set in the world of the book, in which the reader discovered a powerful, ancient bronze key. It was like finding a bit of treasure in a role-playing game that you could use further on in the campaign. The question was: Was this story part of the book's story, or was it just extra, for fun? And if it *was* part of the story—which, Nialla had argued, it had to be, because it was literally, physically made up of parts of the tale—where was the prompt that told you when you got to jump from the events of the book into the scraps-of-cutout-words short story? The whole setup of the books was that you read a section, and then at the bottom of the page you were given choices about how to proceed and directions about which page to go to depending on which choice you made. But there were no such instructions at the end of the scrap-world story. Where were you supposed to reenter the main plot? *Could* you? And what were you supposed to do with that key?

Controversy reigned, because the other thing about Quester's Crossroads was that you could take stuff you collected in one book — potions, tools, codebooks, assorted magical items — into the next one. The author, who everyone figured was a pseudonym for a rotating collection of writers, was silent on the matter. So ever since *The Carry-Witchet,* there were two schools of thought on how to read the volumes that followed: with the scrap-world key, or without. Unlocked, or locked. And it changed things a lot; reading the books unlocked, there were more scrap-world digressions, more information, and occasionally more special items, but each time you used the key, it required you to sacrifice something. That meant there were parts of the story you simply couldn't have if you wanted to use your key (or any other thing you brought back from the scrap world).

And then the QC-fan community really went berserk when someone discovered that Chapter Three in *The Stop-Hole Abbey,* the sequel, had the same number of pages as Chapter Three in *The Carry-Witchet.* For whatever reason, it had occurred to that reader to put the holey pages from *The Carry-Witchet* over *this* Chapter Three — which you couldn't do if you were using the scrap-world key because Chapter Three was a sacrifice chapter if you were reading *The Stop-Hole Abbey* unlocked — to get an alternate Chapter Three, one that gave you a prompt that finally led to the elusive, it's-there-in-the-Table-of-Contents-but-nothing-appears-to-send-you-there Chapter Eleven.

Quester's Crossroads, Nialla often declared, was bonkers in the *most* awesome way.

Nialla passed one of the books to Marzana, then went wordlessly over to claim a chair by the fireplace. Marzana started to follow her, then hesitated. The other seat by the hearth was taken by an older kid she didn't know. As Nialla sat examining every detail of the front cover, the other kid glanced up.

Marzana changed course and headed for the little coffee bar instead, where she took as much time as possible getting a bottle of soda out of the refrigerator, dropping two dollars into the honor jar, and popping it open with the bottle-cap opener mounted under the counter.

Meanwhile, over by the fireplace, the older kid was speaking. "I tried with those, but I hated not knowing what I missed in the sacrifice chapters."

Sorry, Nye, Marzana thought, *but better you than me.*

"I get it," Nialla said, examining the table of contents with the air of someone studying a sacred tome.

"Feels like they just want us to buy two copies," the other kid said. "Feels like a crappy marketing thing."

"I don't think there's a way to do it where you don't sacrifice something at some point," Nialla said distractedly. "I think that's kind of the idea."

The kid refused to take a hint. Marzana steeled herself for the inevitable. She'd seen this before.

"But doesn't that drive you—"

"I am not interested in debating with you whether or not the things I love are crap," Nialla announced in a loud singsong voice, turning the page with a flourish. "Please go back to your own book."

"Fine, I was just—" Nialla stared him down until he turned back to his own reading material, at which point Marzana figured it was safe to join her. As she sat, the kid glanced up again, saw that Marzana had the same book, and visibly debated with himself whether or not to start the conversation anew. Marzana stared down at the cover, focusing on the illustration there: a flourishing marketplace built out of industrial scrap, set within the stone-walled ruins of what looked like some kind of church. At last she felt the kid's eyes shift away from her entirely. Only then did she feel herself begin to relax.

She opened the book at last. Rather than reading, however, Marzana found herself reflecting back on their first effort at finding a real-world adventure.

Nothing happened in the Liberty of Gammerbund. Or, okay, fine, things happened, but nothing *exciting*. Ever. Nothing, as far as Marzana could see, that would give her anything like the thrill of a caper, which is what she really wanted.

Nothing interesting ever happened in the Liberty, yet this didn't seem like it should be true. And it *couldn't* technically be true. In any place where this many people lived their lives in such close proximity, some percentage of them had to be up to something. And you'd think it wouldn't be that hard to cross paths with those people. But of course, there was the complicating factor that a high percentage of people in the Liberty of Gammerbund had absolutely been up to something outside the walls, and had come to this enclosed city-within-the-city for sanctuary. It led those folks to be cautious here. They might still get up to things out in Nagspeake proper, but they tended to wipe their feet of all that before they came home.

Exhibit A: Marzana's mother.

Marzana's mother was the quintessential lady with a past. She went by Barbara, but that wasn't her name. She had taken Marzana's father's last name legally but often didn't use it. When she left the Liberty, she took on new monikers as if they were part of her wardrobe: just as different situations or social settings required different dresses, so did they also require different *noms de guerre*. And you couldn't fault her for her caution; she had been both a thief and a smuggler, and when she'd been a girl not much older than Marzana, already the captain of a hugely successful smuggling crew, she'd had to fake her own death to escape to the Liberty. She and an entire *crew* of her compatriots, some of whom had come to Gammerbund, some of whom had taken new identities, and some of whom had fled Nagspeake altogether. And when she left the Liberty now, it was generally on the kind of errand that caused Marzana and her dad to order pizza and sit up into the wee hours of the morning over coffee and tabletop games, pretending it was just a father-daughter bonding night and not a vigil.

Outside the walls of the Liberty, the woman who called herself Barbara Hakelbarend was a subversive genius, a folk hero, a cipher. At home she was Marzana's mom, and if she had a few uncommon hobbies, well, so did lots of people around here.

Marzana had seen her mother at work exactly once — once that she was aware of, anyhow. That had been this past winter. And being part of that caper had been everything Marzana had dreamed. She wanted more.

But Nialla was right. Nothing interesting ever happened in the Liberty of Gammerbund. And poor Nialla didn't even have a parental legend to live vicariously through — not that Marzana had much material to work with in that department, either. Her mom and dad were big on something called *deniability*, which depended on Marzana knowing as little about her mother's past as possible. Nialla's parents, though, were ultra-ordinary. The Giddises owned a coffee shop. The biggest excitement of the past year was the day the new fancy espresso machine had almost blown up.

A quiet voice spoke from her side. "You left this on the counter." Lucky set Marzana's soda on the little table beside her chair.

"Thanks."

Lucky nodded but didn't leave. She knew how Marzana felt about small talk, so this wasn't going to be that. Marzana closed the book — she hadn't started reading anyway — and looked up. "Did you know there's a little group that comes every week and uses the history room for game campaigns?" Lucky asked quietly.

Marzana shook her head. "What do they play?"

"Risk, right now. Before that was D&D. I don't think they've decided what to do next, but I'm pretty sure this game is winding down. I thought you might be interested in an introduction. The core group is a family of three," Lucky added, breezing past the introduction idea as if she could feel Marzana's hackles already going up. "The kid is an older teenager. Then there's his friend and his friend's sister, who I think goes to Marymead and might be in your grade. Amelia something. Do you know an Amelia?"

There were two Amelias and an Emilia at Marymead Intermediate School. The Amelia in eighth grade was boy crazy to the point where Marzana frankly doubted any big brother would bring her to a game night where another male friend was going to be present. The Amelia in sixth grade was a prodigy at outdoor sports and appeared to require huge efforts of will to sit still in a chair for more than five minutes. Which left Emilia Cabot.

"Is it maybe Emilia with an *E*?" Marzana asked.

"Could be."

"If it's Emilia, I don't really know her, but I know who she is." Marzana was an introvert. Emilia Cabot, though, was a loner. She was one of the Commorancy Kids: the small community of Marymead students who, for whatever reason, boarded there during the school year.

"Well, anyway, they play on Tuesdays at four. No big deal, but if you happened to be here tomorrow, I could introduce you."

"Thanks." Marzana opened the book on her lap again and reached for the soda bottle. "I'll think about it."

Lucky gave a wink by way of acknowledgment and departed.

"You going to come back tomorrow?" Nialla asked without looking up.

"I don't know." Marzana loved games of strategy. And as extended social interactions went, they were surprisingly less painful than most. People didn't expect you to make small talk, and games tended to provide clues to help you work out the necessary conversation, which made it much less stressful. Still, there was a lot of treacherous ground to navigate between the point where you were introduced to a possible gaming group and the point where you were safely seated and embarking on an adventure together. And there was no guarantee that, even if she went through all that agony, they'd invite her to join their campaign. "Probably not." It hurt to admit it, especially since a pre-configured adventure would've been better than nothing right now.

"You should." Nialla carefully set her book face-down on the arm of her chair. "I need a straightedge."

"Already?"

"Yeah. I could really use my X-Acto knife. I can't believe I didn't bring my kit." She got up and headed over to the shelving cart. "Hey, Lucky?"

While Lucky and Nialla assembled the necessary supplies for whatever calculations and/or disassembly the first ten pages of the book required, Marzana turned over the possibility of joining the Tuesday game. But try as she might, she just couldn't picture herself actually doing it. Not any part of it: not the walking in, with or without Lucky, and introducing herself; not navigating the pitfalls of asking if she could play; not successfully being invited to join; not sitting down and taking a turn. No. *Nice idea, Lucky, but it never had a chance.*

Nialla flopped back down into her chair with a metal ruler and began tearing pages from her brand-new book with surgical precision. Marzana watched her with fascination; the boy who'd spoken up before was staring and turning purple in his effort not to comment.

"I can't believe how . . . how ruthless you are with those," Marzana observed. "It kills me every time I have to do anything to them."

"Me too," Nialla said, preoccupied. "But if you don't, you only get part of the story." She looked up suddenly. "It's like you, if you decide to come back tomorrow. It's difficult, but these are the adventures we have, and this is what it takes to be part of them."

Marzana rolled her eyes. "I hate when you get philosophical."

"I know. Especially when I'm both philosophical and right."

There was no good response to that, because it was true. But Nialla returned to her excision without waiting for an answer, because real friends didn't make you waste words on things you both already knew.

The tearing sound of the next page coming out reminded Marzana that they hadn't actually paid yet. With a sigh, she leaned over into the space between the chairs where they'd thrown their respective bags and fished first Nialla's wallet out of her satchel, then her own wallet out of her backpack. She got up and walked over to the ladder where Lucky was back at work with her shelving. "Sorry to keep bugging you, Lucky, but you'd better take our money before we forget."

It was six before Marzana finally made it home. Usually this would've been cutting it a bit close to dinner, but tonight it turned out she needn't have worried. Her parents had a guest.

The Hakelbarends lived in a part of town called the Viaduct, which was a bizarre little district built above and below a very wide, stone-arched bridge. From any standpoint, the bridge was totally unnecessary. It wasn't exactly a bridge to nowhere, because you could actually go up the broad stone stairs on one side, cross it, and come down on the other, but it didn't really *bridge* anything. There was no water underneath, nor any transitways; the space inside the arches was taken up by shops that clustered against the supports, leaving narrow arcades for passage through. It would be one thing if the bridge had been constructed of the same old iron as the Ambrose Bank façade. Old iron operated by its own rules, and structures made of it sometimes did appear more or less out of nowhere and apropos of nothing. But the Viaduct was made of limestone and granite. Somebody—a whole crew of somebodies—had intentionally put it there. It was as if a civil engineer in an age gone by, when designing the Liberty, had thought, *We'll probably want a bridge or two in this place at some point down the line. I'll just stow this one here for safekeeping until we need it.*

But very little open space in the Liberty stayed that way for long. Clusters of tall, narrow houses had been built on the span and the shops had moved in below, and three restaurants had set up open-air cafés along the edges of the broad stairs, with kitchens nestled below at ground level.

Marzana's house, Hedgelock Court, was near the center of the span, a particularly tall and narrow specimen with an assortment of odd balconies that poked out here and there like tree fungus, and a turret that overhung the street below it. That street, Crossynge Lane, also happened to be the most direct route from one side of the bridge to the other, which made it the de facto Main Street of the Upper Viaduct.

She let herself in through the door under the turret (there were other ways in and out of the house, some less obvious than others because, well, *Mom*), went to the combination rack-and-bench by the door to hang up her backpack, and discovered that someone else's coat was hogging her usual peg.

Murmuring adult voices led her past the living room and through a wide arch into the dining room. There was her mother, seated at the far end of the long side of the oak dining table: tall and dark-haired, with eyes perpetually shadow-rimmed, which made her lined face seem paler than it was. There was her dad, deep-voiced and dark-skinned, sitting to her mom's right at the head of the table. He was even taller, tall enough to be seen over the centerpiece of sunflowers and purple grasses, and the room's one window gleamed behind him so that right now he was mostly in silhouette. They were in conversation with a sandy-haired man who sat across from Marzana's mom but had turned a bit in his chair so that his back was to the doorway—a much younger man, if his voice was anything to go by. A stranger, she thought at first, but as the conversation fell away and her parents smiled at her in welcome—welcome, and something else, she thought briefly, filing that impression away to analyze later—the stranger turned and she realized she *had* met him before. Something in her stomach fluttered. Not because of the person, but because of the memories surrounding him.

"Hey, Marzie," her mother said. "You remember Emmett, don't you?"

"Sure," Marzana replied. "We met at Greenglass House."

Greenglass House. The site of Marzana's one and only True Adventure.

two

THE DINNER GUEST

A GUEST FROM OUTSIDE the Liberty. A guest from Green-glass House!

Emmett Syebuck smiled at her. "Hi, Marzana." He was youngish—or younger than her parents, but then her parents were on the older side, anyway—bespectacled, and almost aggressively ordinary in appearance, which Marzana suspected was a look he cultivated. Emmett worked for Nagspeake's customs department and at least occasionally went undercover, as he had during the visit to the inn on the hill below the Liberty where he and the Hakelbarends had first met.

Then Marzana's excitement curdled to cold and leaden fear in her stomach. *Emmett is a customs agent.* She glanced instinctively at her mother, looking for clues as to whether this was a friendly visit or not: Was her mom's face paler than usual? Were her dark-rimmed eyes harder? Was there warning in them?

The worry must've shown. Emmett's smile faded and he held

up a hand. "Everything's fine. I'm not here in any official capacity. I came for your parents' help, actually."

"And we invited him to stay for dinner," Mr. Hakelbarend added. "I was just about to take the roast out."

"Weren't you supposed to play chess with Aunt Marie tonight?" Marzana asked. There was no Aunt Marie, and none of the Hakelbarends played chess.

"No, that's tomorrow night," Marzana's father replied with a wave of his right hand. *No danger here. All is as it's being represented. Don't worry.*

Marzana relaxed. "I'll set the table."

"I'll help," Mrs. Hakelbarend said.

Her husband nodded at a pale wooden cabinet on the wall behind his chair as he got to his feet. "Emmett, there are a few bottles of wine and a corkscrew on the sideboard here, unless you'd rather have soda or a beer."

"Wine's good." The customs agent saluted. "I'm on it."

Marzana followed her parents through a swinging door in the wall behind Emmett's side of the table and into the kitchen. "Everything's really all right?" she whispered.

"Really and truly," her mother assured her as she opened a cabinet and took out a stack of plates. "His visit has nothing to do with me."

"Then what's he here for?"

"He hasn't quite gotten to that part," her father said. "I'll admit, I'm curious. He called this afternoon to ask if he could come by, but he didn't want to say anything over the phone." Mr. Hakelbarend had been a customs agent himself, once upon a time. He pulled on a pair of oven mitts.

Marzana's brain began firing off a whole new series of instinctive danger warnings. Her father could cook, but mostly he made easy stuff like spaghetti and tacos. Her mother was extremely adept at ordering out. Neither of them had made the roast he was about to take from the oven. "Dad," Marzana blurted, "where's—"

"Honora put it in before she went out to her bridge-club meeting. She left a note about when to take it out." He pointed to a cork board on the wall where the note in question was tacked, although *tacked* felt like the wrong word for a note held in place by the curving blade of a paring knife shaped like a bird's beak. The note said in a shaky, spidery hand: *Roast out at four bells on the dot. On. The. DOT.* The final "dot" was underlined three times.

"Dad, it says four bells," Marzana said hastily. "Four bells is—" She did rapid calculations. "Six thirty."

"I know."

"But it's not six thirty," Marzana protested, edging away from him. Nothing good came from ignoring Honora's instructions about dinner. Ever.

"It's six twenty-seven," Mr. Hakelbarend said easily. "Close enough."

Marzana glanced at her mother and noticed that Mrs. Hakelbarend had backed away from her husband too. "Three minutes, Peter," she said in a vaguely warning tone. "We can wait three minutes."

"I'm telling you, she went to bridge club," Mr. Hakelbarend said. He opened the oven door. Mrs. Hakelbarend hugged the plates in her arms to her chest. Her husband reached in. Marzana held her breath. He took out a steaming roasting pan.

The door to the walk-in pantry at the back end of the kitchen burst open, and a grizzled old woman, tall and thin, tattooed and knotty as spent rope and browned to the shade Marzana's mother referred to as "old-sailor ocher," all but fell out of it. She pointed a playing-card holder at Marzana's father, brandishing it like some kind of exotic, fan-shaped weapon. "Did I not leave a *perfectly clear* set of exactly *one instruction* that says the roast comes out at four bells? Because I believe I left a *perfectly clear* set of exactly *one instruction* saying precisely that, and *oh yes, there it is,* I'm looking *right at it,* and there's the clock, and it's no sort of four bells yet, and nonetheless there's you, sir, and may I please know *what* precisely you're doing with *that,* as it's not four bells and there's a clock *right there* as says so?"

"Aha!" Mr. Hakelbarend dropped the roast on the stove, grabbed a spoon from a jar on the counter, and jabbed it right back at her. "I *knew* the wish to catch me out would overpower any actual need for human interaction you might still have in that warped old heart of yours. No bridge tonight after all, eh, Honora?"

"I most certainly do have bridge tonight," Honora said with dignity. "But didn't I just know *someone* here wasn't going to mind my instructions? Because, begging your pardon" — she didn't bother to sound like she cared much about the pardon — "*someone* doesn't, generally." She reached back with her empty hand and flung the pantry door open in triumph, revealing a folding card table and the three other members of her bridge club stuffed in between the shelves of provisions. As the Hakelbarends stared, Mrs. Macready reached up to help herself to some chips from a can on the shelf behind Miss Unwin. Mrs. Ileck steadied the electric camp lantern on the table.

"Hi, there, ladies," Marzana's mother said, waving her fingers over the plates.

"You're having your bridge game in the pantry?" Mr. Hakelbarend asked slowly.

"And good thing, too!"

"Stand down, Honora," Mrs. Hakelbarend said in an amused voice. "We have company."

Honora jabbed the card holder at Mr. Hakelbarend again. "And see you put my good carving knife back where you got it, sir. Begging your pardon, but you're always putting it in the wrong spot in the knife block." Then she shuffled back into the pantry, pausing only to say to Marzana's mother, "That's a good man you've got there, ma'am," before shutting herself and the three other ladies back in with the potatoes.

Marzana shook her head, grabbed a handful of silverware and napkins, and went back out into the dining room. "Everything all right?" Emmett asked cautiously as he pulled the cork from a bottle.

"Our housekeeper's playing bridge in the closet," Marzana said, arranging napkins, knives, and forks. Emmett had been sitting where she usually did, so she set herself a place across the table, next to her mother. "Just a Monday night."

Emmett nodded like this made perfect sense. He set the bottle on the table and peered into the sideboard cabinet. "Are these glasses okay to use?"

"Sure."

Her mother emerged next with the plates and a glass of water for Marzana; a few minutes later her father came out with the carved roast and a bowl of potatoes and carrots.

"Thanks for this," Emmett said, pouring wine for himself and Marzana's parents. "I didn't really plan this trip well. It took longer to get through the warder's office than I'd anticipated."

Marzana's mom nodded. "That'll happen."

"Georgie sends very breathless hellos, by the way," Emmett added in a not-very-convincing casual tone as he handed the wine around and took his seat. "It'll be a while before she gets over her awe of you." Georgie, a thief by profession, was one of the few people in Nagspeake who knew that, on evenings when she wasn't undertaking heists most people would assume to be impossible to pull off, the mysterious master thief known only as Cantlebone could usually be found at Hedgelock Court helping her daughter with math homework.

Mrs. Hakelbarend grinned. "I like that girl."

Emmett grinned back. "So do I."

"Have you spoken to Milo's family since December?" Marzana asked a little impatiently, reaching for the bowl of vegetables.

"I saw them in January at Clem and Owen's wedding. Not since, though. What about you? Thank you," Emmett added, taking the proffered plate of roast from Marzana's dad.

"We've been trying to schedule a time to go stay at the inn for a weekend, but it hasn't worked out yet," Marzana replied.

"I'm sure it's just a matter of time. And school's out here soon, isn't it? It's already out in the city proper."

"In two weeks," Marzana said, trying to rise above the unfairness of those extra fourteen days.

"That should make things easier."

"We hope so," Mrs. Hakelbarend said. Conversation lapsed into murmured thank-yous and clinks of silver on china as they passed plates around. Then Marzana's mother cleared her throat. "So."

"So," Emmett repeated. "Shall I come out with it, or would you prefer to wait until after dinner?" Not particularly subtle code for *How much should I say in front of Marzana?*, she guessed. Marzana caught her father's eye, and he winked consolingly at her. Conversations like this often left both of them out.

"Hard to say," Mrs. Hakelbarend said. "You tell me. Is it appropriate dinner conversation?"

"All fairly aboveboard, actually," Emmett told her. "Potentially awkward, but that's the worst of it."

"Awkward's okay." Marzana's mom set down her cutlery and folded her hands. "Let's have it."

Marzana tried not to let her jaw drop right down into her food. This was different. Ordinarily whenever people showed up at Hedgelock Court for any sort of interesting conversations with her mother, her parents instantly invoked deniability and kicked Marzana right on out of the room.

"All right. Well, I need a favor. This isn't technically my purview — it's not a customs thing — but I have a detective friend who's heading up a case, and he thinks the trail's leading to the gates of the Liberty."

"How, exactly, is the trail leading here?"

"He thinks his suspect has gone into hiding somewhere inside the walls."

Mrs. Hakelbarend raised her shoulders. "Your friend should start extradition proceedings."

Emmett gave her a *Who are you kidding?* kind of look. "The warder almost never approves extradition from the Liberty of Gammerbund."

"No, that's very true. But it's the only advice I have."

Emmett leaned back in his chair. "Interestingly, I suspect in this case, it would probably be granted. But my detective buddy would have to know who he was looking for. He has it narrowed down to three suspects, and there's no way the warder will allow them all to be taken back to the city proper just for questioning." He spread his hands. "Enter Emmett, stage right. My friend has no contacts here. I do." He smiled. "Sort of."

"And your friend knows this?" Marzana's mom said in a flat, warning tone.

"No, of course not," Emmett said quickly. "I mean, he doesn't know anything specific. He's desperate, and we've been friends since primary school. I convinced him to take a break for lunch this afternoon—he'd been working all night; I don't think he'd eaten since breakfast yesterday—and he talked me through the case, hoping for a fresh perspective. I asked if I could reach out to some people and see what I could find out. Now," he admitted, smiling a little apologetically, "he does know, obviously, that my job brings me into contact with, let's say, a number of characters. But I didn't offer any information as to where or to whom I was planning to go, and Thad trusts me, so he didn't ask."

"So what, exactly, is this favor you need?" Marzana's mom inquired.

"I need your help figuring out which of the suspects is the guilty party, so my friend can present his case to the warder. And quickly. We don't have a ton of time."

"So you want me to . . . to what? To investigate citizens of the Liberty of Gammerbund on behalf of the Nagspeake Criminal Investigation Department?" Marzana's mom swirled her wine in her glass. Her eyes were hard. "You know this isn't done, right? Of course you do."

"Yes, of course I do, but you haven't heard what the crime is yet."

"Unless it's murder—"

"It's kidnapping," Emmett interrupted. "An eleven-year-old girl. Taken yesterday on her way home from camp."

Silence fell over the table. Nobody looked at Marzana, but she felt the weight of the room settle on her, along with a whole unspoken speech Emmett was smart enough to know he didn't have to actually verbalize. *Eleven years old. Marzana's not much older than that. Imagine it was Marzana, and you had to wait for some endless, arcane, intentionally obstructive bureaucracy to go through its creaky workings before the good guys could look for her properly. What would you do? What wouldn't you do?*

"I know it's not done," Emmett went on quietly. "But I also know it's not that simple. It *has* been done. Not often, and not publicly, but now and then, when it's merited. Something like it happened just ten years ago. The Liberty found a way, without compromising its sanctuary principles, to handle things when a truly dangerous person tried to claim asylum."

Now that silent weight in the room seemed to shift from Marzana to Mr. Hakelbarend. "Ten years ago it was a murder case," Marzana's father said at last. "But I suspect I would have done the same thing if it had been a kidnapping."

Emmett nodded. "This guy took a kid. He weighs his weight. The whole forty and more."

"No question." Marzana's mom frowned. "But you know I'm not a detective, Emmett. Neither of us is."

He shrugged. "You're what I have. And you have connections. A network."

Mrs. Hakelbarend sighed. "All right. Tell us what you know."

three
THE KIDNAPPING

THE GIRL'S NAME is Peony Hyde," Emmett began, retrieving a satchel from the floor between his chair and the one next to it. He took a manila folder and a notebook from inside it and flipped the folder open to where a photograph was paper-clipped to the top of a page covered with handwriting. Emmett passed the photo to Marzana's mother. It looked like a standard-issue school picture of a pale girl in front of a plain blue background whose dark hair spilled over her shoulders in two long side ponytails and whose teeth glittered with braces.

" 'Hyde,' " Mr. Hakelbarend repeated as he leaned over for a look at the picture in his wife's hand. "That rings a bell."

"Her father is Winston Hyde. If you follow city politics outside the wall, I'm sure you've heard of him. He's a politician — a mayoral candidate, and the favorite to win. City schools finished up for the summer last Wednesday, and Peony was going to start camp today."

It really wasn't fair that schools in the Liberty let out so much later than the ones in the city proper. Marzana stifled her irritation and tried to focus on the matter at hand.

Oblivious to this injustice, Emmett continued. "Yesterday there was a sort of 'Welcome, Campers' shindig at the site—I gather the organizers sort of made a party and last-minute registration drive out of the final setup for the camp. Peony went, but she didn't come straight home afterward. Initially her parents didn't panic—the camp is in their neighborhood, and Peony was given a certain amount of freedom to range during the day. But then yesterday evening, right about when they were starting to worry, a ransom note was delivered. The demands are ridiculous—it's a sum Hyde just doesn't have. He might be the front-runner, but he's not independently wealthy, and his campaign is practically broke—he's the only candidate who's refused to take contributions from D&M—and the whole city knows it. He could maybe cover the amount of the ransom if he diverted every penny his campaign has, but of course you can't just use campaign funds for other stuff, even if it's ransoming your own daughter. So the current thinking is that maybe a political opponent is trying to force him to use those funds illegally and bankrupt his campaign at the same time."

"Who delivered the note?" Marzana's father asked.

"Ten-year-old kid rode up on a bike and handed it to a member of Hyde's security detail. Said a person in a baseball hat had given him a twenty-spot to deliver it. No usable prints on the cash, nothing more by way of description. The kid wasn't even totally sure if it was a man or a woman; he thought it was a man but under questioning admitted he couldn't be positive."

"And the daughter didn't have a bodyguard?" Mrs. Hakelbarend asked, passing the photograph back.

Her husband shook his head as if he knew the answer at the

same time Emmett replied, "Well, he's got some now, but before the kidnapping I think he maybe had one guy assigned to him, and the family didn't have dedicated security. If he'd won and subsequently requested a guard for Peony, she could've had one, but these elections aren't expected to be dangerous. Not in these modern times, at least," he amended grimly.

"Is the kidnapping public knowledge?" Mrs. Hakelbarend asked.

"Nope. But it's bound to be eventually."

"And your suspects?"

"Well, three guys who have reputations for being available for unsavory work such as this are conspicuously quiet at the moment. We haven't been able to locate any of them in the last couple days."

"I'm guessing Hickson Blount is one of them," Marzana's dad put in. "He's been in the Liberty recently. Wouldn't look odd if he turned up again this week."

Emmett nodded. "He is. We also can't find Rose Mirassat, and the third one"—he raised an eyebrow—"is your old buddy Rupert Gandreider. His name came up almost immediately."

"Oh, Rob," Mrs. Hakelbarend said. She spoke in the kind of tone you'd reserve for a wayward child, except her eyes were hard as flint, and Marzana thought she caught the tiny popping sound of her mother cracking her knuckles delicately with her thumb, one finger at a time, under the table. They all knew Rob Gandreider. The last time they'd seen him, he'd been tied up and in Emmett's custody at Greenglass House.

"What happened with that arrest?" Marzana's father inquired, with a trace of humor that suggested he was pretty sure he already knew the answer.

Emmett's eyes narrowed. "*Somebody* left his cell unlocked two weeks ago. Totally by accident. Apparently. He was transferred out of our custody back in January, since his offense wasn't technically a customs matter, so it was a city lockup."

"He just walked out of jail?" Marzana asked. "How is that even possible?"

"Well, there's gross incompetence, or there's aiding and abetting," Emmett said with a shrug. "Take your pick. But look, we have no actual evidence pointing directly to any one of those three, other than Rob's very timely escape. They're just off the radar, and they could be up to anything, or nothing at all. But it's a place to start."

Marzana's mother finished her wine and passed her glass to her husband, who passed it on to Emmett for a refill. "So you want me to try to find those three, if they're here, and work out if one is likely to be involved?"

"Yes, and uncovering a little probable cause wouldn't hurt either," Emmett said. "I'll need every shred of evidence I can find if we're going to make a case for extradition."

"Do you think the girl — what was her name?"

"Peony Hyde," Marzana supplied quietly.

"Thank you. Do you have any reason to think Peony Hyde is actually in the Liberty?"

Emmett hesitated. "No idea. The simplest thing would be to find out from the warder whether any of those three came through with a girl matching Peony's description. But I gather the warder's records are entirely secret."

"There's that," Mr. Hakelbarend agreed, "and there's the further complication that outsiders are the only ones who have to actually declare themselves at the warder's gate. If you live here, you can come in and out by that or any of the other gates, with or without guests, and all you have to do is show your own warrant as a resident of Gammerbund. Rob Gandreider is a resident. The other two aren't, but all they'd need is an accomplice with a warrant to ferry them through."

Emmett nodded thoughtfully. "If you found Peony Hyde, I'd be over the moon," he said. "But really the primary thing I'm hoping for is to narrow down the suspects and help Thad — my friend in Criminal Investigation — to make a strong case for extradition as fast as humanly possible. Assuming one of them actually looks like a probability." He took a bite of his dinner and chewed. "I think she's elsewhere. That's my gut feeling. I just don't believe the Liberty tolerates this kind of thing within its borders, and I think anyone who'd seriously consider kidnapping a public figure's kid would know better."

"Except there's the matter of the ransom the parents can't raise," Marzana's dad pointed out. "Maybe this guy isn't as sharp as he thinks he is."

"Yeah," Emmett agreed. "It's weird. Rob Gandreider, for instance, would know better than to test the Liberty with a kidnapping, but it's possible he's removed enough from city politics up here that he might not know how broke Winston Hyde is. The other two might make a mistake about using this place as a getaway — though it's hard to see how they'd convince an accomplice from the Liberty to make the same mistake — but they'd have to be living under a rock to think they could get any kind of money out of Hyde. And honestly, if you were some kind of shadowy master criminal capable of pulling strings around the city to pull off a job —" He winked at Marzana's mother. "Speaking purely hypothetically, of course — if you could do that, and even if you were also a truly horrible human being, would you pull all those strings to put together a *kidnapping?* When the outcome is so unpredictable and there are so many crazy variables? I mean, you've got a hostage to handle and a ransom drop to negotiate, not to mention the potential sentence is far more severe than for even grand theft. If I were a master criminal and I had the wherewithal to pull a heist together, I'd rob a bank before I'd grab a kid."

Everyone ate in contemplative silence for a few minutes, Marzana included, though inside she was boiling with questions and a rising excitement. Nothing ever happened here. Except *maybe something was*. A kidnapping was horrible, and not the kind of excitement she ever would have wished for. But it was happening, practically right on her doorstep. And against all logic, here was all the information the authorities down in the city proper had on the matter basically being handed to her on a platter, along with the carved roast beef.

At length, Marzana's mother spoke up again. "What about . . . I don't know . . . clues at the scene? Were there any?"

"First, where do the Hydes live?" Mr. Hakelbarend interjected before Emmett, who hadn't quite finished chewing, could answer.

"Printer's Quarter. In the Molendinium neighborhood. Secluded, kind of. Their house is basically at the dead end of Watermill Street. As to clues . . ." Emmett shook his head, then tilted it to the side. *Well, maybe.* "The thing is, we don't know what the actual scene of the crime *was*. The camp checked in kids and any friends they brought to the welcome party, so we know she was there. They claim Peony was accounted for right up until the end of the event, so at first glance it looks like she was taken on her way home. The camp's held on the grounds of an outdoor museum that's more or less adjacent to her school, Watermill Elementary. It's about a mile from her house, but it's a pretty straight shot."

Marzana raised a hand hesitantly, changed her mind and lowered it immediately, then shrank as everyone turned to look at her anyway. Her dad gave her an encouraging nod, and Marzana screwed up her courage. "How could she get kidnapped on her way home if it was a 'pretty straight shot'?"

"A pretty straight shot in the Printer's Quarter is still fairly screwball," Marzana's mom said dubiously. "And if I'm remembering right, Molendinium is as screwball as the Quarter gets." She looked at Marzana. "It's like how we think the walk from here to Marymead is pretty straight, but really we mean it's *straightforward*. You only have to take a couple of streets, but those streets are awfully twisty."

"Exactly," Emmett confirmed.

"And none of her friends saw anything? Other kids? She didn't walk home with anyone?" Mrs. Hakelbarend asked, though it would've been Marzana's next question too.

"Apparently her best friend from school had recently started walking home with a different kid, and she didn't really hang out with that many others. Her parents had been hoping camp would help with that. Plus, I gather only one or two of her classmates live near the Hydes' house."

She must've been lonely, Marzana thought. Lonely and, during that walk home at least, sad.

"Anyway, we can make a pretty good guess about where it happened if it happened between camp and school, but that only narrows it down to a stretch of about a quarter mile. It's a spot where the street runs alongside the old towpath by Millrace Creek. Maybe someone in a boat in the water, someone on one of the bridges—" He made an exasperated noise. "But we can't be sure it happened after the party. They were doing a lot of setup, the counselors were getting to know the kids, and from Thad's notes, they seem pretty disorganized, especially considering they were using an outdoor space with a lot of opportunity for kids to get lost. The camp administrator says she was accounted for all day—that some of the faculty knew her from school, and the rest of them at least knew who she was. But there's no paper record and there's a lot of room for error.

It's possible she was taken from the party. In fact, I think . . ." He shifted papers, looking for something. "Yeah. The administration closed the camp for the week."

Mrs. Hakelbarend leaned across the table and pointed into his folder with her fork. "Is that the note?"

"Oh. Yeah. Well, a copy." He passed reproductions of the note and envelope across the table to Mrs. Hakelbarend, and Marzana leaned over for a look as her mother read.

YOUR *DAUGHTER* IS SAFE FOR
NOW THE PRICE *TO HAVE* HER BACK IS 1000000
WE WILL *SEND INSTRUCTIONS* ON SATURDAY
YOU WILL HAVE ONE DAY *TO PAY*

"The letter itself is on generic looseleaf," Emmett said. "And the text appears to have been cut from a comic book. We think both were Peony's, taken from her backpack. Her parents confirmed that she was reading a graphic novel series called The Sidledywry Knot. Her mom states that she was reading the most recent book—they'd bought it together the day before. That book would've supplied all the text in the ransom note."

"Could your friend pull any prints off it?" Mr. Hakelbarend asked.

Emmett nodded, but his face was grim. "Only Peony's, though. Watermill had done a child-fingerprinting safety event fairly recently, and the prints off the note matched the school's records perfectly. And those prints were all over it, including on the tape holding the words. We're pretty sure the kidnappers made Peony cut out the words and stick them in place herself."

Marzana knew a little about the Sidledywry Knot series; Nialla had been trying to get her to read it for months. Peony, who'd apparently had a falling out with her best friend recently and didn't really have anyone else, had been reading a comic about a crime-fighting bunch of superfriends. Marzana took another bite of her dinner, feeling even sorrier for Peony Hyde than she already had.

It sounded like none of the adults at the table thought the kidnappers had brought Peony to the Liberty. But what if they *had* brought her there? What if she was somewhere in Gammerbund, lonely and lost and scared? And what if—here Marzana let her imagination go a bit, because if she was honest, she didn't really believe this could be possible—the adults in the room were all barking up the wrong trees?

Her mother and father would track down Rob Gandreider, Rose Mirassat, and Hickson Blount and tackle the problem that way: by tackling the suspects. But it didn't sound like Emmett expected them to actually look for Peony herself.

What would it take, she wondered, to track down a missing person if you were starting from zero?

Another of those momentary lulls fell, when everyone at the table paused to get a few bites in. Marzana forced herself to do the same, and even to chew her food at a measured pace like a human in polite society, but her mind was racing. She was itching to call Nialla, but nothing was going to tear her away from that table until they told her to go. She had so many questions, but didn't dare interrupt again for fear of calling attention to herself. She was certain that at some point her parents were going to come to their senses and decide that it would be safest (or whatever) if she wasn't there.

When discussion resumed, Emmett moved on to practical stuff: contact information for himself and his detective friend Thad Something-or-Other, and last-known associates and locations in the city proper of the three suspects. Her mom and dad asked a few more questions. Conversation dwindled. Her dad got up to make coffee, and conversation fell away to nothing for a moment while the coffee grinder growled, and then again as the less-than-dulcet tones of Honora shouting coffee-making best practices came from the pantry.

In the midst of this, Marzana suddenly realized Emmett was talking to her. Her cheeks prickled. "Sorry, what?"

He smiled. "I said, what do you think?"

She shrank a little. Being asked a direct question like this without warning was deeply uncomfortable. Across the table, her mother winked reassuringly. "What do I think about what?" Marzana asked.

"I don't know." Emmett finished the wine in his glass. "I just wondered what you thought of the situation overall. Sometimes outside opinions are helpful. Ideas or questions that might have occurred to you that didn't occur to the rest of us, that kind of thing."

Marzana toyed with her water glass. "Okay, yes. I have a question. What happened with her best friend, the one who stopped hanging out with her?" Once she'd asked the first question, others came tripping out after it. "And if they usually walked home together, that makes me think they lived in the same direction, right? Even if they weren't hanging out, why wasn't the friend walking home by her usual route that day? Why didn't she go home?"

"All good questions," Emmett said. "Here's what I know: the friend was a boy named Hank. Not a *boyfriend*, I'm told, just a boy friend. And I guess it was one of those things where he had started hanging out with some of the boys in their class instead, and he'd drifted away from her."

Marzana nodded. This was a thing that happened. It had

happened in two of her favorite books, and then it had also happened in real life to Nialla back in their first year at Marymead Intermediate, when Nialla's neighbor and best friend at the time had gone to a different middle school and dropped her like a hot potato.

"But how long ago?" Marzana persisted. "How recent was it?"

"Recent, I think, but I'll check. As to why he wasn't walking to his own home by that route that day . . ." Emmett scratched his head. "You know, I'm not sure. I guess I just assumed he didn't go to the party. But I can find out." He felt behind first his right ear and then his left, presumably for a writing implement that wasn't in either place, then found his pencil next to his silverware and scribbled something on a blank page in his notebook.

Marzana watched him write, gratified. "Because if they were planning this thing for a while, they would have factored in this Hank kid, right? They'd have been watching her, probably, but they wouldn't necessarily know all the social stuff happening between them, especially at school. If the split was recent, they couldn't know that Hank wouldn't be there, not at a party campers could bring their friends to. So unless it was a spur-of-the-moment decision to grab Peony on that particular day, there was probably another reason they figured she would be walking home alone."

"Maybe Hank had some kind of a standing Sunday obligation," Mrs. Hakelbarend said, tapping a finger meditatively on the table. "A sport or tutoring or whatever?"

Marzana smiled. *Mom thinks I made a good point.* "Yeah. It seems like there should be some reason the kidnappers knew, even before Peony and Hank stopped hanging out, that he wouldn't be with her that day."

"This is good," Emmett said, finishing his notes with a flourish. "Thad may already have looked into this, but if he did, he didn't tell me about it." He set down his pen and looked at Marzana again. "What else?"

She thought hard. "This is really about money?"

Emmett folded his arms and tilted his head again. "Well, there's a ransom note, and the only demand is cash. Can you tell me more about what you're thinking?"

"I'm not exactly sure, but you said anyone who was paying attention should've known Peony's dad didn't have any money. You said this could be about someone trying to ruin his campaign, but . . . I don't know." She hesitated. Maybe this was just an example of how the real world was more convoluted and less satisfying than mystery novels. Or there was stuff related to campaign money and politics that Emmett and her parents understood that she didn't. "Maybe I just don't get that part."

Mr. Hakelbarend returned with a tray piled with coffee, mugs, and the cream and sugar. "Not sure there's much to offer for dessert. Mrs. Macready's using the cookie shelf as an armrest, and I'm not asking her to move."

"That's all right," Emmett said. "Coffee is perfect. And I should really start home after that. It's a long trip back." He turned to Marzana. "The money doesn't seem like a particularly good reason to go through all the trouble and risk of this kidnapping, does it?" Emmett sighed. "That part of it is deeply strange to me. But for the moment, the ransom note is all we have to go on. Hyde's known enemies aren't the sort to snatch his kid. They're more likely to run attack ads on TV."

"Except you did say he was broke because he was the only guy who didn't take D&M money," Mr. Hakelbarend reminded him. Deacon and Morvengarde: the catalog company that had maintained a monopoly on what legally came in and out of Nagspeake for more than a century. Marzana, as the daughter of a smuggler, had grown up on tales in which the villains were almost always named either Deacon or Morvengarde.

"That's a possibility," Marzana's mom said, nodding. "Deacon and Morvengarde would probabaly very much like to keep anybody who might finally reduce some of their influnce as far from public office as possible."

"You know, that's a very good point. And Winston Hyde's a pretty vocal opponent." Emmett tilted his head. "Kidnapping, though?" he said dubiously. "That's a stretch, even for them." But he didn't look certain. Marzana's parents said nothing. It was clear they didn't think it was *that* much of a stretch.

"Are you taking the bus?" Marzana's dad inquired as he poured himself a cup.

Emmett tapped the side of his nose. "Belowground. That's why the warder took so long with me. I checked in from the inside of the wall. But there's only one afternoon bus from the city proper, and I'd missed it."

Mr. Hakelbarend whistled. "And you said you didn't have connections."

Emmett Syebuck snickered. "They're not *my* connections. They're Georgie's."

"Please bring her next time you visit," Marzana's mom said.

"I will." He rotated his coffee cup in his palms. "Speaking of the next time, there is one other thing I had wanted to ask you, though I recognize it's a long shot."

"A long shot?" Mr. Hakelbarend repeated, skeptical. "Compared to asking us to investigate on behalf of Criminal Investigation downhill, *this* is a long shot, whatever you're about to ask?"

Emmett laughed, but this time it was less amused and more

nervous. "Believe it or not, yeah. Down at CID, people are doing that whole no-thought-is-too-crazy kind of brainstorming, and one of the ideas that came up . . ." He took a breath. "I'll stop beating around the bush. Can you put me in touch with the Snakebird?"

Marzana's mother chuckled. To anyone else it would've sounded perfectly normal, but Marzana immediately felt the false note in the laugh. "No such person, Emmett. You've fallen for a myth. I also can't introduce you to the Tooth Fairy."

"Please." Emmett smiled, but it was a brittle smile with no humor to it at all. "Give me some credit. I may not know who he is, but I know he's out there."

Marzana's father put his hand on her mother's wrist before she could speak again, or worse, laugh that strangely false laugh.

Mrs. Hakelbarend relented. "I'm sorry, Emmett. That was — all I can say is, old habits die hard." She paused, thinking. "I can't introduce you. But I give you my word that if I think it'll help, I'll go to him myself. Is that sufficient?"

Emmett inclined his head. "Absolutely. Thank you." He slid his folder full of notes across the table. "This is for you."

Fifteen minutes later, the customs agent said his goodbyes and headed out into the evening.

"Got homework?" Mrs. Hakelbarend asked as she closed the door and reached for a pile of letters on the table in the entry.

"Homework?" Marzana sputtered. "After all that, you want me to think about *homework?*"

"Why? You got something else you'd rather think about?" her dad asked casually.

Well, gee, Dad, off the top of my head: Kidnappings! Suspects! What the heck is a Snakebird? "Now that you mention it, yes, and

I'm *willing* to put off my scintillating algebra assignment for an hour or so if there's something more exciting on offer."

Mrs. Hakelbarend groaned and held out an envelope from the pile. "Good. Reply to this for me."

Marzana slumped. "That is *not* what I had in mind. I meant—"

"We know what you meant." Marzana's dad took a look at the return address on the letter. "Hannah Jones."

"Must be Nick Jones's kid or grandkid or wife." Mrs. Hakelbarend stuck the envelope in her pocket. "Not the first, and won't be the last. I'll steam it open later and make sure it's not an emergency, then it's back to sender, like the rest."

Marzana made a sad face. "I understand where they're coming from."

Every now and then, her mom got letters from relatives of former crewmates who'd left Nagspeake decades ago. The exodus had been necessary after they'd blown up their ship, the *Lancet,* to evade capture by customs, supposedly leaving all hands dead—including Marzana's mother. As the older ones, particularly the ones who'd left town, began to pass away, their descendants invariably reached out to their legendary captain. *I know we're not supposed to contact you except in an emergency,* the letters always began. *But So-and-So always spoke of you in such glowing terms, we feel we already know you, and we hope you won't mind . . .*

"Oh, I get it. And I'm sure they'll keep coming." Mrs. Hakelbarend kissed her forehead. "Go do your stuff, Marzie. This thing of Emmett's . . ." She glanced at Marzana's dad.

"It's not something we're going to work out over the dinner table," Mr. Hakelbarend finished.

And you're done pretending I'm in it with you, Marzana realized with a sinking feeling.

She left the dining room in a huff, allowing her feet to fall just a bit harder with each step than was strictly polite. At least they hadn't asked her to help with the dishes. Then, belatedly, she realized she should have *offered* to help with the dishes because then they'd have had to let her hang around. She considered taking her backpack into the dining room, but she didn't actually have that much homework, and she never did it there anyway, so it would've just been weird. Instead, she went to her usual spot in the living room, plowed through the work, packed up, and took out *Quester's Crossroads*. She curled up on the sofa to read, and waited.

A few minutes later, her parents strolled in and sat in the pair of chairs across from the sofa. "So," Mr. Hakelbarend said.

Marzana turned a page. "So."

"You okay?"

"I'm fine. There's a sacrifice chapter coming up. Just trying to decide if I'm up for paper crafts tonight or what."

"Uh-huh," Mr. Hakelbarend said. " 'Cause you stomped out of the dining room kinda like you were a little cranky about something."

"Nope." She turned another page, even though she hadn't finished reading it.

"If you say so." He stood again, and so did her mother.

"Dad?" Marzana said abruptly. "What was that thing Emmett said to you about the kidnapper weighing forty?"

Mr. Hakelbarend rubbed his face. "It's a phrase used by customs — strictly unofficially — about how to decide when to pursue a suspect and when to turn a blind eye to whatever we thought they were up to. I think it's an old saying that came over from Britain, and *forty* refers to the reward in pounds attached to bringing in criminals who'd committed capital offenses. So waiting until a smuggler weighed forty meant waiting until they'd done enough mischief to be worth the trouble of pursuing them." He smiled at his wife. "The department wouldn't have the resources to go after big bugs like your mother if it wasted its time and manpower hauling in every citizen who brought a case of breadfruit into town or trucked in a box of rare dahlias or whatever."

"Any other questions?" Mrs. Hakelbarend asked with her own small smile.

Might as well have it out. "Well, yes, now that you mention it," Marzana burst out. "Why can't I help? I get why we have the deniability rules, and I get that you two would rather I didn't grow up to live a life of crime. But this ... this is different. This ... this *case*, or whatever, is unambiguously *good*. Why can't I be part of it?"

Her father sat again, leaned back, and crossed his arms, but not in a defensive way—more like in a *That's a good question; let me think how to explain* way. Her mother sat too, sighed, then propped her elbows on her knees and interlaced her fingers. She said quietly, "It was never just deniability, Marzie. We weren't only trying to keep you on the right side of the law. A job can be unambiguously good and still be dangerous." Mrs. Hakelbarend considered Marzana for a moment, then frowned a little. "You know that, right?"

"Yes, Mom, obviously." And yet, even as she said the words in a properly huffy tone, Marzana realized suddenly that she'd never actually *thought* about that part of it, the *danger* part of it. And from the look on Mrs. Hakelbarend's face, Marzana was pretty sure her mother knew that.

"If we do this," her mom said pointedly, "even if all your father and I do is gather information—we are tangling with people who were willing to take someone's child away from her family."

She let the statement hang there in the room between them. It was effective. So effective, in fact, that Marzana almost missed the obvious counterargument.

Almost.

"But . . . how does not telling me anything protect me?" she demanded. She picked up *Quester's Crossroads* and shook it at her mother. "This is how things always go horribly wrong in books, Mom. Withholding information from the kid. You want examples?"

"Sure thing," Mrs. Hakelbarend said easily. "I'll listen to your examples from literature; then you listen while I tell you about people I know in real life who didn't protect their kids and how awesomely that went. Protecting each other is why the crew of the *Lancet* agreed to sever ties, except in emergencies. Even when people do everything they can to protect their families, things can still go very, very wrong. You don't have to look any further than Greenglass House to know that."

"Touché," Marzana grumbled. Her mother hadn't severed ties with *everyone* from the *Lancet*—there was Honora, and there were others she still worked with now and then—but the Greenglass House example was a good one. "But . . . but Mom, wasn't I good on the Greenglass job? I helped, didn't I? I didn't get in the way, or get into trouble."

"You absolutely were wonderful, sweetheart," Mrs. Hakelbarend said gently. "But you also weren't there when the bad guy pulled a gun. It was awful enough seeing a weapon pointed at someone else's baby. I don't know what I'd have done if it had been pointed at you."

Which was nice to hear, but Marzana was pretty sure it wasn't true. Privately she doubted that *anything* threw her mother off her game. But that wasn't an argument she was going to win.

Her dad cleared his throat. "Look, there's room here for compromise," he said at the same moment Mrs. Hakelbarend said, "Let us think about it." They looked at each other and came to some wordless agreement. Then they turned back to her, a unified front. Marzana sighed. It was so unfair.

"Fine. I await your ruling on this matter." She got up, saluted only a little sarcastically, and headed for the stairs with that same not-quite-a-stomp tread.

As she turned the corner, she heard her father say, "I'm not sure it's fair to expect her to —"

"I know, I know."

A momentary pause, then her father again, in a tone of curiosity, if not disbelief: "Are we really going to ring up the Snakebird about this? And by 'we,' I mean you, obviously, because that bastard's never going to take my call."

Her mother chuckled again. "No, I don't imagine he would. Might not take mine, either. Maybe I'll try his granddaughter Tasha, the one who runs the coffee shop down in Shantytown. I think I heard she's trying to make a name for herself. I've never met her, but . . ." A pause, then louder: "Marzana, I want to hear your feet on the stairs, please."

Marzana sighed again, silently this time, and started up to her room.

If they weren't going to include her voluntarily, then it was their own fault if she had to make do with investigating on her own.

four
OF TRUFFLES AND BACON

EXCEPT NOT *quite* on her own. This was exactly the sort of thing she and Nialla had been hoping for.

Up in her room on the second floor, Marzana flopped onto her bed and reached for her phone. Then she stopped and drew her hand back. Might as well get everything she knew down on paper while it was still fresh. She reached for a blank book and pen she kept on her bedside table, then went to sit on a floor cushion tucked in the window nook across the room.

The window nook was an oddball addition to Hedgelock Court, the result of a previous owner having divided a larger bedroom into two smaller ones. Consequently, there was now one large room with a broad window looking over the roof of the house behind the building, and one smaller room with no windows at all and no good wall in which to put one. So that previous owner had chopped out the entire corner and replaced it with many-paned windows that met in a right angle and rose all the way from the floor up to the ceiling.

From that window nook you could see a slice of the Liberty beyond the Viaduct: clusters of dissimilar buildings piled up on top of one another and lit by a bizarre mix of electricity, gas, and candlelight; a patchwork landscape of shadow and mismatched spills and pops of light that glowed as the twilit sky darkened and a handful of stars began to show.

Marzana sat cross-legged and flipped past assorted failed attempts at writing a journal page each night or recording her dreams in the morning, all of which had fizzled out after about a week. When she came to a blank page, she recorded what she could remember of the text of the ransom note first: Your daughter is safe. The price to have her back is 1000000. We will give instructions on Saturday. You will have one day. After that, she wrote down everything she remembered Emmett telling her parents; then she started listing the stuff she wished she knew. With each new query, she got more irritated with herself. Emmett had invited her to ask questions. If she'd only thought of these then, she might actually have gotten answers.

FIND OUT:

* If Peony's father didn't have the money, and anyone who knew who he was should've known he didn't have the money, then why did this even happen?

* Who were Hyde's enemies, the ones who "aren't the sort to snatch his kid"?

* The party at the camp location seems like it offers more opportunities than the walk home. Find out layout and which other adults were definitely there.

She paused and looked gloomily over the list. It was going to be hard to get this information without being able to interview the people involved. Plus Emmett's detective friend had presumably already looked into all of these things.

This was the wrong tack to take. She shook her head and turned the page. What approach could she take that the adults hadn't already covered? Marzana thought for a moment and realized she was pinning her hopes on the long shot that nobody else really believed: that Peony might be here, in the Liberty. *So focus on that,* she told herself. *If that premise is true, then what questions does it raise?*

She started writing without hesitation. This was easier.

QUESTIONS:

* How would kidnappers have gotten to the Liberty?

* How would they have gotten in with an unwilling Peony without raising suspicion?

* Where would they have taken her to keep her out of sight? Is there a part of town that's better for that kind of thing?

* How would they have gotten her there without raising suspicion?

* How many conspirators would this require? How much would they all have to know?

She tapped the eraser end of her pencil on the top edge of the notebook three times, then added another bullet and wrote in all capitals: WHO THE HECK IS SNAKEBIRD AND WHAT WAS ALL THAT NONSENSE WHEN EMMETT ASKED ABOUT HIM?

Marzana snapped the notebook shut hastily as an authoritative knock sounded on her door. Honora's knock. "Come in," she called.

Honora strolled in, walking the rolling walk she'd never quite managed to lose even after thirty years as a landlubber. "Begging your pardon, miss, but I made some cider for the ladies and thought you might not turn your nose up at a cup or so."

Honora and the ladies typically had somewhat more potent sustaining beverages while playing bridge, but not even bridge night was enough to make Honora break the tradition of bringing a cup of cider—hot in the colder months, lukewarm in the warmer—to the daughter of her former captain. "Thank you, Honora," Marzana said, reaching up to accept the cup.

"What about a story tonight?" Honora asked, folding her hands behind her back. "Or would you rather get back to your writing?" She nodded at the notebook in Marzana's lap.

Marzana sat up straighter, her heart knocking against her ribs. The kidnapping had entirely pushed the evening's other meaningful event from her mind: the letter from Hannah Jones.

Marzana wasn't the only one who felt for the families who reached out in search of their relatives' pasts. Honora felt it too, though she did her best not to let it show. The former *Lancet* crew members who'd come to the Liberty of Gammerbund still kept in touch, sometimes even still worked together, because the Liberty afforded protections that didn't exist outside its walls. But everyone else had had to sever ties. Honora certainly understood all this, but she also clearly felt the pain of it.

The former captain's steward would never, under any circumstances, have protested any decision her commander made; Honora's loyalty to Marzana's mother was absolute. *Except* on days when letters came. On those days, Honora protested in secret. For every letter the captain refused to answer, she told Marzana a story.

"Do you have time?" Marzana asked. "What would the ladies say? Aren't they waiting?" *Please have time. Please have time. Please.*

Honora snorted. "Amy Ileck cheated worse than an Eel Street powder merchant in the last rubber," she said disdainfully.

Marzana snickered; Mrs. Ileck was one of the matrons at Mary-mead, and she was an absolute terror. So she also cheated at cards. Marzana filed that away for later use.

"And Henny Unwin was her partner and said nothing," Honora continued, looking like she wanted to spit. "But for all that, if Lula had played even halfway decent, we'd still have won, because Amy's idea of cheating is, in a word, dumb. So to hell with the covey of 'em. They can wait."

Marzana set her journal aside and turned to face the old lady, not daring to believe her luck. "Yes, please, then."

Honora grunted her assent and sat at the edge of the bed, think-ing. "I've told you about the time with the truffles, have I?"

"I don't think so." Marzana wrapped her arms around her knees and leaned back against the window. There was no "think" about it. There had been twelve letters, and therefore twelve stories. Marzana had spent the night after each one had been told repeating it to her-self until she had committed it to memory. There had been nothing about truffles so far.

Honora snickered. "It was a transport commission," she said, crossing one bony ankle over her knee. "We was to take the barky out of city waters to meet a boat offshore, take possession of a cargo of white truffles, and bring it in to a warehouse in Shantytown. And weren't we all pleased about it! It was time-sensitive, of course. Food jobs mostly always was. And o' course at that time Deacon and Mor-vengarde had a blockade up in the waters just off Nagspeake, so there was that complicating things." Deacon and Morvengarde again, up to more of the shenanigans that made smuggling such a big a part of Nagspeake's past and present, was almost always the villain when Honora told a story.

"So Captain V."—to Honora, Marzana's mother would always be Captain V.—"negotiated a bonus, which it was that if we managed to run the blockade, in addition to our payment, we got a nice cut of the cargo itself. We were to have two twenty-pound bags if we managed the job without incident.

"Now, there was a bit of a mystery about the contract, on account of it had come thirdhand through a broker who wasn't known for being clear about details, and owing to that it was anybody's guess as to whether we were to be carrying white chocolates or white fungus. Mostly we figured it was chocolates, because two twenty-pound bags of the other sort of white truffles would've been worth enough to retire on. Still, a nice treat of fancy-pants chocolates wouldn't have gone amiss, and the payment for the job was high enough to start with. So out goes us to meet the ship.

"And of course there was the blockade." She flashed out three fingers, each tattooed to show the underlying bone. "A triplicity of Morvengarde ships patrolling out past the battery." Honora waved her hand. "But luck was with us, and that night there was buckets on buckets coming down from on high like a blessing, a good whip of wind to spin it every which way, and a fog-wreath curling around everything for good measure. Them blockadeers hadn't a chance, not with Holy John and Saint Ben up in the heavens—the cross-trees, you get me—"

"I get you."

"Best lookouts for a storm, they were," Honora said nostalgically. "And it was Miss Meg at the tiller, who could take a schooner within a biscuit-toss of a wall of rocks and not break the tiniest bead of sweat or mess up that bright pink lipstick she always wore. So with a minimum of adventures, there's us pulling up alongside the ship out there in the Atlantic in all that blow."

She raised a single finger on which the bone tattoo was further decorated with scrimshaw as delicate as filigree, and her voice dropped a note or two. "But there's something amiss, and we can all of us hear it. And even as we're fending off the side of the ship, every man jack among us is crossing ourselves or scratching on the stays or whatever the hell we can reach to scratch on and those down on deck afraid to look up in case there's corposants or worse up in the rigging. Because it's a din as can only come from hell or beyond: screams and shrieks and noises like the cries of the damned as the torture comes on. And yet, there's the crew of the hell ship there, tossing us ropes and waving and calling through the wet like they ain't floating in a tub full of nightmare hullabaloo.

"So we does what we does, making fast and preparing to take charge of whatever it is this cursed ship's carrying in her belly and just praying it ain't a bunch of souls in bags. And the situation being what it is — the night, the noises, the all-of-it — it's your mother who goes up first, and I go up alongside with Tumbler Fletchwood and the Nicks — Nick Jones and Nick Larven and Nick Nackatory, that was — and we say our hellos, except for Tumbler, who's alternating psalms and snippets of apocalyptic poems under his breath for luck and can't be bothered with pleasantries. Meantime, we look around all syrup-ticious-like. And it's a shipshape deck and no mistake, but there's no cargo in view, just a wide-open hatch amidships and a line ready to bring something up out of it and those screeches pouring up and out like the reverse of all the wind and rain coming down. 'Heave!' shouts the bosun's mate, and round goes the winch, and with those screams still shredding up the night, up comes a sling with the first bit of our cargo." She leveled her sharp eyes at Marzana. "And *what* do you think it was?"

An expectant hush stretched between them. Marzana considered for a moment, figured out a pretty good idea, then debated whether or not it would spoil the effect if she guessed correctly.

Probably. She shook her head. "Not a clue."

Honora sat back in satisfaction. "Pig," she announced with a grin. "Cutest little monster you've ever seen. Only about yea big" —she held her hands about two feet apart—"but squealing like it had a complaint to lodge with the devil. And Captain V. goes over and looks into the hold, then leans back and says just 'Ah.' Then she sighs and folds her arms and looks up at that pig in the sling. So Nick Jones and Nick Nack and Larven and Tumbler and me, we go and look too. And it's all pigs. All these little white pigs. White *truffle-hunting* pigs."

"About twenty pounds each?" Marzana hazarded.

Honora tapped her finger to the side of her nose. "You have it." She scratched her head. "We never did figure out why they were contraband. There's no truffle hunting to be done in Nagspeake. But we did the job we was contracted for, and at the end of it, we got our bonus. Not two twenty-pound sacks of fungus nor two twenty-pound sacks of chocolates, but two twenty-pound sacks of pork still on their trotters." She cackled in delight. "We called them Anthony and Francis, which was a very literate joke to do with ham that Tumbler explained to me once but which I've forgotten, and they was ship's pets aboard the *Lancet* right up until the very end. I believe they lived out their retirement on a farm someplace in the States." Her voice softened. "Wherever it was Nick Jones retired to, I think it was."

She clapped her hands on her knees, the universal Honora signal that either a story had come to its conclusion or she was about to stand up, or both. Marzana applauded. "Thank you, Honora."

"Pleasure, miss." Honora nodded once, then stood, adding grimly, "Now I'd better see about the ladies." From the sound of it, she might well have been talking about prisoners in a brig rather than card players in a cupboard. It was just remotely possible that Honora had locked them in while she was gone.

When she was alone again, Marzana picked up her journal. She set it on her knees and leaned her arms on the flat surface as she looked out over her own private slice of the Liberty.

Honora had told the truffle story as if it had been a grand joke, but even though Marzana had gotten only twelve — thirteen, now — stories, she understood that it was what Honora had left out that really made the tale work. Pink-lipsticked Meg, the pilot and her mother's first mate, had to be able to take a schooner within a biscuit-toss of rocks because the back way out of Nagspeake by water was almost impossible to navigate under the best of circumstances unless you knew exactly what you were doing, never mind in a storm heavy enough to provide cover for running a blockade — a thing that, Marzana happened to know, didn't miraculously become *easy* just because it was raining, merely *possible*. The *Lancet* had had no crow's-nests, so those two lookouts up in the crosstrees had been out there standing on the yards with nothing but their own balance and whatever rigging they could hold on to in order to keep them in place as the ship tossed and heaved and the weather battered them, and they'd still been able to keep watch. Just getting to the punch line alive would've been an adventure. Then they had to get back home.

And they had. They always had.

It was this kind of thing that the writers of the out-of-town letters her mother always marked "Return to Sender" were looking for. Hannah Jones, related somehow to the Nick Jones who'd been a member of that boarding party—Hannah, who might even have met the pigs Anthony and Francis without ever suspecting that they, too, had adventures in their past. Jessie Colporter, whose letter last month had come in a fancy blue envelope from Key West, Florida. Somebody named Moth Fletchwood, who'd written three times last year before he'd finally taken the hint and who was presumably related to the Tumbler from this most recent story, the one who recited poems for good luck and had given the pigs their "very literate" names. Marzana had thought about writing back to them herself: *It's not you. She doesn't tell me anything either. I have to get all my stories from Honora Catharping.*

"And nothing ever happens here," Marzana said quietly. She looked down at the journal's marbled cover, visible between her wrists. Well, right now something *was* happening. She grabbed her phone from the bedside table and dialed Nialla, twisting the cord around her finger as she waited.

Three rings, then, "Hello?"

"Nye. It's Mars. I don't want to say much now, but I think I have something."

"Something like what? A cough? A fever? A knot in your back?"

"Something like an adventure." Marzana paused, listening for sounds in the hall. "But I think I'd better tell you at school. Someone might hear."

"You call me just to tell me you have something like that to tell me but you can't tell me until tomorrow?" Nialla demanded, exasperated. "Why would you do that? What kind of person does that?"

Marzana grinned. "Meet you in the usual place."

"Bite me. Fine." Nialla hung up, but Marzana could hear the smile in her words even through the phone.

five

MARYMEAD

THEY MET ON Tuesday morning as they always did: in front of the iron fence that ran the length of Marymead Interme-diate School, a brick nine-story mansion on a street called Pastern Wynd in the neighborhood of Pastern Rows. The iron out front was the old, shifting kind, so every now and then—if it had recently reorganized itself into a different style of fence and if she wasn't paying attention—Marzana almost could've walked right past the school without realizing it. What always saved her was the fact that Marymead students since time immemorial had been in the habit of leaving locks on the fence as mementoes, some haphazardly hand-engraved with names and dates and others enameled with a rainbow of sparkly nail-polish colors. The locks moved with the iron, but they were always there.

The mansion had been renovated and turned into a tall, loom-ing middle school. It had some quirks, because the original owners of Marymead, the Cotgrave family, had placed some interesting conditions on the bequest of the house to the Liberty Education Department—but once you got used to them, it was a pretty normal school.

Nialla was sitting on the bottommost of the wide stairs that led up to the door when Marzana arrived. She pointed an accusing finger at her. "You."

Marzana put up her hands. "Wait. Listen."

"*You* listen." Nialla got to her feet. "Actually, no. You *talk*. Talk *now*." Marzana looked around. The tiny front yard and the wide stairs were rapidly filling with students. Nialla shook her head. "No, ma'am. Don't even think about telling me 'Not now.'"

"If I couldn't tell you last night because someone might hear, how am I supposed to tell you in the middle of the entire student population?" Marzana demanded.

"This is infurating. Come on." Nialla grabbed the strap of Marzana's backpack and hauled her up the steps, through the entry hall with its huge chandelier, and from there on to the Great Saloon, which was open overhead all the way to the second floor, muttering all the way, "If we hurry, we can maybe get to homeroom before it fills up. Otherwise it'll have to wait until study period after lunch." There were no quiet corners or opportunities for privacy in the dining hall, and many a secret had been let loose into the school population by someone unwisely trying to share it with someone there.

"'Kay. Meet you back here in a minute." This, too, was a daily ritual: parting ways to run to their lockers and meeting back up again at the massive hearth at the back of the saloon.

But Marzana's locker, which was always temperamental, refused steadfastly to open. It was also geographically inconvenient—there were huge square turning staircases to either side of the saloon, but Marzana's locker was by the one that was farthest from their first-period classroom. By the time she and Nialla made it to their seats, they were only seconds ahead of the late bell. By the time the free-study period between lunch and algebra finally arrived, both girls were quietly going out of their heads.

They rendezvoused as they always did on the second floor, which housed some faculty offices and the art department, but that the students generally called the study story. The big, high-ceilinged Library was there, complete with ladders, galleries, and some rather inappropriate art that the Cotgrave family had specified must be left in place. (It was one of those bizarre conditions of the bequest of the house, and the director of Marymead circumvented it by means of some very heavy velvet brocade curtains.) There was a second, smaller library called the Study, and another, similar room called the Parlor. It was in the Parlor that Marzana and Nialla met at their usual couch, which faced a window looking out over the roof of the Orangery, an old-fashioned conservatory greenhouse that was the centerpiece of Marymead's back courtyard. Beyond the Orangery to the right, a miniature set of Italian fountains burbled; to the left lay a small English knot garden; and visible over the Orangery roof was the canopy of a Japanese camphor tree.

"This had better be good," Nialla said crankily as she threw her bag down on the floor between the couch and the window. "You have no idea the suspense I've been in. You're a monster."

"It's good." With a quick glance around to make sure nobody was paying them any special attention, Marzana took out her notebook. "It's a kidnapping."

Nialla's mouth dropped open, and her eyes popped gratifyingly. *"What?"*

"Shhh." They huddled closer, and Nialla listened breathlessly without interrupting even once as Marzana went over everything she'd heard at dinner the night before. "And they don't think she's here," Marzana finished. "They're not even really considering it. So that's what we're going to investigate."

"Okay." Nialla took a deep breath. "I'm going to ask you a question, Mars, and I want you to promise you won't take it personally."

"Fine," Marzana said impatiently. "What?"

Nialla hesitated. "Is this . . . is this real, or are we playing?" Marzana folded her arms tightly against her ribs. "I mean," Nialla said hurriedly, "I know the . . . the kidnapping's not a game. I mean us. Is there really anything we can do, or is this just us trying to — to play along or something? Don't be mad."

"I'm not mad," Marzana said. "I'm just thinking." Nialla nodded, chewed a cuticle. Marzana mentally reviewed the same things she'd fallen asleep considering the night before. It really all came down to one question in two parts: What were the chances? The chances that there was anything to find here in the Liberty that her parents weren't already going to uncover, and the chances that Marzana and Nialla could find it, if there was?

Finally she looked up. "I mean, the thing happened. It's an actual thing that's happening in real life, Nye! It's what we've been wanting, isn't it?" She grabbed Nialla's shoulders and shook her. "In the place where nothing happens, something's actually happening!" And she laughed, feeling almost giddy. Then she felt horrible, because of course this wasn't a game. There was a real kid somewhere, lost and scared. What kind of terrible person laughs with joy about a kidnapping? "I mean —"

"No, I get it. Don't start. You don't have to worry about every word with me." Nialla's dubious face broke into a smile. "All right, then! It's on. It's afoot. Where do we begin?"

The door opened, and Mrs. Ileck slouched in. For whatever

reason, the public-address speakers in the Parlor were perpetually broken, and Mrs. Ileck was the fail-safe to make sure everyone got to their next classes on time. She grabbed the pull attached to the clapper of the old brass bell by the door and gave it a series of hearty pulls. "Move along, scamps."

The girls gathered their books, and Marzana gave Mrs. Ileck a weak smile as she passed under her severe stare and out into the hall. "How'd bridge finish out last night, Mrs. Ileck?" she asked, trying to lighten the mood. The old lady scowled, and a second too late, Marzana remembered the cheating Honora had mentioned.

"Just fine," Mrs. Ileck said tightly. "Get out."

The girls hurried down the hall and around the corner and then, once they were out of sight, made their way in a more leisurely fashion up to the math department and their algebra classroom on the third floor. There, instead of ancient and fluffy-haired Mrs. Agravin, a much younger stranger—a substitute teacher, apparently—was busy writing his information on the board. Marzana and Nialla glanced at each other, then threw their bags onto their respective desks, which were side by side in the back row by the window.

"All right," Nialla said quietly as she slid into her seat. "If this is real—"

"Shhh."

"If this is real," Nialla repeated in a whisper, "then where do we start?"

"I don't think—" Marzana's words died away. She nodded toward the front of the classroom and whispered, "Nye. *Look.*"

Nialla tilted her head and frowned at the board. "His name's apparently Mr. Otterwill?"

"Yeah, but—" Marzana lowered her voice even further. "I'm looking at his bag." It was a messenger bag, which Mr. Otterwill had set on Mrs. Agravin's desk. Sewn onto the flap, right above the buckle, was a large embroidered patch shaped like an upside-down shield, with the point uppermost. The background was a wavy, variegated blue. Stitched onto the blue was a spoked circle, its lower arc tucked neatly into the curve at the bottom of the patch. With the wavy blue behind it, it seemed obvious that the circle was meant to be a water wheel, the kind that powers a mill.

Nialla leaned this way and that as the incoming students came in and took their seats, blocking her sightlines. "Oh. *Oh.*" She leaned close. "The girl's school was called—?"

Watermill Elementary. "Yup." Nialla didn't miss a trick. It was nice not to have to explain every little thing to your partner.

"You think he worked there?"

"I'm going to find out."

"I can do it, if you want," Nialla offered.

"Maybe neither of us will have to," Marzana whispered back. He'd almost certainly give the class some version of the *I'm your substitute; let's get along until the boss gets back* speech. They always did.

The second bell rang, and the class settled itself. Mr. Otterwill turned and faced them. He had brown hair tinged with just a little gray above his ears, and Marzana figured he fell somewhere in that nebulous age range between her parents and Lucky: he might've been a weathered thirty-something or a young-looking fifty.

"Hey, there," he began with a smile that was friendly but also a little hard: *I'm a nice guy but don't push me around.* "I'm Brian Otterwill, and I'm standing in for Mrs. Agravin for a bit. Unfortunately she came down with a spot of something, and she's in the hospital at the moment."

There was a general murmur of dismay. Mrs. Agravin was (a) deeply loved by the Marymead population and (b) old as the hills. A kid named Samir in the front row put up his hand. "What does she have? Is she okay?"

Mr. Otterwill made a sympathetic face. "I'm sorry; I don't have a lot of details. For what it's worth, I heard food poisoning, which isn't usually that big a deal, but I gather since she's elderly, they're just being extra cautious." He smiled ruefully. "In the meantime, it's you and me for a while." He perched on the desk, hands in pockets. "I'm pleased to be here with you, though I wish it were under better circumstances. I'm not from the Liberty myself. It was a bit of a happy surprise, winding up here at Marymead."

Here we go. Marzana reached for a pencil to give her fingers something to do rather than twitch. More hands went up. She dropped the pencil again and sat back, arms folded, to wait.

"Where are you from?" asked Lucy, the girl in front of Marzana.

"Oh, just the city proper," Mr. Otterwill said. "I live on the Slope. I suddenly found I had a week free, and just as suddenly this opportunity came up. I do have family here in Gammerbund, so I took the job, and here I am."

Why hadn't one of the usual substitutes from the Liberty been called in? And how did a teacher "suddenly" find he had a week free the first week of summer? Wasn't that kind of a given, having that week off? Marzana clenched her teeth. This was a question that needed asking. But would it be weird that she knew that city-proper schools were already out? Maybe he'd had a vacation planned that fell through. Or . . . had there been something strained in his voice when he'd mentioned that suddenly free week? Maybe he'd been about to get married and his fiancée had called it off. Maybe he'd been planning to repaint his house and it had burned right down to the ground. Maybe, maybe, maybe . . .

Meanwhile, a number of other kids had raised their hands, which was predictable. Some of Marzana's classmates had never been out of the Liberty. "What's your part of the city like?" asked Alex Moody.

Mr. Otterwill considered. "Well, you know where the Slope is —it's the east face of Whilforber Hill, so it's all built on the incline. Streets are steep. I live on one of those long stretches of row houses that go on and on. To get to my usual school, I cut through—" He hesitated. "Can you keep a secret?"

As a group, the class bristled, and you could almost hear the silent, piqued protest *We're from the Liberty; keeping secrets is what we do* that every kid thought about saying but didn't. Marzana used the shifting and huffing as a cover to reach into her bag and extract a piece of scrap paper. She scrawled a few lines, folded the page, and palmed it.

Apparently Mr. Otterwill was not insensible to the indignance his last question had caused. He chuckled and held up his hands. "Okay, okay, yes, I forgot who I'm talking to. Here's the secret. There's one stretch of connected row houses that goes on for literally miles. We call it Ulie's Divide. You don't want to have to go around it to get where you're going, especially if you're running late. And if I'm honest, I'm usually running late." Giggles from the class. Marzana reached down to tie her shoe and flicked the note she'd written under Nialla's desk.

"Yes, yes, a teacher with lateness issues. Contain your amusement, I beg you," Mr. Otterwill said drily. "Well, I live north of the Divide, and the school where I usually teach is south of the Slope."

Nialla paused in the act of retrieving the note to glance up and catch Marzana's eye. The Printer's Quarter was south of the Slope. So was the district called Bayside, but if Marzana's sense of the city's geography was right, Bayside would be a long, long haul from Otterwill's neighborhood. If he walked to work, it was probably in the Printer's Quarter. And Peony's school was in the Printer's Quarter. So far, so good.

"But—" the substitute continued, "and this is a big secret, so, you know, keep it under your hats—there are false-front houses in the Divide. A handful of them, scattered along the length of the row. If you know where they are, you can just walk in the back door, through the house, and out the front door. Or vice versa. So that's how I get to and from work: cutting through these hidden-passage houses, twice a day."

The group was suitably impressed. More hands went up. Marzana silently begged someone to ask the one thing she wanted to know before the class went off the rails about secret passages and whatnot. Nialla's hand shot up and started waving. Mr. Otterwill nodded her way. "Yes?"

"Did you teach middle school?" Nialla asked. The class groaned, and other hands started waving preemptively.

"Nope, elementary school, actually, so this'll be a nice change," Mr. Otterwill said, playing to the room.

Ask the follow-ups, Nye, Marzana silently begged.

"What school?" Nialla asked before he could move on to the next kid. And then, the question Marzana had written on the note she'd passed, "Aren't all schools down in the city out for the summer already? How was this a surprise week off?"

This time, Marzana was certain that something in Mr. Otterwill's cheerful expression flickered. "Place called Watermill," he said. "And yes, classes finished last Wednesday. But I'd planned—" He hesitated. "I had a job at a summer camp, and they canceled the first week."

Oh, snap. Marzana forced herself to sit still and not keel over with excitement. Mr. Otterwill turned to the front corner where Ed

Tivrutsky and Loxi Chell were both bouncing out of their seats. "Uh . . . you, then you," he said, pointing, "and then we should probably do some math at some point."

Nialla flicked Marzana's elbow, her lips silently forming the words *Oh, my God!* While Ed and Loxi asked more questions about the passage houses, Marzana leaned into the aisle, unable to take her wide eyes off the substitute. "Is he possibly talking about the same . . . ?" Nialla whispered, again mouthing the final word, *camp,* rather than speaking it aloud.

"I think yes," Marzana whispered back. "He clearly knows about . . . what happened. It's not public, but I bet there was no way to keep it from people who were there that day, especially if the police had to question them."

"We need to know more. But how?" Nialla wondered. "We can't ask him. If the kidnapping isn't public, there's no way we'd be able to explain how we knew about it."

Marzana tapped her pencil on her desktop. "I don't know."

Up at the front, Mr. Otterwill clapped his hands. "All right, enough with the interrogation. I have some . . . I believe the technical term is 'busywork'? . . . I'm supposed to give you." Amid protests from the class, he flipped off the overhead lights, then turned on the projector by the desk to reveal a page of problems in Mrs. Agravin's small, slightly wobbly handwriting. "There's a whole trove of in-case-of-substitute-teacher stuff here," Mr. Otterwill said, "but once I'm up to speed on where you guys are, if I'm still here tomorrow, I can try to come up with something more fun than these problem sheets. For today, though—" He tapped the projector, then settled into Mrs. Agravin's chair. "Let me know if you have any questions."

Oh, I have plenty, Marzana thought, watching him pick up a copy of their algebra textbook. *As soon as I figure out how to ask them.*

By unspoken agreement, she and Nialla didn't make any further attempts at conversation for the rest of the class; you couldn't hide whispers or pass notes when the entire room was heads-down and quiet.

Marzana was halfway through the first problem set when she got the idea. It was not a comfortable idea, but it was so obviously, instantly right that she stifled the twitchy nerves it immediately sent spiking through her and started working out how to turn the idea into a plan. By the time the bell rang, she had a pretty good sense of what to do next. She didn't like it, but she had it.

"Well?" Nialla asked breathlessly as the current of escaping algebra students swept them out into the hall.

"I think . . . I think maybe we're going to need help."

"What kind of help?"

"We might—" Marzana stopped talking for a moment as Naz, Lucy, and Loxi came out of the classroom giggling. Marzana and Nialla followed at a slower pace, wading through a sudden wave of sixth-graders toward the huge staircase that led to the language arts classrooms, one flight up. "I think there's a way we can find out more about Mr. Otterwill," Marzana said. "But we might need . . . an inside man."

"What kind of inside man? Inside what?"

They started up the stairs, which were old and massive, with carved banisters and green carpet that was probably meant to dull the thud of hundreds of footfalls. Like the math department below it, the fourth story of Marymead House had once been a bedroom floor, back when it had been a residence; the school had knocked out a dozen or so walls to convert the original assorted bedrooms, boudoirs, salons, and dressing rooms into six classrooms. Marzana looked down the crowded hall, her eyes seeking the back of a particular head. *There.* She caught Nialla's eye and nodded her chin as a blond girl with two braids tied with purple ribbons crossed from the girls' bathroom to one of the classrooms.

"Emilia?" Nialla mouthed. Marzana nodded. Nialla looked puzzled for a moment, but just for a moment. Then her eyes snapped upward and she stared, apparently at one of the eels stamped into the pressed-tin ceiling over their head. But Marzana knew she was thinking a couple stories farther up, to the floors that were home to the Commorancy Kids' dormitories.

Marzana often wondered about the other kids who went to her school. They all wondered about one another—or, more to the point, they wondered about one another's parents. Whispers of rumor and speculation did occasionally flutter through the halls of Marymead Intermediate, but you didn't ever ask outright. It wasn't done, because it was tacitly understood, even in middle school, that people in the Liberty might have complicated feelings about discussing themselves or their families. Still, there were guesses. And the most irresistible subjects of speculation were the Commorancy Kids —the student boarders at Marymead.

The Commorancy Kids lived on the sixth and seventh floors. They didn't precisely keep to themselves, but there was an aura about them of loftiness, almost of ownership. Of mystery. Because *why* did they live there during the year, and not at home?

It could have been the simple fact that while Marymead was one of the best schools in Gammerbund, it was also stuck in the middle of one of the most geographically inconvenient parts of town, where the twisty streets were too narrow for the vintage buses that were the only public transportation in the Liberty. But every year, plenty of more interesting theories circulated quietly around the school. And, of course, everyone thought the Commorancy Kids secretly knew everything. They were widely assumed to roam the halls of the school at night like specters, getting up to hijinks and into everyone's student records. This year, there were fifteen Commorancy Kids, and Emilia Cabot was one of them.

If there was anything useful to be learned about their new substitute teacher in the school's records, and if there was anyone who would know how to get at that information, it would be one of the Commorancy Kids. And although neither Marzana nor Nialla knew any of them well enough to just walk up and ask them to break into the principal's office as a favor, maybe, just maybe, they could interest someone in a caper. Plus, Emilia Cabot played strategy games. That gave them something in common and suggested Emilia might have a good mind for puzzles and problem-solving.

It wasn't much, but it was something.

Nialla gave Marzana a dubious look. "You're just going to go up and . . . ?"

"Obviously not," Marzana retorted. "But I was thinking I'd go to the game at Lucky's bookstore tonight after all and see how I feel. Then maybe I'll talk to her."

"Oh, my Lord, now I want to come," Nialla breathed. She hugged her book bag to her chest and spun in delight, nearly whacking a shorter kid who happened to be passing by in the face with her elbow. "This is so exciting. Are we . . . are we putting together a *crew?*"

"Maybe," Marzana said reluctantly. "I mean, if we're going to do this—"

Nialla nodded. "We should do it right. We'll need resources. We'll need people who can do the stuff we can't."

"So you'll come tonight too?" Marzana asked hopefully.

Nialla's face fell. "I can't. I have to watch Toby."

"You could bring him!"

"I could *not* bring him. You don't try to recruit an asset with somebody's six-year-old brother in tow."

Marzana sighed. "Fine."

Nialla linked her elbow through Marzana's. "It'll be okay, you know. It always is, once you get over it. True or not?"

The second bell rang, giving Marzana the cover she needed to make a face rather than actually give an answer before the two girls parted ways: Marzana for Mr. Lewis's language arts classroom, and Nialla for Ms. Snyder's Advanced Poetry and Prose.

The problem was, Marzana *didn't* know that to be true. She could never tell if it, whatever *it* was (*it* was almost always some kind of social interaction that Marzana had been forced to have with someone who wasn't Nialla or one of her parents or Honora), had been okay or not. She needed Nialla to tell her. She needed to be able to ask, *Did I do okay?* before she could be sure.

Half the problem was the not-knowing. Not being able to trust, afterward, that however things seemed in the moment, they hadn't been awkward. Not being able to remember every single detail, every single moment, or to be able to rewind it with sufficient accuracy to be certain that she hadn't said anything stupid, meaningless, or awkward or that might be taken the wrong way or that could be twisted around to bite her. That she hadn't accidentally said aloud any of the things she thought she was just musing silently to herself. *Did I do okay?* was really a whole intense cloud of questions and assessments.

Nialla, fortunately, understood that. And she knew that if Marzana didn't ask, she'd obsess over the details for the rest of the night, even waking up in the darkling hours if her subconscious decided the matter hadn't been settled to its satisfaction. So they had an agreement: Nialla would always tell the truth when asked, and Marzana would always trust the answer.

At first it had seemed too simple. Just to decide to believe and let go? Impossible. But, improbably, it worked. Marzana's anxious, self-conscious brain needed to hear from someone it trusted that it could shut off its panic response. It wasn't enough for Marzana to reassure herself. But if Nialla did it, Marzana could sleep.

Tonight Nialla wouldn't be able to do that for her though. So the choice was this: Did her wish to pursue the adventure outweigh her wish to avoid the anxiety of speaking to people she didn't know without a friend she could rely on to put her out of her misery afterward?

Yes, yes, it did. But without Nialla, it was going to be a long night.

As she took her seat, Marzana glanced two rows over at Emilia, wondering with multiplying butterflies in her stomach whether she should talk to her after class and ask if it was okay to show up to the game at Surroyal Books, or whether she should just show up. In the end she opted for the latter, if only to save herself from having to figure out how to start the conversation. This was the kind of thing Marzana needed a few hours and a bit of rehearsal to prepare for.

six

EMILIA

MARZANA AND NIALLA parted ways in the marble-floored entry foyer of Marymead, promising to check in by phone that night. Then Marzana ducked into a nook between the foyer and the dining hall, dropped a coin into one of the two pay phones hidden there, and dialed Hedgelock Court to tell Honora that she would be at Lucky's after school for a game, and depending on the play, she might be late for dinner. Honora, who hated phones and could never quite get the hang of not being weird on a call, shouted at the top of her lungs that she'd pass the word to the captain and rang off with her usual abrupt and clattering hang-up.

Marzana replaced the receiver, straightened, yanked decisively down on the straps of her backpack to tighten them, and started off for Surroyal Books, taking a roundabout route at a leisurely if not actually reluctant pace. She needed time to prepare.

This isn't a big deal, she told herself as she walked. *People do it all the time. And if it was a really private game, they wouldn't play it in a bookstore. So it's not a big deal. It'll be fine.*

It didn't *feel* fine, but Marzana was pretty sure that was just her mind messing with her. *Focus on the words,* she thought. *Figure out the words and it won't be as scary.*

She could skip the "Hi, my name is Marzana and I heard you had a game going and I was wondering if I could join" opening statement, because presumably Lucky would introduce her and handle that part. Unless . . . unless she ran into Emilia Cabot first, in which case it would be strange if she didn't say something. Marzana looked around, just in case Emilia was nearby, walking a parallel but separate course to Hellbent Street. No sign of the blond braids with their purple bows. Marzana breathed a sigh of relief.

"Hi, Emilia," she said to herself, speaking the words as soundlessly as she could. "Lucky told me there was a game here on Tuesdays and suggested I come by and see if I could join in."

Simple enough. So why was she already starting to breathe faster? Why did it feel as if a bear had crawled into her rib cage to crouch heavy on her stomach and squeeze her lungs in its massive grip?

Because it wasn't the words she could predict and practice for that were the problem. It was what came after those, which meant she had to plot out answers to all the possible replies Emilia was likely to give. And then Marzana tended to get hung up on planning for the negative responses, as well as trying to guess at the unknowable, unpredictable responses she couldn't have anticipated but that theoretically could happen and probably *would* happen the one time she didn't plan for them. And — good news/bad news — neither the negative nor the wildly unpredictable happened that often. Fortunately, things were rarely as bad as she feared. Unfortunately, she was nearly always underprepared to reply when the response was positive. And, unless she prepared, she had zero instincts for small talk, which resulted in exchanges like the one that had occurred the last time Nialla had been out sick and the only open seat at lunch was at the table where Naz, Lucy, and Loxi sat.

MARZANA: Hey, guys. Can I sit here? It's just that there are no other—

NAZ: Sure.

MARZANA: Oh. Cool. Thanks.

LUCY: We were just talking about the new Oracular Records Department movie and whether they'll make it more grown-up than the books are. Naz says probably not.

MARZANA: . . . Oh.

LOXI: I don't care. I'm seeing it anyway.

NAZ: Yeah, because you'd see anything with that guy in it.

LOXI: What can I say? My love is real.

MARZANA: *(Awkward chuckle. She has no idea who That Guy is.)*

LUCY: . . .

LOXI: . . .

NAZ: . . .

MARZANA: *(In desperation)* Um, I need ketchup. Does anyone else need ketchup? I'll go get ketchup.

All four look down at their trays full of standard-issue cafeteria pizza and corn niblets.

NAZ: No, thanks.

LUCY: I'm fine.

LOXI: Ketchup with pizza? Is that good?

MARZANA: . . . Probably not.

LOXI: I'll probably skip it, then.

MARZANA slouches away in defeat, trying frantically and

failing to think of something, literally anything, to say when she gets back.

This event, which Marzana thought of as the Ketchup Pizza Incident, had happened in sixth grade, and the memory still smarted. Hijacked by it now, she lost two blocks' worth of time rerunning the interaction again and again and working out different ways she could've played it. And then, far too soon, she saw the gold awning with its gray antlers and realized she'd planned for absolutely nothing beyond the initial hello. The bear in her belly stretched, bounced on her gut, and jammed its muzzle up into her throat.

Marzana shook her hands out once, twice, then forced herself to grab the door handle and go into the bookstore.

Lucky looked up from the register counter and beamed. "Hey, you! I didn't know if you'd come!"

"I did," Marzana pointed out, completely unnecessarily.

"Well, come on back," Lucky said, strolling around the counter and reaching for Marzana's shoulders. "I'll introduce you. I don't think your friend from school's here yet."

Emilia wasn't there yet? *But I didn't plan for talking to anybody else!* Marzana protested inwardly. There it was: the eventuality — an obvious one, in this case — she hadn't considered. The others were strangers, and older: two degrees of difficulty she wasn't ready to tackle without preparation. What if Emilia didn't come today at all? But Lucky was drawing her forward, through the poetry section toward the room that held the history books, a fireplace that shared a chimney with the decorated hearth out front, a chandelier made of ceramic antlers, and the big oak table where presumably the game-playing group set up. And then there they were: two ladies, one Asian with glasses and the other white with a blue sequined headband, and a pale, freckled boy who was probably in high school. They all looked up as Lucky and Marzana approached.

"Hey, guys," Lucky said cheerfully. "This is my friend Marzana." Marzana fought to swallow past the bear and make her face as pleasant as the bookseller's introduction voice. "Marzana's a game player too," Lucky went on, "and yesterday I mentioned that there was a group that came on Tuesdays. Since I think you told me last week you were going to start something new today, I suggested she come by and see if she could join. I hope that's okay. She's a classmate of—"

Almost before Marzana could begin to puzzle out what she should say, the faces of the two women broke into wide smiles. The boy, cooler and more aloof, kept his smile smaller and narrower, but it looked genuine enough. "Oh, of Emilia's?" asked the headband lady.

"Yes, ma'am," Marzana said.

"Wonderful to meet you. I'm Lily, and this is Maria and Jeffrey. Emilia and Alex usually get here a little after us."

Lucky vanished with a wink as Maria waved and Jeffrey managed a noncommittal "Hey."

"You're welcome to play," Lily continued, taking a box from a tote bag. "We just finished a long game, so we decided today we wanted to do something we could finish in one sitting."

"The Sneaksby Gambit," said Maria, the lady with glasses. "Do you know it?" Marzana shook her head. "Well, neither do we, so no worries. I picked it up last night." Maria examined the box. "Looks cool, though, doesn't it?"

Marzana nodded. "Yes, it does." This was good. As long as they just kept asking questions, she could manage.

"All right, well, how about if you lot try to figure out the instructions?" Lily suggested. "I'm going to get beverages. Jeffrey? The usual?" Jeffrey nodded an affirmative as he reached for the box and pulled off the lid. "Marzana? What can I get you? My treat."

"Oh. Thanks — Lucky has those grapefruit sodas?"

"You got it."

Marzana sat next to Maria on the bench closest to the fireplace, and the two of them waited while Jeffrey unfolded the instructions and proceeded to haltingly explain the functions of the two different decks of cards, the handful of markers in assorted colors, and the sets of five each of pewter trolley cars, sailing ships, figures in bowler hats, monsters in sailor suits, and tiny gates with doors that swung on minute hinges.

"Oh, hey, Marzana."

She glanced up. Emilia and a tall boy who might have been her twin (minus the braids and bows) entered the history room on Lily's heels, hands full of coffee cups, soda bottles, and snacks.

"Hey," Marzana said, reaching up to help with the bottles Emilia was carrying.

"Are you playing?" Emilia asked, passing a soda to Marzana and another to her brother.

"Yeah," Marzana said. "If that's okay."

"Fine by me," Emilia replied, pulling out the chair at the end of the table opposite the door. "That's my brother, Alex," she added as Alex took the seat next to Jeffrey and favored Marzana with a short wave. "He's at the upper school. Commorancy, like me." She reached across Alex and plucked the instructions from Jeffrey's hands. "How's this all go, then?"

It was that easy.

The game took about three hours, and it was perfect: complex enough that there wasn't a mess of downtime that required small talk to fill it, but not so complex that six first-time players couldn't manage. Emilia turned out to be a force to be reckoned with during game play. The Sneaksby Gambit was a cooperative game, meaning they were all more or less on the same team, so it was good for everybody that she was such a shark. Marzana decided she'd rather not wind up playing against Emilia at anything if she could help it. But if Emilia agreed to help with her and Nialla's investigation, she was going to be an excellent addition.

They took a break an hour in. Maria excused herself to use the restroom, Lily said something about stretching her legs, and the boys slouched out of the room for more snacks. Emilia and Marzana were left alone.

Emilia glanced at her with curiosity. "Surprised you came out," she said. "You always seem to want to keep to yourself. Except for Nialla, I mean."

"I do," Marzana admitted. "This was really scary for me. It was nice of everyone to let me play and not make a big deal out of it."

Emilia nodded. "Everybody here's nice."

Now or never, Marzana thought. The others would come back soon, and at the rate the game was going, she'd have to hurry to get home before dark. *Don't overthink it. Just talk.* "I wanted to talk to you about something," she blurted, scooting down the bench to Emilia's end of the table.

Emilia blinked, momentarily startled by the outburst. "Okay, shoot."

"Nialla and I are doing this thing and we want you to join us," Marzana said rapidly. "We think you can help us, but it's not exactly . . . well, it's the kind of thing we could get in trouble for. But we're doing it because someone else is in trouble."

A brief flash of something crossed Emilia's face. It was there and gone so quickly that it was hard to pin down, but chief among the emotions Marzana thought the expression might have contained was at least a touch of suspicion. "Why me?" Emilia asked.

It was not the question Marzana had expected to follow her opening salvo. "Um . . . well, because you're in the Commorancy, honestly."

Emilia gave her a long, considering look. "Only because of that?"

Marzana felt her skin starting to prickle with embarrassment. The true answer was *yes*. The right answer would've been Emilia-specific, something that would make her feel like Marzana and Nialla had chosen her for who she was, not where she lived during the school year—but she just didn't know Emilia that well. Feeling a little like she was in danger of entering Ketchup Pizza territory, Marzana managed a nod. "That, and that we knew you played strategy games. I thought you might be up for the challenge of something real." *Please don't be offended. Please don't be offended.*

The other girl said nothing for a moment. Marzana held her breath. "Who's in trouble?" Emilia asked at last.

Marzana exhaled with relief. She lowered her voice. "A girl was kidnapped a couple days ago down in the city proper. We think she might be here in the Liberty."

Emilia held up three fingers. "Who is it, why do you think that, and how do you know all this?" Her eyes flicked down the table and toward the doorway, and Marzana had the sudden thought that, even among friends, even when playing games, this girl probably always chose her chair strategically. "Quick, because I hear Alex coming. He walks loud."

Marzana couldn't hear anything, but it made perfect sense that, in addition to being a shark and a strategist, Emilia would also have supersensitive hearing. "It's a long story. I have inside information I can give you, but it would take more time than we have right now."

"And you need me because . . . ?"

"We want to know more about a substitute teacher named Mr. Otterwill."

The other girl nodded. "I see."

Now even Marzana could hear that the boys were on their way back. "Can we meet tomorrow in the Parlor during study period? We can tell you everything then."

"Not the Parlor. Too public. Sixth-floor common room. Meet in the dining hall after lunch and I'll show you."

"Perfect," Marzana said as Alex and Jeffrey returned and tossed handfuls of snacks onto the table in between the Sneaksby bits and pieces.

Emilia gave another short nod, then reached for a bag of pretzels. Marzana sat back, trying to decide whether she could be relieved or not. This was not the total, terrifying mess she had expected. Of course, Emilia hadn't said yes—just that she wanted to hear more. But it was a good first step.

"So?" Nialla demanded, skipping all accepted phone-answering protocol. "How was it?"

Marzana, sitting in the window nook in her bedroom with the cord of her phone stretched as far as it would go, swallowed her planned *Hey, Nye, it's Mars; how's the babysitting going?* "How did you even know it was me?"

"Nobody else calls me," Nialla said indistinctly. A sound had arisen in the background that Marzana couldn't quite identify: it might've been coming from Toby's electric keyboard if the batteries were almost dead, or Toby might have been attempting to play "The Wheels on the Bus" with a colander and a whisk.

"It went fine, I think," Marzana replied, jerking the phone away from her ear as Nialla abruptly screamed her brother's name far too close to the receiver. *Fine,* of course, was nothing but a guess, and she was by no means sure, even after having mentally reviewed every interaction she had been part of that she could remember on the walk home. Over and over. Game play and conversation. Everything she'd said to Emilia during the break—although that part, oddly, had been the easiest to decide had gone more or less the way she'd hoped. It had been too brief, with too little time to obsess and worry—she'd had to stick to the facts, with no small talk to trip her up.

The whisk-percussion stopped. "Quick, tell me before he starts again," Nialla ordered.

"I think she's in," Marzana said cautiously. "We're meeting tomorrow during study period to go over what we know. You too. Only not in the Parlor. In the sixth-floor common room."

"I didn't know there was a sixth-floor common room," Nialla said wonderingly. "And we're allowed up there? This is already paying dividends."

"Yeah."

"So how did it go down? What did you say? Did they let you play?" The tiniest of pauses. "How was it?"

Marzana gave her a quick narration, then hesitated over the last question. "It was . . . fine. Scary. You know. I knew it would be, going in. But everyone was really nice, and with Lucky introducing me, it probably wasn't as awkward as it could've been, so that helped. And of course they were about to start a new game, so it wasn't inconvenient or anything."

"Good! Congratulations!"

"Yeah, thanks."

"So," Nialla began. "TOBY! GET OFF THE COUNTERTOP RIGHT THIS MINUTE, TOBY!"

"Ouch," Marzana said mildly.

"Sorry. So I have a thing I want to talk to you about."

"Um. Okay, that sounds cryptic."

"No, no." Nialla laughed, but awkwardly. "I mean, you might hate it. But hear me out. Since we're putting a crew together."

"Are we, though?" Marzana asked dubiously. "Or did we just recruit one person to do a specific job we can't do?"

"Well, that's kind of what putting a crew together is, isn't it?"

"I . . . guess?"

"So since we're putting a crew together, I have a suggestion. Someone I think we should add to the team."

Marzana frowned into her phone. "Okay."

Nialla hesitated, then said in a rush, "I think we should ask J.J." Her voice got smaller and smaller with each word, until Marzana almost didn't catch the name at the end.

"Who?"

"J.J. You know."

"I really don't." Marzana tried and failed to come up with a J.J. she was aware of at Marymead. "Is he in our grade?"

Nialla hesitated. "Well, yes, he is; he's just . . . not at our school."

"I'm still not putting a face to this name, Nye."

She sighed. "I think you just know him as Julian. Julian Mowbry."

"Julian Mowbry?" Marzana thought for another moment. "I'm still not—oh. Oh. *Julian?*"

"Yeah, *Julian*. He goes by J.J. now."

Marzana rolled her eyes so far back into her head, she felt a sharp stab of headache. Julian was the boy best friend who had so abruptly ditched Nialla back in the sixth grade. "And *why,* exactly, should we ask J.J.?"

"Hear me out."

"You already said that. If the deal is that we're recruiting people to do jobs we can't do, what job is it J.J.'s supposed to do for us? I didn't know we had any other jobs lined up."

"It's not a job so much as he has a skill we—I think would be useful."

"What skill?" Marzana asked, thumping her head gently against the wall.

Nialla cleared her throat. "Magic."

"Magic."

"Yeah."

Marzana shook her head to clear away visions of a kid in a black cape wielding a wand with paper flowers sprouting from one white-tipped end. "Please tell me that by 'magic,' you mean J.J. is currently enrolled at Hogwarts."

Nialla laughed awkwardly. "No, I mean the other kind of magic."

"Rabbits and top hats."

"Yeah. Only no, it's not like that." Nialla made a frustrated noise. "He can explain better."

"*Can* he?" Marzana held the phone away from her head and scowled at it for a second, as if Nialla could see her expression through the receiver. "You already told him, didn't you? You told him about the crew we're putting together."

"No," Nialla protested lightly. Silence. "Yes. Yes, I did. I cannot tell a lie."

Marzana groaned. "Nialla."

"Mars, hear me out."

"If you say that one more time, you're off this caper. I mean it."

A deeply aggrieved exhalation from the other end of the line, then: "Will you just let him explain?"

Marzana said nothing, let the silence stretch for a moment before she asked, "Is he there now?"

"No, of course not." Of course he wasn't. Mrs. Giddis would've had kittens if Nialla had invited a boy over while both parents were out of the house.

Marzana picked at a flaking bit of paint low on the bedroom wall, near the baseboard. "He was so mean to you, Nialla," she said finally.

"That was a long time ago," Nialla said quietly. "And he wasn't mean. Sometimes people just grow apart."

Marzana snorted. "That's your mom talking."

"Okay, yes, it *was* my mom talking, but that doesn't make it wrong. It's true."

For a beat or two, there was nothing but the sound of cartoons in the background and an occasional *click-click* Marzana immediately identified as the sound of Toby playing with Legos. *Julian wouldn't know what that sound was just from hearing it,* she thought bitterly. *He probably doesn't know you at all anymore.*

"Will you just talk to him?" Nialla asked.

Marzana closed her eyes. "Yes. If you want."

"I think you'll see what I mean."

"Sure. Fine."

"I'm sorry I said anything to him before I asked you," Nialla said in a very small voice.

"I said it's fine."

"You were talking about something else when you said that. You said fine, you'd talk to him."

Marzana ground her teeth together. "It's fine! Apology accepted."

"Thank you."

"Okay. When do I meet the Great Mowbrini?"

Nialla laughed. "Tomorrow after school. He can meet us at Surroyal."

"I'm so glad you have this all arranged," Marzana said sourly. "While we're on the subject, just so we don't have any other surprises, is there anyone else you're planning on dragging aboard?"

"No. Cross my heart. Next one's your pick."

"Oh, super. Thanks. By the way, exactly how big is this crew going to be, do you think?"

Cartoons and Lego-clicks while they both considered this question. "As big as it needs to be," Nialla said seriously. "But I don't know yet what else we're going to need. You?"

"Nope." The piece of paint Marzana was picking came away under her fingernail, and she examined the new spot of robin's-egg blue that peeked through. She sat back. "If it gets much bigger, though, we're going to have to come up with a name."

"How big does a crew have to be before it needs a name?"

Herself, Nialla, Emilia, J.J.— assuming J.J. turned out not to be the best-friend-ditching twit Marzana assumed he was. That made four. "I think if we hit five, we start talking names."

seven
FLETCHWOOD

"EVERYTHING OKAY?"

Marzana glanced up sharply from her breakfast. "I'm fine, Mom." Mrs. Hakelbarend was looking at her with slightly narrowed eyes and her head skewed just a little bit to the right. It was an expression Marzana recognized, and she set down her fork and immediately focused on appearing as guileless as possible. It was . . . not easy. "What?"

"Oh, you know. You're just plowing through that bacon like I might take it away if you stop to breathe or anything."

Marzana shrugged. "It's good bacon."

"It's not good bacon. I burned it."

Huh. Marzana looked down at her plate. She'd been so focused on the day ahead, she hadn't even noticed. "It tasted good to me." Though now that she was paying attention, she could smell the burned grease in the kitchen, and there was a slight but distinct gray fug hanging a few feet over the dining table.

Her mother's eyebrows descended a quarter-inch lower over her eyes, but Marzana got a surprise reprieve as the sounds of Honora discovering the evidence of bacon failure spiraled up in the kitchen.

"If I've said it once, sir, begging your pardon, I've said it a hundred times, or a dozen at least," Honora said waspishly, "but bacon is much better done in the oven, sir. I'm certain I've said it, begging your pardon, sir. Doesn't get on the range top, like, or smoke up the galley."

"I didn't make the bacon, Honora," Mr. Hakelbarend said on the other side of the door, his voice mild. "That was the captain."

"Sir, now, I've known the captain since she was a girl in pigtails, not meaning to be argumentative." She broke off speaking as the sound of the coffee grinder started up, and Marzana and her mother shared a knowing look. Right about now, Honora would be clenching a spoon handle between her teeth to get her calm back before she informed Mr. Hakelbarend that optimally he should've ground the coffee at the #4 fineness setting, begging-your-pardon-sir-but-not-really, *not* #6, which was what Marzana's dad preferred. But even biting a spoon wouldn't keep her from commenting for long. Fortunately, the doorbell rang before Honora's restraint gave out.

"I'll get that," she announced through clenched teeth as she stomped out of the kitchen and through the dining room. "Number four. Number *four*."

A moment later, she returned wearing an expression on her face that Marzana was unaccustomed to seeing there. Regret, maybe. "Which it's a pair of young men to see you, Captain."

"Did they give any names?" Mrs. Hakelbarend looked up, noticed the look on Honora's face. "I see they did. Who are they?"

"I believe they're relations of old Tumbler's," Honora said delicately.

"One of them wrote," Mrs. Hakelbarend guessed. "Moth, I think the name was?"

"That's him, ma'am. Moth Fletchwood, and a Christopher Fletchwood's with him."

Marzana's mother took a deep breath. "Bring them in, if you please, Honora." The steward touched tattooed knuckles to her temple and stomped out.

"He's the guy who wrote all those times last year, huh?" Marzana asked.

Her mother nodded but didn't have time to say anything more before Honora was returning with two young men in tow. The older one, who Marzana thought was somewhere around twenty-five or thirty, was slender and tallish, though not as tall as her father; green-eyed and fair with light-brown hair that he wore swept up from his forehead and back, giving him an extra two inches of height. The other looked a couple of years younger and was just a bit shorter and stockier, but with the same coloring. Neither looked a thing like a sailor, but then again, Marzana reminded herself, she probably didn't either. Maybe they'd been raised away from the water, just like she had. Children of sailors, but not sailors themselves.

The younger carried a small bouquet of daisies. The older one had a porkpie hat in his hands, and he worried the brim between his fingers as Marzana's mom stood.

It was always interesting, getting a glimpse of her mother the legend. Gone was the middle-aged mom who'd been comfortably folded into a dining chair with one foot propped on the next chair over. In her place was a commander, standing with the easy, confident stillness of one who feels no need to waste motion. This lady seemed a foot taller than she usually was, and she somehow managed to tower over even the taller of the newcomers, despite the fact that he had three or four inches on her, hair included. Instantly she commanded the room.

Without realizing it, even Marzana sat up straighter. She spotted her father leaning in the kitchen doorway with his arms folded and an admiring, almost goofy grin on his face. He caught Marzana looking, made a vaguely embarrassed face, and winked.

The older guest fidgeted with his hat. "Captain . . . er, Mrs. . . . ." He paused, helpless.

"Hakelbarend," Marzana's mother supplied, holding out her hand: a fluid, economical motion. " 'Mrs.' is fine. And you are?" Despite the proffered hand, her voice was a little on the flinty side.

"Moth Fletchwood." He grasped her hand gratefully. "This is my brother, Christopher."

He pulled the younger man forward to stand beside him. Christopher held out the bouquet. "Ma'am."

Marzana's mother accepted the flowers, only to have Honora whisk them away a second later, muttering, "I'll get 'em in water," as she ambled into the kitchen.

Moth spoke up. "You sailed with our father, I think. Henrik Fletchwood."

Mrs. Hakelbarend inclined her head. "I knew him, yes."

Christopher's nervous face broke into a wide smile, but something about this answer made his brother frown. "Tumbler. I think you knew him as Tumbler," Moth said.

"I know who you mean." Mrs. Hakelbarend smiled fleetingly. "He moved to someplace on the Chesapeake, didn't he?"

Christopher nodded. "A town not far from Annapolis. There's a Magothy River up there. He said just the name made him feel closer to home. Reminded him of the Magothy Bay back here."

Moth cleared his throat. "I wrote to you, ma'am. I don't know if the letters ever reached you before they . . . well, they all came back."

"They did." Marzana's mother hesitated just the tiniest fraction of a second. "Do you know why I sent them back?"

Moth's face tightened. "No, ma'am."

She didn't actually say, "I think that's a lie," but she gave him a long look that got the message across just fine.

"He left us your information," Moth said. "Instructions on how to reach you. If—"

"If?"

"If it was an emergency," Moth finished lamely.

Mrs. Hakelbarend nodded. When she spoke again, her voice was a touch less flinty. "When did he pass, Moth?"

Moth crumpled the brim of the hat, then released his grip. It was Christopher who answered in an unsteady voice, "Two years ago."

"I'm sorry to hear that." She put a hand on his shoulder for just a moment, then took it back. "And when did you get into town?" she asked, sharing the question out between the two of them.

Christopher looked to his brother. Moth shook his head, as if momentarily confused by the question. "Ah. A while. I've been here since . . ." He paused, changed gears. "I was really hoping you could tell me—us—a bit about him. About your days together. He was getting a bit vague at the end. He couldn't hold the thread of a story."

"That's unfortunate. He wasn't that far on in years, was he?" Mrs. Hakelbarend asked. "Sixty or seventy?"

"Sixty-eight, when he went," Christopher confirmed.

"I hadn't seen him since—" She turned to Mr. Hakelbarend. "Do you remember when it was that he came back through Nagspeake? Coming up on fifteen years ago now. Would've been eleven or twelve years after the Endgame." *The Endgame* was how she always referred to the events leading up to the destruction of her ship and her crew's subsequent escape from the city proper.

"I think it was eleven years after," Marzana's father said. "The statute of limitations had expired, but only recently, I think."

"I remember that," Moth said. "I was ten or eleven. My mother was afraid he wouldn't come back. I never knew whether she was worried about some kind of danger or whether she thought he might leave us and go back to his old life."

Marzana's mother relented just a little. "I'm sorry she worried about that. She didn't need to. A handful of people came back through Nagspeake around then. It was about tying up loose ends — being able to leave the city for good, but on their own terms. Now, certainly there was some danger. There's no getting around that. There always is, in Nagspeake. But Tumbler loved you. Loved your mother. He was writing to her the whole time, during that return trip: a poem for every place he wished he could show her, he said."

For all that she refused to talk, her mother never forgot a detail. Marzana's heart gave a pang at the thought of all Mrs. Hakelbarend could've shared if she'd wanted to.

Christopher's face shone. "She still has all those poems."

A momentary silence fell. The Fletchwood brothers waited, hardly daring to breathe. Marzana could see her mother warring with herself — with the rules she'd set and so steadfastly maintained. "Even back when we sailed," Mrs. Hakelbarend said at last, "Tumbler looked like he'd been carved from rock, but he was a very gentle soul. Though I don't imagine that's telling you anything you don't already know. He was easy to love." She glanced over her shoulder toward Honora, who had returned from the kitchen to put the vase of daisies on the sideboard and was now standing with her feet apart and her hands clasped behind her back like a soldier at ease. "Wouldn't you say so, Honora?"

"I would indeed, ma'am. We all cared for him very much, sirs, if I may say so."

"He was mad for puzzles," Mrs. Hakelbarend went on. "He taught me everything I know about locks. He saw them as their own special subset of conundrums, and he could open anything. Absolutely anything." Her thin, stony smile morphed into something more genuine. "He loved poetry, though he was forbidden Whitman after the crew realized that, in the poem he most liked to quote, the captain was dead."

"'O Captain! My Captain!' that was," Honora supplied darkly. Then she made a soft nasal sound, glanced around, and darted out of the room to find a genteel place to spit for luck.

"Did he . . ." Christopher hesitated. "Did he leave anything behind?"

Moth darted a glare at him so sharp, Marzana felt herself flinch in sympathy. Marzana's mother frowned. "What do you mean, did he leave anything behind? You mean when he passed? How would I know that? Didn't he leave a will?"

Between the eyeball daggers his brother was shooting at him and Marzana's mom's confusion, the younger man was reddening fast. "No, I meant—I mean, yes, he did, and we have all that, but . . . I meant did he leave anything behind here in Nagspeake, that time he came back?"

"Too late for that," Moth muttered.

"Well . . . he left people," Mrs. Hakelbarend said. "Everyone did who left the city. There was no big unclaimed treasure cache, if that's what you're asking. Your father probably lost the security deposit on his flat, and anything he left in it was gone too, of course, long before he made that one trip back here. If he'd left anything meaningful behind that I didn't know about, I imagine he would've collected it on that trip if it was still around to be collected."

"You're right, of course. And that's not why we came to see you," Moth said pointedly, still glaring at his brother. "I hate to intrude on your breakfast any longer, Ca — ma'am, but before we go, could you . . . could you possibly tell us any stories? Just one or two."

Marzana's father disappeared discreetly back into the kitchen. He knew what was coming. His wife's reply was swift and decisive. "No. I can't."

Moth's face fell. Mrs. Hakelbarend put a hand on his shoulder: a comforting hand, and a steering one. The interview was over. "We made these rules, these agreements, for the safety of everyone," she said, walking with Moth at her side out of the dining room and toward the front door. Christopher trailed a step after them, looking broken. Marzana followed as far as the entrance to the dining room. From there she could still see and hear what remained of this conversation. "It was especially important for the safety of the ones who stayed in town."

"But after all this time," Moth protested, a mutinous edge coming into his tone. "What does it matter? You said the statute of limitations on your . . . your *adventures* was up over fifteen years ago."

"If Tumbler told you anything about Nagspeake, he'll have told you that there are interests in this town that don't care a fig for statutes of limitations."

Moth shrugged out from under Mrs. Hakelbarend's hand and stared at her, visibly struggling with his reply. His voice, when he found it, was angry. "But you can't think I'd *ever*—"

Mrs. Hakelbarend stopped walking in the foyer and faced the

young man, but Christopher stepped between them before anyone could speak. "We just wanted to ask. Had to. We're sorry to have—"

Moth shook his head in disgust. "Why are *you* apologizing to *her?*" Marzana recoiled a bit at his expression. He was understandably red-cheeked, but mixed in with the embarrassment was a fair amount of rage.

"You know where to find me in case of an emergency," Marzana's mother said distinctly, holding out her hand again. "I'm sorry I can't give you more than that. And I'm very sorry for your loss."

Moth Fletchwood looked down at her palm. He didn't shake it. Instead he grabbed the doorknob with clumsy fingers and stalked out into the daylight.

Christopher took her hand before she could lower it and clasped it tightly. "I'm sorry." Then, before Mrs. Hakelbarend could reply, he followed his brother out.

Marzana's mother pondered the door as it shut behind the Fletchwoods. "I suppose it's getting to be that time."

"What time?" Marzana asked.

Mrs. Hakelbarend sighed and returned to the dining room. "Men and women I shipped with are passing away. And their children and grandchildren want to know who they were." She smiled at Marzana. "That legendary escape—if I do say so myself—is never going to die, but it's easy to forget there were real people involved. We pulled off our grand illusion, but in the aftermath, we were still living, breathing human beings who had to find someplace safe to go. They couldn't all just change their names and addresses and go on in the city. They couldn't all escape to the Liberty and go on with their lives the way Honora and your dad and I did."

She sat and looked at Christopher Fletchwood's daisies on the sideboard. "That escape had zero deaths, but there were casualties.

Families were broken. Whole identities died so the corresponding humans could live. Many of those who stayed—if they stayed in less . . . *forgiving* parts of Nagspeake than the Liberty—had to walk away from everyone they'd known before. They lived in fear that the wrong person might recognize them. The ones who had family either picked up and moved the whole kit out of town, or they severed ties for the safety of all. Think of that."

She lifted her coffee cup and went into the kitchen for a refill. Marzana trailed afterward. "So these people who've been contacting you—family of crew—you think all of them are reaching out now that their relatives are dying?"

"I know so." She refilled her cup. "Remember, I've been reading the letters before I send them back, because I did say crew and their families should reach out to me if they're ever in serious trouble. But these letters are all coming from family who just want the truth. And I'm not insensible to that." She passed the coffeepot to Marzana's father, who was leaning against the counter. "Some of the crew must've left dead letters behind," Mrs. Hakelbarend said, adding a spoonful of sugar and stirring. "*Not to Be Opened Until I'm Returned to the Dust* sort of thing, with reminiscences or who knows what, but apparently including my name and how to find me. It's dangerous, and everyone knew they weren't supposed to do that—and certainly if those letters had anything about me in them, they also ought to have included instructions not to look me up unless it was an emergency."

"But people are human," Marzana's father said, and Marzana got the impression he intended the reminder to be for her mother's benefit as much as for Marzana's. He swirled the coffee in his mug. "They don't follow instructions they don't like, and here we are."

Her mother inclined her head. "I owe them. I know that. And while it's dangerous to romanticize what we did, I also do believe my crew comprised patriots and heroes, and I want their families to know." She smiled. "To be proud. Even if it's dangerous."

Marzana smiled too, but what she was actually thinking was that if her mother really felt that way, it was strange that she was so hesitant to share those stories with her own daughter. She knew better than to point out that bit of hypocrisy just now, so instead she asked, "What do you mean it's dangerous to romanticize it? If you believe they were heroes and patriots, it isn't romanticizing it to tell those stories, is it? It's just true."

"It's dangerous because you can forget that we were real people. That we weren't perfect. That there were real consequences, that it wasn't all swashbuckling adventure, and who we were really fighting against and why." She sighed. "So what else could I tell those kids? Tumbler was a sweet guy. He loved poetry. He loved a good brainteaser. He was a whiz with locks. Taught me everything I know."

Honora stumped in, opened her mouth to order them all elsewhere, then shut her mouth as the doorbell rang again. She groaned and stumped back out.

"Please let that be someone who just wants to sell me magazines." Mrs. Hakelbarend glanced at her watch. "You're going to be late, Marzie."

Marzana grabbed her mother's wrist and looked at the time. "Yes. Yes, I am." Her father held out a piece of toast. Marzana took it, stuck it in her mouth, and headed out of the kitchen to get her bag and her shoes.

She found Honora in the foyer closing the door behind Nicholas Larven, her mother's former lieutenant and one of the very few shipmates besides Honora who still worked with the former Captain V. "Hi, Mr. Larven."

"A fine, fine morning to you, my dear." He tipped his trilby hat and gave a short, courtly bow. Nick Larven did not remotely resemble a sailor. He looked like a fussy old man with a too-fancy mustache and a too-neat suit—a bit of a dandy, was how her mother put it. Today he was dressed in dark pinstripes with a single blue flower in a tiny silver buttonhole vase and his gray mustache waxed to points. But he was the kind of dandy who carried a sword in his cane, a steel plate in his hat, and a collapsible grappling hook on his key ring. He was upwards of sixty, but he was strong as a wolf, and he could be as merciless as one when the occasion required. According to her father, back in the days when Mrs. Hakelbarend had earned her legendary status as Captain V., Mr. Larven had been her crew's most formidable muscle. It would be hard to imagine now, if she hadn't seen it herself, him disarming a much younger man—Rob Gandreider, in fact—with a single candlestick.

Given the kidnapping, this was unlikely to be a social visit. And of course, he *would* show up just as Marzana had to haul her tail to school. She clenched her teeth, shouldered her backpack, and stalked out into the morning.

eight

THE MAGICIAN AND THE CAMOUFLEUR

THE MORNING PASSED in much the same way as it always did. The Marymead fence had sprouted a collection of iron bells, using the students' locks as clappers. Nialla brought sugar cookies she'd somehow managed to make in between Toby incidents. They ate one each as they walked up the stairs to home-room and decided to save the rest for the meeting on the sixth floor.

Marzana wondered if Emilia would join them for lunch, but she didn't. She sat with a handful of the other Commorancy Kids at her usual table on the far side of the dining hall under a sprawling Venetian glass chandelier, one of three that were relics from the days when this had been the Cotgrave dining room. It wasn't until five minutes to the bell that she got up, dumped her tray, and strolled over to where Marzana and Nialla sat at the end of a table by the window. "You guys about done?" she asked.

Boy, Marzana thought, *Emilia's poker face isn't just for game night.*

She glanced at Nialla. "I am."

Nialla got to her feet. "Sure thing."

Emilia nodded. "Then let's blow this popsicle stand."

They grabbed their bags, dumped their trash, and followed Emilia to the nearer of the two big staircases. Since the lunch bell hadn't rung yet, the stairs were mostly empty. "You haven't been up here before," Emilia said as they reached the second floor and started up to the third. "The Commorancy floors upstairs, I mean."

Marzana shook her head. "Nope."

"They're nothing special." Emilia glanced over her shoulder at them. "I mean, people think it's mysterious or whatever. They're just dormitories. I feel like I should make sure you temper your expectations, in case you were expecting the Gryffindor common room or something."

"I wasn't," Marzana assured her as they passed the third floor.

"I kind of was," Nialla grumbled.

"Well, sorry to disappoint." She sniffed the air as they continued upward, then glanced at Nialla's book bag. "Do you have cookies in there?"

"Yeah, but now that I know we're not going to Gryffindor tower, I'm not sure I'm sharing them."

"Would it help if I told you there actually is an Owlery?"

"Yes," Nialla and Marzana said together.

"Oh." Emilia said nothing for two more floors. The other two followed her breathlessly, in part because of the prospect of an Owlery and in part because there were just a thumping lot of steps. They paused for a momentary break at the turn in the stairs just above the fourth floor, scooting back into the wallpapered corner to make room for some kids heading up to the language and social studies classrooms on five. "There isn't one, though," Emilia admitted at last.

Finally they arrived at the sixth floor. "Most of the dormitories are upstairs on seven," Emilia said, leading them into a wide space between the two staircases. It was mostly open, like the Grand Saloon on the first floor. The same big brick chimney that rose from the saloon's huge hearth up through the house, floor by floor, stood like a column in the center of the room here, with fireplaces cut into it front and back.

"Is this the common room?" Marzana asked, looking around at the scattered chairs and tables, some of which were cluttered with abandoned textbooks and in-process projects. She paused to read a note taped to the top of a diorama of a room built into a shoebox: HARRIET, DO NOT TOUCH THIS! WE ARE NOT ADDING A DEATH RAY. I LOOKED IT UP AND MATTHEWS DIDN'T INVENT IT UNTIL THE '20S. PETER. And then, Harriet's scrawled reply: PETER, HE ANNOUNCED IN 1923 THAT HE'D INVENTED IT. SHOW ME WHERE IT SAYS HE DIDN'T INVENT IT EARLIER. XO HARRI. Standing on a toothpick tripod next to a matchbox desk was, in fact, an item made from a single rigatoni noodle blackened by marker that looked suspiciously like a tiny death ray.

"Nope," Emilia replied. "We call this space the Inglenook, even though it's not remotely a nook. It's whatever it needs to be: study spot, dining room, workshop. Same thing upstairs. Our common room's there," Emilia said, pointing ahead to a pair of yellow doors. "Each floor has one. This floor also has our kitchen and pantry, a bathroom, the babysitter's office, that kind of thing."

"There's a *babysitter?*" Nialla asked, aghast.

Emilia made a face, then nodded toward an office off to the right. "Resident nurse. Someone has to make sure we're not getting into trouble up here when everyone else goes home, running with scissors and eating the detergent and whatnot."

The yellow doors had probably once been sunflower-colored

and bright, but they had darkened and the paint had cracked with time. The effect was surprisingly nice, like looking at the fissures on the surface of a painting made with thick-daubed strokes of color. Marzana and Nialla followed Emilia through them and into a room that filled up almost the entire front of the floor. Two sets of doors led out onto the balcony; between them, a huge picture window faced onto Pastern Wynd and stared into the windows of the two tall, skinny houses across the street from Marymead. There were a number of round tables, three clusters of big cozy chairs, two wood-burning stoves, and some nice tufty rugs underfoot. The paintings on the walls looked like they might've been done by students, some recently and some long ago.

"This is nice," Marzana commented. The novelty of being on the sixth floor and the aches in her legs from hiking all the way up here were almost drowning the nerves that had been ramping up since before lunch. Almost.

Emilia surveyed the room. "It's clean for once. That's a pleasant surprise."

"I'm surprised it's empty," Nialla said. "I'd be up here all the time if I had a private common room."

"I asked to have it for this period today," Emilia said, crossing to the trio of chairs that looked out the picture window.

"You asked to have it?" Marzana repeated. "To yourself? How does that work?"

Emilia shrugged. "It's easier than you'd think. There are only fifteen of us, and we try to take care of each other. If somebody needs privacy, we find a way. Nobody abuses the privilege."

"That's amazing." Nialla picked a seat and sighed as she settled into it. "It's so quiet. I could get used to this."

"Well, don't get too used to it." Emilia sat, and Marzana followed suit. "So let's have it. Tell me about this kidnapping."

"Okay." Relieved that they'd somehow skipped small talk altogether, Marzana took her journal from her backpack and went page by page through everything she'd learned about the crime from her parents and Emmett, along with the questions she'd written down on Monday night. Out of habit so old she didn't even really have to think about it, she skirted any mention of the connections between Emmett and her parents, or exactly why Emmett had come to the Hakelbarends in the first place.

Emilia was a good listener, or at least her impassive poker face made it look like she was. "And who's Mr. Otter-something?" she asked at last. "You said you needed to know about a substitute teacher. Mr. Otter-something."

"Otterwill," Nialla supplied. "He's subbing for Mrs. Agravin, and he came from Peony Hyde's elementary school. *Aaand,*" she said, drawing out the word for dramatic effect, "he's visiting family in the Liberty here on short notice because he had a summer job working at a camp, and that camp canceled its first week — this week — yesterday."

"Which your parents' friend said was the case with Peony's day camp, which was located right by the school where she went and where this guy worked, and which they said was at least partly staffed with people who knew her personally." Emilia had been paying very close attention.

"Exactly," Marzana said, gratified. "We think he has to know something. The kidnapping hasn't been reported to the public, but probably the teachers at the school would've been interviewed, and for sure any counselors who were there on Sunday to set up."

"Sure, but there's not likely to be confirmation of any of that in whatever records Marymead has for him," Emilia pointed out. "If they have any records at all. Unless he's subbed here before, I can't imagine there'll be much. Just personal information. Contact stuff. If the notice was that short, there might not even be a résumé, and if there is, I doubt he'd have taken the time to update it to include a camp from which a kid maybe just got abducted."

"You're probably right," Marzana agreed, "but it's a place to start."

Emilia nodded. "Seems reasonable. You want me to look tonight?"

Marzana hesitated. "You can really do that?"

"Crack into the faculty records?" The poker face fractured at last as Emilia smiled a little. "That's why you asked me, isn't it?"

"Well . . . yeah. But . . . but you can really *do* it?"

"What can I say?" Emilia raised both hands, palms up. "The legends are all true."

Nialla shook her head. "I think you might be my new hero." She leaned over, got the foil package out of her bag, and opened it with an air of formality. "I bestow upon you these cookies, even if you have no owls."

The three girls took a cookie each. Then they looked at one another. "So?" Marzana said finally. "All for one, or something?"

"All for one," Emilia confirmed, holding up a crooked pinky finger. Marzana linked hers to it.

"And all for three," Nialla said, slipping her pinky in too. Emilia looked at her with concern. "Don't worry." Nialla laughed. "One for all. It's just something my brother used to say. All for one and all for two." They each took a ceremonial bite. Nialla laughed again, this time a little nervously. "I can't believe we're actually doing this."

"Anyway, it'll be all for four if J.J. comes aboard," Marzana pointed out. She paused to finish chewing. "Nialla's neighbor," she explained to Emilia. "He might join us too."

"We're meeting him at Lucky's this afternoon," Nialla said. "Can you come?"

"Sure. What's his deal?"

Marzana glanced pointedly at Nialla, who squirmed slightly and bought herself a minute by cramming the rest of her cookie into her mouth. "He's into magic," Nialla said a little defensively when she'd finished chewing and couldn't put off answering any longer.

Emilia's poker face didn't falter in the slightest. "Magic."

Nialla sighed. "Listen, you'll understand when you talk to him."

"Can he throw playing cards to do damage, or something?"

"No!" Nialla exploded. "Well, maybe. I don't know. But—just let him explain tonight. I'm telling you, it's a good idea, bringing him aboard."

"'Cause weaponized playing cards would be pretty useful, maybe. Depending on how serious things get." Emilia patted Nialla's shoulder peaceably, which was smart, because Nialla's face was starting to go impressively red. "Yeah, I wanna come and talk to the magician. What time?"

"Meet outside on the front stairs after school at three?" Marzana asked. "We can walk over together."

"Yeah." Emilia smiled slowly. "But let's not meet outside. Find me in the trustees' hall as soon as you can after dismissal."

Marzana frowned. The trustees' hall was just outside the gymnasium, which had once been the ballroom of Marymead House. The gym was at the back of the ground floor, and it opened onto the courtyard, which might've been a convenient direction in which to go if the courtyard didn't have a twelve-foot wall around it. If, however, they were going out the front door eventually, the cramped hallway, crowded with too many lockers and kids in too small a space, was a crummy meeting spot.

But before Marzana could ask why on earth they'd meet there, an old-fashioned buzzer rang over the common room's open double doors. Emilia popped to her feet, impassive expression right back in place. "Better get moving. You kind of have to haul tail to get to the lower classroom floors from here before the second bell."

Two hours later, Marzana and Nialla lingered in the hallway that ran in between the gym and the saloon, watching other kids packing up to head home. Short bays of four lockers each projected perpendicularly into the hall on both sides, with a wide break for the excessively grand double doors to the gym. Rows of gilt-framed, grim-faced Cotgraves and Cotgrave relations and descendants and other trustees of Marymead, past and present, hung above the lockers on both sides. The girls picked a spot against some lockers on the saloon-side wall to wait, and a moment later, Emilia materialized from out of the current, her satchel over one shoulder. "Hey."

"Hey," Marzana replied, still without a clue as to why they were here. She fidgeted and gestured vaguely toward the entry hall. "Should we . . . ?"

Emilia shook her head once. "Just wait."

The crowd in the hall began to thin out. Emilia checked her watch in a careless fashion, then put up three fingers with which she proceeded to soundlessly count down: three, two, one. She held up a fist, and at that very moment, one of the massive doors beside them swung open and Mr. Pratt, the gym teacher, came out with a student in tow.

"—happy to discuss it, Kevin," Mr. Pratt was saying, "but it's table-tennis day, so I have to be quick about getting the flag down. You're welcome to walk with me." He and the student trooped down the hallway and disappeared around a corner.

Emilia stretched, then affected a look of surprise and annoyance. "Darn it, did I leave my coat in there?" she asked in a bored tone. "Come on, I bet I know where I left it. I'll be quick." And without waiting for an answer from the other two girls, she yanked the door open and slipped inside. Marzana and Nialla exchanged puzzled grins and followed.

The gym was another casualty of the Cotgraves' stipulations about their bequest. The school was not permitted to move or alter any of the family's collection of fancy-pants lighting fixtures, so the former ballroom's massive gaslit chandelier, which for whatever reason had never been converted to electricity and always seemed to be giving off a low, persistent hissing sound, still hung midway between the two suspended backstops and had to be hauled up and out of the way whenever it was time for basketball. A stage had been installed in the wall to their right (post-Cotgrave, thank goodness, Mr. Pratt often snarked, or the school would probably have been stuck with actual footcandles there). The lights were out, but there was plenty of illumination coming in from the glass-paned French doors directly across the room (also not ideal for a room with frequent airborne objects moving at high velocity), which led to the walled courtyard. There was a second set of smaller double doors on the wall across from the stage, but they didn't really lead anywhere but to the administrative offices.

"Are we going out through the courtyard?" Nialla asked dubiously.

"More or less," Emilia replied, crossing to the French doors. "Quick, now."

"How?" Nialla asked as she and Marzana followed, but Emilia didn't bother to answer. The doors were already open; Mr. Pratt kept them that way in good weather to try to protect the glass, much to the fury of Mr. Sopwith, the gardener, who considered them to be the first line of defense in protecting the Orangery from escaped volleyballs and the like. Emilia led them outside into the courtyard, took a look around to be sure it was empty, then made a rapid turn to face the outside wall of the gym, where Mr. Sopwith kept a big work shed full of supplies. She took a little pouch from her satchel. It was about the same size as the one that held the little scout-knife multi-tool that Marzana's father had given her for her last birthday —*I should really start carrying that,* she thought—but when Emilia flicked her case open, instead of a knife, she extracted a pair of lock-picks.

"Wait a minute," Nialla whispered, glancing around in a panic. Marzana looked up instinctively toward the dozens of windows that overlooked the courtyard—but the shed was so close against the wall, the girls were probably invisible to anyone looking down.

"No time to wait." Emilia spoke fast as she went to work on the lock below the chipped glass knob using a practiced bit of twitchy fiddling with the picks. "Mr. Sopwith locks the side gates on either side of the house and goes out front during dismissal to make sure nobody picks the flowers on their way home. The only way back here for the next half hour is through the gym, but Mr. Pratt's fast getting the flag down. He's who we have to worry about."

"And the table-tennis club," Marzana said, remembering Mr. Pratt's words as he'd left the gym.

"Yeah, not really," Emilia said, turning the knob. With a creak of old hinges, the door opened. Emilia swept an arm toward the cluttered inside of the shed. "Be my guest."

"That's impressive," Marzana muttered, hurrying inside with Nialla right behind her.

"Meh," Emilia said, pulling the door shut behind them. The scent of potting soil and chemicals filled their nostrils. The shed was dim but not dark, due to two green-tinged skylights in the roof, and it was almost obsessively neat and organized and large enough for the three of them to move around one another comfortably.

"For some reason, that lock gives me trouble," Emilia said, reaching for a key that hung on a hook beside the door. "There's a copy of this key upstairs in the Official Commorancy Key Collection — it's just a ring full of rando keys collected over the years by boarders at Marymead — but somebody else was using the collection this afternoon."

"How, exactly, do I apply to be a Commorancy Kid?" Nialla asked as Emilia relocked the door from the inside and rehung the key.

Emilia grinned. "Get on the waiting list. And move off *that*." She pointed at the ground, and Marzana and Nialla discovered a wooden trapdoor set into the middle of the floor, the rest of which was made of the same paving stones that lined the courtyard outside.

Nialla backed up into a corner stacked with terracotta pots, and Marzana edged back against a pegboard hung with handheld tools. Emilia bent and lifted the hatch to reveal a brick-walled hole with a short ladder bolted to one side.

"You're kidding," Marzana said, staring down into the dark. Trapdoors in sheds? Collections of mysterious keys? She turned to Nialla. "All this time we've been bored out of our minds, thinking there was nothing exciting going on anywhere, and meanwhile our classmates are getting up to shenanigans right under our noses."

"Bored? Here?" Emilia considered them as she took a flashlight from her bag. "Someday I'll give you a proper tour of the school." She passed the light to Nialla. "Take this. I'll close up after us."

Nialla switched the flashlight on and tucked it under her chin. "Nothing down there better be carnivorous." She swung her feet into the hole and began her descent.

Emilia leaned on the hatch. "If there is, I haven't met it yet."

Marzana climbed down next, following the jittery beam and feeling the thrill mount as she descended. As they waited for Emilia at the bottom, Nialla bounced giddily on her toes at Marzana's side and swept the light around the space: a tunnel that began at a wall just behind the ladder and seemed to open out into a bigger chunk of darkness just a little ways up ahead. This—this was *exciting*. Marzana reached out and grabbed Nialla's free hand, at which her friend, unable to hold her own glee in any longer, actually hopped twice in delight.

They just barely managed to compose themselves as Emilia dropped down between them a moment later. She took the flashlight from Nialla. "Onward."

The air down there was musty and humid, but it had a vague, familiar, citrusy green note to it. "I can smell the Orangery," Marzana said as they walked down the tunnel toward the place where it widened. Her voice echoed.

"Yup." Emilia's light played over a tangle of iron and copper pipes and assorted antique valves and gauges that seemed to go on for yards and yards. "Most of the plants and fruit trees up there need tropical conditions year-round. The Orangery is heated from under the floor. This is where all the works are." She swung the flashlight wide, revealing a sort of walkway at the periphery of all the plumbing. "This way."

They followed Emilia and her flashlight through the perfumed tunnel and into a stretch with a more minerally smell to it. Emilia pointed to another jumble of pipes. "Those are the fountain water-works. Nearly there now." At last the beam of the flashlight fell on a set of stone steps. Emilia trotted to the top and hastily picked the lock on a small wooden door set into an old brick wall. She pushed the door wide, leaned to the side so that Marzana could squeeze in next to her, and trained the beam of the flashlight downward to il-luminate a derelict little platform about a foot below that jutted out over a wide, dry cement trough. "Thataway."

"Where are we now?" Marzana asked as she climbed down onto the platform. It looked like a small pier.

"Private dock," Emilia confirmed as Nialla dropped down to join Marzana. "Underneath Eald Brucan Lane." She flashed the light from side to side, revealing an arched red-brick ceiling over a tunnel marred here and there by the jut of more sad little dry piers, but with no end in sight in either direction. "I don't know when there was last water in this canal—maybe not since the Cotgraves—but this is where Eald Brucan gets its name: from the old brook that used to run below it. We can take this all the way to right under where West-ing Alley meets Hellbent, and come down basically across the street from Surroyal Books."

"Down?" Nialla asked, looking up at the arched brick ceiling of the tunnel. "Don't we have to go up at this point?"

"Well, not at *this* point," Emilia said, and the tunnel vanished into darkness as she leaped onto the pier, tucked the flashlight be-tween her chin and left shoulder, and used her picks to relock the door they'd come through. "At this point we go straight." She stood and jumped down into the dry canal. "All will become clear. Shall we?"

They filed down the center of the canal for about ten minutes, until they reached a pier whose corresponding door was painted with an address in flaking gold paint that glittered when the flashlight's beam found it: 5 WESTING ALLEY. This door wasn't locked at all. They followed Emilia through it and up into a basement full of washers and dryers that sat at odd angles to the wall, dark except where small windows near the ceiling let in shafts of dusty light. "Apartment building," Emilia explained. "Abandoned. Mostly."

There it was again, that sudden, cresting thrill. "What does 'mostly' mean?" Nialla inquired.

"It means it would look very weird if anyone came out the front door, so we're going to climb up a few floors and come down the fire escape."

"Isn't there a back door?"

"Yes, but it's padlocked from the outside, and I presume none of us are magicians or we wouldn't be going to interview one. Plus," Emilia added, "this route is much cooler. If you thought the waterworks were exciting, this is going to be something else."

Marzana's nerves had been fizzing along at a high degree of excitement ever since Emilia had begun to work on Mr. Sopwith's shed door, but now they ramped up to an even more extreme pitch. She was used to a low-grade jangling borne of her general worries about all the social interactions that somehow she just couldn't seem to get through the day without. But this was different. She'd felt it before, once or twice — most notably, of course, at Greenglass House — but in general she had come to believe the feeling wasn't to be found at home in Gammerbund. Yet here they were, and much to her shock, there had been excitement literally under her feet all this time. She just hadn't known where to look.

They found a stairwell behind a pitted metal door and

marched up six floors. Emilia stepped out into the hallway without so much as a pause to see if the coast was clear. "Come on," she called, when Marzana and Nialla hesitated. "Our skulking days are over."

They joined her in a hallway tiled in black and white squares, and Emilia pointed with a flourish to a sign on the door of the apartment immediately across from the stairwell they'd emerged from.

BONEASH AND SODALIME'S GLASS MUSEUM AND RADIOACTIVE TEASHOP

"This is a . . . museum?" Nialla said, glancing from the sign to the end of the deserted hallway.

"And . . . radioactive teashop," Marzana finished warily. Then she realized they weren't standing in darkness anymore. "Wait." Bare and dusty bulbs screwed into rusted, unremarkable ceiling fixtures flickered overhead. "The lights are on. Won't someone notice?"

"They're always on," Emilia said. "Wait until you see this." She turned the knob, and, as with the building's entrance in the canal tunnel, the door opened easily. In the room beyond, there was still more light, and in its warmer illumination, a sea of pastel-colored glass surfaces glittered.

"It's a real museum," Emilia said, waving them forward. "Everything's labeled; everything's got a history. Somebody maintains it, but I've never seen anyone here, other than people I happen to bring with me. Oh, and listen, it's about ten minutes to four, so we should probably not hang out in there or we'll be late for the magician. We can come back another time for a proper look around."

Marzana edged forward, drawn irresistibly by the weirdness of a museum of any kind being kept in a mostly abandoned apartment building whose front and back entrances were apparently never unlocked. But Nialla hung back. She tapped the word RADIOACTIVE on the sign. "What about that?"

Emilia waved a careless hand. "Nothing to worry about. There's a display about it in there. Apparently in the States they used to make a kind of glass with uranium. It's supposed to be pretty harmless. Still," she said, eyeing the room behind her dubiously, "I've never quite worked myself up to drinking the tea."

Marzana gaped at her. "You can really *have tea* here? But you said there's never anyone around!" Unable to resist any further, she pushed past Nialla and Emilia and into the museum.

From bottles of every shape and size to jewelry and electrical insulators and pipes and bits of decorative sculpture, glass covered nearly every surface—but tidily, precisely: plates standing on the floor in perfectly balanced stacks; saltcellars in the shapes of animals or shoes or wheelbarrows displayed with neatly printed tags on furniture and collections of lenses laid out in rows in display cases; masses of glass hanging from the ceiling in the form of lighting fixtures both fancy and plain and unlit mobiles made variously from art glass, champagne flutes, and teacups. A shoe rack beside the door held four different pairs of glass slippers. A shelf a few feet above it held four glass display heads, each different from the rest, wearing an assortment of felt hats. There was white glass; glass tinted pale milky blue and green and pink; painted glass; blown glass; pressed glass in patterns of hobnails or concentric circles or darts and arrows and diamonds. There was opaque glass in the colors of custard and bisque, or shaded from yellow to pink like a citrusy sunset. And everywhere, in between and around and over and under all those other colors and styles, there was glass in distinctive shades of yellow and green. Some of it was transparent and some was not, but every piece seemed faintly to glow.

In the middle of the room stood a table neatly laid with tea things made of gleaming glass the cloudy, bluish-green color of Marzana's toothpaste back at home. The teapot was steaming faintly. Marzana could smell the freshness of the scones on the plate beside it. Three cups and three saucers had been set out. The centerpiece was a vase of painted crystal, filled with blown and sculpted flowers so detailed that Marzana was almost convinced she could smell their perfume, too. A glass bee perched on one delicate petal.

Emilia came to stand beside her and looked at the table over folded arms. "The number's always right too," she said, nodding at the scones. "The first time it was me and the girl who introduced me to the place, and there were two cups. When I come alone, there's just one. Once I came with three others for my birthday, and there were four cupcakes, and you won't believe this, but one of them had a candle in it."

If anyone else had told her this, Marzana would've called that person a liar. But coming from Emilia, this somehow seemed at once entirely astounding and entirely possible.

A momentary silence fell as Marzana and Nialla looked around in wonder. "Are you really bored all the time?" Emilia asked quietly. "I don't understand. Not when there are things like this in the Liberty."

Marzana lifted her shoulders, feeling a vague sense of remorse at the words she'd chosen before—but only a shadow of what she thought she might have felt if not for the thrumming wonder and exhilaration still coursing through her. "I didn't know," she said simply. "I didn't know there were things like this."

Emilia shook her head. "But *how?* How have you not noticed? Don't you know where you live?"

"That's not fair," Nialla protested. "How on earth would we ever have found *this?* If we hadn't been shown, I mean. *You* had to be shown. You said so. How would you have found it?" She looked back at the sign on the still-open door announcing the presence of the museum. "Speaking of which, how does *anyone* find it? How do visitors get here? *Do* they? Does anyone else come here?"

Emilia considered. "Well, like I said, I've never seen anyone, and the front and back doors are padlocked, so your guess is as good as mine. The canal door is always unlocked, and if we had kept going up on those stairs, the roof doors are usually open. And of course, there's the fire escape." She shrugged. "It's a mystery. But we have a date with a magician. Let's not be late."

She closed the museum's front door and passed through the main room toward the arched entry to the kitchen, where there was a whole new collection of glassware. She topped short of going in and paused beside a table holding a tapering horizontal display of glass bowls, some rimmed with gold and all nestled one inside the other from wide to narrow with a spoked wooden wheel at the narrowest end. The sign above it read FRANKLIN ARMONICA, and for no apparent reason, there was a bowl of water on the table, next to the display.

"I'm going to say this," Emilia stated, "but it might tick you off. I like you guys, so I hope it doesn't, but I think it's something worth thinking about."

She paused for only a second or two — not long enough for a reply, but plenty long enough for Marzana to be taken aback by the businesslike way Emilia dispensed with sentiments that would have stymied her for hours and, in the end, almost certainly would've kept her from speaking up at all.

"To answer your question from before, Nialla: If I hadn't been shown this place, I might never have found it, that's true. But then again, I might have. For sure I would have found someplace or something just as amazing. I'd have found an adventure of some kind, even if it wasn't the kind I thought I was looking for. *Because I go looking for them.* I open doors, I look through windows, I explore alleys and hallways, I assume every staircase has something interesting if I follow it up or down, and if I meet someone who seems interesting, I ask them where they've been and what they've seen." Emilia gave the wheel at the end of the row of bowls a spin, and the glass glittered as the column turned. She stuck her thumb in the bowl of water and held it to the gold rim of one of the bowls. It gave off an eerie, gorgeous sound, a single, wavering note that hung in the air like a dream and pierced Marzana's heart with aching joy. "You could do all that too," Emilia said as the note died slowly away. Then she disappeared into the kitchen.

Marzana and Nialla stood, still riveted by the ghost of the Franklin armonica's note, which hadn't quite vanished from the world yet. "You know," Nialla said slowly, "she's not wrong. It would never have occurred to me that I was allowed to try that armonica thing out."

"Come *on*," Emilia barked from the next room.

Marzana gave her body a little shake to get herself focused again. "Right." But both girls paused as, on their way to the kitchen, they drew even with the tea table. They exchanged a glance, and then each took a scone. "Thank you," Marzana whispered. The scone was warm in her palm. She picked up the last remaining one. "Let's take this for Emilia."

The kitchen was long and narrow. At the end of the room, on the far side of the collections of soda and coffee siphons and an assortment of laboratory glassware, Emilia waited beside an open window leading to a fire escape coated by old flaking paint. Her impassive expression cracked into a smile as Marzana handed her the scone.

They ate as they climbed floor by floor down a fire escape that, for whatever reason, spiraled rather than switchbacked to the alley below. The neighboring building was close enough that Marzana could reach out without stretching at all to trail her fingers against the brick. And then, one last climb down the final stretch of ladder that reached almost all the way to the paving stones of Westing Alley, and they were on the ground. The scone was cranberry and quince, and it was wonderful.

They arrived at Surroyal Books five minutes before four, but J.J. still beat them. Riding high on the deliciousness of the trip from Marymead to the bookstore, Marzana barely felt a shred of nervousness right up until the moment they passed under the ringing bells over the door. Then Nialla brightened and waved at a boy with curly black hair who looked up from one of the chairs by the fire. He waved back and got to his feet. Marzana barely had time to start to formulate an opinion about the notorious Julian Mowbry before another boy in one of the other chairs got up too and followed J.J. over to the three girls.

"Hey," Nialla said.

"Hey," J.J. replied, super-casual. Marzana wanted to roll her eyes, but she restrained herself.

This was fortunate, because Nialla immediately waved a hand in her direction. "J.J., this is Marzana, and our partner, Emilia."

"Nice to meet you," J.J. said. He nodded at the other boy, who was olive-skinned with sandy, sun-bleached hair: young-sailor coloring, Mrs. Hakelbarend would've said. "This is my friend Ciro. You'll want him for this thing too."

Marzana felt rather than saw Nialla and Emilia's eyes flick her way. She kept her voice even, though it was difficult. Remembering Emilia's earlier air of this-needs-to-be-said-so-I'm-just-gonna-say-it, she ginned up her courage, pitched her voice to what she hoped was an effective blend of businesslike and annoyed, and snapped, "No offense, but we aren't even sure we want *you* for this thing yet." It came out angrier than she'd intended, but then again, Marzana was *furious.* She'd told herself she didn't need to worry about this whole interaction because it was going to be up to J.J. to convince her to let him come aboard, which meant all the worry about what to say and what not to say should've been on him. Now he'd thrown Marzana right off her game.

"Okay, okay, everybody calm down." Nialla pushed Marzana with one hand and J.J. with the other, herding them toward the history room with the table and the antler chandelier and the semi-privacy. "Let's go talk."

Marzana allowed herself to be moved along. Emilia and Ciro followed a pace or two behind.

They passed Lucky along the way, dusting shelves in the poetry section. "Afternoon, all," she said, waving a linty cloth. "How's everybody?"

"Fine," Marzana said over her shoulder as Nialla propelled her along. "Okay if we use the history-room table?"

"Be my guest."

"Thanks."

Remembering Emilia's strategic seat choice from the night before, Marzana stalked to the chair at the far end of the table and folded her arms as the others filed in after her. "So talk, then." She glared at J.J. "You first. I hear you're a *magician.*"

"Yeah, I am," J.J. replied, sounding a bit defensive as he sat on the bench to her right.

"And what kind of *magic* do you do?" She knew she was being a little snotty. She didn't care.

J.J. snorted. He snapped his fingers. The bulbs in the antler-chandelier light went out, and the room, which had no windows, went almost fully dark.

"Whoa," Nialla said appreciatively. Marzana kicked her under the table.

"I do several kinds," J.J. said calmly. She followed his voice and spotted his silhouette near the door, where the only light left was dribbling in from the rest of the bookstore. The chandelier clicked back on, and J.J. lowered his hand from the switch on the wall and sauntered back to the table. "Mostly close-up magic, but also some stage magic."

Marzana looked from him to the switch he'd somehow thrown from ten feet away. "And how'd you manage that feat?"

J.J. gave her a pitying look. Then he relented, possibly because he remembered he was supposed to be convincing her to let him join the group. "I half-flipped the switch and attached a thread to it when we walked through the doorway," he explained. "When I snapped my fingers, you looked over here"—he waved his left hand—"so you didn't see me pull the thread and tug the switch the rest of the way."

"And you removed the thread when you went over to turn the lights back on," Emilia guessed. He nodded.

"What made you go to all that trouble the second you walked through the door?" Marzana asked.

"I assumed you'd want to see something, and you'd be expecting me to do some kind of card trick or close-up vanishing or something basic like that." He shrugged. "This wasn't any more difficult. It just took planning. That's the kind of stuff I'm good at. I can look at a space and figure out how to use it, to make it do what I want it to, and to make other people in the space think what I want them to think."

"Illusions." Nialla gave Marzana an expectant smile.

"Illusions," J.J. confirmed. "Though the word 'illusions' always makes me think of dudes in shiny suits with mysterious tunes playing in the background."

"Okay," Marzana said reluctantly. "I guess I can see why Nialla thought you might be useful." She laughed a little self-consciously. "Despite what she said—I mean, she told me it wasn't *magic*-magic, but I was still kind of hoping you'd turn out to actually be—you know. A real magician or whatever. That you could really do that stuff."

J.J. looked at her, perplexed. "But I can. That's the point. That's what all the planning is for. I can walk into a room, look around, and figure out how to make whatever bit of magic I want to happen, happen."

"Right, I get it. But I mean . . ." Marzana waved her fingers. "A mage or sorcerer, like from an RPG. That would be pretty epic."

"I know what you mean." The magician in question shook his head. "But look—the reality is even better. When I do a trick, it's me doing it. *Me,* not some nebulous power that does it *for* me. Give me a spool of thread and some wax, and I can do things you wouldn't believe. What's more impressive, snapping your fingers and having instant results, or actually figuring out the possibilities and mechanics on the fly and producing the same effect?"

"I get it," Marzana repeated, though it was more directed at Nialla than at J.J. Nialla was still staring at her in that expectant *See what I mean?* manner, and Marzana really wanted that to stop as soon as humanly possible.

"But the really epic thing?" J.J. went on, leaning across the table.

"Even if I *tell* you the miracle is just a piece of thread, I can still make you believe in it. I can make you believe I have to be lying about the string. That I have to be doing it for real. *That's* actual, legit magic."

Marzana nodded, pointedly ignored Nialla, and turned to the other boy at the table. "All right, then . . . Zero, was it?"

Ciro gave the smallest of sighs. Apparently he'd gotten that before. "Ciro, with a *C*. Ciro del Olmo."

Out of the corner of her eye, Marzana thought she saw Emilia sit up a touch straighter, but when she glanced over, the other girl's face was just as blank as usual. "And what's your deal?" Marzana asked, turning back to Ciro.

His face was almost as impassive as Emilia's. "My skill is hidden information."

"Hidden information, like what?" Marzana asked. "Like codes and ciphers?"

He nodded, but in such a way as to make clear that codes and ciphers were not remotely the extent of what he was talking about. "Like codes and ciphers, but also steganography and camouflage and plain old lying."

"Tell them about your folks," J.J. suggested, pushing Ciro's shoulder in encouragement.

"Hang on," Emilia interjected quietly. "This can't be about our parents. I can't talk about that."

"Neither can I," Marzana said, looking away from Ciro and J.J. to glance at Emilia curiously out of the corner of her eye.

"Doesn't matter, because you're already in," Ciro said. "I can talk about my father because he's dead, and my mom — well, if knowing where I learned what I know will help convince you to let me join up, I'll tell you."

There was a momentary silence around the table. "I'm sorry

about your dad," Emilia said at last. Marzana shot her a grateful glance. Of course that was the right thing to say, but it hadn't even occurred to her.

Ciro nodded. "Thank you." He looked to Marzana again. "Well?"

Marzana fidgeted. "Do you *want* to tell us?" She was deeply uncomfortable with the idea of any of them having to share more than they wanted. *This is the Liberty, after all. We keep our secrets. And we know better than to try to pry secrets out of others.*

Ciro looked at her with an unexpected mixture of anger and pride. "Yes."

"Okay, then." This situation was *so* awkward. "Go ahead."

He folded his arms defensively. "On both sides of my family, I have experts in hiding information and finding information that's been hidden. My dad and his family were camoufleurs. There have been del Olmos in Nagspeake since before the Revolution."

"What's a camoufleur?" Marzana asked.

"Someone who camouflages things. So for instance, there's a pretty great story about how my however-many-times-great-grandfather came to Nagspeake from Acapulco." Ciro leaned on the table. "I do have some Latino ancestry—my first name comes from my great-uncle—but the first guy in my family to call himself del Olmo was actually a Korean named Songhan who came to Mexico in the eighteenth century as a sailor on one of the Manila galleons, which used to go back and forth between there and the Philippines. But conditions on the galleon were horrific, so he deserted the ship in Acapulco. Then a year or so later, he got into trouble—the kind that had bad guys scouring the city for him."

"You should tell them that story," J.J. interjected. "*That* story's awesome."

Ciro shook his head. "It is, but it's a longer story, and it's not the point. What matters is that Songhan figured the best way to escape was by sea. He had a locksmith friend who was sailing to Nagspeake with his wife in three days, and his friend said the captain would take passengers. But that was expensive, and Songhan was broke."

"Couldn't he have signed on as a sailor?" Nialla asked. "If he'd been one before? Weren't ships always looking for good sailors back then?"

"He could have, but he thought he'd be safer if he went as a passenger, because then he could hunker down and hide in his cabin until the ship left port, and no captain would allow anybody to come aboard and hassle someone who'd paid for safe passage. But again: expensive. And then," Ciro continued, "he learned from his buddy that the ship had a problem that might keep it from departing on schedule. The trouble was the ship's elm-tree pump, which is just what it sounds like: a pump made from the trunk of an elm tree. This ship's pump had broken, and the crew had replaced it with one made from a different kind of wood. But since then, the ship had had nothing but bad luck, and now the crew was ready to mutiny if they didn't get a new pump made from an actual elm tree. Only Mexico doesn't *have* elm trees, so the ship was stuck.

"Songhan's friend introduced him to the first mate, and Songhan asked how much a new pump would be worth. The first mate said if he could produce an elm trunk within two days, he'd pay Songhan's passage himself, and the crew could finish the pump at sea. He was basically asking my ancestor to work a miracle. And," Ciro said with a grin, "Songhan did it. He produced the trunk and got his passage, and the crew took to calling him Songhan del Olmo: Songhan of the elm. He liked it so much that when he got to Nagspeake he kept it, and there have been del Olmos here ever since."

"How did he find the elm if there weren't any in Mexico?" Emilia asked.

Ciro grinned even wider and spread his hands. "Nobody really knows. But the del Olmos forever after were camoufleurs of some kind or another. My great-great-grandfather went to the United States for a while during the Second World War and painted warships in this crazy, colorful, wild patterning called *dazzle* that was supposed to fool U-boats so they didn't know where to fire their torpedoes. My grandfather designed a bunch of the old Belowground Transit stations that were supposed to blend into their surroundings, and my father painted some warehouses in Shantytown that were camouflaged to look like tenements, along with some other things in the city that had to be hidden in plain sight. So I presume that back in the day, Songhan did what all his descendants went on to do: he made one thing look like another, and he did it so effectively that even a bunch of superstitious, paranoid sailors who thought their lives depended on it couldn't tell the difference." He cleared his throat. "And on my mom's side, I'm descended from Annamaria Gallfreet."

A momentary shocked silence settled over the room. "The Spinster?" Nialla said in a whisper.

"Really?" Marzana asked, trying unsuccessfully to keep the disbelief from her voice. The Spinster was a legendary figure from two centuries before. She'd been a weaver by trade, but the story went that she had also dabbled in codes and code breaking during the Napoleonic Wars. Now and then her tapestries showed up in museums around Nagspeake, and supposedly if you knew how to look, there were secrets to be found in them. The Spinster was a heck of an impressive ancestor to claim.

Ciro nodded. "My mother's family has been working in codes

and ciphers and languages and programming for more than two hundred years."

Something clicked. "The cell phones?" Marzana asked, aghast.

Ciro nodded again. Nialla clapped a hand over her mouth. J.J. sat back, looking very satisfied. Even Emilia's poker face cracked for a minute, but it wasn't into surprise, rather a brief *I knew it* smile, and Marzana recalled how she had sat up just a bit straighter when she'd heard Ciro's last name.

It wasn't totally Deacon and Morvengarde's fault that Nagspeake was stuck, technology-wise, in the previous century. But it was *almost* totally their fault. They had a monopoly on the rights to lay cable and fiber. They had a monopoly on the rights to provide internet service and to build cell towers. They had a monopoly on the rights to sell the phones themselves, which were not only exorbitantly expensive but were basically guaranteed not to work, because D&M refused to put in the infrastructure, and the government down in the city proper . . . well. There were a dozen reasons they couldn't—wouldn't—do anything about it, the biggest of which was that anyone who opposed D&M was guaranteed not to get any D&M campaign money, and D&M had a lot of that to pass around.

But in the past few years, someone in the Liberty had been quietly chipping away at this problem. Internet access was spotty, but with the right hacks in the right places, you could just barely get it to work. Cheap and functional cell phones had been circulating. There was too much packed into too small a space in the Liberty to do much digging, but makeshift cell towers had appeared, moved, reappeared elsewhere. The resulting shadow network didn't work very well—or at least, it didn't yet. Marzana's mother, for instance, had access to whoever was supplying the phones, but she refused to rely on the devices during real jobs. And of course—deniability at work—she'd never told Marzana who that person was.

Now Ciro glanced at the door, then reached slowly into his pocket and took out a small gray rectangle. He set it in the middle of the table. The others leaned in to take a look.

"Does it really work?" Emilia asked.

"Of course it does," Ciro said defensively. "Mostly. I mean, the only person who ever calls me is Mom, and she doesn't seem to have any trouble. Usually." He looked down at it a little doubtfully. "The camera works great, at least."

"So are we in, or what?" J.J. asked, all but bouncing on the bench.

Marzana glanced at Nialla's hopeful face, then Emilia's impassive one. "Can you and Ciro give us a minute?" she asked.

"Sure." J.J. said breezily. He and Ciro got up and headed back toward the bookstore's main room. J.J.'s confidence was getting on Marzana's nerves. Maybe that was part of his magician thing, she thought grumpily. Maybe you had to be confident to convince people to believe you were doing the impossible.

When the boys were gone, Emilia cleared her throat. "Did you want me to go too?"

Marzana shook her head. "No, you get a vote here."

"We're voting?" Nialla clapped quietly. "Then you don't hate the idea."

"I don't hate it, but I'm still mad at you. Don't think just because I'm willing to put it to a vote that you're off the hook here. Especially since they're basically a package deal. We can't very well take one and not the other."

"Why not?" Emilia asked.

"Because . . ." Marzana hesitated. *Because it would be a jerk move* was what she'd been thinking, but Emilia had a point. They weren't doing this for fun and games. *Aren't we?* a small voice in Marzana's head inquired. *No, we're not,* she replied firmly.

"Because I think whichever we take will just tell the other everything he finds out anyway." Marzana looked curiously at Emilia. "Why? Do you think we should take one and not the other?"

Emilia shook her head. "I was just asking. Making sure I understand where we're all coming from."

"Okay. So what's your vote?"

Emilia's poker face wavered for a moment as a frown settled between her eyes and vanished just as quickly. "As long as they're not going to come in and try to take over just because they're boys. I quit a game group once because that kept happening."

To Marzana's surprise, Nialla nodded seriously. "Agreed. I vote yes, but only if we don't keep voting on everything. I hope you keep asking for our input, Marzana, but if we're really doing this, somebody has to be in charge, and as far as I'm concerned, that person has to be you."

"Seconded," Emilia said.

In charge. Out of nowhere, the bear that showed up periodically to go on a rampage in her gut came tearing through her insides. It only made sense — somebody had to at least nominally call the shots, and while the idea of being that person was utterly terrifying to Marzana, the idea of it being anyone else was fundamentally unacceptable. She took a deep breath to try to at least signal to the bear to chill out and take a nap. "All right, I accept your terms and I also vote yes."

Emilia got to her feet. "Shall I go?"

"Sure."

She disappeared, and Marzana immediately began stringing

words together in her head, but Emilia and the new recruits were back before she'd gotten farther than *We've discussed it and we've decided . . .*

"So?" J.J. asked without a moment's hesitation. "Have you determined our fates?"

Everyone was looking at her, including Emilia, who had taken the chair at the opposite end of the table, and Nialla, sitting on the bench to her left. The bear was still sniffling around, kicking her gut and pawing at her throat. Marzana swallowed its claws down and nodded. "We have. But we want to be very clear about what we're doing and how we're doing it. If you agree, we'd be glad to welcome you aboard."

"Sweet." J.J. dropped onto the bench opposite Nialla. "Tell us what the deal is, boss." Ciro sat at his side without a word, listening.

Boss. Was that a good indicator that he already understood that she was in charge, or was he being sarcastic? "Well," Marzana said, screwing up her courage, "you hit on the first thing." The words *Not to be bossy, but* came instinctively to her mouth, but she caught them before they escaped and swallowed them back. "I'm in charge. If at any point we disagree about the best strategy, I make the final call. I make the decisions about when to call in the adults, and if I decide things get too dangerous, we stop."

J.J. nodded immediately. Ciro raised a hand. "I have no problem with that, but I want to know more about what we're doing before I decide if I'm coming aboard or not."

Marzana balked. "After all this, *you* aren't sure?"

Ciro shrugged. "I've told you about me, but *you* haven't told me anything. Not about the . . . the *thing,* whatever this thing is, and not about you. I agree with you and Emilia that we shouldn't have to tell each other anything we're not comfortable sharing, but if you're heading out to rob banks tomorrow, then no, I've got better stuff to do with my time that won't get me arrested."

He had a point.

"Okay," Marzana said. Then she stopped talking for a minute as Emilia rapped twice on the table, sharply, just before Lucky and one of her customers came in looking for a book in the medieval history section. Marzana had a second to wonder just how awkward this looked — five kids suddenly going silent the moment an adult walked in — before J.J. leaped into the void.

"I thought so too," he said carelessly, as if picking up the thread of a previously existing conversation. "That was before I took the test, though. It wasn't the worst test I've taken this year . . . also not the easiest. Sometimes I think the difference is whether I have one of those annoying soft-lead pencils instead of my usual ones." He leaned back with his hands laced behind his head. "My sister likes the soft-lead ones. Sometimes we get our pencils mixed up at home, and then the whole day is shot because the school store is absolutely never open when you need it to be. Part of the thing is, those soft-lead ones won't hold a point, and I need a good point on my pencils for tests. I think my average went up by, like, ten percent after I got myself one of those fancy two-stage sharpeners. You know the kind I'm talking about?"

The customer, who had been showing signs of maybe wanting to browse, changed her mind, stuck her book under her elbow, and headed back for the front of the bookstore. Lucky followed, shooting a bemused glance over her shoulder as she went.

J.J.'s flood of test-and-pencil blather tapered off. "You were saying?"

Marzana looked at him in something akin to wonder. That much small talk, just off the top of his head? "How did you *do* that?"

"He has a gift," Ciro said drily.

Oh, right. Marzana snapped her fingers. "It's a magician thing, right? Patter, or whatever it's called."

J.J. grinned. "Yes. Yes, that's exactly it."

Ciro rolled his eyes. "Actually I just meant he's a bigmouth."

Emilia shifted in her seat. *"Anyway."*

"Anyway." Marzana cleared her throat. She opened her backpack, which sat on the floor by her chair, and took out her journal. "We want to solve a kidnapping. And we think we could use your help."

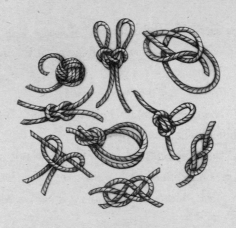

nine

STRATEGIES

WITH EMILIA KEEPING watch for more shoppers, Marzana told the story for the third time. When she'd finished, she looked from J.J. to Ciro. "So? What do you think? You want in?"

The boys glanced at each other. "Yeah," J.J. said in an *Are you kidding?* tone. "Sign me up. Nothing interesting ever happens around here!"

Ciro was slower to reply. "Your mom and dad are working on this too?"

"Yes. They're working on a different angle, though."

"But they don't know you're working on it."

"No." Marzana gave him a defiant look. "When we have something to give them, we'll give it, obviously."

"Obviously." Ciro cracked the smallest, briefest smile imaginable, then got all serious again. "Okay, I'm in too. So what's our plan now? What do you need us to do?"

That was the question. "Well, so far we have exactly one lead."

"Your math teacher."

"Yes. Emilia's going to see what she can find out about him from the school records," Marzana began. J.J. and Ciro both glanced at Emilia, impressed. "But what I'd really like," she continued, "is to find out if he can tell us anything about the situation with Peony at the school." She looked around the table. "Don't you think there had to be some way the kidnappers knew she'd be alone that day? She'd been walking with a friend for weeks before that. The split was new."

On opposite sides of the table, J.J. and Nialla shifted in their seats. J.J.'s face was pink.

"Makes sense to me," Ciro said, pushing through the silence. "But if nobody is supposed to know about the kidnapping yet, how are you going to ask?"

"I haven't figured that out yet," Marzana admitted. "If anyone has any ideas, I'm all ears. In the meantime, what other angles can we work?"

Nialla spoke up. "I want a crack at the ransom note. I have an idea."

Marzana flipped to the page where she'd written the text of the ransom note. "It's right here, more or less."

Nialla shook her head. "I need to see exactly what the note looks like on the page, in detail. I need my own copy, really. Do your parents have a copier?"

"Nope."

"And I guess there's no way you're getting their copy out of the house."

Ciro raised a hand. "I've got this." He put his phone on the table again. "I told you the camera works, right? Just invite me over. I can take a picture of the note and print it at my house. Can we do it tomorrow?"

The bear clawed its way back up, but Marzana managed to mutter, "Sure." This was going to take so much figuring out, both in terms of conversation and logistics. She couldn't decide which was scarier: the prospect of small talk, the fact that she'd have to explain his presence to her parents, or the problem of getting him into their study upstairs. But all of those were challenges for later.

Ciro glanced at Nialla. "You live near J.J., right?"

"Two doors down. The house with the six chimneys, first-floor flat."

"Then I can have it to you tomorrow night."

"Perfect. Also, does anybody have any money?" Nialla asked, rummaging in her satchel and pulling out her wallet. "I've read the series Peony was reading, but I got it from the Library. I'm going to need my own copy, and I've only got . . ." She peered into her wallet. "Yeah, just a few clams on me."

"That's a good idea," Marzana said. "I want to read it when you're done."

"Then we'll need two copies, because mine's not going to be in one piece when I'm finished with it. Unless one of you guys happens to have the Sidledywry Knot books already."

Nobody did—Emilia had read them as well, but also from the Library. Between them, they had what they figured would be enough money for a copy of the book Peony had, as well as the first one in the series so that Marzana and anyone else who wanted could start the series from the beginning. Nialla pocketed the cash.

"Okay, that's three angles to pursue," Marzana said. "There's one more I—"

"Incoming," Emilia reported, then pivoted neatly to browse the Ancient History shelves.

"The thing with pencils," J.J. said thoughtfully as two college-age kids wandered in, "is that it's not just the lead that'll mess you up. It's the eraser. Yesterday I had what looked like the perfect pencil for my physics test—"

"Wait," Emilia interrupted, "you're taking *physics?*"

J.J. spread his hands open. "What can I say? Anyway, I thought I had the perfect pencil—I mean, it was the kind I like; it was brand-new, or anyway it looked brand-new; I had a nice point on it, thanks to one of those awesome two-stage sharpeners—but then I went to use the eraser, and it did that thing where the rubber just smears the line all over the place. I don't even know what makes that happen. Like the eraser dries out or something?" He whistled low, shaking his head. "I had to borrow a pencil from Mrs. Turin, and her extra pencils are all stubby and they have almost zero eraser, which is kind of worse because then sometimes the metal ring scrapes the paper, plus by the time you sharpen them enough to put a good point on them, there's not enough pencil left to hold comfortably. Yeah, it was a bad day yesterday."

"I have to ask," Marzana said, still marveling at his ability to spout meaningless jabber apparently without forethought. "Why don't you just carry, you know, more than one pencil at a time? If it's this big a deal."

J.J. looked thoughtfully at her. "I ask myself that all the time. I think it comes down to this: I like the uncertainty. It's exciting."

Ciro scratched his chin. "Our lives are sad, aren't they?"

"A little," Marzana agreed, watching the two interlopers make their way back out of the history room.

"Clear," Emilia said, but this time she stayed facing the Ancient History shelf. The bookstore must have been getting busy. Time to wrap up.

"Before we disband for the night," Marzana said quickly, "the last idea I had was about how you'd get into the Liberty in the first place if you were dragging along a kid you'd kidnapped. It's possible the kidnappers have Liberty warrants, but even so, presumably if they brought Peony here, she'd have been either fighting, restrained, or unconscious. How would they have gotten her through the gates?" She pointed at Ciro. "You reminded me of something. There's a Belowground Transit station in the Liberty. They could've come in that way."

The others turned and stared at her. All but Ciro, whose face cracked into a very odd smile.

"The Belowground doesn't exist anymore," J.J. said immediately. "Hasn't since long before we were all born."

"Yes, it does," Marzana retorted. "It absolutely does. It might not be fully operational, but all the infrastructure's still there. The guy who brought this case to my parents came via the Belowground."

"I didn't know there was a station in the Liberty, though," Emilia said.

"There are two," Ciro said, still smiling. "I know that for certain. Like I said, my grandfather worked on them."

Marzana gave him a thoughtful look. "Your grandfather the camoufleur."

"Yup. Every Belowground station was meant to blend into the environment. The original idea was just that they weren't supposed to stick out — you know, they were supposed to have some of the character of whatever neighborhood they were in, really feel like part of it. But once they hired Granddad — well. Granddad was the guy you hired if you wanted to completely hide something, and I guess he had a hard time reeling himself in. The stations here are probably all right out in the open, but they would still be almost impossible to find if you didn't already know where they are. That's my guess, anyway."

"And do you know where they are?" Nialla asked.

Ciro's smile faded a tiny bit. "I don't. But I can probably find out. All Granddad's stuff is in my parents' attic."

"Can you look tonight?" Marzana asked.

He nodded. "I'm pretty sure."

"All right. Anything else we can think of?"

"I don't have a job," J.J. complained.

"Incoming," Emilia said again, pulling a heavy paperback off the shelf.

"What I really like," J.J. said without hesitation as a trio of customers came in with their arms full of books, "are those pencils that have the replaceable erasers. The school store used to have those, but I think some kid got some stuck up his nose and they stopped selling them."

"Some kid stuck erasers up his nose?" Ciro frowned. "I bet it was Jimmy Costak."

J.J. nodded. "Who else?"

"Why?" Emilia asked. "Why the heck would anyone do that?"

"He was trying to shoot them out his nose at the girl who sat in front of him," J.J. explained.

Nialla shook her head in disbelief. "That's disgusting."

"Yeah, we told him he should have just asked her out the normal way."

The customers, who'd clearly hoped to grab seats at the table, sighed and departed.

"I don't have a job," J.J. complained again, as if the eraser conversation had never taken place.

"It's just the first day," Marzana said consolingly. "We aren't going to crack this case in a single sitting."

"Well, when do we meet again?" he asked.

"Not tomorrow, because we have to do the ransom-note thing. How about Friday, same time?" Marzana suggested. "Then we should plan to get to work again on Saturday morning. If we're going to do any good at all here, we have to move fast. That's the day the kidnappers are supposed to send ransom instructions to the family. We need to be ready for anything."

J.J. was aghast. "You want me to miss *cartoons?*"

Marzana gave him a pitying look. "We all have to make sacrifices."

They exchanged phone numbers. The boys and Emilia said their goodbyes, and that was it. Marzana suppressed a sigh of relief, then immediately worried that she might have seemed too eager to be rid of her compatriots. But as she began the laborious process of reviewing every moment she could remember, it seemed to her — tentatively — that this first meeting had gone really well.

She and Nialla went together to the graphic novel section, where Lucky — bless her — had copies of every book of the Sidledywry Knot series that had been released so far. Nialla selected the first and the most recent, and they took them to Lucky at the register to pay.

Lucky looked up from the invoice she was reading. "Study group?" she asked casually.

"Sort of," Nialla said, handing over the cash she'd collected.

"Hmm." Lucky rang up the books, bagged them, and passed back some change. "You know, if the history room is too distracting, there's a spot that gets less foot traffic that you could use next time. If you're planning on meeting again."

"We might be," Marzana said, matching Lucky's casual tone. "Where's the better spot?"

Lucky turned her face up and nodded at the little mezzanine that overhung the register desk, enclosed by windows made from round panes like glass bulls'-eyes. The room beyond the windows was dark. "There's another table up there, along with some empty shelves where I've been meaning to move the Philosophy and Poetry sections, but I haven't had time." She handed the bag of comics to Nialla. "If you guys wouldn't mind moving a few books to those shelves after you meet, you're welcome to use the space."

"Deal," Marzana said, grinning. "How do we get up there?"

"The stairs between Biography and Plays."

"Can we start Friday after school?"

"Anytime. You'll be doing me a huge favor. I'll mark which sections go where for you."

This was what they'd been missing: a headquarters.

"You know what this means," Nialla whispered as they left the bookshop amid the tinkling of the front-door bells.

Once they were out on the street, she took the first Sidledywry Knot book from the bag and passed it to Marzana. "It probably means a few things," Marzana replied, tucking the book into her backpack. "Which thing were you talking about?"

"There are five of us now, plus we have an HQ. We're gonna need a name." She raised a hand, half wave, half salute. "Get on that."

"Nialla." Marzana grabbed the strap of her friend's satchel as she turned to go. Nialla paused, her face sympathetic, and Marzana could see that she knew what was coming. Marzana worried the strap, unable to let go. "Did I do okay?" she asked, forcing the question up and out into the world.

As it did every time she asked it, the question brought both fear and relief. Fear because she was mortally afraid of the answer, and Nialla would tell her the truth, even if it was bad. Relief because Nialla would tell her the truth, even if it was bad, and then she would *know*.

Nialla smiled, took Marzana's fidgeting fingers off her satchel, and squeezed her hand. "Better than okay. You did great. I promise."

The relief was like a gulp of cold water after a long run. Marzana let out her breath. "Okay. Thank you."

It shouldn't have been the name part that stuck in Marzana's head on the walk home. She had plenty of more serious, more important stuff to ruminate upon. How to ask Mr. Otterwill the questions they needed to ask him. How you got a kidnapped girl into a walled city. Where you might keep her once you had. How Marzana was going to sneak a boy her parents had never so much as heard of into their study for a look at the copy of the ransom note. But it was the name she kept coming back to, if only because having to say "Hey, I'd better assemble Emilia and Ciro and J.J. and Nialla" was going to get real annoying, real fast.

They needed a name. They were pursuing strategies. This was real.

So what kind of name did they need? Something efficient, elegant. Cool, but not trying too hard. Something she could say out loud and not worry about it being overheard.

Marzana was still turning this over in her mind when she hung up her backpack in the entryway at Hedgelock Court. Voices were murmuring in the living room. She followed them and found her parents deep in conversation over a pot of coffee. Mrs. Hakelbarend, listening intently to her husband, looked up as she entered and held out one arm. Marzana slid under it and leaned against her mother's side and into a kiss on her temple.

"Anyway, no record of Rob, but the other two, the nonresidents, came through the main gate on Monday, the day after the kidnapping. Each was alone, according to the warder," Mr. Hakelbarend continued. "No visitors, no companions. Not conclusive, but I guess at this stage any information is good information, until we figure out what we really need to know. Can't rule them out, but if either is involved in this thing, it suggests, as we thought, that Peony Hyde might not be in the Liberty."

Marzana shifted a little. Had they considered the Belowground? Surely they had. Despite everything, she still couldn't quite bring herself to believe she was going to think of anything her father, with his background in law enforcement, and her mother, with all her decades of experience outside the law, had not.

Then she sat up straighter. *Not* my *connections,* Emmett Syebuck had said about how he'd managed a ride on the Belowground to visit the Liberty. *Georgie's.*

Georgie was a thief Marzana and her family had met at Greenglass House. Her connection would be—could only be—the conductor who had delivered Emmett to the Liberty on the Belowground. Marzana had never met him, but she knew someone else apart from Georgie who had. Reaching out to that person out of nowhere might be slightly weird, but . . . she thought back to Emilia in the glass museum, talking about how she found adventures every day because she went out to meet them.

All Marzana had to do was make a phone call. If it had been up to Emilia, she would have done it without hesitation, even if it felt slightly weird. Just one phone call. No problem.

She sure as heck wasn't leaving this room yet, though. Not while her parents were talking.

"I have Nick looking for Rob," Mrs. Hakelbarend said with satisfaction. "I give it twenty-four hours before Nick trots him back here from whatever hole he's hiding in."

Her father chuckled. Even Marzana snickered a bit at the idea of anyone evading her mother's fussy, mustachioed comrade for long. Nick was a force to be reckoned with.

"Times like this, I really miss Meg," Marzana's mother added, pouring herself more coffee. She turned to Marzana. "How was your day?"

"Good."

"Did the game group meet again tonight?"

"No, I was hanging out with Nialla." Which was a technically true, if incomplete, statement. "So nothing new, then?"

"Not really," Mrs. Hakelbarend said. "Our networks take time. I have high hopes that Rob might know something, but until he surfaces—"

"Or Nick dredges him up," Marzana's father put in.

Mrs. Hakelbarend nodded. "I've put out other feelers, but I'll admit the waiting is not my favorite thing." She glanced at Marzana's dad. "I'm not patient enough for this kind of work. Not used to it."

He sighed and leaned back in his chair, stretching his legs out and propping his feet up on the coffee table as he stared up at the beams in the ceiling. "Nobody feels good about having to wait for investigations to bear fruit when there's a kid involved."

"Isn't there a deadline?" Marzana asked in a halfhearted effort to play dumb. "For the ransom, I mean."

"Sunday," Mr. Hakelbarend said darkly. "The note says the Hydes will get instructions on Saturday; then they have one day to pay."

Deeper in the house, the kitchen door banged open. Mr. Hakelbarend took his feet off the table so fast, it was a miracle he didn't kick over the coffee. Honora stalked into the living room. "Begging your pardons," she announced, "but it's half an hour to dinner." She peeked into the coffeepot. "Shall I do up another, then?"

"Not for me, thank you, Honora," Mrs. Hakelbarend said. She got to her feet and headed for the stairs. "Half an hour it is. Excuse me."

Marzana's dad set his empty cup on the tray. "No more for me, either, Honora. Thank you."

"The number-four grind," she said loftily as she carried the coffee things away.

Marzana got up too. Now that the part of the discussion she was allowed to overhear was done, she had work to do, and a half an hour might just be enough time.

"Gonna try and finish homework before dinner," she announced.

"Good luck," her dad said, reaching for a newspaper. Marzana darted out, in such a hurry to set this new idea in motion that she almost forgot to take her backpack with her.

Up in her room, she rifled through the assortment of papers and notebooks and whatnot in her desk until she found a scrap of paper with a phone number written on it tucked in a drawer. She carried it over to her bed, where she sat and practiced a few lines before picking up the phone receiver (cautiously, in case her mom was on the line), trying to channel Emilia the whole time: *If I meet someone who seems interesting, I ask them where they've been and what they've seen.*

At last, Marzana dialed the number scrawled in blue marker. The dial tone was scratchy, as it always was. She counted the rings until a woman's voice answered.

"Greenglass House. This is Nora."

Marzana took a deep breath. "Hi, Mrs. Pine. This is Marzana Hakelbarend. You know, from Christmas?"

"Of course, Marzana! Hi."

"Can—hi." She shook her head, flustered, and forced herself to regroup. "I was wondering if—can I talk to Milo?"

ten

MILO

'M SO HAPPY to hear from you!" Mrs. Pine said with what sounded like genuine delight. "Of course. You and Milo were going to try to schedule a game, weren't you?"

"Um. Yes, we were . . ." Marzana let her voice trail off, hoping that would be enough small talk. *Just get Milo.*

"I know he's really looking forward to that. Unfortunately, he's at camp this week. He's not back until Sunday."

Marzana bit down a noise of frustration. "How is he at camp? Doesn't he have school?"

"City schools started summer vacation this week."

Oh, that's right.

"Well . . ." She hesitated, kicking at the leg of her bedside table. "It's . . . sort of really important. And . . . time-sensitive. Is there a way I can call him? Or can you have him call me?" *Don't ask why,* she begged silently. *Don't ask why, please, please, pretty please.*

"Well, I can call the office there," Mrs. Pine said slowly. "I think they really only want campers to make calls in emergencies." She paused. "Is it an emergency?"

Well played, Mrs. P. Well played. Marzana took a deep breath. "Sort of."

Silence for a moment, then: "Is it something I can help with? Or Ben, if it's a game question or something like that?"

"It's—" Marzana stifled another grunt of irritation. Mrs. Pine would certainly know how to get hold of the conductor, but would she share that information with Marzana? There was no way that request wouldn't make her curious—but would she be curious enough to bring it up to Marzana's mom, even though as far as she knew, the two of them hadn't spoken since Christmas?

Possibly. Marzana could practically hear it: *How to get hold of the conductor? Let me just see if I can find out. I'll get back to you. Hey, while you're on the phone, I'd love to say hi to your mom, maybe invite her down for dinner. Is she available?* Maybe if Marzana said it was for a school project? But no, the Belowground Transit—or at least the fact that any part of it was still functional—was a pretty big secret. Mrs. Pine would probably just refuse to tell her.

All of which raised an equally difficult point: Even if Marzana and her crew did somehow manage to get in touch with the conductor, what reason was there to think he'd help them?

Meanwhile, at the other end of the crackly line, Milo's mom was waiting for an answer.

"I just . . . wanted to talk to Milo," Marzana said helplessly, voice thick with frustration and the humiliation of not having thought this through at all. "Never mind. Goodbye."

Just as she was about to replace the receiver, Marzana heard Mrs. Pine speak rapidly. "Wait a second, sweetie. Don't hang up." Marzana heard a soft tap—Mrs. Pine setting the phone down, probably

—and then another momentary silence. She rubbed at her prickling eyes. *I'm going to have to plan way better before my next attempt at getting information from anyone,* she thought. And then Mrs. Pine spoke again. "Give me your phone number, Marzana. I'll call and leave a message for Milo, and then he can call you."

Marzana's heart leaped. "Oh, thank you." She rattled off her phone number.

"I'm not sure what his schedule's like or when he has free time. Is there any time that definitely won't work for you?"

"I'm here tonight. I leave for school tomorrow at seven, and I can be home by four. I'll be home all evening. Friday afternoon I'm busy after school . . . Saturday I'm not sure, but if I have to, I can be home all day." The other members of the group would just have to find useful things to do without her if that became necessary.

"I'm writing all that down." Mrs. Pine's pencil scratched away, blending in with the noise of the connection. "Okay. Got it. No promises, but I'll do my best."

"Thanks, Mrs. Pine. I really appreciate it."

"Happy to help. Sure there's nothing else we can do?"

"I'm sure." *Don't ask to talk to my mom. Don't ask to talk to my dad.*

"Then have a good night. Come visit us soon."

Marzana slumped in relief. She said her goodbyes and hung up, feeling shaky. *Dodged a bullet there,* she thought. *I am not good at improvising.* This was helpful to know, though—she'd have to be much better prepared for awkward questions before she wandered into a conversational minefield like that again.

Which, she realized, was likely to be tomorrow, when Ciro came over. How was she going to explain the sudden arrival of a boy her parents had never heard her mention before?

"It's a problem for later," she muttered, reaching for her backpack as she glanced at her bedside clock. Twenty minutes left until dinner. She sped through her homework, then took the graphic novel they'd bought at Lucky's downstairs to read. She'd just gotten to the point where teenage math whiz Casie Patrick, having just been recruited into the legendary secret crime-fighting syndicate called the Sidledywry Knot, arrives for the very first time within view of the crumbling mansion called Cartonfield, the Knot's base of operations, only to witness it exploding in a sudden and blinding fireball, when her parents entered the dining room.

"Well, that's a bummer," Marzana murmured, marking her place with a scrap of paper.

Mrs. Hakelbarend went to the sideboard to open a bottle of wine. "Marzana?" her dad called as he headed for the kitchen. "What's your poison?"

"Seltzer, if there's any," Marzana said as she dropped the comic under her chair.

Honora yanked the door open just as Mr. Hakelbarend reached for the knob. "Which it is under control, sir, begging your pardon. Vittles is up in five. You can sit."

She disappeared and reemerged a minute later with Marzana's seltzer, then went back again to retrieve dinner: a wooden trencher carrying an assortment of small, perfectly done flatbread pizzas with different toppings that looked at once mouthwateringly delicious and totally out of place being served by a weatherbeaten old sailor. As the sailor in question whipped out a gleaming, curved mezzaluna knife and proceeded to carve the pizzas into neat slices, the phone rang in the parlor.

"I'll get it," Mrs. Hakelbarend said, sliding out of her seat and heading for the living room. "Please, God, let it be Nick."

A moment later, Marzana's mother reappeared in the doorway with a bemused smile on her face. "Marzie," she said, tossing her head back toward the living room. "For you. It's Milo Pine."

Marzana got up so fast, she whacked her knee on the bottom of the table and nearly knocked over her glass. "Be right back. Or . . . I might be a minute, if that's okay," she amended. "I think he's calling from camp. I can't really ask him to call back."

Her mom waved a hand. "Take your time."

She darted into the living room and picked up the receiver, which lay on an end table by the sofa. "Hello?"

"Marzana? It's Milo. Sorry to call at dinner, but the phone was free and I wasn't sure when I'd have the chance again. Mom said you called and it was some kind of emergency." He sounded a little bewildered, which of course he did. In the background, a low hum of kids' voices droned. Marzana caught random snippets: *meatloaf* and *no way I'm eating that* and something about a jar of fungus that under different circumstances she would definitely have wanted to know more about. But not tonight.

"Hi, Milo." Marzana twisted the cord. *Not prepared. Not prepared.* Then she remembered two things: First, that Milo was not all that much more social than she was, and second, that the best interactions she'd had lately were the ones where she'd skipped trying to make small talk and gone right to the facts.

"I'm sorry to bug you." She lowered her voice and cupped her hand around the receiver. They shouldn't be able to hear her from the dining room, but better safe than sorry. "I need your help. I need to know who your friend who works on the Belowground is, and how to get in touch with him."

The line crackled. "Brandon?" Milo asked at last, sounding even more dumbfounded than before.

"Do you know more than one?"

"No, no. Brandon Levi is his name. How you get hold of him . . . my mom would've known. Why didn't you just ask her?"

"Because I don't want adults involved," Marzana said in a harsh whisper.

"But Brandon is —"

"Okay, because I don't want *my* adults involved," she corrected herself. "There's a thing that's going on, and I think . . . I think the Belowground might be a clue. I'm hoping your friend can help."

"And you don't want to tell your parents." Milo sounded wary, which was hardly fair, considering what he had gotten up to last winter right under his own parents' noses.

"They're busy," Marzana said helplessly. "And . . . I need this, Milo. I want to do it myself. As much of it as I can, anyway."

A very, very brief pause. Marzana looked over her shoulder, listening for voices in the dining room.

"Okay," Milo said. "I get it. I'm pretty sure my parents would have his phone number somewhere, but if asking them is out, I can think of two other possibilities. I don't know how well either of these will work for you, but here goes." He paused as the cafeteria noise spiked behind him. "The first," Milo continued when it quieted again, "is that he's a fighter in addition to being the conductor, and he usually talks about taking bouts on Morbid Street, down in Shantytown. I'm pretty sure there are a handful of fight houses there, but I also think he's fairly well known. So in theory, you could phone around there and try leaving messages."

Marzana groaned inwardly at the prospect of more awkward phone calls, but this at least was doable. "Morbid Street fight houses. Got it. What's the second option?"

"The second option is to call him from a station."

"From a station," Marzana repeated. "There's a call system?"

"Yes. I'm not sure if it's the same in each of them, or even really whether they all have one, but in the station by our house, it looks like a doorbell. Brandon installed them himself. Or he's in the process. It's sort of an ongoing project, I think. And even ours doesn't always work. The iron interferes."

"Weird."

"Yeah. Some stations he can't even get to because of the iron. I don't know what the state of your local one is."

"Brandon brought somebody here to visit my parents just this past week. Emmett, that guy from Christmas."

"Well, then your station must be functional. So probably there's a call button, but it might not look like much." He paused. "Come to think of it, your *station* might not look like much. They all sort of vanish into their surroundings. Do you know where it is? I guess you can't ask your folks, huh?"

"No, I don't know, but I know someone who does."

"Ottomy?" Milo said in a questioning tone, like he was trying the word out. "I think I've seen that on the old transit map inside our station. Part of it's torn and part of it's water-damaged, but I think, if I'm picturing it right, that's the name of the one in the Liberty. Ottomy Something. Ottomy Street, maybe?" He laughed. "So all you have to do is find a hidden train station, bust into it, and locate a bell that might or might not be there, then wait for him to show up from wherever else in the city he is. Easy-peasy."

"Piece of cake." Marzana hesitated. It felt like she ought to say something else. In the absence of any better ideas, she settled on the most basic truth. "This is helpful. Thank you."

"You're welcome." Now Milo paused. "I don't know what you're up to," he said at last, "but I wish I could help."

"Me too," Marzana admitted. "If you weren't at camp, I'd have begged you to come visit for the weekend."

"Marzana, what's —"

Another spike of sound behind him. Between that and the crackling connection, Marzana lost track of his voice for a moment. "What did you say?"

"I said," Milo repeated, "what's going on?"

She hesitated, lowered her voice even further. "A girl was kidnapped. Don't worry," she said quickly, as a sound like a gasp made it down the line. "My mom and dad are already on it. I'm just . . . trying to help. And they won't let me."

"Okay," Milo said after a moment. "Well, then I hope this does some good."

Marzana nodded, even though he couldn't see it. "Me too."

"Brandon's a good guy. If he can help, I bet he will. Hey, what's your address?"

"Hedgelock Court, Number 230, the Viaduct. Why?"

"No reason." A pause, presumably while Milo wrote it down. "Might send you a postcard."

"Um. Thanks?" Marzana glanced over her shoulder again. "I'd better get back to dinner. You too, probably."

Milo snorted. "It's meatloaf tonight. Why is there always meatloaf at camp? It's the worst."

"Can't help you there."

"Yeah. Well. Good luck."

"Thanks. You too." She hung up, sprinted up the stairs to her room, and scribbled Brandon Levi, Morbid Street fight houses, and Ottomy Street into her journal. On her way back to the dining room, she took a detour to the study and pulled a big old atlas from a shelf of similarly antique books. Turning to the index, she searched the O's.

There was no listing for Ottomy Street. She replaced the atlas and took down the middle book of a three-volume dictionary. There was "ottomy," right after the entry for "Ottoman Empire": *ottomy (n.): skeleton (obsolete).*

Marzana put the dictionary back and hurried down to rejoin her parents.

Her mom pushed the big wooden trencher of pizza toward her place as she sat. "How's Milo?"

"Good," Marzana said, taking a pepperoni slice, a pesto and chicken, and one with shaved ham and arugula. "Is Honora not eating with us tonight?" It was a rhetorical question. Mrs. Hakelbarend always made a point of setting a place for Honora at the table with them, but with very few exceptions, the fourth setting had always disappeared by the time the old steward actually served dinner.

"Nope." Marzana's mom reached for another slice. "Noticed your book," she said casually. Marzana stiffened, her toe instinctively finding the graphic novel under her chair. "That's the one Peony Hyde was reading, isn't it?"

Marzana nodded. "Well, it's the first book. I think Emmett said she was up to the most recent one. This whole thing reminded me that Nialla's been on me for a while to try the series. She really likes it."

Mrs. Hakelbarend nodded as she chewed and swallowed a bite. "Well, if anything interesting occurs to you as you read, let us know."

"Sure." Marzana took a bite too. Maybe the fact that she'd been reading the book in plain sight would make it less suspicious. A question occurred to her. "You guys might know this. I was wondering: Is a 'knot' a usual name for a team or a gang, or did they come up with that just for this series?"

It was her father who answered. "It comes from old thieves' cant

—a sort of secret language of the underworld. That term's been around a long time."

"What's on your mind?" her mother asked, watching her closely.

"I was thinking how lonely Peony must have been," Marzana said, entirely truthfully. "She'd just lost her best friend, and she was reading a book about a crime-fighting team. They were sending her to camp to try to make new friends. It seemed . . . sad. I hope . . ." Suddenly there was a lump in her throat. "I hope she's okay, is all."

Marzana's mother reached for her left hand, and her father reached for her right. "We're going to find her," Mrs. Hakelbarend said, and for the first time, Marzana noticed that the circles perpetually lurking under her mother's eyes were darker than usual. Her mother was worried about this girl that none of them knew too. Marzana glanced at her father and saw the same worry pooling under his eyes, visible even with his much darker skin.

"Promise?" she asked quietly.

Her parents looked at each other. "Promise," her mother said after a moment. The hesitation was small, but it was enough. You didn't ask *Promise?* when you wanted truth. You asked it when you wanted comfort, and parents weren't dumb enough to answer a comfort question with honesty. Marzana took her hands back and ate another bite of pizza in hopes that it would knock the lump back down again.

That night, when the usual knock came on Marzana's door and Honora peeked in with her tray of cider, Marzana was ready.

"Honora?" she asked, accepting the proffered cup. "Tell me some kinds of knots."

"Knots?" Honora repeated, blinking curiously. "Meaning tying knots, that sort?"

"Yes. If you please."

The old sailor sat down next to her and scratched her grizzled head with one tattooed hand. "Well, what are you needing the knot to do? There's knots for all things, but no *one* knot for all things, if you take my meaning. Matters what you plan to do with it."

"I'm not actually planning to do anything with it." Marzana picked up her journal, open to a fresh page, and a pen. "I just need to know names. It's for school. Interesting names," she added as an afterthought. "Interesting knots. If possible."

"Ah," Honora said, in a tone that implied of course schoolwork would be frivolous enough to demand one make a list of knots without bothering to know what they were for. "Well, then. If that's all. Sure. You have a few basic types of knots: bends, hitches, loops, plaits, sennits and splices, stoppers . . . running knots, slipped knots, binding knots, whipping knots . . . that's to keep rope from fraying . . . decorative ones to pretty things up . . . but you want some names of specific ones, do you?"

Marzana was already writing. She nodded without looking up. "Yes, if you please."

"Well, you want a bowline on there," Honora said, looking over Marzana's shoulder at the list she was making. "Can't do a day at sea without a bowline. A chain sennit looks right pretty if you care about that — something like a nice braid. I'm also partial to a good killick hitch, me — nothing better for attaching a rope to something oddball. Then you've got your highwayman's hitch, your blood loop and your half blood knot, your left-hand bowline and French bowline and Spanish bowline and your bowline-on-a-bight. You've got all sorts of butterflies: butterfly bend, butterfly coil, butterfly loop. And there's cat's paw and catshank and dogshank and sheepshank; and monkey's fist—you see those sold for key fobs in souvenir shops; and the ones that sound like pubs: the wall and crown, the savoy, the hunter's bend, the square turk's head, and the simple Simon under. And then," she said nonchalantly, "you have your sneaky-boots knots. Thief knots and grief knots. Suitable for sneaky-boots girls who might not be telling the whole truth about a thing."

Marzana glanced up at Honora, who was leaning with her chin on one fist and her elbow on one knee, looking at her with dark amusement. Marzana wrote *Sneaky-boots* neatly on the page, then listed *thief knot* and *grief knot* below it. "What makes them sneaky-boots knots?" she asked innocently.

"They look like a reef knot, which is a very common knot everyone knows how to tie if they ain't some sort of whipjack posing as a sailor." She felt her pockets, then looked around. "You have a bit of cordage handy? A shoelace, perhaps?"

"Maybe." Marzana hopped down, opened her closet, and rifled through the assorted shoes on the floor, looking for a pair of sneakers that had lately been feeling a bit snug. She stripped the pink shoelace out of one and tossed it to Honora.

"You know how to tie a reef knot, of course," the steward began. Marzana bit the inside of her mouth, praying Honora didn't look up and spot the ignorance on her face. This was the kind of thing Honora always assumed the daughter of a smuggling captain had to know, but in fact it was precisely the kind of thing that fell through the cracks when you weren't actually, actively preparing your child for a life either at sea or on the wrong side of the law.

Fortunately, though, Honora didn't wait for confirmation. "Left over right, then right over left," she said, taking one end in her left hand and crossing it over and under the end in her right to form a loop. Then she brought the ends back toward each other and crossed the one now in her right hand over, then under, the one on the left. "Fair it a bit," she said, working the knot into a tighter, more compact shape with her fingertips, "and there you are." She held the shoelace up: a wide loop hung from the knot, and two loose ends poked out either side. "See how it has four legs? Two legs that become the loop, two legs that are ends, and one of each on each side of the knot."

"Got it."

"And notice the two loose ends are both on the top of the knot, so to speak."

To the right and the left, the loose ends stuck out horizontally above the legs of the loop. "Yes."

"Right. Well, this is a wonderful common knot. If you were a sailor tying your ditty bag shut, you'd most likely tie it with a reef knot." Honora undid the knot and smoothed the shoelace out. "But, if you were concerned that Jimmy Stickyfingers in the bunk below had been eyeing your antique shoebuckle what's proven to be lucky over the course of fifteen missions and you wanted to know if he or anyone else had been searching your dunnage for it, then instead of an ordinary old reef knot, you might use a sneaky-boots knot to find out. F'rinstance."

She looped the cord in her left hand, then threaded one end through the loop: in, out again, over and under and through. "Fair it a bit"—she tugged the knot into shape—"and see what you have." She lay the knot over her index finger for Marzana's inspection.

"It looks . . . the same," Marzana said at length. "But you tied it totally differently."

"Because it ain't the same." Honora lay the knot out on her palm, smoothing the four legs out to either side. "Look again. This isn't a reef knot. It's a *thief* knot."

It took her a minute, but then Marzana spotted it. With the reef knot, both loose ends were on top. This time, the loose end was on top on the right, but on the left-hand side, one of the legs of the loop had the upper spot. "I see. The loose ends are in different places."

"It also isn't as reliable." Honora tugged the loop legs, and the knot slid quite a bit before it tightened, even though she'd already faired it. "The grief knot's slipperier yet. A good one for reminding you: knots in before knots out, always." She undid the thief knot and performed an even fiddlier bit of threading to produce a knot that looked like the first two, only twisted slightly. As with the thief knot, it had a loose end both above and below, though because of the twist to the knot, the four legs didn't lie nicely off to either side this time. Honora didn't bother to fair it; she tugged the loop ends once, and the whole thing came easily apart. "But then the point of these knots isn't whether they're reliable; the point is whether your shipmates are."

She tied another neat left-over-right, right-over-left reef knot. "If a stickyfingers is getting into your dunnage when you aren't looking, he's not likely to notice you've used a thief knot to tie your bag shut. He'll see a reef knot because that's what he's expecting, so that's what he'll use to retie your bag, never having noticed the difference, even if the knot falls apart under his fingers like a reef knot never would when he goes to open it. But when *you* see *his* reef knot, you'll notice, because you'll know it wasn't the same knot you left, and then you'll know someone has been all up in your dunnage. Savvy?"

"I do," Marzana said, tapping her pen thoughtfully on the page full of knots. "That's interesting. Thanks, Honora. This is exactly the kind of thing I need."

"Welcome, I'm sure," Honora said drily, getting to her feet with a creak of old knees. She handed Marzana the shoelace. "A grief knot's also called a *what knot* sometimes. I always thought that was funny." She closed the door gently after her, leaving Marzana alone with her cider and her shoelace and her list of knots. Her eyes lingered on the three names listed under *Sneaky-boots knots: thief knot, grief knot, what knot.*

She fell asleep still turning the names over and over in her mind, until they became knots in her dreams, symmetrical slithering tangles of rope woven from night, from stars, from the wind that slid through the narrow roads and high-walled alleys of the Liberty and under the spans of the Viaduct like the water that had never flowed there but seemed as though it should have, binding Gammerbund and everything in it up into a round monkey's fist. And there the entire district hung, ensnared, until Honora came stumping over the hill with a marlinespike in one hand, grumbling that she'd have been there sooner but the Mister had put the spike away in the wrong bit of the knife block yet again, as if she hadn't told him a dozen times and more exactly where it was meant to go when he was done with it. But instead of taking her marlinespike to the knot to pick it apart herself, she came to stand behind Marzana, who was suddenly there too, staring at the round knot that held her home within it like a pearl in an oyster. As together they watched the slowly spinning knot, Honora braided Marzana's hair with the marlinespike and her knobby old fingers, murmuring, "Knots in before knots out; chain sinnet looks nice if you care about that." And then, when Marzana's hair was neatly knotted into six chain-sinnet braids, Honora handed her the marlinespike. "Have at it, Sneaky-Boots," she said with a wink, and as Marzana stood there, marlinespike in one hand, staring at the knot and wondering where to begin, her alarm went off, and it was Thursday morning.

eleven

HOORAY, HOORAY, HOORAY!

THURSDAY DRAGGED, to an impossible degree. Neither Marzana nor Nialla had any classes with Emilia until Marzana's language arts class near the end of the day. They could have met up during the free study-hall period again, but they hadn't arranged it in advance, and Emilia was curiously absent from both the hallways and the dining hall.

Marzana and Nialla fidgeted study hall away from their usual spot in the Parlor, skipping the sofa itself in favor of the floor between it and the window. Marzana sat cross-legged, attempting to tie a grief knot in her pink shoelace. Honora's demonstration the night before had been too rapid to follow, but Marymead's Library had two books on knots. One of them lay open in her lap.

"You don't think she got caught, do you?" Nialla asked quietly from the floor by the window, where she had been staring down into the courtyard. Marzana suspected she knew what had been going through her friend's head. *We were down there.* Under *there. There's a whole* world *under there.*

"I mean, even if she got caught, she'd still be in class, wouldn't she?"

"No idea."

They sat in silence for a moment. "How's your graphic novel lead going?" Marzana asked at last, pulling the loose ends of the twisted grief knot she'd tied and watching it fall neatly apart.

Nialla made a face. "Can't really do much until I have the ransom-note copy. So far, all I've done is log all the occurrences in the book of the words in the note. But the good news is, every issue is hand-lettered, so I should be able to figure out exactly where each word came from."

"I started reading the first one yesterday," Marzana said, looping the lace left-over-right, right-over-left, into a reef knot. "And I think maybe I have a name."

"A name?" Nialla repeated, confused.

"Yeah. You know. A name for us."

"Oooh, really?" Nialla perked up. "What is it?"

Marzana grinned. "Saving it for when we meet."

Nialla pouted, but only for show. "Fair enough."

Mrs. Ileck flung open the door and rang the old bell. The girls gathered their bags and headed up the stairs to algebra. Still no Emilia — this was another time when they sometimes caught sight of her in the halls. Today, though: no go.

Mr. Otterwill was there again, writing a problem set on the board, apparently having moved on from Mrs. Agravin's busywork. "Any ideas?" Nialla whispered as they took their seats. "I just know there's stuff he could tell us."

Marzana shook her head slowly. "We have to figure something out by tomorrow. If we're going to do any good at all, we have to do it this weekend. The payment's due on Sunday. Things change then."

Nialla shuddered. "I hate to think what you mean by that."

"Me too."

After algebra was language arts, and still Emilia didn't show. "Should one of us try to go up and see her?" Nialla asked when they rendezvoused to walk home.

"I should have offered to take homework to her," Marzana muttered. "I bet there's some way the teachers send it up anyway, though."

"Do you think if we just went up there, anyone would turn us away?"

"No idea." Marzana considered. "But I have a feeling Emilia knows what she's doing. Somehow I think if she's not putting in an appearance today, it's because she doesn't want to be seen. I'm inclined to give her space."

"If you say so," Nialla said doubtfully. Marzana frowned a little, wondering if Nialla thought she was just being timid. But Nialla caught the look and waved one hand. "I'm sure you're right. No big deal. Listen, I'm going to go straight home by the shortcut and finish logging words. That way, assuming Ciro can still get to me tonight with the copy, I can start on the real work."

"Which is what?" Marzana asked as they walked down the stairs.

Nialla gave her an enigmatic smile. "Saving it for when we meet. Turnabout is fair play." She waved and headed for an alley to the south. It was a more direct route home for her, but it meant Marzana had to walk the whole way back to the Viaduct alone. Which wasn't a bad thing, really. She still had to figure out how she was going to introduce Ciro to her parents.

He was waiting when she got to the west stairs, leaning against one of the stone balusters and eating a shave ice from a vendor who kept a stall on one of the lower risers. "Hey," he said as she walked up. "This stuff is amazing. Currant-mint. Have you had this?"

Marzana frowned. "Of course. I walk past it every day."

He slurped the last bit of melt from the cup and tossed it in a trash can. "If I walked by here every day, I'd eat this stuff fourteen times a week."

She had no reply ready, so she just nodded. "Sure. This way."

They walked up together, passing through the tables and chairs of the restaurants that had their outdoor café seating to either side on the wide stairs: first the wrought-iron tables of the High Teashop, and then through the green-checked tablecloths of the Updraft Café, and finally under the umbrellas of the Piper Gates Chophouse before they reached the green stones that paved Crossynge Lane. Marzana filled in Ciro on Emilia's absence, but after that, neither of them spoke much. *Too much silence.* "I figured I'd just tell Mom and Dad we're working on a project together," Marzana said as they walked. "They don't know every kid in my class this year. I don't think they'll ask too many questions. We're doing plays in language arts. Maybe we could be planning a set." She could tell she was speaking too fast. But then she was out of words, and that was worse.

Ciro didn't seem to notice her awkwardness, but he didn't seem to like the idea. "It's an option."

"Not a good one?" Her cheeks began to burn. "Well, you said plain old lying is one of your specialties. If you've got a better cover, I'm all ears."

"I don't have a better one." Ciro flashed a reassuring smile. "It's just that I think one of the keys to good lying is not to lie when you don't have to. We could come up with an elaborate story, or we could make it so much easier. We can just tell your folks the truth: I live near Nialla, and that's how we met: through her. No lies required."

"So you're saying I basically tell my mom and dad, 'I met this boy and invited him over to hang out after school'?" Marzana asked, aghast. "Just like that? They're going to assume that means I *like* you or something. I'm going to get so much crap for this."

"Yeah, probably." Ciro grinned. "Do you care?"

Kind of, yes, she did. Still. *We all have to make sacrifices,* she'd told J.J. "I guess not, but it's going to be so *awkward.*"

"It was going to be awkward anyway. This conveniently explains that, too."

Marzana sighed. "It's the perfect cover."

"Good." Ciro looked around at the tall, overhanging houses that blocked any view of the city beyond. "You know, I don't think I've ever actually been up here before."

"Well . . . welcome."

They walked a little way in another uncomfortable silence. Uncomfortable to Marzana, anyhow, who spent the whole time trying to think of something to say, then discarding everything that came to mind as pointless. Ciro, she realized, didn't seem bothered by the lack of conversation at all. He merely glanced this way and that, reaching out occasionally to touch a frond of some trailing plant.

"Oh," Marzana said, as it suddenly occurred to her that there was something she needed to ask. "Did you manage to find any of your grandfather's Belowground stuff?"

Ciro shook his head apologetically. "Nope. Or yes, sort of. Mom drafted me into a thing the second I walked in the door. She needed me to find a bunch of my old baby clothes for a shower she's going to tonight, so while I was looking for them, I did a pretty thorough search of the attic. I know where Granddad's stuff is; I just didn't have a chance to look at it or even bring it down because Mom was in such a hurry for the baby stuff. But she'll be out of the house tonight and I'll have the whole place to myself. I should have everything you need by the time we meet on Friday."

"Great." She stopped in front of Hedgelock Court and rooted in her pocket for the key.

"Wow," Ciro said, looking up at the tower that overhung the street. "This is . . . impressive. And weird."

"It gets weirder," Marzana said, opening the door and ushering him inside. She tossed her backpack on the floor of the foyer, then stopped. There were angry voices coming from the living room, but muffled in a way that happened only if you pulled the almost-never-used pocket doors closed. Marzana couldn't quite make out the words, but the voice speaking right now was her mom's, and the tone was unmistakably dangerous. She hesitated for only a moment, debating whether or not to announce their arrival, before a sharp cough — loud but fussy; that had to be Nick Larven — silenced her mother's voice.

Nick Larven plus dangerous Mom tones meant there was someone else in that room too, and not just her father. Mr. Hakelbarend might well have been with them, but that voice was not one Barbara Hakelbarend used with anyone she liked. Which meant Nick had probably done exactly what she had sent him to do: he'd brought Rob Gandreider in for a little talk.

One of the doors scraped open, and Marzana's mother stalked out into the hall. "Marzie," she said grimly, "welcome home. Do me a favor and stay clear of the living room for a bit?"

"Erm. Sure." Her mother's eyes flicked over at Ciro. "Mom, this is —"

Mrs. Hakelbarend snapped her fingers. "You're Katia del Olmo's kid, aren't you?"

So much for any subterfuge. "Yes, ma'am," Ciro said. "I'm Ciro."

Marzana stiffened. "Huh. Didn't know you knew his mom." Thank goodness they hadn't tried to claim to be classmates. She prepared herself for any of the potential awkward follow-ups that had to be coming.

Fortunately, her mother had bigger fish to fry. Mrs. Hakelbarend glanced over her shoulder, back toward the living room. "Well, tell your mom I said hello. I have to get back. You guys need anything, Honora's probably around somewhere." She gave Marzana a look that spanned a whole spectrum of silent conversation. Chief among them were apology — although whether it was an apology for not being available to make snacks when a friend came over or an apology for the likelihood that it was going to get loud in the living room, Marzana couldn't be sure — and warning, which was clear enough. *Keep out of the way.* That much Marzana didn't have to be told aloud, anyway. Rob could be a nasty customer.

"Well," Ciro said when they were alone again, "maybe this isn't going to be as hard as we thought."

At that moment, Honora appeared in the passage from the dining room. "Afternoon, miss. And sir," she added, not blinking an eye at Ciro's presence. She'd probably been listening just out of sight. "Just to say I'm in the kitchen if you need anything."

"Thank you, Honora." A sudden thud from the living room echoed down the hall. It sounded as if someone had slammed something — a book, say, or an uncooperative witness — onto the coffee table. "I think, under the circumstances, that we'll go watch TV in the upstairs study," Marzana said as they all pretended very carefully to have heard nothing at all.

"That seems a sound plan," Honora agreed. "I'll bring up some cookies, shall I?"

"If you please. This way, Ciro." She started up the stairs, listening hard for any actual words emerging from the noises below.

Ciro followed. "Who's the guest?" he asked under his breath.

"I have a pretty good idea," Marzana whispered back as they reached the second floor. "The room we want's right over the living room. We might be able to hear something." She led him down the hall to the study. The whole way, she tried stringing silent sentences together. Without being able to say them out loud, though, it wasn't very helpful. She thought back to J.J.'s effortless impromptu speeches and wished she had even a fraction of his confidence.

It was too much. Just inside the study doors, Marzana stopped short—so short, in fact, that Ciro nearly ran right into her. She blushed, and both of them took a step back. "What's up?" Ciro asked, pretending fairly convincingly that nothing weird had happened.

"I'm really bad at small talk," Marzana blurted.

Ciro tilted his head. "I hadn't noticed."

"Because I haven't *made* any small talk," she pointed out.

"Did you think you had to?" Ciro asked curiously. "Why?"

Abruptly she realized that was a good question. "People seem to expect it," Marzana said after giving it some thought.

Ciro frowned, considered, shrugged. "I don't." He narrowed his eyes at her. "You're thinking about the Pencil Speeches, aren't you?"

"A little," Marzana admitted.

He rolled his eyes. "Yes, J.J. can spout meaningless drivel on command. But it's *meaningless*. That's the point. You said it yourself:

It's patter. It's a tool he has, and he's good at it, but it's as much illusion as any other magic he does. And," he added, "much like making coins appear out of people's ears, if he did it all the time, he'd be insufferable."

That was probably true. Marzana tried to decide whether it made her feel any better and couldn't quite make up her mind. Either way, standing here in the doorway was weird. "Okay." She stood aside and waved an arm into the room.

Ciro bowed his head briefly and stepped past her into the study. "Say what you need to, or what you want to," he said, glancing around the room. "You're the boss. But you don't have to make conversation on my account. Fair?"

His eyes came back to her on the *Fair?*, and Marzana couldn't have explained why, but something about the moment was exactly like asking Nialla *Did I do okay?* and being told *Yes.* There was no good reason it should've worked, but somehow it did.

"Fair," she said, and felt a weight fall away.

When Hedgelock Court had taken itself seriously as a stately house, this had been the library. About a third of the space occupied the lower half of the turret and projected out over the street. The rest of the study sat directly over the living room. In addition to having bookshelves set into several sections of the turret walls, it had a big walnut dining table that her parents used as a desk, a blocky chaise lounge and an overstuffed chair that faced the carved cabinet that hid the TV, and—most important—a fireplace that shared a chimney with the one in the room below where her parents were currently entertaining their guest. Marzana opened the doors of the media cabinet. She tossed Ciro the remote. "Find something, please."

"Is the lady with the tats likely to throw cookies from a box on a plate, or bake them?" Ciro asked as he dropped onto the chaise and began pushing buttons. "How much time do we have? And is she going to feel like she has to chaperone?"

"She'll bake them, but she keeps dough already made in the freezer," Marzana said, kneeling and leaning carefully into the fireplace. There was no hearth here, just a massive, time-polished piece of sandstone set into the hardwood floor. "The dough will have to defrost a little and the oven's got to preheat, so she can't put them in right away. She'll bring drinks and fruit or something up first to tide us over, so I'm guessing we have five minutes before that happens. Fifteen minutes after that, she'll come up asking if we want refills. And fifteen minutes after *that*, we'll get cookies, when they're out and cooled just a bit."

"Which answers my chaperone question, too." Ciro paused on a classic movie channel, and a man calling himself Rufus T. Firefly began to sing about the wonderful changes he had planned for Freedonia now that he was president.

"Yup. Chaperoning at a distance. Not that she'd think of it that way. I don't get up to much." Marzana leaned back in, listening. The voices were faint, but she could make out actual words now. "Ciro, can you hear any of this from there?"

He paused for a moment, then shook his head. "Not over Groucho."

"Groucho?" she repeated, preoccupied. If Ciro couldn't hear the voices from downstairs from where he was sitting, then neither would Honora when she came in.

Ciro's reply was wounded. "I can deal with no small talk, but please tell me you've heard of the Marx Brothers."

"Of course I've *heard* of them. I've just never watched a whole movie."

"Well, you're in luck. This is the best one, and whatever noise comes up through the chimney will blend right into the craziness."

Marzana nodded, satisfied. She dusted her hands off on her jeans and sat awkwardly in the big chair. "My mom recognized you. Do you . . . recognize her, or know how your mom knows her?"

"My mother . . . knows a lot of people," Ciro began carefully. "Not all of them are real open about who they are or what they do. Mom doesn't usually introduce us."

"But I bet you don't forget a face," Marzana guessed.

"I don't usually forget a face," he admitted. "I think I've seen your mom, yes." He kept his eyes on the Marx Brothers. "You said you couldn't talk about her. I'm guessing you get the same speech I do about deniability. Is that . . . accurate?"

"Very. I hate deniability," she added in a grumble.

"Yeah. But your mom's working on this thing too, huh? That's what you said yesterday."

"Yes." Marzana contemplated the boy sitting cross-legged on the chaise. When she'd told him and J.J. about the kidnapping, she'd framed it simply: *This happened; my parents are investigating.* She'd avoided saying much about Emmett and the fact that he'd asked them specifically to investigate suspects, because admitting that her own parents were working with authorities from the city proper was a dicey thing to do.

Still, Ciro had told the truth about his own family. The Spinster was a legend in the Liberty, but she'd been dead for centuries, so it made sense that he was comfortable talking about his connection to her, and she didn't see any reason he couldn't have told anybody about his dad and grandfather. But fessing up to his mother's shenanigans . . . well, he'd trusted Marzana, Nialla, and Emilia (and J.J., though Marzana assumed that, as Ciro's best friend, he already knew) with some pretty sensitive information there. Not everybody in the Liberty would understand what her parents were doing, even given the seriousness of the situation. But Ciro, she thought, probably would.

"An agent from down in the city asked for their help in tracking down a few suspects they thought might be involved in the kidnapping. I think Mom and Dad and one of Mom's lieutenants have one of those suspects in the living room. I think it's more or less an interrogation." There was a creak in the hallway. Marzana clammed up fast, and a moment later — five minutes on the dot from the time she'd predicted it — Honora stalked in with a tray in hand.

"Cookies'll be up in about a glass's time," she said. "Thought you'd like something in the meanwhile." She set the tray down on the ottoman between the chaise and chair with a rattle of lemonade glasses and apple slices and stalked out again without another word to either of them, though Marzana thought she heard her mutter, " 'Hooray for Captain Spaulding,' " on her way out.

"Wrong movie," Ciro said under his breath as he reached for one of the apple wedges on the tray. "This is *Duck Soup*. Captain Spaulding's from *Animal Crackers*."

"I had no idea Honora was a Marx Brothers fan." Marzana got to her feet and tiptoed toward the door of the study. She heard the stairs protesting faintly at the far end of the hall as Honora stomped back down. "Okay. Let's move. I'll find the note; you listen and see if you can make out anything they're saying."

Ciro hurried over to the hearth. Marzana darted past the big table by the bow window, which was clean of papers and neat as a pin as always, and headed for a low cabinet full of various-sized drawers that stood against the wall opposite the fireplace. Her mother was too cautious to leave things out even in her own home — deniability always making life difficult—but she wasn't totally paranoid. Some of the cabinet's drawers were locked, but Marzana was willing to bet that since this particular case was a mostly legal enterprise, Mrs. Hakelbarend wouldn't have gone too crazy with security. She wasn't disappointed. She found Emmett's folder tucked in the top flat file drawer within half a minute of looking: a thin, perfectly ordinary-looking manila folder with *PH for BK&PH* printed on the tab and a paper clip fastening something to the inside of the top cover.

"Ciro." Marzana waved him over without touching the folder and pointed into the drawer. "Take a picture for me."

"Nice instincts." He took his phone from his back pocket, and Marzana watched with interest as he thumbed it on, turned on the camera, and documented the folder's exact placement within the drawer from three angles. "Good?"

"Good." Marzana lifted it out gently, carried it to the table, and opened the top cover with care, so as not to disturb the paper clip. There they were: the school photo and the color copies of the ransom note and envelope that Marzana had seen at the dining table, all tucked under the clip and facing a page covered with notes in both of her parents' handwriting.

And then she heard herself make a small noise as she spotted a tiny drawing in the left-hand margin of the page. Her father's work, no question—he was a doodler. Marzana could picture the scene: her mother pacing by the study window tossing out ideas, her father sitting at the long table making notes and sketching this quick shape during a thoughtful pause. As she looked down at the drawing—a bird with an abnormally long, snakelike neck—a word she'd heard on Monday but that she hadn't thought of since came sharply back to her. *Snakebird.*

"What is it?" Ciro asked.

"Tell you later," she said quietly. "Camera again, please."

Only when she was satisfied Ciro had enough images that they'd be able to exactly replicate the arrangement of the papers did she slide the copies out from under the clip.

YOUR *DAUGHTER* IS SAFE FOR
NOW THE PRICE *TO HAVE* HER BACK IS 1000000
WE WILL *SEND INSTRUCTIONS* ON SATURDAY
YOU WILL HAVE ONE DAY *TO PAY*

The words had been irregularly cut from their original pages and affixed to a piece of ordinary looseleaf paper with clear tape. The "1000000" and a couple of the longer words had been assembled letter by letter. Thanks to the distinctive comic-book lettering, it didn't look serious. It looked like a prop from a movie that wasn't planning to give the audience too close a look. It looked all wrong, like a letter containing deadly serious news that the sender had typed in a totally inappropriate font.

She set it on the table, and Ciro climbed up on a chair in order to get the best straight-down picture he could. Then he nodded at the rest of the papers in the folder. "Shall we . . . ?"

"Absolutely." It didn't take long to photograph the rest of the contents. There were three pages of her parents' handwritten notes, a few pictures of a street that ran along a canal with a little towpath and a bridge, and two typed and stapled pages of notes that presumably Emmett had brought with him.

When Ciro was finished, he scrolled through the images and they carefully replaced everything, putting the paper clip precisely where it had been before and stacking each page exactly as it had been relative to both the folder and the page below it — or as close to exactly as they could manage. Then Marzana carried the folder to the drawer and placed it inside, and they double-checked the photos again to make sure it was positioned correctly. She closed the drawer, let out a deep breath, and glanced at Ciro, who was grinning like some kind of maniac.

"That was fun," he admitted, shoving his phone in his pocket.

She smiled back. "Yeah, it was." Marzana held out her hand and watched her fingers quiver. "My hands are shaking a little."

He held out his own, palm down. "Mine too. So now what? Fireplace? I didn't catch much before you found the folder."

Marzana glanced at the clock. It had been eleven minutes since Honora had dropped off refreshments. A glass's time, Honora had said, before the cookies would be done: thirty minutes. Maybe she could preempt another visit before then. Marzana went to the ottoman, got the two glasses of lemonade, and passed one to Ciro. "Here. Bottoms up. I'll go for refills, and I bet then she doesn't bother us again until the cookies are done."

The two of them chugged their drinks. "So who am I going to be listening to?" Ciro asked in between gulps.

"My mom. Her associate, Nick. Possibly my dad. The guy they're . . . *talking* to is Rob Gandreider, I think." She paused to finish draining her own glass. "He's a Libertyman, but he was in jail in the city proper until just recently. I'll fill you in on the rest later."

Ciro nodded as he drank, then handed over the empty glass and returned to the fireplace. Marzana left him there to eavesdrop while she headed down to the first floor.

The voices in the living room were much quieter than they had been. Marzana restrained herself from going over to press her ear against the closed door and followed the cinnamon-and-nutmeg smell of Honora's snickerdoodles through the dining room to the kitchen.

The steward was sitting at the little breakfast table, sipping from a coffee cup with a battered copy of a book called *How to Cook a Wolf* clutched in her knobby, tattooed fingers. She looked up as Marzana entered and took in the empty glasses. "Thirsty, were you?"

Marzana shrugged. "It was good lemonade. There was an interesting flavor in there."

Honora gave her a considering look, then harrumphed in a peculiar way that somehow managed to convey surprise and pride all while both looking and sounding completely dismissive. "Juniper," she said. "In my day we spiked our lemonade with good strong Hollands, but since it's frowned upon to feed gin to children in these heathen times, juniper syrup's the best I can do." She stalked to the freezer and added a few ice cubes to each glass, then pulled a pitcher of lemonade from the fridge and a hand-labeled bottle from a shelf. She poured a bit from each into the two glasses and stirred the concoctions briefly with the handle of a wooden spoon before presenting them to Marzana. "I'll be up with the cookies in a bit."

"Thank you, Honora." Marzana took the glasses and forced herself to walk at a normal pace until she was out of the kitchen and through the dining room. Then she sprinted up the stairs and into the study.

Ciro glanced up and waved briefly from the fireplace, where he sat cross-legged, his face tight with concentration. Marzana deposited the glasses on the tray and hurried over to join him. Together they sat as the disembodied voices drifted up through the chimney.

". . . not saying it's impossible that you did." That was Marzana's father's voice. "But I am saying that *if* you did, there's no record of it."

"I can't help it if the blasted gatekeeper didn't do his job." Yes, that was definitely Rob Gandreider. He sounded surly but tired. "I wasn't going to remind him, was I? I'd been arrested, if you recall. It was an *escape,* for the love of all that's holy. And unless you're planning on turning me in, I don't see what it has to do with you. Of course, once a city cop, always a city cop."

Marzana's father laughed. "That's rich, coming from a fellow who was actively moonlighting as a customs asset less than six months ago."

"Once a city cop, always a city cop," Rob repeated coldly. "Plenty said it when you turned up here."

"And if I'd been there when they said it," Mr. Hakelbarend retorted, unconcerned, "you'd have heard me say that they were welcome to come and say it to my face. But they, unlike you, were too smart to do that." A moment's pause, then Marzana's father's voice spoke again in a different tone. "Say it again, Rob. Say it right to my face."

Silence. Rob wasn't stupid.

"I would think that you would recognize the seriousness here," Marzana's mom said. "For kidnapping, the Liberty will extradite. They just will. The thing is, that takes time. The other thing that takes time is raising a ransom if you're not rich, and the girl's parents aren't. So this isn't likely to resolve itself quickly. I worry that if the girl isn't found by the time an extradition happens, it won't be extradition for kidnapping. It'll be extradition for kidnapping *and* suspected murder. And if you haven't cleared your name before then," Mrs. Hakelbarend continued, "well, Rob, I'll find you and hand you over myself. That is a promise, and I think you know I can keep it."

Murder. "I never thought of that," Marzana whispered. Somehow, though she'd recognized that things got much more serious if the ransom wasn't paid on time, the idea that the kidnappers might just up and kill their captive outright had never occurred to her. "What are we doing sticking our noses into this?"

"Trying to help," Ciro said quietly. "That's what."

"What on the bleeding earth made you think this was me?" Rob demanded in the room below. "You still haven't explained that. Sent a damned bagman after me here—*here!* Not *out there,* but *here,* on our own home grounds!—and why? You say I'm a suspect, but let me ask you: Do you really think I'd go to all the trouble of breaking myself out of the city hoosegow just to turn around and commit a crime on city turf? What, did I just pick up a job on the way home? A *kidnapping?* Exactly how stupid do you think I am?"

"I don't think you're stupid," Mrs. Hakelbarend said darkly. "And yeah, put like you just put it, you'd have to be stupid to do this. But not if it went down the other way around. Not if that door at the lockup that oh-so-conveniently got left open for you to saunter through *got left open* in exchange for your agreeing to play some part in the snatching of this girl. Every caper needs a good fidlam ben, after all." The phrase *fidlam ben* wasn't familiar, but the pause that followed it was. Marzana could perfectly picture her mother staring her prey down for dramatic effect. "So maybe we should start there. Who left the door open for you, Rob? How about you walk us through that?"

Another silence. Marzana hadn't heard Nick speak yet, but she had no doubt he was there: quiet, menacing, ready. Her mother would be perched at the edge of whatever surface she was sitting on, leaning forward with her elbows on her knees, her eyes hard and the rest of her face almost smiling—Marzana had seen her do that more than once, and it was unsettling as all get-out—her body totally still the way a predatory cat could be totally, almost invisibly still, right up until the minute it lunged. Her father would be standing close by, his arms loose and his hands in his pockets, looking relaxed but somehow also obviously ready in case Rob tried to make an unwise move.

"Who said anyone opened the door?" Rob replied at last, but some of the bravado had gone from his voice.

"Had it from a customs officer and a detective who were in pretty strong agreement on the matter," Mr. Hakelbarend told him. "What, you saying you picked that lock? What kind of lock was it again? Nick?"

Nick Larven spoke for the first time, his voice managing to be both jolly and flint-edged. "That was the Hever Street Prison, wasn't it? Not the worst accommodation you can get down in the city, that. Still, if memory serves, they installed new Ward's locks late last year. Brand-new models, they are. Ward's calls them Saturns, but all the gents I know who've ... *encountered* them refer to them as Hell-cats, as they knot up picks like a cat knots yarn. I managed to get my hands on one, in fact. Been working on it for two months, and I can't so much as move a tumbler." He laughed. "Here's a deal for you. That lock's in my Gladstone bag out in the hallway. What say I just run out and fetch it right now, and if you can show me how to pick a Hellcat, Rupert, I'll quit my employment this minute and sign on for whatever job you've got lined up next."

The wisp of sound, barely audible, that whisked up the flue might have been a sigh. "The man who opened the gate was a guard. His uniform patch said Flynn, but I never learned his first name. He said he suspected if I tried the door at a certain hour, I might find it was loose, provided I was willing to lie low for a couple weeks before I came back here. That's all. Lie low, and not return to the Liberty until this past Sunday. It did occur to me that he might be setting me up, but I figured without bars between us, I could probably manage him if he tried to retake me. He didn't, though. I never did figure out what the point of it all was, but I wasn't about to look a gift horse in the mouth."

"He *was* setting you up," Mr. Hakelbarend said. "As a red herring. The kidnapping took place on Sunday, and according to our contact, your name was all over the discussions almost as soon as it happened. You were literally their first suspect."

Rob swore, but the word was muffled. Marzana pictured him dropping to a seat with his face in his hands. "So now what? I'm telling you, this wasn't me. Not in any way. On the honor of my warrant." His Liberty warrant, he meant — the paper that proved he was a permanent citizen of Gammerbund. Marzana and Ciro glanced at each other. Nobody would lie against the honor of his or her warrant.

The adults apparently thought so too. "How about we start with you not disappearing when you leave this house?" Mrs. Hakelbarend said. "I'll pass this to the investigators in the city and let them follow up. But you stay visible — to us, at least — in case we have any other questions. Don't go off-grid. And you come straight back to me if you hear anything that suggests whoever took this girl has any connection to the Liberty other than you."

"Stay visible?" Rob snorted. "If it'll clear my name of suspicion in this thing, you tell me what to do and I'll do it." His tone turned sober. "I'll put my ear to the ground, Babs. If I hear anything, it's yours."

"I'd appreciate that."

"Now can I get an ice pack or something? I think this is going to bruise."

"I'll make you one to go," Marzana's father said. "Come on."

The scraping that followed was the sound of the pocket doors opening. There was no further discussion. The interrogation was over.

Marzana got thoughtfully to her feet, returned to her chair, and reached for her lemonade. "That was interesting." Ciro nodded as he followed. He took a wedge of apple, bit, and chewed. In the background, the Marx Brothers were oddly silent as Harpo pretended to be Groucho's mirror image.

"We should write that down," he said at last. "Before we forget."

"Yeah. Be right back." Marzana hurried to her room and grabbed her journal and pen. She paused in the hallway to listen for footsteps on the stairs, but there was nothing.

Back in the study, she and Ciro reconstructed as much of the conversation as they could. After that, on the assumption that Honora's cookies had to be out of the oven by now, they settled back into their respective seats to at least pretend to watch *Duck Soup*.

Sure enough, Honora surfaced about five minutes later with a plate of warm snickerdoodles and two mugs of milk. "Enjoy, now," she said, swapping them for the contents of the last tray.

Figuring it might look suspicious if she didn't seem at all curious, Marzana followed Honora to the door. "Is everything okay?" she asked in an undertone.

"Things is calming down," Honora said cautiously. "So to speak." Her eyes flicked down to Marzana's legs, then back up. "You might try and not get that on the furniture," she commented with one eyebrow arched up high. Then she touched her knuckles to her forehead and took herself downstairs again.

Marzana glanced at her knees. A dusting of soot showed where she'd knelt to lean into the fireplace. "Shoot." She sat and scrubbed at her pants with the hem of her T-shirt.

Ciro shook his head. "This doesn't bode well, does it?"

Marzana flopped back with a groan. "Amateurs. We are such amateurs." She looked down at her hands. "I better just go wash. And maybe get pants that won't turn state's evidence on me."

Ciro reached for a cookie. "I'll be here."

After Marzana changed, they watched the end of the movie, figuring it would be weird if they didn't. Then they headed downstairs, Marzana carrying the empty cookie plate and Ciro carrying the mugs. This time, voices were coming from the dining room, but it was just ordinary conversation. Or maybe not *quite* ordinary: the flow of talk stopped abruptly when they reached the dining room doorway. Her parents and Nick Larven were there. Of Rob Gandreider, there was no sign.

"Well, hi," Marzana's mother said brightly.

Mr. Larven got up and enfolded Marzana in a hug. "Hello, my dear. Lovely to see you."

"Hi, Mr. Larven. Um, this is my friend Ciro."

"I'll take those." Mrs. Hakelbarend took the plate and mugs. "Ciro is Katia del Olmo's son," she added on her way to the kitchen.

Both Mr. Larven and Marzana's father made pleased faces. "Nice to meet you." Marzana's dad got up and reached across to shake Ciro's hand. "Oh, of course." He turned to Marzana's mom as she returned. "Katia lives not far from the Giddises, doesn't she?"

Ciro spoke up. "Just around the corner, sir."

"Well, that explains that." Mrs. Hakelbarend sat again. "Ciro, are you joining us for dinner? We're having pasta. Nick's staying too. Easy as pie to add another place."

No way. Apart from how exponentially awkward this was going to get if they had to go on with this pretense much longer, Ciro had to get going if he was going to print all the pictures he'd taken, get the photo of the ransom note to Nialla, *and* raid his attic before his mother got home. Marzana felt stirrings of panic and embarrassment whirling together in the pit of her stomach as she tried to think of something to say to decline for him.

Ciro spoke up first. "Nope," he said easily. "I have a project due tomorrow. But thank you."

"I'll walk you out," Marzana said, hoping she didn't sound too relieved.

Mrs. Hakelbarend made a disappointed face. "Another time, then. Hi to your mom." Marzana's dad gave a short wave, and Nick twirled his mustache in a melodrama-villain way that Marzana suspected he'd been practicing for years.

She all but dragged Ciro out into the hall. "They seem nice," he managed, clearly trying not to laugh as he allowed himself to be hauled to the front door.

"Har, har." Marzana opened it and shoved him out. "Tomorrow, then, at the bookstore?"

"Yeah. Same time, after school?"

"Yup. See you then." She hesitated, then added, "Thank you. You know how to get home?" She pointed down Crossynge Street. "Straight that way until you get to the stairs."

"Got it. Tell Honora I said 'Hooray, hooray, hooray!'"

"I don't know what that means."

"It's from the song she was quoting earlier. Hooray for Captain Spaulding. Now, if you'll pardon me." He leaned back inside and reached past her to grab his bag. "I have some projects to finish." He lowered his voice. "Want me to just give printouts of everything to Nialla tonight so she can give them to you first thing tomorrow?"

"Perfect."

Ciro saluted, and she watched him until he had descended to the street. Then she shut the door, squared her shoulders, and steeled herself for a return to the dining room and certain humiliation.

Fortunately for her, conversation had returned to the interrogation, and with Ciro gone, this time her parents didn't clam up quite as quickly. "So next we tell Emmett to look into this Flynn character," Mr. Hakelbarend was saying, "and to find out from his detective buddy where the idea of Rob as a suspect originated." He looked at his watch. "Maybe I'll do that right now." He got up and gave Marzana's shoulder a squeeze as he passed her on his way to use the phone in the parlor.

Mrs. Hakelbarend looked at Nick. "You know I can pick a Hellcat, right?"

Nick made a face. "I was under the impression that if I followed the patent trail far enough, I'd find you invented the design."

Marzana's mother said nothing, merely shot Marzana a glance, then grinned into her wineglass. Marzana smiled weakly, wondering what the right response to that was, considering she hadn't officially been party to the conversation they were referencing.

"Which is, of course, why it pains me to tell you I have managed to open mine no less than three times," Nick continued apologetically.

"Out of how many tries?"

Nick sighed. "Regretfully, I'm not good with numbers."

"You're a doctor, Nick," Mrs. Hakelbarend said drily. "Don't doctors have to be able to count higher than three? For dosages or whatever?"

"It's a paradox." Nick winked at Marzana. "Strangely, I am good with paradoxes."

"I have no idea what you're talking about," Marzana lied. "Are we eating soon?"

"Five minutes!" Honora barked from the kitchen.

"Five minutes it is," Mrs. Hakelbarend called back. She stretched her arms over her head and exhaled. Her eyes fell on Marzana. "So," she said casually. "Will we be seeing more of Ciro around here?"

"I claim sanctuary," Marzana mumbled.

Honora bustled out of the kitchen with a basket of rolls. "He's a Marx Brothers fan," she said crisply. "Can't say fairer than that."

"And there you have it." Marzana caught Honora's eye. "By the way, he said to tell you 'Hooray, hooray, hooray.'"

Honora made another of her harrumphing noises — surprised and pleased, this time — then plunked the basket down in front of Marzana, who, recognizing this for the distraction it was intended to be, grabbed a roll and studiously ignored everyone else in the room until the adults took the hint. Mr. Hakelbarend returned from his phone call just as Nick launched into a story about something absurd that had happened at the lab of one of his favorite chemists. Mrs. Hakelbarend raised both eyebrows. Marzana's father nodded once and murmured, "At CID." After this briefest of pauses, Nick continued his tale as if there had been no interruption at all.

Marzana let her mind wander as she tore her roll into halves, then quarters. The afternoon in the study had produced plenty of new information, but it was knots that she found occupying her thoughts. Out of nowhere, she remembered the dream from the night before: Honora braiding her hair with a marlinespike as the Liberty of Gammerbund, bound up in a decorative knot made of night and wind, swung like a pendulum.

Thief knot, grief knot, what knot.

I worry that if the girl isn't found by the time an extradition happens, her mother had said to Rob, *it won't be extradition for kidnapping. It'll be extradition for kidnapping* and *suspected murder.*

Amateurs, Marzana had said to Ciro. *We are such amateurs.*

Her father didn't mention the call he'd made again until the phone rang after they'd finished dinner, just as Honora arrived at the table with the coffeepot and another plate of snickerdoodles. "I'll get it, Honora," Mr. Hakelbarend said, rising and striding into the parlor before the old steward could object. He was gone only a few minutes.

Marzana kept her eyes on the cookies and pretended not to pay attention as Nick asked, "And so?"

"Well," Mr. Hakelbarend said with a chuckle, "I actually got hold of Emmett at his CID friend Thad's office, which happens to be just down the street from the jail where Rob was being held. So Emmett and his friend went over for a talk with Flynn himself: Captain Morris Flynn of Sovereign City PD, who—this will surprise you not a bit—was also the person who first raised Rob's name as a suspect." He reached for the coffee Honora had poured in his absence. "And I'm guessing Thad put thumbscrews on him or something, because he broke fast. Apparently he had taken bribes from one or two or five people, and he got a phone call from someone who had all the details of his many illegal acts and claimed to have evidence. That someone—he says it was a female voice trying to sound like a male, and I don't see any reason he'd tell the truth about his own crimes but lie about that—ordered Rob's release, right down to the specific date and time, in exchange for keeping quiet."

"A female voice?" Mrs. Hakelbarend repeated. "Rose Mirassat, maybe?"

Nick dunked a cookie into his cup. "I'm trying to picture dear Rose making that sort of phone call, and I'm having difficulty. I can't see where she'd get that sort of information about a city cop, either. It's not her line. She's a confectioner, for heaven's sake."

"And this would have been difficult information to get, even for a carrier," Mr. Hakelbarend said. "Flynn vomited out a handful of names of people he'd taken bribes from, and they were five very different criminal entities — not folks who generally play nicely with each other or who would be likely to band together to force a dirty cop's hand, even if they'd had some shared reason to do it. Also not folks who'd have any reason to mix themselves up in a kidnapping. Not by a long chalk."

"Well, it doesn't seem likely that Peony's abduction was pulled off by just one person," Marzana's mother said, "so there's no reason to assume the person who made the call was the same person who originally collected the information about Flynn's bribes. But this does suggest that one of the players has access to a significant trove of data."

"That sounds more like Hickson Blount," Nick said.

"Maybe," Mrs. Hakelbarend agreed, but she sounded unconvinced. "Let's talk to him next, if you can find him. And it probably wouldn't hurt to invite Rose by, though I tend to agree with you that this sounds less and less like Rose's kind of gig."

"Consider it done," Nick replied gallantly, brushing a single cookie crumb from his lapel as he stood.

They said their goodbyes, Marzana receiving a gentle tap on the crown of her head as he passed her on his way out of the dining room. But she stayed seated and quiet as she finished her last cookie, listening as her parents lingered in the hall behind her after seeing Nick to the door. She was not disappointed.

"I actually think this new information rules Hickson Blount out," Marzana's mother said. "He's not that good. There can't be many people who would have had access to this level of data, not from such varied sources."

"But we do know of at least one person who could," Mr. Hakel-barend said quietly. "You gonna make that call you told Emmett you might?"

Marzana turned nonchalantly as her mother made a sound of resignation. "Seems like I should, doesn't it? If he didn't provide that information, he'll know who did." Frowning pensively, she cracked the knuckles of her left hand with her thumb. "I'll try Tasha. Of course, if her grandfather's involved, she'll politely decline to help."

"And if he *did* give the caller the information?"

"If he did," Mrs. Hakelbarend said grimly, "then we have a huge problem."

Marzana didn't have to wonder who her parents were talking about, not with the image of the sketched bird fresh in her mind.

Can you put me in touch with the Snakebird? Emmett had asked. *I may not know who he is, but I know he's out there.*

And then, her mother: *I'm sorry . . . I can't introduce you. But I give you my word that if I think it'll help, I'll go to him myself.*

Her parents returned to the table and began to gather the coffee and dessert dishes. Marzana made her face as blank as Emilia Cabot's. In her mind, the swinging knot of Gammerbund began to come apart as a strange, serpent-necked bird landed upon it, knocking it off its trajectory, and, with a long and needle-sharp beak, began to pick it apart.

Thief knot, grief knot, what knot.

"Marzana?"

She looked up abruptly. Her mother held out her hand for Marzana's plate. "Thanks." She could see her mother watching her out of the corner of her eye as she gathered the last of the dishes, but Marzana couldn't begin to tell what she was thinking.

Marzana went up to her room just a bit earlier than usual after dinner and rifled through her desk drawers for anything that looked like it might be useful to someone who, like Emilia, was in the habit of finding adventures on a daily basis.

She found a pocket flashlight and the multi-tool her father had given her, added a pocket notebook and a space pen that would write at any angle (also a gift from her dad), and, after a moment's thought, tossed the shoelace she'd been practicing knots with onto the little pile. Then she rooted around in her closet for a little cross-body purse she never used because it was too small for books. The components of her beginner toolkit fit inside with room to spare, which was good because Marzana was pretty sure she'd wind up adding more to it.

She hung the purse from her doorknob, then took the first Sidle-dywry Knot book over to the window nook. It was past eleven when she finally set it down, finished. By the end, with most of the original Knot destroyed in the explosion that consumed Cartonfield, Casie —having changed her name to Nell Southsea to preserve the fiction that she, too, had perished in the conflagration—and the few survivors had begun rebuilding the syndicate from the ground up. With almost no resources, they had dedicated themselves to the two endeavors that presumably would drive the rest of the series: bringing to light the conspiracy that the Knot had been attempting to unravel before it had been destroyed, and locating the traitor or traitors who had betrayed the organization and allowed it to be so devastatingly attacked.

But really, Marzana thought as she closed the first book, the story that mattered was about the friends Casie/Nell pulled together to populate the new Knot. Not all of them were even precisely friends—but they were all in it together, all working as one toward the cause of justice. And the new recruits were *kids*. Because in the world of the book, it was clear that the adults had been lost long ago: they were powerless, or hopeless, or corrupt, or they just didn't care enough about anyone other than themselves to do the work. If there was justice to be found, it wasn't coming from the grownups.

This was the fictional world Peony had been living in before she had been taken: a world full of friends who had your back, even when the adults couldn't be trusted. Who did she think would be coming for her now? Was she sitting somewhere, lost and lonely, and praying the adults in her life were better than the ones in her book?

twelve
NEXT-DAY POST

WHEN MARZANA STUMBLED down the stairs Friday morning with her newly assembled kit in the purse slung over her shoulder and her journal and the first Sidledywry Knot book under one arm, she found a package waiting for her on the dining room table.

"What's this?" she asked her mother, who sat lazily braiding her long, dark hair into a single plait as she stared down at the morning paper.

"Search me," Mrs. Hakelbarend said as she wrapped an elastic around the end and picked up her coffee. "It must've been delivered at some unholy hour of the morning. It was on the doorstep when I went out for the paper."

Marzana took the package and turned it over: a small rectangular box wrapped in crumpled newsprint. It had been sent next-day post, and the shipping label covered most of the sender's information. All but the first letter on the first line: *M*. Marzana peeled the label carefully back, and the rest of the name revealed itself letter by letter. "It's from Milo."

"Milo from Greenglass House?"

"Yeah." Marzana tore away the newsprint. Beneath it was an oatmeal box, taped shut, and inside that, a bunch more newsprint. Then, finally, stuffed at the bottom, a second parcel the size of her palm: something small and hard, wrapped in a piece of green construction paper and tied with twine.

"What is it?" Marzana's mother inquired, leaning around the bowl of flowers in the middle of the table for a better look.

"Still working on that." Marzana untied the twine and slipped off the construction paper, noting briefly that there were words written on the inside. And then, the thing within lay in her hand. Or really, the two things: a gold-colored metal vial, and tucked inside that . . . Marzana shook whatever it was out and examined it: a figurine about the height of her thumb, in the shape of an owl with a girl's face. Carved on the base was the word *Sirin*.

"It's . . . a bottle, and . . . I think this is an RPG miniature," Marzana said, turning the Sirin owl over in her fingers. She set it down, reached for the green paper, and flattened it to read the note.

Dear Marzana,

I can't come help out myself, but I didn't come to camp alone.

Two things:

1)   Don't lose this vial.

2)   Keep the Sirin figure inside it.

She knows I'm sending her, but we're not sure whether she'll come through immediately or not. Sometimes she loses time and we don't really know why.

oh — three things.

    3)   Send the vial back to Greenglass House when it's time.

    Good luck,
    Milo

Very little of it made any kind of sense to Marzana, except that Milo had sent this—whatever this was—to her, thinking it might help with the investigation. And he'd gone to the trouble of sending it next-day post from summer camp. How did you even manage that?

"And so?" Mrs. Hakelbarend inquired.

"We're working on putting a game together," Marzana said, folding up the note and tucking it in her pocket. "This is a character Milo wants to use." She passed the Sirin owl across the table. "I guess I'm going to be the game master."

"I can never keep these character types straight," her mom said. "What's this?"

"I'm not actually sure." The only game Marzana definitely knew that Milo played was Odd Trails, so it was probably from that. But the figurine, with its bird's body and girl's face, didn't immediately bring any specific player class to mind. Nor did the name Sirin. "I'll have to look it up." She passed her mother the vial. "He said to keep it in this, though I have no idea why."

She gathered the box and newsprint and carried them into the kitchen to the recycling, then made herself a bowl of cereal.

"Super quiet around here," she observed as she carried the bowl back into the dining room.

"Honora went to the market," Mrs. Hakelbarend said, passing back the Sirin figure in its container. "Your dad headed out early."

Marzana tucked the vial into her pocket. "Work stuff?"

Mrs. Hakelbarend lifted her mug, smiling enigmatically. "Ma-aaybe."

"I really want to ask what all that was with Rob last night."

"And I really want to ask about Ciro," her mother said, turning a page of her newspaper. "Wanna trade?"

Marzana scowled while she finished chewing a spoonful of cereal. "Sure. You go first."

"What do you want to know?"

What didn't she already know from the previous night's eavesdropping? And what did she logically have to ask so it wasn't obvious that she already knew more than she should? "Well, did he do it?"

"If he had, do you really think we'd have let him walk out the door?"

"I didn't know you let him walk out the door. He was here, and then he was gone. So he didn't do it?"

Mrs. Hakelbarend's smile faded into a thoughtful frown. "I'll put it this way: I don't think he did the job himself. I think it's possible he is, or was, involved somehow, but I also think it's possible his involvement is unintentional."

"Does he know who did do it, then?"

"I believe he does not." She tapped her fingers on the tabletop. "This smacks of someone pulling strings. I think Rob was set up to be a suspect. Frankly, I think we'll find the same thing is true of Hickson and Rose when we track them down."

Marzana nodded as if this were all fascinating new information.

"Do you still think the people who are really behind it are in the Liberty now?"

Her mother said nothing for a moment. She took a sip of coffee. "I honestly have no reason to think so, Marzie. I never did." Her expression darkened. "If they are, then I'm glad to help, because the asylum laws that protect the Liberty won't survive if kidnappers and violent criminals are allowed to shelter here. But I'll tell you this much: If there's someone causing problems in Nagspeake, and that person can't immediately be dragged in to face the music — if there's trouble finding them for even five minutes, everyone always assumes they've gone to ground in Gammerbund. And obviously" — she raised both arms to indicate herself — "that is sometimes true. But not everyone here is a lawbreaker. Not even *most* everyone. And not everybody gets sanctuary. The monsters don't get sanctuary, and for the most part, they know it, so they don't even ask. The city proper needs to start taking a much closer look at itself if it really wants to get serious about tracking them down in town."

"Wow," Marzana said. "Downer, Mom."

"Yeah. I'm in a bit of a mood today." Mrs. Hakelbarend straightened and flashed a hundred-watt smile. "My turn."

"Shoot," Marzana said, turning her attention to her cereal.

"Why did I not know you had a —" Marzana raised her head and her spoon in warning. Her mother closed her mouth for a moment. "Why was I totally unaware of someone you were apparently good enough friends with to invite him over for a movie?"

"Well," Marzana said, "maybe I didn't invite him over before now because I was afraid you guys were going to make a big deal of it. And," she added, remembering Ciro's advice that a good liar told as few lies as possible, "you were kind of busy yesterday when we got here."

Mrs. Hakelbarend nodded and sipped her coffee. "Fair."

Marzana made a production of glancing at the clock on the sideboard. "I believe I have time for precisely one more query, Mother."

Mrs. Hakelbarend gave her a long look, and it occurred to Marzana to wonder whether her mom was about to fling a point-blank question in her face: something along the lines of *Just what the heck do you think you're up to, Marzana?* or *Exactly who do you think you're fooling here, young lady?* or possibly something as pointed as *Did you find whatever you were looking for in my study?*

Instead, though, her mother went nonlinear. "Are you okay?"

Marzana blinked, surprised. "What do you mean?"

Mrs. Hakelbarend turned the mug between her hands. "I find investigating a kidnapping very upsetting. Your dad feels the same way. I think we're both having a hard time compartmentalizing our feelings as parents, and because I'm really not sure how much good we're going to be able to do—since, like I said, we're really just not sure there's any Liberty connection—I think we both feel a little helpless and frustrated. I guess I wanted to make sure you weren't having a similar experience. Not stressing or worrying or feeling anxious because of it."

"I . . . hadn't thought of it like that at all, actually," Marzana said. It was a lie—hearing the words "suspected murder" had knocked the breath out of her—but she couldn't bring that up. Plus, if her mother suspected anything about this had shaken her, Mrs. Hakelbarend would clamp down on every scrap of information. Marzana would get nothing else from her.

"Well, good. Don't start now. Forget I said anything." Mrs. Hakelbarend got to her feet. "I believe that's the end of my time." She reached for Marzana's bowl and spoon. "I'll take care of these."

"Thanks, Mom." Marzana hesitated. "I promise I'm okay."

"Good." Her mother leaned over and kissed her forehead, the long braid brushing Marzana's wrist. Marzana touched the end of the plait. They didn't look much alike, she and her mom, but they had the same dark-rimmed eyes, and in the right light you could spot the same just-barely-there reddish highlights in their hair. She could see the faintest tinge of them now.

On impulse, she got to her feet and hugged her mother tight. Then she disentangled herself. "I better get going." She grabbed the book and her journal and darted for her backpack. If she hurried, she'd get to school with a decent amount of time to spare. Hopefully Nialla had something to report.

Marzana had barely closed the door behind herself out on the front stoop when a voice spoke from her side. "Hey." She started, and turned to find a girl who looked just a little younger than she was standing on the sidewalk, leaning against the stoop railing as if she'd been waiting for Marzana to emerge.

There was something distinctly familiar about this girl. She was pale and lightly freckled, with curly reddish hair that poked out in a fringe from under a green-and-blue knitted beanie. As Marzana looked down at her, she had the strangest feeling, like back when Nialla had started wearing glasses the week after they'd first met. The *I know you* awareness had come well before the actual recognition.

But the recognition was there. "Hey," Marzana said as she studied the girl. She wore jeans, and a T-shirt with UP IN THE AIR, JUNIOR BIRDMEN! on it that Marzana had definitely seen somewhere before . . . but where?

Up in the air. Marzana glanced at the girl's beanie, struck by a sudden memory of a different hat altogether: a fur-lined aviator's cap. And . . . a Christmas tree.

The answer hit her, and she almost tripped over her own feet as she took a step toward the girl, who had begun to smile as if watching Marzana figure things out was the best game she'd played in days.

She knows I'm sending her, but we're not sure whether she'll come through immediately or not. Sometimes she loses time and we don't really know why.

"Oh, my God," Marzana said, grabbing the railing to regain her balance. "You're — are you *Meddy?*"

And the girl, who was not just a girl but a thirty-something-years-dead ghost somehow sent to Marzana in the *mail*, of all things, nodded. "That would be me."

thirteen

DUMBWAITERS

SIX MONTHS AGO, Marzana's one and only other adventure had taken her to Greenglass House. There, of course, she'd met Milo. And somewhat after that, in a rather dramatic reveal, she'd met his friend Meddy, who, it turned out, was the child of one of Mrs. Hakelbarend's famous smuggler colleagues who had lived in Greenglass House, too. But that had been long ago, before both the smuggler and his daughter had died.

And here Meddy was again, looking like any kid on the street.

"What are you *doing* here?" Marzana demanded, hopping down the last steps as she fumbled in her pocket for the vial. She held it up. "Is this — did this —?"

If there was anything stranger than meeting a ghost over Christmas vacation, it was having that ghost arrive on your doorstep by mail six months later.

"Yes. And now that I'm here, you'd better give it to me. It's what lets me move around away from Greenglass House, though I'm still figuring out how." Meddy plucked the vial from Marzana's fingers.

Marzana snapped her fingers. "It's a reliquary! Like in Odd Trails—what's the thing that can move away from the character that summoned it using a reliquary?"

"A scholiast." Meddy sounded pleased. "Exactly. By the way, I should remind you that right now, to the world at large, it looks like you're talking to yourself. So maybe pretend to tie your shoe or something and talk quietly."

"Right." Marzana dropped to fumble at her laces so fast, she banged her knee on the pavement. "Hey—can *anyone* else see you right now?"

"I think just you," Meddy said. "But it seems that once I show myself to people, they can see me from that point on, which is why I wanted to wait until you were outside to manifest. Otherwise your mom would've seen me, since I showed myself to her and to your dad back in December." She squatted and watched Marzana work loose the double knot in her right shoelace as she spoke. "Milo figured out the hack with the vial right after you all left Greenglass House in December. I—ghost me, anyway—I'm tied to the inn because ... well, because I died there. But Milo found this"—she held up the vial between forefinger and thumb—"in the attic at Greenglass House. And we already had this." She shook the little owl-girl figurine out onto one palm. "My dad had it made especially for me, so it's able to represent me, like a relic; and the vial, which must've been in the house for ages and ages, works as a reliquary. I don't know how much you remember about scholiasts in Odd Trails ..."

"Not much," Marzana admitted as she began to slowly retie her shoelaces. "I've never played a harbinger, and only harbingers can summon a scholiast, right?"

"Right. And usually scholiasts are tied pretty closely to their harbingers. They have a range of a hundred feet. Unless you have a reliquary, that is, in which case you can do an exploit called Spooky Action at a Distance. The harbinger can give the reliquary to someone else, and the scholiast follows the reliquary rather than the harbinger."

"And that's *real?*" Marzana asked in quiet disbelief. "I mean, it works for ghosts?"

Meddy sighed. "I understand so little about myself as a ghost, you'd be amazed. I sort of have to piece the rules together as I go. And I thought Milo was crazy for thinking you could apply role-playing-game rules to the real world. But he pointed out that Odd Trails is based on legends and folk stories, so there could be some underlying truth to it. There usually is, you know, with folklore. So we decided to give it a try, and much to my personal shock, it works. Mostly. I'm still sorting out the details." She winced and rubbed her nose. "There have been some . . . painful surprises."

Marzana grinned as she finished retying the knot. "Meaning you occasionally walk into walls?"

"That's *precisely* what I mean." Meddy glanced at a giant watch on her wrist. "Were you on your way somewhere?"

Oh, right. School. "Yeah, actually." Marzana got reluctantly to her feet.

"Great. I'll walk with you, and you can fill me in on exactly what the heck is going on."

"But I'm going to look like I'm talking to myself, right?"

"True, but unavoidable. Maybe make it look like you're doing it on purpose. Practicing a speech for school or something."

Marzana, who often discovered that she'd been talking to herself while working out what to say or what she should have said during some social interaction real or imagined, nodded. "I can do that." She started down the sidewalk, and Meddy fell into step at her side. It was rush hour on Crossynge Street, with a steady flow of passersby on foot and on bicycle, but none of them seemed in any way interested in a middle-schooler apparently talking to herself. "So you were at camp with Milo?"

The ghost girl nodded. "I haven't been able to leave Greenglass House in decades. It was good to get away for a while." She looked around, then up at the tall, narrow houses looming overhead. "And this is the Liberty of Gammerbund, huh? Why, exactly, am I here? Milo said someone was kidnapped, but that's pretty much all."

"I think that's all I managed to tell him," Marzana admitted. Then, pausing whenever it felt like any particular person or group out on the street was too close for comfort, she relayed the key points as briefly as possible. "I can fill you in on the rest later. We're all meeting after school at Lucky's bookstore—you remember Lucky—but Emilia can probably find us a private place to talk during our study period."

"I'd like to help," Meddy said, sidestepping a kid who nearly zoomed a toy plane right into—through?—her. "I'll do whatever I can. But I'm not . . ." She hesitated, looking for the right word. "Powerful. I can walk through walls and stuff . . . sometimes, anyway." She took the vial from her pocket and rattled it in her palm. "The reliquary lets me move through space almost like you do, which is good for, say, leaving Greenglass House, but bad for maximum mobility through solid objects. If *you* hold the reliquary, I can pass through things, and carry stuff with me too. Objects, clothing, whatever." She looked happily down at her T-shirt. "This is new, for instance. That guy Sylvester who came to Greenglass House with you at Christmas had the same shirt, and I really liked it, so Milo found one for me. But I can only go so far from the reliquary before I'm tugged back. If *I'm* holding the reliquary, I can go any distance, but the reliquary won't go through solid surfaces, so neither can I. It's really taking some getting used to."

"So you can't go and find the Belowground conductor for us, for instance," Marzana said glumly. "Or at least, not any faster than I could myself if I went down into the city proper."

Meddy pointed a finger. "Bingo. And you understand, of course, that I don't have, you know, *magic* or anything."

Marzana snorted. "That's okay. We have a magician."

Meddy gave her a sideways look. "A magician like a sortileger or a mage or something? Or like a dude who does birthdays?"

"I suspect he's at least done his own birthday."

The ghost grinned. "This is gonna be great."

Impulsively, Marzana grinned back. "Yeah, I think it is."

Nialla was pacing beside Marymead's front stairs when Marzana hurried up to her with Meddy in tow, panting from having basically speed-walked the entire two and a half miles from the Viaduct. "Oh, my God, Mars," she breathed, grabbing Marzana's arm. "You guys did it! I can't *believe* you guys did it!"

"I take it Ciro managed to drop off some goodies last night."

"Yes. I have everything here." Nialla was incandescent with impatience as she shook her satchel meaningfully at Marzana.

"And did you take a look?" Marzana asked.

"I took a look at *everything*," Nialla replied. "Not that I understand it all, but I can give you a rundown before class. Let's go to your locker first."

Marzana looked around. She and Meddy had made really good time getting to Marymead, and the schoolyard was still pretty quiet. The kids who'd come for before-school commitments had gotten there half an hour or so earlier, and the big rush of students arriving for the regular start of the day would begin in about ten minutes. Nobody was looking their way. She turned to Meddy. "Can you . . . ?"

"Can I what?" Nialla asked, confused, at the same moment that Meddy nodded and replied, "Sure thing." The ghost girl leaned sideways, pointedly sticking her face between Marzana and Nialla.

There was nothing else to see, but something happened, because Nialla did a thing Marzana had not realized could truly, actually happen: she jumped out of her shoes. Nialla staggered backwards, leaving her slip-on sandals on the pavement where she'd been standing a second before. "What . . . who . . . what just . . . ?"

Meddy flung her arms wide. "Tarncap Reveal!"

"Nialla," Marzana said, "this is Meddy. She's joining the crew. Meddy, this is my best friend, Nialla."

Meddy waved a hand. "Hi."

"Hi," Nialla replied weakly. Then, "Meddy?" she repeated. Recognition flickered on her face. "From winter break? But . . . you mean that was true? *Literally* true? All of it?"

Marzana took Nialla's arm. "It's okay. Put your shoes on and let's go inside. In the meantime, tell me about Ciro's prints. And remember that only you and I can see Meddy, so be subtle about talking to her."

Meddy took out the reliquary and handed it to Marzana. "Take this for now, would you?"

Marzana zipped it into the purse that held her adventuring kit. "Of course."

They walked up the stairs, Nialla tripping on every other step as she tried to simultaneously watch Meddy out of the corner of her eye and maneuver her own feet, all while holding in the questions she was clearly burning to ask. She hauled open one of the front doors, held it for Marzana and Meddy, and followed them into the nearly empty front hall. "I don't even know where to start. A lot of the notes describe what you told us already—the stuff what's-his-name, Emmett, told your parents." She looked to Meddy. "Did she tell you everything already, or should I go over it?"

"I think I'm caught up as far as possible, not including whatever new stuff you have," Meddy replied.

"Okay, well, in addition to the *old* stuff, there's a lot I don't understand, which I think must be their potential leads. It's a bunch of names I don't recognize. But *you* might, Mars."

"What about the ransom note?" Marzana asked quietly. "Will it be helpful for the theory you had?"

Nialla's expression sharpened. "Yes. I think so. It still might be nothing, but the copy gives me what I need to test it. We'll see. Ciro said your parents were questioning somebody last night," she added in an undertone.

Marzana swallowed her reply and stifled a startled yelp as they turned the corner around the stairs and nearly walked into someone leaning against the end of the first row of lockers. Then she stifled another squeal, this one of relief. "Emilia!"

"Top of the morning," Emilia said, her expression deadpan as ever. "Thought the two of you might show up early."

"It's the three of us, actually," Marzana told her.

Meddy waved from beside Emilia, whose head snapped around,

nearly whipping Nialla across the face with one of her braids. Her poker face didn't crack, but she spat out a very evocative swear word. "What the heck is going on? Where did *she* come from?"

"This is Meddy," Marzana said for the second time. "Meddy, Emilia."

"She's dead," Nialla blurted. "A ghost."

"Awkward," Meddy said, "but accurate."

"Um." Emilia extended a hesitant palm. Meddy shook it, and Emilia stared down at their clasped hands. "Interesting. Nice to meet you, I guess." She took her hand back and examined her palm. "Where did we come by a ghost? You're not from Marymead, are you?"

"Camp care package," Meddy replied. "In reverse."

Emilia tilted her head, considering. "I have so many questions."

Meddy raised an eyebrow. "You don't seem particularly surprised, though."

"Yeah," Nialla added, frowning at Emilia. "What, exactly, does that mean: 'You're not from Marymead'?"

Emilia shook her head. "Later, Nialla. We don't have time for me to blow your mind right now."

Well, if there were ghosts at Marymead, Marzana figured, the Commorancy Kids would know. Marzana made a mental note to come back to that another time. Emilia was right; they were on a tight timetable. "Hey, where were you yesterday?" Marzana asked her. "We were worried stiff!"

"Really?" Emilia gave her a curious look. "Why didn't you come up? I faked sick because I spent all night doing stuff. But I'm fine."

"We can . . . we can just come up?" Nialla asked dubiously. "Just like that?"

"You can if you're visiting someone." Emilia turned to Meddy. "I live here," she explained. "Me and a handful of others. Anyway, for future reference, my room is 7R2. Back of the house, overlooking the knot-garden side of the courtyard." She straightened and tossed her head at the locker bank. "Need anything before your first class? You have Topham for homeroom, right?"

"Yes to Topham, and I guess I can skip my locker," Marzana replied. "Nye?"

"I'm good."

"Let's go, then." Emilia led them away from the lockers and down the hallway between the gym and the back wall of the saloon again, toward the far side of the house.

"Would you look at these sourpusses?" Meddy said, staring up at the portraits above the lockers as she brought up the rear of the group. "Though these names are magnificent." Now Meddy's voice was coming from above. The other three girls turned sharply, and Marzana looked up to see the ghost girl leaping across the tops of the banks of lockers, pausing after each soundless, loping jump from one little bank to the next to read the labels on the frames. "Ophelia Anella Cotgrave, Nadia Almiretta Cotgrave-Cormorant, Maurice Worcestershire Cotgrave . . . Everybody going by all the names they have, apparently . . . Ezra Montcalvo Cormorant, Maeve-Alice Cotgrave . . . But so crabby-looking." Meddy jumped down, and even Emilia winced as she landed, but the ghost girl hit the floor without so much as a whisper.

"This is going to take some getting used to," Emilia observed. She glanced up at the portraits with a half-smile. "Funny you should mention those. The Cotgraves used to own this house. These are all previous owners and trustees and so forth." She cocked her head, and Marzana heard the creak of the front doors, along with a murmur of voices. The school day was about to begin. "Time's short," Emilia said. "This way."

Just past the gym, a narrower hallway met the one they were following. Tucked into the right angle formed by these passages were the administrative offices, and Emilia paused there for a quick glance to be sure they were still alone. "The principal will be there already," she whispered, starting forward again and leading them down the narrow hall between the offices and the back wall of one of the staircases, which was lined with more lockers. "And probably the guidance counselors—they always show up early—but not Miss Palkowick, and that's the only person we care about right now. School secretary," she explained to Meddy. "Quick, now." The voices of incoming kids were impossible to ignore. Somebody with a locker in this row was going to pop around the corner any minute.

The hall ended at a pair of swinging doors covered in green leather. Emilia hurried through them and into a service hallway with faded blue wallpaper, smooth stone floors, and occasional overhead fixtures with bulbs that gave light in mismatched tones of yellow and blue. It was a door and a passage Marzana had seen a million times during her years at Marymead. Now, as she and the others followed Emilia through, she realized she actually had no idea where the passage went.

Emilia steadied the swinging doors, then nodded to the left, toward the front of the school, where a narrow staircase led downward and the hallway beyond it ended in the entrance to what Marzana's mental map of the school told her had to be the dining hall. "The cafeteria's that way, and the stairs go down to the kitchen and pantry and whatnot," Emilia explained to Meddy in a whisper. "The science labs and music rooms are down there too, but students use a staircase on the other side of the house to get to those." She turned and pointed toward the back of the building. "What *we* want is over here."

At *that* end of the hallway, on the right-hand side, the wallpaper was interrupted here and there by what looked like dark wooden cabinets with dull gold drawer pulls near the bottom edges. Nialla got it first. "Dumbwaiters?"

"Yup." Emilia walked down and hauled up on the handle of the nearest one to reveal the cabinet inside. "In we go."

"What?" Marzana blinked. "In there? *All of us?*"

"I don't actually take up any room," Meddy put in. "It looks like the three of you'll fit with no problem."

"But will it *support* three of us?" Marzana asked.

"We're just climbing in to climb through," Emilia said. "But it'll hold. These dumbwaiters have been safety-tested by generations of Commorancy Kids, with necessary adjustments made where needed. Look." Emilia reached in and pointed to a handle that had been fitted on the inside of the dumbwaiter, opposite the one she'd used to lift the door from the outside, and then to a button that looked like it had to have been installed by someone other than a licensed electrician. "I've seen these things hold five kids at once." She climbed in and scooted over. "Get in."

"I'm trusting you on this one." Marzana squared her shoulders, put both hands on the lower edge of the dumbwaiter, and hoisted herself inside. The inner cabinet shifted, but not enough to make her doubt Emilia's assurances. Nialla followed, and Marzana looked past her into the hall for Meddy. "Already in," the ghost girl said, her face looming pale out of the shadows an inch in front of Marzana. "Sorry. Didn't mean to startle."

"Keep your voices down," Emilia whispered. "And can one of

you pull the door shut?" Meddy did, while on the other side of the cabinet, Emilia leaned against a second door for a moment. She gave a satisfied nod and hoisted it open, revealing nothing but another dark surface. But this surface swung easily outward at a touch, opening into a room that seemed immediately familiar, even though Marzana couldn't quite place it.

Smallish, old-fashioned wooden desks were scattered around the space, along with green embroidered brocade chairs that looked suspiciously like they might once have been part of a bigger set in someone's fancy dining room. Mentally mapping what they'd passed right before Emilia had led them through the dumbwaiter, Marzana snapped her fingers. "This is the back office, isn't it?" That meant the outer surface Emilia had pushed open to let them into the room had to be the big portrait of Jane Agatha Marymead in its ornate gilt frame.

She glanced out at the office's door, which was presently closed, its frosted window dark.

"Miss Palkowick opens up her office at eight on the dot," Emilia said, following Marzana's eyes. "Which means we only have a few minutes, because she's absolutely never late." Emilia hopped out, gesturing at the dark window in the door. "If she's early, we'll see the light go on in the outer office first, and then we'll have about thirty seconds to get back to the dumbwaiter while she starts a pot of coffee. Forty, if by some miracle it's unseasonably chilly out and she has a sweater to take off. Is it chilly today?" she asked hopefully as first Nialla and then Marzana dropped lightly down into the office.

"Not really," Nialla said, glancing around.

"I'll keep watch," Meddy said. She strode across the room and straight through the door without bothering to open it.

"Holy moly, that's weird," Nialla mumbled.

Marzana nodded, wondering how Milo had played it so cool when Marzana had visited Greenglass House, not giving Meddy's presence away for days. *Focus.* "What are we doing here? Mr. Otterwill's records?"

"He doesn't have much." Emilia headed for a small bank of battered lateral files. "Employee records are here." She dragged the top drawer open, plucked out a manila folder, and opened it. Marzana and Nialla looked on as Emilia moved the very small pile of papers around. "Name, address, the usual stuff. Copies of his ID documents and his Liberty work warrant. Notes that they called the principal at Watermill for references, blah blah. But this might be useful." She pointed to a page mostly covered in handwriting, along with a single sticky note that read *Watermill/R. Burroughs, 4pm,* along with a phone number with a Printer's Quarter exchange.

Marzana scanned the notes on the page: *Employee in good standing, advises on two extracurricular clubs, currently teaching science but can easily handle general and specialized math at secondary school level . . .* This was probably the Watermill principal's phone reference. "What am I looking at?"

"Two things." Emilia pointed to a line near the top. *Recomm. Victor Cormorant.* "This is the person who recommended Mr. Otterwill as a substitute."

Nialla tapped her fingers on her cheek. "Why does that name sound familiar to me?"

"The portraits back in that hallway," Marzana said immediately. "The one's whose names Meddy was reading. I don't remember a Victor, though."

"There isn't a Victor in the portrait hall," Emilia said. "But yes, there are a handful of Cormorants — they married into the Cotgrave family at some point. The thing is, I think *Victor* Cormorant specifically sounds familiar to me, but I can't place it. I was hoping the name would ring a bell to somebody else."

Nialla stared down at her feet, then back up at Emilia. "I do think I might have seen that name somewhere else — Victor specifically — but I honestly can't think of where it might've been."

"Keep thinking about it. Maybe it'll come to you. If we both recognize the name, then we both must have seen it around the school somewhere. I'll try to track down the Cotgrave genealogy today during study period. There's a ton of that stuff in the Library, and if all else fails, the school historian will know."

Meddy poked her head — only her head — directly through the surface of the door to stare at them. "You have a school historian? What school has a *historian?*"

"The Cotgraves made it a condition when they bequeathed the house," Emilia said. "One condition of many, all of them weird. I'd give my right big toe to see the actual documents."

"How loudly were we talking?" Marzana asked nervously.

"Not loud at all. I was leaning right against the door." Meddy's head popped back out of sight.

Emilia made a quiet throat-clearing sound. "There's also this —"

"Oh, I see it," Marzana whispered. She touched an arrow leading away from the phrase *two extracurricular clubs.* At its other end were the words *math competition club, comics club.* "Comics."

"Exactly," Emilia said with satisfaction. "What if Peony Hyde was in that club? Mr. Otterwill would for sure have known what she was reading, and maybe even about her breakup with her friend. And if he really was at the camp party that day . . . I think this makes him a serious suspect."

Marzana glanced around the room, looking for the copier. "We should make a copy of this."

"Can't. The copier is loud." Emilia closed the folder and dropped it neatly back into place in the drawer. "But I made notes last night. I'll bring them this afternoon."

Meddy appeared without warning from the direction of the office door. "Incoming."

Marzana's heart thudded into a higher gear. On the other side of the frosted window, a light clicked on, turning the dark square a dusty, dimpled yellow.

"Yup, that's our cue," Emilia whispered briskly, sliding the file cabinet gently closed. "Let's go. We'll be seen if we leave by the hallway, so we should take the dumbwaiter straight upstairs. Gotta get it moving before she comes in, because you can just barely hear the first lurch from the outside."

They hurried back to the dumbwaiter, and Emilia waited without any apparent concern as Meddy vanished herself into the dark cabinet and Marzana and Nialla hoisted themselves up. Then she followed, pulling the painting in its frame back toward the wall as she went. It snapped into place with a soft click, and Emilia drew the inner door down and hit the button she'd shown them before. The dumbwaiter lurched upward, making Marzana and Nialla grab for each other. But after the initial jerk, the ride smoothed out, and Emilia's voice, muttering rhythmically, could be heard over the soft creaks of the slow-moving contraption.

"*Mrs. Kerwallow sometimes may follow her cows trotting over the hill,*" she murmured.

The idea flitted through Marzana's head that it was possible they'd just locked themselves in a moving box with a crazy person.

Then Meddy began to laugh, a strange, slightly out-of-control giggle. It reminded Marzana of babysitting for a four-year-old who'd laugh that way seconds before giving in to some ill-advised impulse like launching himself off the couch and onto the floor in a belly flop. *Oh, my God, what if they're both insane? Milo Pine, did you send me an insane ghost?* Marzana and Nialla glanced at each other.

"What?" Meddy asked, wiping her eyes. "You guys can't feel that? That is *crazy.*"

"Feel what?" Nialla demanded.

"Something about the way this thing is moving," Meddy managed, speaking in gulps between laughs. "Crazy. Crazy crazy *crazy.*"

Oblivious to everything else, Emilia continued reciting: *"But only on days when the old cow sashays, for she's certain they dance a quadrille."* She poked the button crisply on the last syllable of *quadrille.* The dumbwaiter stopped. "Timing's important," she explained in a whisper. "It's the only way to know where you are from the inside."

She hit the button a second time. The dumbwaiter shot into motion again, and Emilia continued her recitation. *"Mrs. Kerwallow takes walks in the hollow, in search of a creature that sings."* Meddy began giggling again as Emilia went on, *"But only on nights with stars glowing bright, for the critter likes glittering things."* Emilia pushed the button and glared at the silently shaking Meddy. "All right, yes, it's hilarious. Is the coast clear, or what?"

Meddy pulled herself together, gulping deep breaths. "I can't believe you guys can't feel that," she wheezed. She disappeared through the door, then leaned her head back in and announced, "All clear."

"Thanks." Emilia pushed up the door and swung open another framed picture on the other side. This time Marzana recognized where they were immediately: Mr. Topham's history room.

Meddy stood beside the dumbwaiter, shaking her head. "Your school is *so* weird."

"There's been a dumbwaiter behind this map all that time," Nialla said wonderingly as she climbed past Emilia and down. "Who knew?"

Emilia's expression cracked briefly into amusement. "Lots of us. Welcome to the club. All right," she said crisply, sitting on the edge of the dumbwaiter with her legs dangling as Marzana followed Nialla out into the empty classroom. "I had a thought, but you guys will have to do it because I don't have Otterwill for math. One or the other of you is reading *Sidledywry,* right?"

Marzana and Nialla nodded. "Both of us," Nialla said.

"Well, you can test our hypothesis about Peony being in Mr. Otterwill's comics club. Find some way to bring the series up. See if he reacts. It's something to try."

Nialla nodded. "I can do it."

"Right. See you later, then. Lockers after school, same as before?"

"Yeah, we'll—" Marzana stopped, confused, and looked around. "Wait." This classroom, hers and Nialla's homeroom, was at the front of the house. The administrative offices and the dumbwaiters were on the same side of Marymead, but they were at the back. "The back office and Topham's classroom aren't vertically in line with each other. Are they?"

"Nope," Emilia said. "They aren't. It's all in the timing."

Marzana folded her arms. "Come on. Are we in this together, or not?"

Emilia hesitated. "The easy answer is, there must be horizontal shafts between floors."

There must be implied that Emilia didn't actually know it to be true, and the existence of passages between the ceilings and the floors above them seemed like the kind of thing the kids of the Marymead Commorancy would make it their business to confirm or refute. "But you don't think it's the right one," Marzana guessed.

"Yeah." Emilia shrugged. "Well, we've never found any. But we do know that the dumbwaiters' works are made of old iron. We think—in the Commorancy, I mean . . ." She paused again, her blank expression cracking briefly into something very interesting, a blend of defiance and vulnerability: *You won't believe this, but I don't really care.* "We think that the iron can reconfigure the house when it wants to. Open up new paths."

"No way," Meddy breathed as the words "Shut up!" erupted from Nialla.

Marzana gaped, trying to imagine moving tendrils of old iron shifting entire classrooms out of the way of passing dumbwaiters. "It would have to do more than open up new paths. It would have to move around—or just move—whole *rooms.*"

"Yeah," Emilia said, with the *Believe me or don't* challenge set firmly on her face. "That's exactly what it would have to do."

"But . . . but we'd feel something, wouldn't we?" Marzana persisted.

Emilia shrugged. Then she glanced thoughtfully at Meddy. "Maybe some of us did. Shut the map after me, will you?" She swung her legs back into the dumbwaiter and pulled down the door. A very soft thump told them she'd hit the button and was off again.

Marzana shook her head as she reached out and swung the framed map back into place against the wall. *Click.* "I know old iron moves, but is it really possible that it can also manipulate space with well-timed nursery rhymes?"

Nialla turned on the light switch by the door, then walked

back to her desk and sat, still looking dazed. "Ask Mrs. Kerwallow, I guess."

"Well, I *definitely* felt something," Meddy muttered. "*So* weird, your school."

The classroom door opened, and Mr. Topham wandered in. He reached for the light switch, frowned to find it already on, then did a full-on double-take when he spotted Marzana and Nialla in their seats. He glanced at the clock on the wall, then at his own watch. "Morning, ladies. You're here early."

Marzana and Nialla waved as if nothing were out of the ordinary. Between the desks, Meddy waved too. Then she turned to face the two of them. "Hey, listen. Mind if I do a little exploring? Maybe I can shadow this Mr. Otterwill character. Marzana, tug your ear if yes; Nialla, scratch your chin if no."

The two non-ghosts glanced at each other. Nialla shrugged. Marzana reached up, pretended to adjust a braid, and tugged her ear once.

"Cool, cool. I'll meet you where we ran into Emilia at the lockers downstairs, if I don't find you in class first."

Marzana glanced at the teacher, but Mr. Topham was focused on unpacking his briefcase. She reached into her pocket and wiggled the gold vial just below the level of her desk. *Will you need this?*

"Probably a good idea." Meddy plucked it from her palm. "Thanks, Marzana." And with that, the ghost of Greenglass House pocketed her reliquary and sauntered past their oblivious history teacher and out into the hall.

Nialla glanced at Marzana. "Today's an odd day."

"Feels off, somehow," Marzana agreed as she got out her folder.

"Yeah. Not in a bad way, just . . ."

Marzana nodded. "I know exactly what you mean."

fourteen
GENUS *ANHINGA*

MARZANA SPENT study period that afternoon working on her knots in the Parlor while she looked over the notes Ciro had photographed at her house. Nialla spent it figuring out how to talk to Mr. Otterwill about the Sidledywry Knot — assuming Mrs. Agravin hadn't returned and he was still subbing for her.

"We haven't actually seen any evidence Mr. O.'s into comics, have we?" Nialla asked. "I mean, that we could refer to when talking to him."

"Casie's some kind of math nerd, right?" Marzana mused. "That's how she got recruited in the first place." She set a page of notes aside and picked up her shoelace. So far, there wasn't much she hadn't already known from Monday night's visit with Emmett, and of course the notes didn't include the results of the conversations she'd overheard the night before. She kept finding herself staring at that tiny image of the serpent-necked bird.

"Casie," Nialla repeated. "Oh, right. She's Nell Southsea after the first book. I keep forgetting she had a different name at the beginning. Yeah, a math angle could work. There's a thing in the fifth book where she uses this weird mathematical paradox — something about a Grand Hotel and pigeonholes and infinite guests. I can ask him about that."

"Perfect." Marzana tugged on a thief knot to fair it. They really were pretty things, knots. A momentary recollection of the dream of the needle-beaked snakebird picking one apart flitted through her mind, and she pushed it away.

"Before class, or after, you think?"

"I think before, if we can get there fast enough. That gives us a whole forty-five minutes to see how he acts, and then you can always go up after class and ask for more information if we think we need to twist the knife again." She tried to go back to reading and found herself staring at the bird again. "This Snakebird thing is driving me crazy."

She looked up at the wall clock. In ten minutes Mrs. Ileck would fling open the Parlor door and ring the bell. Plenty of time. Marzana started shoving her stuff back in her bag, tucking Ciro's printouts more carefully into her journal. "Running to the Library real quick," she said in response to Nialla's questioning glance. "Meet you outside when the bell rings." She darted out of the Parlor, turned left just past the larger of the school's two art classrooms, then took another left down a short, wide hallway lined on one side with study tables. On the opposite side was one of the two entrances to the Library.

Marymead had a lot of impressive rooms, thanks partly to the overall architectural design of the building, which shone even in the humblest social studies room, and partly to the Cotgraves' stipulations about what changes could and could not be made. The Library and its little sibling, the Study, had been left nearly untouched, and they were both pretty magnificent.

The doors Marzana had come through stood between two pairs of interior spiral staircases, their iron wrought in textures of bark and leaf, that rose to the Library's gallery level. It was old iron, but in this room, its shiftings were subtle: each spiral evoked a different type of tree and changed to reflect the seasons, with buds appearing in the spring and unfurling through the summer into leaves that faded away throughout autumn to reveal bare branches in the winter. The gallery ran all the way around the room, where the rows upon rows of bookshelves were interrupted at regular intervals by the heavy velvet curtains that tastefully hid the Cotgrave family's collection of questionable art. Two more old iron staircases led up to the gallery from the opposite side of the room. The primary Library entrance was on the wall to Marzana's right, and to her left, four big windows overlooked the courtyard.

All three terminals for the digital catalog were in use, so Marzana went straight for the massive antique card catalog. It was better, anyway. The digital search was mind-numbingly slow—thanks again, Deacon and Morvengarde—so Miss Caton, the head librarian, kept the cards painstakingly up-to-date, and incoming students quickly got proficient at using them. Marzana flipped through one of the *B* drawers until she found what she wanted, then hurried across the room, darting past the research tables to one of the staircases on the west wall, taking care not to let her feet pound too loudly on the iron risers.

The section she wanted bore an antique label that read *Birds and Birding* in addition to a later librarian's numerical classification. The books on the shelves here were a mix of Cotgrave inheritances and newer school acquisitions; figuring things in the birding world didn't change that much over time, Marzana reached for the prettiest option on the shelf, a volume with a tooled-leather cover that looked like it had been there a long while. The title, *Stanton's Aviary*, had been stamped on the cover in gilt, and when she blew the dust from the top, Marzana discovered that the edges of the pages on all sides had been decorated with images of birds' eggs.

As she descended to the lower floor, Marzana checked the clock over the main-entrance doors to see if she had time to borrow the book. Just then, against the trickle of students beginning to leave early for their next classes, Dr. Eddowes, the school historian, entered with Emilia at his side. They walked rapidly to a stretch of bookcases between the lower-level windows and beneath another Cotgrave-trustee portrait. Marzana grinned as she remembered Meddy's comment on the crankiness of the Cotgrave and Cormorant trustees down in the hall. This painting was no exception: the sitter was much younger than the others, a girl who appeared to be in her late teens, but she looked like she was trying very hard to seem older by affecting an expression of cold disdain.

The historian located a slender volume on the shelf below the cranky-girl trustee and passed it to Emilia. She opened it, and they exchanged a few brief words. Then Dr. Eddowes, always in a hurry, glanced at his watch and pointed emphatically at the spot from which he'd taken the book. Marzana couldn't make out the words he spoke, but the gesture conveyed *Put it back where you found it, Miss Cabot* with perfect clarity. Then he darted out of the Library, dodging kids with the ease of long practice.

Emilia decamped to the nearest table. She looked up as Marzana passed by on her way to the circulation desk. "Anything good?" Marzana asked.

"Cannot predict now." Emilia glanced at *Stanton's Aviary*. "Whatcha got there?"

"Birds," Marzana said. Emilia nodded and turned to her own

reading. There was no time to explain further. They had two minutes until the first bell; they could catch each other up later.

Marzana checked out the *Aviary* and returned to find Emilia rapidly copying a genealogical diagram from her book, which wasn't a book at all, but a big leather folder holding a single wide page that folded in the center. The family connections had been drawn as a literal tree, its shape reminding Marzana of the camphor tree in the courtyard behind the Orangery. Occasional tendrils reached all the way into the margins, where they sprouted into blossoms containing the family crests of the various stately old families that had married into the Cotgrave lineage.

Marzana sat beside her and opened the *Aviary*. It was definitely old, the paper thick and textured, so that the words seemed pressed in rather than printed onto it. Black-and-white woodcut illustrations decorated pages here and there, along with a smaller assortment in color that had been done on different paper altogether and pasted in along with a page of translucent vellum for protection.

The birds were arranged alphabetically, and in the latter half of the *S*'s, she found the entry for *snakebird*. Really she found the illustration first: a bird with a crane's snakelike neck and long, sharp beak, and the stubby legs and webbed feet of a duck. *Snakebird (colloquial): any bird of the genus* Anhinga, *so called for its serpentine neck. A predatory waterfowl able to alter its natural buoyancy when in water, sometimes showing only its head above the surface.* Abruptly, Marzana stopped reading as she remembered that she and Nialla needed to get to math as early as possible.

Emilia looked up from her drawing and raised a questioning eyebrow.

"Nialla and I have to be upstairs early," Marzana whispered. "I forgot."

Emilia nodded. Then she appeared to notice for the first time the entry Marzana had been reading. She frowned; then her eyes popped wide. As Marzana watched in confusion, Emilia reached out and dropped her index finger straight down on the word *snakebird*. Then she glanced back at the page she'd been copying. "That's why," she said softly. "*That's* why I knew it."

Marzana, stunned, stared from her book to the Cotgrave family tree in the folder. "What?" she whispered.

"I know why I knew the name Victor Cormorant." She tucked the family tree back into the folder and closed it. "No," she said pre-emptively as Marzana opened her mouth to demand more information. "You have a job right now. Go meet Nialla."

"Don't you have to put that back?" Marzana whispered under her breath as Emilia shoved the folder in her backpack.

"Yes, and I absolutely will, but thanks for the reminder." Emilia hurried back to the shelf where she'd found it and began shifting the books to hide the gap. Marzana turned back to the *Aviary* and quickly read the rest of the brief entry.

Snakebird (colloquial): any bird of the genus Anhinga, so called for its serpentine neck. A predatory waterfowl able to alter its natural buoyancy when in water, sometimes showing only its head above the surface. Generally silent. Subsists on fish, which it impales upon its sharp, piercing bill. Often seen with wings upraised and outstretched in a fan over its head, for which reason it is often confused with a related species, the cormorant.

The bell rang just as Emilia returned and scowled at the open book. "Mars, *why* are you still *here?*"

They found Nialla in the hallway outside; then all three sprinted up the steps. "Talk now," Marzana said as she ran.

Emilia gave her a disbelieving glance. "You're kidding, right? I can't talk and run stairs."

They parted ways on the next landing, where Emilia had to continue up to her social studies class. Marzana and Nialla raced to Mrs. Agravin's classroom and stopped outside the door to compose themselves.

"So?" Nialla huffed. "You find something?"

"Maybe," Marzana managed. "Never mind that now. Focus on your thing." Her heart began to pound harder, even as her breathing began to settle. They were about to confront the only actual suspect they had. "You ready for this?" she asked.

Nialla nodded seriously. "Born ready."

Inside, they found Mr. Otterwill erasing the previous class's notes from the projector.

"Hey, Mr. Otterwill," Nialla sang out. "You have a minute?" Marzana, whose job it was to observe and take notes, perched silently on a nearby desk as a couple of other early students began to drift in.

Mr. Otterwill blinked. "Sure. Remind me of your name?"

"Nialla." She reached into her backpack, pulled out Sidledywry #5, and slapped it onto the projector surface. Immediately the cover of the book splashed up on the whiteboard. "I've been reading this series, and I thought you might be able to explain something to me."

Marzana watched the substitute teacher look from the projection on the wall down to the book before him. He said nothing, just lowered his left hand to the cover. "I'm sure you don't know the story," Nialla said casually. "But it's basically —"

"I know it," Mr. Otterwill said flatly. He looked down at the book for a minute longer. "You want to know about the Paradox of the Grand Hotel, right?"

"Yes! That's so cool!" Nialla exclaimed, hamming it up. "How did you know? Have you read them?"

"Yes. I'm the adviser for a comics club at my regular school." There was definitely a tinge of something in his voice. Wariness? Sadness? It was hard to say. "I had a couple students who read this series."

"I really like it. I like how the main character builds herself a new knot. You know, after she loses everyone in the first book." Nialla hesitated, and Marzana thought she could guess the calculations her friend was doing. How close to sail to the truth in order to try to get him to give something away? Marzana could almost feel her own blood pressure going up, and she wasn't even having to work out what to say next.

But Nialla didn't have Marzana's hangups about speaking to people, and Marzana had forgotten that Nialla also didn't have to fake that particular connection to Peony. "It makes me think of myself a little," she admitted. "I lost a friend a couple years back. I mean, that sounds dramatic—he's not dead or anything, but we were best friends for a long time, and then we suddenly weren't close anymore. Do you have any idea what that's like?"

Mr. Otterwill stood so still, it was as if he'd been frozen in place. "I have an idea."

Nialla didn't reply right away. Marzana held her breath. *Say something else,* she begged him silently. *What are you thinking? Say something!*

But he didn't.

"Well, I didn't have to assemble a whole superteam," Nialla said when the pause threatened to get awkward, "but I did have to find a new best friend." She smiled at Marzana as three of their classmates wandered in, chattering and laughing. Class was about to begin. "Anyway. The Grand Hotel paradox. You were going to explain it."

Mr. Otterwill shook his head with the air of someone shaking himself awake. He glanced at his watch. "Not now. I'll explain it at the end of class, if there's time. Just in case there are other students reading Sidledywry." He turned away and walked over to his desk.

Nialla chirped, "Okey-doke," and headed back to her seat. Marzana lingered a minute. It was a fairly clear dismissal, but it was also more of a tell than any he'd given yet. Something about the way he leaned over the desk made her think it was sadness rather than wariness she'd seen — but she wouldn't have wanted to bet on it. Either way, as he reached for his coffee cup, Mr. Otterwill's hands were trembling.

He looked up and caught her watching. "Is there something else . . . I'm sorry, I don't recall your name, either."

"Marzana." An impulse struck, and she forced herself not to second-guess the idea or waste time stressing word choices. "It's so cool that you happen to be into comics, too. We could've gotten stuck with somebody who does nothing but hand out worksheets. How'd you wind up here, again? I mean, since you aren't from the Liberty. How'd you happen to get the job?"

"How — oh." His tight face relaxed a bit. "Just timing. I'm staying with my great-uncle. He has a connection to the school, and he happened to be in the office when the call came in that Mrs. Agravin wasn't well. He recommended me for the position."

Whatever Marzana had expected, this wasn't it. She forced herself to nod and say, "Cool," as if this answer was sufficient but uninteresting, then walk, not run, back to her seat to join Nialla as the rest of the class trickled in. Ignoring her friend's urgent glances, Marzana took out a pencil and piece of notebook paper, scrawled Victor Cormorant is his great-uncle on it, and took advantage of the arrival of the two kids who sat in front of them to pass the note across the aisle.

Nialla erupted into a fit of fake coughing, at the end of which she crumpled the paper into the smallest possible ball, popped it into her mouth, chewed, and swallowed.

Just as he'd said he would, Mr. Otterwill saved a few minutes at the end of class to explain the mathematical paradox Nialla had asked about, which had to do with how you fit an extra person into a hotel with an infinite number of rooms already occupied by an infinite number of guests. It was interesting, but it didn't seem to offer any additional insight into Mr. Otterwill himself, or to the case at large. But Marzana and Nialla didn't linger afterward to discuss the paradox or any of their other discoveries, because Marzana's next period was language arts with Emilia. With any luck, if they both got there early, there'd be time to find out what Emilia had remembered about Victor Cormorant. Marzana had an idea, though she couldn't figure out how it might be possible — not when it meant Emilia knew something so secret that Marzana's mother had refused to divulge it to Emmett.

Emilia hadn't read the entry in *Stanton's Aviary*. She hadn't had time, and even if Marzana was wrong and Emilia, in addition to everything else, was a speed-reader, it hadn't been the word *cormorant* she'd pointed to. It had been the title of the entry. Whatever she'd remembered, it was the word *snakebird* that had brought back the memory of how she knew the name *Victor Cormorant*.

The snakebird Emmett had asked her mother about had

obviously been a person—a person with an identity so secret that Marzana's mom had tried to claim to a customs officer whose job it was to know about all the secret, shady individuals in Nagspeake that, whoever he was, he didn't exist.

Clearly Emilia had heard the word before and when she'd seen it again, she'd connected it instantly to Victor, even without reading the final line of the *Aviary* entry: *Often confused with a related species, the cormorant.* Where had she heard of the Snakebird, and how on earth could she also have already known who he was? And, most important, how did the Snakebird connect to Peony's kidnapping?

From the way Emmett had asked her mother for an introduction and the conversation between her parents she'd overheard the night before, it seemed that the Snakebird was some kind of intelligence expert. Marzana's knowledge of Nagspeake's underworld was limited by her parents' reticence, but she knew that there were people who specialized in information. Hickson Blount apparently was one of these; the Snakebird, clearly, was a higher-level one. No, *highest*-level—her mother had said that if it was he who'd supplied the information used to blackmail the cop who'd released Rob Gandreider, then they had serious problems.

On the fourth floor, Marzana mumbled a reply to Nialla's goodbye and hurried to her classroom. Emilia was waiting outside. As Marzana approached, she waved her over to a nearby water fountain. "Buy you a drink?"

"Pretty please, talk now," Marzana begged.

Emilia gave a faint smile. "I thought I'd seen Victor Cormorant's name around here because of the Cotgrave-Cormorant connection. But I realized that's not where I heard it. I heard it in a totally different context. He's what's called a carrier—someone whose profession is information." She lowered her voice. "You know. Underground stuff."

Marzana dropped her own voice to the lowest whisper she could manage. "And he's called the Snakebird?"

Emilia nodded. "Your bird book jogged my memory. Where'd *you* hear that name? Part of the original conversation that started this whole thing? Why didn't you mention it before?"

"I think I just forgot it that first day. Then my parents brought it up again last night, plus there was a mention in the notes Ciro copied. I was going to mention it when we met at the bookstore. But how did *you* know it?" Marzana asked.

Emilia made an apologetic face and gestured around them. "There's no way I'm talking about that here. Maybe when we get to Surroyal. Let me think about it."

"All right," Marzana agreed reluctantly. Then she grinned. "How about the family tree, then?"

Emilia sighed. "No luck. The most recent family members shown on it are Catriona and Oliver Cotgrave—they're the ones who donated this house to the department of education—and their daughter Nadia and her husband, Ezra Cormorant. He's the only Cormorant on there." She wrinkled her nose in annoyance. "I asked Dr. Eddowes if there was something more up-to-date, with all the more recent Cotgraves and Cormorants on it, and he got very defensive. Said he'd been meaning to do it for a while but hadn't found the time, and beat an even hastier retreat than usual, which perhaps you noticed."

"I did. Well," Marzana said crisply, "I can shed a little light. Not sure how he's related to Ezra and the Cotgraves, but Victor Cormorant is Mr. Otterwill's great-uncle."

Emilia gave her a long, impassive look. "All right, I'll say it. I'm impressed. How'd you find that out?"

"I . . . I just asked," Marzana replied as the second bell rang and they headed for the classroom door. "I asked how he got the job."

"You just asked?" Emilia repeated, and Marzana suspected the other girl understood perfectly well how big a deal this was. "You did?"

"Well, yeah."

Emilia smiled. "Good work."

fifteen
THE THIEF KNOT

ARZANA, NIALLA, EMILIA, and Meddy arrived as planned in the spot by the lockers where they'd met up that morning, then snuck out again through the gym and into the garden shed.

Marzana took her little flashlight from her newly assembled toolkit. Nialla had brought one too. Meddy seemed to be able to see in the dark just fine, and the ghost girl was as delighted with the world under the courtyard as Marzana and Nialla had been. "Hold this," she said, passing Marzana the gold vial reliquary so that she could explore the space with more freedom. She disappeared into the tangle of plumbing under the Orangery by walking straight through the nearest knot of pipes as if it wasn't there to stand in her way.

"So what were you up to all day, Meddy?" Nialla asked her when she reappeared a few minutes later.

"Seeing what more I could find out about Mr. Otterwill," Meddy said as they climbed down one by one onto the little pier over the dry canal. "I tracked him down in the teacher's lounge this morning. I explored a little during his classes, and when he wasn't teaching, I followed him around. I only walked into doors twice," she added, pleased with herself. "After all these years, it's hard to adjust to the fact that I can't just skate through things when I'm carrying the reliquary."

Nialla chucked her on the shoulder. "Congratulations, I guess."

"Thank you. Anyway, while he was having lunch, he asked another teacher if she knew if the school had heard from Mrs. Agravin. Apparently nobody has, but they told him the whole story. Monday night, her sister—or, at least, someone claiming to be her sister—called to say Mrs. A. had come down with something, and because of her age, she'd been taken to the hospital just to be safe."

Was that female caller, Marzana wondered, the same person who'd called Captain Flynn of the SCPD and blackmailed him into releasing Rob Gandreider from his cell?

"That much he said he already knew; he said when he was hired, they told him he'd be there until at least Wednesday, but now he's just supposed to check in every morning, and had the other teacher heard whether there'd been any updates?" Meddy continued as they made their way along the canal toward the pier at 5 Westing Alley. "Apparently the sister had expected Mrs. Agravin to be released sometime late Tuesday; then she would take Wednesday to rest and probably would be back on Thursday, but definitely by Friday. The sister said she'd call Wednesday night with an update, but as far as anyone knew, no one had called. But then it starts to get weird. Miss Whoever-You-Mentioned-Earlier, Miss Pal-something—"

"Palkowick," Emilia supplied.

"Right. She wanted to send get-well flowers, but the sister hadn't said which hospital Mrs. Agravin had been admitted to. I gather there are only a couple hospitals in the Liberty, so she just called around to each one on Tuesday afternoon, but she couldn't find her. The sister had said Mrs. A. would be discharged Tuesday, though, so Miss Palkowick just sent flowers to her home and didn't think about it again until, I guess, yesterday afternoon, when the sister hadn't called with an update like she said she would. This morning they started trying to reach Mrs. A. by phone, and they haven't gotten hold of her yet. I think they're beginning to be just a bit worried." Meddy nodded ahead of them, to Emilia's back. "And so . . ."

"So Meddy found me at lunchtime," Emilia called as she hoisted herself up onto 5 Westing's pier. "And I got Mrs. Agravin's address."

"You managed to get her address from the office during school hours?" Nialla asked, impressed. "With Miss Palkowick at large?"

Emilia opened the door with its gold-flaked address, her face dramatic in a shaft of dusty light from somewhere beyond. "I have my ways."

During the climb up to the fifth floor of 5 Westing Alley, Marzana and Nialla told Meddy about the discoveries they'd made before math class. Then, with no little pride, they introduced Meddy to Boneash and Sodalime's Glass Museum and Radioactive Teashop. Today four places had been laid on the table, along with four little half-moon-shaped pastries whose thick, rolled-crust edges made perfect handles, ideal for when you wanted to eat a rhubarb pie and climb down a narrow spiral stair at the same time. "Meddy," Nialla said as she hoisted herself through the kitchen window, "do you think it could be a ghost who keeps this place and sets out the tea?"

Meddy looked a little sadly back at the single pastry they'd left on the table. "I don't think so. I think another ghost would have known I don't eat. Though I did used to love rhubarb."

A few minutes later, they dropped one by one to the stones of

Westing Alley and strolled out to Hellbent Street. At Surroyal Books, Lucky, occupied with a customer, barely looked up long enough to wave. Marzana exhaled a short breath of relief. Like Marzana and her parents, Lucky had been introduced to Meddy at Greenglass House, but if she noticed her at all today, she didn't make the connection between the girl in the green-and-blue cap and Milo's otherworldly buddy. Which was good. They could save that reintroduction for another time.

Marzana explained the bargain they'd made with Lucky for space on the mezzanine, and since neither of the boys had arrived yet, she, Nialla, and Emilia got to work moving armfuls of books, leaving Meddy to put them in order on the shelves upstairs, where no one would notice books disappearing and reappearing in different places as the ghost girl picked them up and put them down.

About ten minutes later, the bells over the door rang again. Marzana paused in the act of carrying an armful to the stairs and waved to J.J. and Ciro. "This way." She held out her books to Ciro, who repositioned a long tube he'd been carrying in order to accept the new burden. She pointed him at the doorway to the mezzanine. "Take these up for me. J.J., come help me get the rest of letter *E*."

"What are we doing, exactly?" J.J. asked as Marzana loaded him up.

"Earning our Batcave," she replied, sweeping the rest of the books off the shelf and herding him up the stairs.

On the mezzanine, she found introductions already under way. Ciro, looking dazed, shook hands with Meddy. He glanced over his shoulder as Marzana and J.J. deposited their books on the shelf. "Oh, wow. J.J.—this is Meddy."

J.J., straightening his stack of books into a neat horizontal row on one of the shelves marked POETRY, managed to miss the dramatic reveal. He looked up at her. "Hi, Meddy. Do you go to Marymead too?"

"Not exactly, no," Meddy said with a smile. "Are you the magician, by any chance?"

J.J. grinned. "Yeah, that's me."

"Cool. Can you do this one?" Meddy flickered once, then disappeared.

J.J. squealed in a highly undignified way and grabbed the nearest person, who happened to be Emilia. She patted his head. "There, there."

Marzana knocked her knuckles on the table. "Come to order, everybody." The setup was similar to down in the history room, with benches on the long sides of the table and chairs at the short ones. With only the slightest hesitation—This was getting easier!—she took the chair at the end facing the stairs and sat. One by one, the others followed her lead: Nialla and Emilia to Marzana's left and right, J.J. next to Emilia because he was still a little shell-shocked and she had to more or less steer him to his seat. Meddy sat next to Nialla, and Ciro took the chair at the opposite end.

And then they all looked at Marzana.

She swallowed. "As the first order of business, I'd like to welcome Meddy to the group. I met her over Christmas, when I went caroling to an inn called Greenglass House with the Waits." Marzana looked down the table at her. "Some of us are here because we grew up hearing about adventures our parents had, and we jumped at the chance to finally have one ourselves. But we have a rule that nobody has to talk about their parents if they don't want to, and some of us feel like we can't say anything specific. You don't have to either, Meddy—but I want you to know you're in good company."

Meddy tapped her fingers on the tabletop. Unlike when she had jumped from the lockers that morning, the soft sound her fingers made when they struck the surface was perfectly normal, as if she had ordinary, solid fingers to drum with. She looked around the table, silently assessing everyone there. Then, "My real name is Addie Whitcher," she said slowly. "My father was Doc Holystone."

Ciro whistled, long and low. Even Emilia deigned to look impressed, though she averted her eyes almost immediately. J.J., however, turned to Meddy with an expression of deep sorrow.

"I'm so sorry," he said. He made a twitchy sort of motion with his hand, as if he'd had the impulse to reach for hers but stifled it. And then Marzana remembered that Meddy had seen her father die, only moments before falling to her own death.

Meddy turned to J.J. in surprise. "Thank you."

"So you're . . . what, a ghost?" Ciro asked. "What's that like?"

"I'm not sure I have all the rules down myself." Meddy held out her hand to Marzana. "Reliquary? This is how I get to leave the house," she explained when Marzana held up the vial. "If Marzana has it, I can do a lot of cool ghosty stuff, but I can't go that far from her. If I hold it, I can go any distance, but my ghostly capabilities are pretty well squashed. I'm still making sense of it."

Marzana cleared her throat. "Okay. Secondly, Nialla and I decided the day we started assembling this group that once we hit five members, we'd need a name. Well, we're at six now. And I have a name. We are a *knot*."

"Like in the Sidledywry books," Nialla said, nodding in approval. "A knot, like a crew."

"Yes." Marzana took the shoelace from her pocket and smoothed it out on the table. "But we're not just any knot." With five pairs of eyes on her, she tied a reef knot in the lace and held it up.

"Reef knot," Meddy said instantly. Marzana felt a momentary, entirely unexpected pang of jealousy. Apparently not everyone with dubiously employed parents had their underground educations totally neglected.

"Yes." Marzana untied it, then performed the fiddly-looping tie of a grief knot, taking care not to pull it so tight that it came undone, and held it up. "And this is a grief knot." She glanced at Meddy. "You want to explain?"

The ghost girl shook her head. "Your show."

"Well, a grief knot looks like a reef knot, more or less. It's a kind of trap, like leaving a strand of hair on a drawer pull to see if anyone opens it while you're not looking."

"Very cool," Ciro said. "One knot masquerading as a different one. I like that."

Marzana smiled. "I thought you might. A grief knot isn't good for much but traps. It's fiddly and weird and it has a funny twist." She tugged to unravel it, then tied the slightly stabler thief knot. "This one's also a trap, just a bit more sturdy." She tossed the thief-knotted shoelace on the table. "That's us: fiddly and weird, and who knows if we're good for anything, but we're going to try." She looked from face to face. "We're the Thief Knot."

"The Thief Knot," Nialla repeated thoughtfully. "I can get behind that."

Meddy nodded, and so did Ciro. "You know I'm down with it," he said.

"Me too," J.J. agreed.

"Works," Emilia said. "What's next?"

"Well, let's go around the table." Marzana looked at J.J. and Ciro. "We have kind of a lot of new information from Marymead, plus the stuff from Ciro's pictures. We're going to need to go through those a bit more closely than I managed to today, because all this other info came up. Shall I start?"

"Might as well," J.J. grumbled, "seeing as how I didn't have a job yesterday."

"I have some new stuff too," Ciro said. "It can wait, though."

"Okay." Marzana opened her journal and took out the prints of Ciro's photographs. "Well, you remember we have a teacher at Marymead who taught at Watermill, Peony's school, and who we think was supposed to work at the camp that threw the party Peony went to before she was taken?" She nodded to Emilia. "Emilia cracked into his file at Marymead."

Together, J.J. and Ciro broke into slow but very impressed applause.

"There wasn't much there," Emilia told them, as if this made the actual feat any less extraordinary. "But there were a couple interesting things. Mr. Otterwill ran the comics club at Peony's school, for one thing, and we're pretty sure he knew her, and he knew what she was reading."

"How'd you figure that out?" J.J. asked.

"Nialla basically waved the book under his nose and got a reaction," Marzana said.

Nialla smiled modestly. "Hold your applause. But I think—Mars, you were watching, am I right about this?—that he looked more sad than anything else."

"Sad about what?" Ciro asked. "Do we think he's involved, or do we think he just knows she was kidnapped? Like you said before, if he worked at the school and was part of the camp faculty, the police would have interviewed him."

"I'm not sure, but at this point we absolutely have to treat him as a real suspect," Marzana said, "because of the other thing we found out. It has to do with a relative of his, the person who recommended him on short notice to sub for Mrs. Agravin. A guy named Victor Cormorant."

Ciro's head came up sharply. "Cormorant. I've—" He looked around the table. "Why is that name familiar?"

J.J. shook his head. "It doesn't mean anything to me."

Nialla, however, said frustratedly, "I don't know, but I thought I recognized it too."

"Okay, this is weird," Emilia exploded. "I also knew the name, and until I figured out *how* I knew it, I thought Nialla and I must just have noticed it at school. There were a couple Cormorants—Ezra and Nadia—who were trustees and have big portraits up on the wall. But that's actually *not* how I know *Victor* Cormorant, and you guys almost certainly can't have the knowledge about him that I do. So where have *you* seen his name?"

"And why would it be familiar to Nialla and Ciro, but not to J.J. and me?" Suddenly, a possibility occurred to Marzana. She reached for the printouts of Ciro's photos. "You two are the only ones who've read these thoroughly. His name's got to be here."

Ciro snapped his fingers. "I think you're right." He took the pile from Marzana and shuffled to a picture of a page she recognized as her parents' notes rather than Emmett's. "Here."

"That's it," Nialla said, and she and Ciro each poked an index finger at one line in a list of people to contact, written in Marzana's mother's handwriting. Marzana wasn't surprised she'd missed it— during study hall, she'd been fixated on a different page altogether, the one with the snakebird drawing.

The first entry on the list read *Rob/Rose/Hickson:* Emmett's three suspects; no surprises there. The next two names were known quantities: a friend of her mother's who worked for the warder of the Liberty and one who worked for a local newspaper, both of whom Marzana figured Mrs. Hakelbarend wanted to talk to merely in the interest of leaving no stone unturned. The second-to-last read simply *Tasha*. But the final one was *Victor Cormorant*.

"So that's one mystery solved," Ciro said, looking up at Emilia. "Who is he, then?"

Marzana took *Stanton's Aviary* from her bag and passed it to Emilia, who thumbed through to the *snakebird* entry and placed it in the middle of the table. "Underworld types who specialize in information are called carriers. They deal in knowledge, passing information about anything and everything, including information about likely jobs that might be attractive to *other* underworld types. There's a very powerful knowledge-broker in Gammerbund called the Snakebird." Emilia tapped the bird. "His real name is Victor Cormorant."

"I'm guessing his identity isn't common knowledge," J.J. said, glancing at Marzana curiously.

"Nope," Marzana and Emilia said at the same time. Marzana found the page with her father's sketch on it and slid it up next to the *Aviary*. "But my parents know. And Emmett, the guy who came to my parents about the kidnapping, asked to be introduced to him. It seemed like Emmett just wanted to find out if the Snakebird had any information that might shed light on the case, but my parents seem to think it's possible he's involved. And, like I said, Victor Cormorant got Mr. Otterwill the substitute-teaching gig. Cormorant's his great-uncle. Mr. Otterwill is literally staying with him while he's in the Liberty."

"Your folks don't know about that connection, though, do they?" Ciro asked. "So why do they think Cormorant might be part of all this?"

"It has to do with *him*." Marzana tapped Rob's name on the first line of the list. "These three are suspects. They're the ones Emmett originally asked my parents to look into. Rob's a pretty small-time crook, but he's the kind of guy who has connections to what my dad would call bigger bugs. He gets caught up in stuff. He was locked up in the city proper, and a couple days ago someone blackmailed a cop to let him go. Mom thinks the knowledge behind the blackmail had to come from somebody big. Maybe the Snakebird."

"Let's go back to the three suspects." Emilia took out her own spiral pad and pen. "What else do you know about them?"

Marzana considered. "Apparently Hickson Blount is also a carrier, although my mom said she doubted he was good enough to have been the source of the blackmailer's information. And I heard a colleague of my parents say that this wasn't Rose's kind of thing because she was a candymaker, though I don't see what that has to do with anything. Presumably they all pretend to have straight jobs, right?"

"I remember your mom said something about that Rob guy that I didn't understand," Ciro put in. "About how every job needs a good fiddler or something, only I don't think it was fiddler."

"It wasn't, but it was something like it. Fiddling Ben?" Marzana hazarded. She looked to Emilia, figuring if she knew about famous carriers, she might know this term too.

Emilia, however, shook her head. "I've got nothing."

It was Meddy who spoke up. "Not a fiddling Ben. A *fidlam ben*. That's a generalist, like our buddy Rob. Your basic, all-purpose ne'er-do-well. And Rose must be a *confectioner*, which is a counterfeiter. I can see why your folks didn't think a counterfeiter would fit into this scheme. But a master carrier like the Snakebird would."

Emilia nodded. "The kidnappers pulled a lot of strings—probably more than we're aware of yet, and it would've taken a carrier to know which strings to go for and how hard they'd need to be hauled on to get a result."

"Okay, then. The Snakebird's officially a suspect too." Marzana looked around the table. "Who's next?"

"Me," Meddy said, rapping on the tabletop. She repeated what she'd learned about Mrs. Agravin. "It might be worth making a trip to her house to check on her."

"I want to go," Nialla said. "I love Mrs. A."

J.J. raised a hand. "Well, I've got nothing to report because I didn't have a job, as you remember, so I call dibs on being part of the mission to Mrs. What's-Her-Name's house. Where is it, by the way?"

Marzana turned to Emilia, who flipped back a page in her pad and consulted the jottings. "Whipping Hyde."

"I'll go too. But can we pause a minute?" Ciro got to his feet. "I need a map for when we get to what I have to report. I'm sure this bookstore's got some for sale. Be right back."

He hurried down the stairs. Meanwhile Emilia tore out a page from her pad, wrote down Mrs. Agravin's information, and passed it to J.J. A moment later, Ciro came back, clutching not a folded map but a book under one arm.

"Bought a gazetteer," he said, putting it on the table between them and opening it to the index. "More detail." He trailed a finger down the list of neighborhoods, streets, and landmarks until it stopped on *Whipping Hyde,* then turned to a two-page spread of the entire Liberty. They all leaned over the atlas as he located and pointed to an irregular splotch of pale orange that was Miss Agravin's neighborhood.

"It's not too far from the Viaduct," Marzana observed. "J.J., can I come with you guys?"

"You're in charge here. Should we go tonight?"

"Yeah. The ransom has to be delivered by Sunday, so tonight and tomorrow are all we've got." Marzana turned to Ciro. "But first, what do you have to report?"

Ciro reached under the table and produced the tube he'd brought with him, along with a battered old manila envelope from his backpack. "I mostly spent last night printing things off my phone. But I also did some excavation in the attic. This is everything I could find of my grandfather's stuff from back when he worked on the Belowground."

He removed the cap at one end of the tube, reached inside, and withdrew a handful of rolled paper, some of it thin enough to be almost transparent, some a vivid, saturated cobalt. Ciro unspooled the outer page and stretched it open on the table. Marzana turned in her chair, grabbed four small books from the poetry shelves, and passed them down the table for Ciro to use for weights. He muttered, "Thanks," as he positioned them around the blueprint.

In one corner of the flattened page, the name *Padraig del Olmo* and the words *Oldeye Overlook* had been printed in old-fashioned lettering similar to the "fancy copperplate" Honora used to label things around the kitchen. The drawing was of a pavilion seen from the front: something like a band gazebo, only fashioned from saplings whose branches knitted themselves together overhead to form the roof.

"There are a whole bunch of these," Ciro said, unrolling a

second blueprint over the first: a more ordinary-looking brick façade that Marzana thought looked somehow familiar. Here the line under Granddad del Olmo's name read *Sanctuary Cliff.* "I assume most of them are for stations down in the city proper, but they're only labeled with names and numbers, not actual locations. Without a map of the system, it's impossible to say where they are, and there was no complete map with Granddad's stuff. But again, there were two Liberty stations, so theoretically two of these could be local."

Meddy spoke up. "I can tell you where that one is," she said, pointing at the drawing of the brick building on top. "It's in the woods behind Greenglass House."

"That's why it looks familiar," Marzana said. "I passed it with the Waits on our way to the inn at Christmas."

Meddy grinned at her. "Milo would love this. I wish he could be here, too. Southwest side of Whilforber Hill," she added for Ciro's benefit. "A little more than halfway down to the river."

"Good to know." Ciro dug his own notebook from his backpack, opened it to a page already labeled STATIONS, ran his finger down the list he'd written below the heading, and wrote Greenglass House on the line next to Sanctuary Cliff.

Marzana leaned across Nialla for a look at his list. "Those are all the stations?"

"Not necessarily," Ciro said. "Just the ones that I found drawings for. And I don't know for sure that all of these even wound up being the final plans. Some of them might just have been proposals. Like, there are two completely different blueprints labeled *Whitesmith's Row.* Wherever that is, presumably the city wouldn't have built two separate stations there."

"I'll bet Whitesmith's Row is in the Quayside Harbors. There used to be a big metalworkers' quarter there." Meddy pointed to a line where Ciro had written Coup de Grâce/Hacker's Bluff. "And this is definitely in Shantytown."

"Can I see?" Marzana reached for the notebook and scanned the list. Sanctuary Cliff, Misericorde, Whitesmith's Row ... There. Not Ottomy *Street*, but Ottomy *Stalls*. "This one's in the Liberty," she said, pointing. "Milo said he'd seen this name on the map in the station at Greenglass House."

"Ottomy Stalls . . ." Ciro leafed awkwardly through the remaining rolled blueprints, then pulled one free and slipped its corners underneath the books. "Here. This is a huge long shot, but does anybody recognize it?"

They all leaned over the drawing. It looked like a storefront —just like any old alleyway storefront, complete with a striped awning and a big glass-front window with the words *Ottomy Stalls* on it in arcing gold letters. "It looks like it would fit right in on a market street," Nialla said. "That's all I can figure."

"All right, so we think we've sort of identified four," Ciro said, taking his notebook back from Marzana. "Maybe we can eliminate a few more stations from the running. Speak up if anything sounds familiar: Yellow Inlet. Coldside Farm. Salton Square." He glanced around the table: nothing. "Hornblende Park? Saint Horace Rye?"

Emilia shifted in her seat. She said nothing, and her face betrayed nothing, but everyone looked at her nonetheless.

"What?" Marzana asked. "Saint Horace Rye, or Hornblende Park?"

For a moment, Emilia said nothing. Then she sighed the tiniest, quietest sigh. And then, without any other warning, she crumpled. Her face dropped into her arms, and Marzana had a brief glimpse of tears streaming down her cheeks.

They all sat there, stunned, looking at the quietly sobbing girl and then around at one another. J.J., on Emilia's left, caught Marzana's eye over Emilia's hunched shoulders. "Hey," he said, sounding helpless. "Hey, it's okay. Whatever it is." He patted her back, an awkward, wooden *thump-thump* with his palm. Still, it was something, and it managed somehow to break the horrified spell that had fallen over everyone else.

Nialla jumped up and rushed around the table. She scooted onto the bench on Emilia's right and put both arms around her. Emilia leaned into the hug and continued her almost soundless crying with her face buried in Nialla's shoulder.

Marzana fidgeted, completely at a loss about what to do. If it had been her, she'd have wanted privacy for a cry like this.

Across the table, Ciro pressed a palm to his eyes for a moment. When he took his hands away, his expression was full of regret. "Hornblende Park is a cemetery," he said softly.

Meddy spoke up. "Your last name's Cabot, isn't it? Your dad is Alexander Cabot." Then she glanced at the line where the cemetery's name was written in Ciro's notebook and corrected herself awkwardly. "Or . . . was?"

"Yes." Emilia lifted her head off Nialla's shoulder with a ragged breath. "To both."

"How do—did—you know her father?" Marzana whispered to Meddy, who stared back at Marzana as if she'd admitted to having twelve toes.

"*You* don't know who Alexander Cabot was?" she demanded in an undertone.

"No," Marzana said defensively. "Why should I?"

Emilia had been the first person to say she couldn't talk about her parents and what they did. The name Alexander Cabot meant nothing to Marzana, but Meddy clearly knew who he had been. Suddenly Marzana wondered if she'd misinterpreted Emilia's reaction to being invited to join the knot. Perhaps that "Why me?" had not meant what she'd thought.

"*Why?*" Meddy repeated, incredulous. "Only because he saved your mom's life once."

sixteen
SECRETS AND FINDINGS

ARZANA STARED BACK. "Excuse me?"

"Alexander Cabot saved your mother's life once," Meddy repeated. "If the story is true."

Emilia sniffled. "It's true."

"Hang on." Marzana turned to stare at Emilia. "How do *you* know who my mom is?"

"For someone who can crack into the school files, it would've been easy enough to find out," Ciro observed quietly.

Marzana shook her head. "My mom's name wouldn't be in my file. Not her real name, anyway."

"I didn't snoop in your school file," Emilia protested. "I've always known who your mom is." She took a shuddering breath. "Dad told me."

This was intolerable. Marzana pounded her fists on the table, got up, and stalked to the far end of the bookshelf behind the table with her arms wrapped tightly around herself. She'd hoarded the stories she knew—the ones she got from Honora when the steward was feeling mutinous and the very occasional ones she got from her parents themselves, each of which had felt like a victory because it was like pulling teeth trying to get her mom and dad to tell her anything—but here were Emilia and Meddy, whose fathers apparently had just . . . just *told them things*. Just *told* them, the same way Marzana's parents told her the weather when she came downstairs in the morning for school.

"I know what you're thinking," Meddy said, coming to stand at her side. "Don't do it."

"What do you mean?" Marzana snapped.

Nialla spoke up, her voice urgent, worried, soothing, as she rose from the table. "Mars—"

"I mean our parents are dead," Meddy snapped back. "I can only speak for myself, but I'd trade any story—no, *every* story I know about my father to have him back."

"Me too," Emilia put in from the table.

Marzana whirled. "No. Don't do that. Don't play that card with me. You know why?" She felt a tickle on her cheek, swiped at it, and wiped the tiny bit of damp off on her jeans. "Yes, my parents are alive. But if the unthinkable were ever to happen—and who says something won't go horribly wrong someday? It could—and if something ever happened to them, I'd be left without knowing. I'd be left without the stories, without the memories, without the knowledge and the skills and the *names,* Emilia! If not for all these names—Victor Cormorant, Ottomy Stalls, just random names I've never heard before, names I'd probably never have come across if not for this kidnapping—I'd never have known there was this connection between you and me. And *you've* known this whole time and you didn't tell." Nialla's arm slid around her shoulder, trying once more to soothe, and Marzana shrugged it impatiently off. She wiped her cheeks again. "I know who my parents are — who they were before they came here — but I barely know what that means. I know what everyone else thinks it means — what Violet Cross meant to the city —"

There was a sudden sharp intake of breath from the boys at the revelation of Marzana's mom's real name. She ignored it and plunged on. "I know what *she* means to people who tell the stories that still go around Nagspeake, whether they're accurate or not," Marzana said through clenched teeth. "But I don't know what it all means to *me*. Not from my mom and dad themselves."

Nialla fidgeted at her side, clearly desperate to put her arms around Marzana and pull her away from this argument. Marzana ignored her. She looked fiercely from Emilia to Meddy, daring either to argue.

Emilia held her gaze. "You should take that up with them. Seeing as how, you know. You *can.*" She sucked in a deep breath, wiped her face clean of both tears and visible emotion, and took the gazetteer from Ciro. And as Marzana watched Emilia flipping through the maps, she felt an uprushing swell of anger, disappointment, and humiliation.

This. This right here. *This* was the kind of thing that kept her up at night. This was how it felt when all her fears about talking to people suddenly became reality. She'd screwed up. And worst of all, now there was no way she could ask Emilia to tell her the story. She'd found a window in the deniability screen — an amazing, unexpected window — and she'd slammed it shut.

Emilia, meanwhile, seemed bent on demonstrating that the conversation was quite seriously and definitely over. She dropped the gazetteer open to the two-page spread of the whole Liberty of

Gammerbund and planted a finger on the left-hand side. "Hornblende Park is here. Ciro, where's the blueprint?"

Ciro moved the atlas aside and extracted the Hornblende Park drawing from the pile. "Should've maybe guessed," he said, laying it on top. Now that they knew this station was either in or near a cemetery, it was clear its entrance had been designed to look like a mausoleum.

Emilia took another shuddering breath. "I know where that is. I've passed it, visiting Dad's grave." She sat back. "So that's one. What's the other one called? Ottomy something?"

"Ottomy Stalls." Ciro cleared his throat. "I didn't see any listing for a place called that in the index. But I'm with Nialla. 'Stalls' makes me think of a market."

"Thanks," Nialla said miserably.

Marzana came back to the table, still smarting, still with her arms tightly folded. She picked up the gazetteer, taking care not to link eyes with any of the other girls. The spot where Emilia had identified Hornblende Park was in the northern part of the Liberty, not far from the wall. "Presumably you wouldn't put two train stations in the same part of town," she said as she examined the facing page.

"That implies some organization and logic," J.J. said. "If there was logic to this, they wouldn't have built one of the stations in a graveyard."

Ciro shook his head. "There is a logic to that. They had to avoid the iron."

Everyone turned to look at him. "The iron?" J.J. repeated. "You mean the old iron?"

Marzana's face was still hot with shame, but she made herself speak up. "Milo said something about that. The Belowground conductor he knows doesn't have access to certain stations because of the iron, and the call button at Sanctuary Cliff doesn't always work because of it. 'The iron interferes'—that's what he said."

"Yeah. That's why you have stations in places like this. Cemeteries almost never have old iron in them." Ciro picked up the manila envelope, which had been lying there forgotten ever since he'd taken the blueprints from the tube, and pulled out a stack of typewritten letters. "This is correspondence about the Belowground, mostly about deadlines and fiddly changes to plans and red tape they were dealing with. But there's also some discussion where they rule out certain sites because there's too much iron underground. And there's one where they're debating moving a whole line because there's new interference. Like what your friend was talking about."

"Interference?" Nialla repeated. "From old iron? We're talking about the same thing, right? I know old iron moves a little in its way, but I didn't think it actually *interfered* with anything."

"It tinkers with stuff," Ciro confirmed. "It messes with my mom's cell towers all the time."

"It definitely moves more than you think it does," Marzana said, shifting a bit in her seat as everyone's eyes came back to her again. "Especially underground. There are whole structures down there, and they shift. Mom—" She hesitated. "She learned it the hard way." This was one of the few stories Marzana did know; the behavior of one of those underground old iron structures was the reason her mother had undertaken the caper at Greenglass House just before Christmas, bringing Marzana's dad, Nick Larven, and Marzana herself along for the ride. She glanced sharply at Emilia, remembering an earlier conversation while momentarily forgetting that Emilia probably hated her right now. "And you said—"

"The dumbwaiters. Yeah." Emilia nodded. "I can totally believe the iron would really cause problems if you were trying to build anything as elaborate as a subway system, especially since nobody knows what makes it move." She gave Marzana a brief, grudging smile.

Marzana returned the smile with a heavy dose of silent apology and slid back into her seat. "*Ottomy* is an old word for a skeleton," she said. "I looked it up after Milo first mentioned it. Maybe it's another cemetery, in a different part of town." Belatedly it occurred to her that referring to skeletons was maybe not the right thing to do when you'd just been discussing a friend's dead father. She darted a quick look at Emilia, but the poker face was firmly back in place, so Marzana slid the Ottomy Stalls drawing out from under Hornblende Park and soldiered on. "Except nothing about this looks like it would fit in a cemetery."

"Hey." Nialla tilted her head. Marzana followed her gaze to the corner of one of the blueprints sticking out farther down in the pile. Nialla tugged at it gently, then yelped. "Hey. *Hey.*" She pointed at the box in the corner: *Cotgrave Wall.*

"Whoa!" Emilia reached across to help Nialla lay the blueprint on top of the mess of drawings and letters.

Marzana leaned in for a closer look. It looked nothing like a train station. Two spiral staircases rose up from the ground floor to a gallery above, where two great doorways gaped like huge rectangular eyes. The space below the balcony, between the staircases, appeared to be filled with, of all things, *books.* "That looks really familiar."

Emilia leaned in next to her and gave a single, short chuckle. "It ought to look familiar. Instead of doors on that upper level, imagine giant paintings of weird nudes. Or rather, imagine curtains covering said paintings of weird nudes."

And then Marzana realized what she was looking at. "No *way.*"

"Somebody fill me in," Meddy said, "because I have no idea what's happening right now."

"It's the Library at Marymead," Nialla told them. "Except now, there are paintings where these doors are. The school keeps them behind curtains because they're . . . ah . . ."

"They're giant paintings of weird nudes," Emilia repeated. "There's no other way to put it. Giant. Weird. Nudes. The family that originally owned the house—the *Cotgrave* family—negotiated as terms of the sale that all of the home's paintings would never be removed, not even for cleaning."

"Those paintings must be hiding the old entrance and exit to a private Belowground station." Nialla looked at Emilia. "You didn't know about this?"

Emilia shook her head. "Nope. I'm trying to figure out how it's even possible. There's no room for a—" She stared at the drawing. "This is going to break my head, but who cares? My stock is going to go through the roof with the other Commorancy Kids if there's really a hidden station in Marymead."

"Your school is so weird," Meddy muttered again.

"So there are three Liberty stations, not two?" J.J. said.

Ciro scratched his head, looking confused. "It seems that way. Unless one of these was proposed but never built. That's assuming Marzana's friend Milo is right and we take Ottomy Stalls as a given." He paused, then suddenly began to laugh. "Good grief, I just had an Emilia moment."

"What the heck is an Emilia moment?" Emilia demanded.

"I thought Victor Cormorant's name was familiar because of the pictures I took, but it wasn't only that. Look." Every other blueprint had the architect's name in the same box as the name of the station.

This one, however, was different. Ciro pointed to a second box in the opposite corner from the one that contained the name *Cotgrave Wall.* This second box did not have *Padraig del Olmo* in it. Instead, the members of the Thief Knot stared in disbelief at the name *Ezra Cormorant.*

"Wow," Marzana said softly. "These flipping Cormorants really get around, don't they?" She leaned back and folded her arms. "Okay. So we have a route into the Liberty that opens up in Marymead, along with a missing Marymead teacher and a substitute from the kidnapped girl's school who was recommended for the position by his great-uncle, a legendary information broker who is also the — what? — son or grandson or some descendent of the architect of the station in the school, who also happened to be married to the daughter of the last Cotgraves to own the house."

"That," Meddy said meditiatively, "is a lot of stuff pointing back at your weirdo school."

"I suspect," Marzana said, thinking hard, "it's the other way around. All the school connections are arrows pointing back at Cormorant." She looked at Ciro. "What else?"

He shrugged. "That's it from me."

"If Ciro's done, I have something." Nialla opened her bag and took out a mostly destroyed copy of Sidledywry #5 and a folder, from which she pulled Ciro's photo of the letter with the kidnappers' demand. "This, of course, is the ransom note. And we know the police think the kidnappers made Peony cut out the words and glue them down herself. Well . . . maybe because before this craziness started I was five chapters into *Quester's Crossroads* — that's this other series," she explained, turning to Meddy. "You find your way through the story by solving puzzles and little mysteries along the way. Sometimes you have to actually cut up the books to figure it all out. So I got to thinking."

Nialla opened the comic and fanned through the pages. Here and there, words had been snipped out. She opened the folder again, this time pulling out an envelope.

"I went through and replicated what Peony did." Nialla shook a little flurry of colorful paper snips from the envelope onto the table-top. "These are the words she cut out to make the text of the note, and I'm ninety-nine percent sure I was able to identify the exact spots in the book she took the individual words from."

"How?" Ciro asked, pulling the ransom-note copy across the table for a better look. "Some of these words, sure — 'daughter,' 'price,' 'Saturday' — those probably only occur once within the comic." He frowned briefly, as if something had occurred to him, then shook his head. "But others — 'you,' 'your,' 'is,' 'for,' 'to' — I bet there were lots of those. And what about the words she had to spell out herself? And all the zeroes — those are individual *O*'s, right? How could you be sure you got the right letters?"

"Because," Nialla said triumphantly, "the guy who does the lettering for the series does it by hand. No two words are exactly the same. No two *letters* are even exactly the same."

"Nerd," J.J. said mildly.

"Correct." Nialla stuck out her tongue at him. "Fortunately. Because as a result of my nerd-tasticness, I'm pretty sure I know exactly where Peony got every word and letter she used. And that brings me to the first weird thing about this note and how Peony made it. She spelled some of the words out letter by letter when she didn't really have to. 'Daughter' actually *is* in the book, but she spelled it out anyway. Same thing with 'have,' 'back,' and even 'instructions.' There are instances she could've used, but she spelled them out instead. Plus a lot of the time, with more common words, she didn't take them the first or even the second time the words appeared. She took some from deep in the book when she could've found them earlier. Why? Imagine this girl, alone, scared, and the sooner she finishes this note, the sooner it goes to her parents and the sooner they do what it says and she goes home. Why was she so haphazard about it?"

"But she was in the middle of the book, right?" Emilia asked. "Maybe she remembered later instances because she'd read them more recently. Or for common words, maybe she just opened the book at random, knowing they'd probably be there somewhere."

Nialla inclined her head. "That's possible, I agree. And it would be the simpler explanation, except for the second weird thing." She began turning the colorful paper shapes over and around so the words from the ransom note showed in the right order, which took her a minute, because most of the slips seemed to have words on both sides. Then she set the photograph of the actual note alongside the clippings. "I tried to replicate exactly what Peony did. Look how sloppy her cutting was. These pieces are totally irregular."

It was true. Some words and letters she had extracted neatly; others she'd snipped out wildly. Some she'd cut out too closely, so that tiny bits here and there had been nicked off letters that stuck up tall or hung low. With other words she'd done the exact opposite, so that once or twice you could see the evidence of the first letter of the next word in the comic, or the words above and below. The word "price" had been removed in a circle.

"You sure she wasn't just cutting the way a little kid cuts?" J.J. asked. "Maybe they gave her safety scissors to work with so she couldn't stab her way out or something. You can't be real precise with those."

"She's eleven, not five," Nialla objected. "I mean, yes, it's a possibility; it's also a possibility she was sloppy because she was scared. In any case, I did what she did. Check this out." She opened the book to the first page with a cutout and held it up for everyone to see. "Here's the void left by the word 'send.'" She pulled the matching word from the pile she'd poured from the envelope. "*This* 'send.' Note that Peony left a lot of extra space around the word." She tapped the circle of page visible through the hole in the book. "And here's what's revealed on the next page, under the hole she left taking that Sunday out: 'avenue.' Trimmed a bit at either end, but almost perfectly framed by her weird cutting job."

Marzana stared. "You think she did it that way to leave a message?"

Nialla grinned. "That's exactly what I think."

Ciro whistled again, but he looked uncertain.

Emilia frowned, definitely unconvinced, then made a *Well, maybe* face.

But J.J. shook his head decisively. "No way. No *way*. That would've taken so much effort. So much time. Wouldn't the kidnappers have noticed what she was doing?"

"Maybe, maybe not. What if they aren't people who deal with kids much? Maybe they just assumed that it would take a kid a long time to find and cut out all these words."

"Why did they do that?" Emilia asked quietly. "Force Peony to make her own ransom note? That would give me nightmares for the rest of my life. And isn't the ransom note the kind of thing you'd have prepared ahead of time?"

Ciro spoke up. "They're hiding behind Peony. If they'd picked something else—anything else—to cut the text from, it would've been a clue about them. Instead, all we learn is stuff about Peony:

stuff her parents already knew. Her fingerprints. Her paper. Her book." His brow creased again in that same brief, dissatisfied frown for just a moment.

"Plus," Marzana added, thinking of every substitute teacher she'd ever had, "it's busywork. They have this kid on their hands. Keeping her occupied means less annoyance for them. But you were thinking something else just now," she said to Ciro, "and before, when you were talking about the common words and the uncommon ones."

Ciro nodded. "Yeah, something's bothering me, but I'm not sure what it is. Something about the words . . . something about this note giving us clues about Peony instead of about the kidnappers . . ." He shook his head. "I don't have it yet. Sorry."

"Wait, back up," J.J. interrupted. "Nialla. I'm not saying I buy this, but *was* there actually another message when you put together the words beneath the cutouts?"

Nialla's grin faded. "I haven't worked it out yet. But I think so." She turned to Ciro. "You said hidden things are your forte. If I skip the trip to Mrs. Agravin's place, could you stick around and take a look at what I've got, help me find the message?"

"You bet."

"All right, then. You guys work on secret messages, we'll go check on Mrs. Agravin, and . . ." Marzana glanced at Emilia, then Meddy. "How about you guys?"

"I'll come with you and the magician," Meddy said.

"Emilia?"

The blond girl shook her head. "I really want a look at the paintings in the Library, now that I know there might be something behind them. You have no idea how much effort it's taken to keep sitting here. I can't see how it's possible there's room for anything in those walls, even a staircase — but if there's a station under Marymead, it's a way the kidnappers could've brought Peony into the Liberty. And if Victor Cormorant's involved, there's no way he doesn't know about that station—not when it was designed by a relative to go in a house that used to belong to his family." She straightened suddenly in her seat and looked around at them. "Maybe Mrs. Agravin saw something, maybe even saw them bring Peony in, and they had to get her out of the way."

"Get her out of the way?" Nialla repeated, stricken. "You don't mean—"

"I don't mean *that*," Emilia said quickly. "Just . . . what if she saw something?"

"All right, then. I feel like we should move more books for Lucky, but time's short." Marzana looked at her watch. "Let's do, like, ten minutes of shelving, then split up. I'll try to check in with everyone later tonight, but whatever happens, let's rendezvous here again tomorrow morning," Marzana said. "Plan to be here when the bookstore opens at ten. It's the last day we've got before the ransom is due."

They packed up their various notebooks, envelopes, maps, and document tubes, then spent a very focused ten minutes moving books bucket-brigade style. By the time Marzana, J.J., Emilia, and Meddy headed down the stairs armed with Ciro's gazetteer full of maps, the entirety of the poetry section was in place on the mezzanine shelves.

Marzana was the last to go, and she'd just about reached the bottom when she heard Ciro call her name.

"'Hooray for Captain Spaulding,'" Marzana said as he trotted down and met her on the last step, and then immediately felt awkward about it.

But Ciro grinned, and it looked genuine enough. He reached

into his back pocket and held out his cell phone. "Take this, just in case. If I'd known you were going off on a mission, I'd have swiped one of Mom's spares."

She looked down at the phone. "Who on earth am I going to call?"

He shrugged. "Emergency services. The police. The bookstore phone downstairs. Your parents. I don't know. I hope nobody; my mom checks the call log. But if you guys are going out to follow a lead — and this is an actual lead —" he added in a tone of vague disbelief, "then you should have a way to call for help, and you shouldn't hesitate to use it."

Marzana took the phone gingerly. "How does it work?" But it was pretty self-explanatory. There was a button for *on,* buttons for dialing, a button for *off.* Simple enough.

"This one opens the camera." Ciro pushed a button on one side, and the screen went from black to showing a crisp image of Marzana's foot.

"Thank you."

Ciro nodded. "'Hooray, hooray, hooray!'" he said briskly. Then he reached out and gave the end of one of her braids a gentle tweak. "Good luck."

Emilia waved goodbye and vanished into Westing Alley, leaving Marzana, J.J., and Meddy to continue on down to the end of Hellbent Street and toward Whipping Hyde. For a while, Marzana walked in silence. Her well of conversation had run dry, all except one question, which she didn't quite know how to ask. Not yet.

Fortunately, Meddy had plenty to say. "So how far is this place?" she asked no one in particular.

"It's about a ten-minute walk to the bus; then we take that for about another twenty," J.J. said. He glanced at his watch, then at Marzana. "The next one comes at five thirty. Supposedly. Do you need to call your parents or anything? We probably have time, and there's a pay phone on the next block. You're going to be way late getting home."

"I guess." She patted her pockets for change. "I should've asked to borrow the bookstore phone. Ciro gave me his cell for emergencies, but this doesn't really qualify. What about you?"

"Yeah, I'll call after you, if there's time. But we won't be too far from my house, and anyway, my parents work late."

Meddy looked at her own watch, then up over the tops of the looming houses at the sliver of sky. "You're saying it's not six yet? Feels like eight or so."

"It always feels later than it really is around here," Marzana said. "This is one of the older neighborhoods in Gammerbund. Lots of narrow streets and shadows."

"And a lot of old iron, too," Meddy added, slowing just a bit to touch the trailing end of what looked like a vine but was actually a bit of ornamental ironwork that had separated from a fire escape.

They reached the pay phone. Marzana found some change to dial home while J.J. took a deck of cards from his pocket, halved it, and spun the halves around in his palm, pretending not to care that Marzana and Meddy were watching out of the corners of their eyes.

Honora picked up on the fourth ring. "Hedgelock Court!" her creaky old voice barked in its customary too-loud fashion. "Hakelbarend residence!"

Marzana winced and angled the earpiece away from her head to compensate for Honora's phone voice. "It's me, Honora. Can I talk to Mom?"

"Captain's not in," Honora retorted, sounding a bit put out for some reason. "Left a note for us, though. Gone for a game of squash. Might be home late."

"Huh." *Gone for a game of squash* was code. It meant that whichever parent signed the note had gone out on the kind of business that generally required deniability.

"Mom, or Dad?"

"Both."

Well, that explained Honora's salty tone; she was crabby about having been left behind. "Well, I'll be home late too. Going to a friend's house for dinner."

"A friend, is it?" Honora asked, brightening. "Your friend the Marx Brothers fan, is it? Ciro, that was?"

Marzana clamped her hand down over the earpiece a second too late to muffle Honora's voice and rolled her eyes at the silently laughing J.J. "Might as well tell her yes," he whispered, splitting the deck in two and shuffling the halves together, flawlessly alternating cards from each side, one after another. "Otherwise you'll have to explain away a second boy she's never heard of who's suddenly inviting you over for dinner."

"Yes," Marzana muttered into the phone, one hand over her eyes. "But could you not make a big deal about it, please?"

"Bus is coming," Meddy called. "Is this ours?"

"Yes," J.J. replied. "But more importantly, I don't think either of you understand how impressive that shuffle was." He tucked the cards in his pocket.

"Gotta go," Marzana said into the phone. "Honora—you don't know anything about this squash game, do you? Where it is, who else is there, anything?"

"All I know is that if someone had told me earlier in the day that everyone in the house was planning on being out of it this evening, I wouldn't have roasted a chicken."

"I'm sorry," Marzana said, but she knew the complaint was neither directed at her nor really a complaint. Honora was telling her that whatever errand had called Marzana's parents out of the house, it had come up fast. It had been unexpected.

"Be home before I worry," Honora said.

"Aye, aye," Marzana replied, then hung up as the bus arrived.

seventeen

OTTOMY STALLS

IT WAS A DOUBLE-DECKER BUS, blue and gold — tall in height but short in length, the better to avoid getting stuck at any of the many tight corners on its route. J.J. took a pass from his wallet and held it out for the driver to punch with a little silver handheld device, then proceeded to the vehicle's upper level. Marzana dug more change out of her pocket and dumped it in the hopper as she followed him with Meddy on her heels.

The lower level was crowded with commuters, but there was nobody up above. They took seats near the back just in case: J.J. and Marzana on either side of the aisle, and Meddy in the seat right in front of Marzana. When they were settled, J.J. took out his deck of cards again and swiveled sideways in his seat to face the girls. "So what kind of magic can a ghost do?" he asked, performing another fancy, perfectly alternating shuffle in his hands. He looked up with a grin, which faded when neither Marzana nor Meddy looked properly impressed.

"I can shuffle, if that's what you're asking," Meddy said drily.

"Okay, first of all, this? What I'm doing?" He did the alternating shuffle again. "This isn't just a shuffle. It's a *faro* shuffle. It's *challenging*. Plenty of people can't do a faro at all, let alone a perfect one. Fun fact: If you do eight perfect faro shuffles, it returns the deck to exactly the order it was in before you started." He held out the cards to Meddy. She looked down at them, then up at him. "Don't make me say it." He sighed.

"Fine." Meddy picked one.

"Now put it back." The ghost girl obeyed, sliding the card into the middle. "Now observe." J.J. raised one finger, lifting it away from the top of the deck. One card rose up. He snatched it and spun it to face Meddy and Marzana. "That yours?"

Marzana glanced over. Eight of diamonds. Meddy looked unimpressed. "I think you know it is."

J.J. sniffed. "You sound like you think you can do better."

"You're asking me if I can do card tricks?" Meddy looked at the deck thoughtfully. She took it, shuffled it, and passed it back to J.J. "Shuffle, cut, whatever you want. Pick one."

J.J. shuffled, cut the deck in half, shuffled again, and handed it back. Meddy fanned the deck, and he selected a card.

"Show it to me," Meddy ordered.

J.J. flipped the card in his fingers with a little flourish to show them the ace of spades.

"Yes, yes," Meddy said impatiently. "Ace of spades. Very impressive." She held the deck back out. "Put it wherever." J.J. tucked it back into the deck somewhere around the middle.

"Okay." Meddy put the deck on her knee, squared it up neatly, and quickly placed her finger on the top card before the jolting of the bus could shift the stack. As they watched, her finger sank straight through the cards in slow degrees until finally, thoughtfully, Meddy paused. "I think . . . yes." She gave her half-buried finger a gentle flick, and a single card shot forward out of the deck and into J.J.'s hands.

He turned it over. "Ace of spades."

Meddy fanned her hands. "Ta-*daa*." Her flourish was cut short as the bus went over a bump. J.J. grabbed the cards before they could fly everywhere.

"Okay, okay, you get points for flair there." The bus lurched again, and J.J. almost lost his grip on the deck. Marzana glanced around. They were emerging from the old part of town into Ten Churches, the neighborhood to the south. "That's my school," J.J. said, pointing to a low building off to their left. "My house is just about ten minutes away."

Marzana nodded absently. She knew this neighborhood. It was Nialla's, too, after all. Right next to the school J.J. had pointed out was the primary school Nialla had gone to, right up until her parents had decided to transfer her to Marymead in the sixth grade.

Meddy, however, was looking around as if transfixed. Marzana followed her eyes, wondering what was so interesting. Houses — yes, piled up on top of one another as they were throughout the Liberty, but here at least the brick streets were wide enough for a bus, which meant fewer deep shadows and more sky. J.J.'s school actually looked like an educational institution and not a refurbished mansion. All right, yes, the roof had been built upon, like the roof of most every other low edifice in Gammerbund, but somehow it was only a nice little park up there rather than another three or four stories' worth of building.

And there was the old iron, of course. Marzana had grown up with it, and if you grew up with old iron, you did sort of stop seeing it as unusual. On the other hand, while you could forget to notice it, you could never fail to spot it if you were looking. Wrought whorls of metal climbing buildings like vines; lampposts that leaned at odd angles or that partially swallowed whatever stood beside them: trees, gates, corners of buildings; fences that followed unlikely routes, rising up out of the ground like sea serpents breaching and diving, breaching and diving, rather than lying in nice straight lines around a yard.

There was a lot of it here, now that she was looking. But surely Meddy wouldn't find that strange. Greenglass House stood alone on its particular bit of hillside, but the nearest district, where presumably Meddy would have spent a lot of time, was the Quayside Harbors, which had more old iron than any other place in Nagspeake.

And then Marzana remembered that Meddy had been dead for decades — occasionally present in Greenglass House but never, in all that time, able to leave until just recently, when she and Milo had worked out their hack with the reliquary. Of course she was gaping at everything like a tourist. She'd probably forgotten what the rest of Nagspeake looked like.

The bus slowed, stopped, leaned, and made a sound like a cough as its lower doors opened for whoever was getting on or off. Marzana glanced at her watch. J.J., still flipping cards absently in his hands, spotted her looking. "Probably ten minutes more."

"Thanks." That was plenty of time. Marzana turned to Meddy. "Tell me about Emilia's dad saving my mom."

Meddy looked at her, surprised. "Why don't you ask Emilia? Why didn't you just ask her back at Lucky's?"

"Because I was mad at you both, obviously, and then you were both mad at me, and I was afraid if I asked, I'd screw it up somehow."

The ghost girl sighed. "I wasn't mad at you. I was just trying to point out that it was a bit unfair of you to act like you have it harder than someone who's actually lost parents, just because your parents keep secrets." She smiled a sad, sympathetic smile. "All parents keep secrets. Especially parents in our folks' line of work."

"No, it's everybody's parents," J.J. put in. "My folks are boring as anything, and they still manage to keep secrets. I have no idea what they think they need to be secretive about, or why they think I care, but somehow they still do it."

Here was yet another of the many reasons Marzana got stressed out when she talked to people. She'd asked a perfectly simple question—assuming Meddy knew the answer, which clearly she did —and instead of getting that answer, Marzana had somehow found herself on the receiving end of a lecture. This wasn't the conversation she'd wanted to have. "I'll ask Emilia," she said, forcing her words to come out evenly. "But for now, *just tell me, would you?*" Her voice twisted up into a yell despite her best efforts. *Calm. Calm.* She took a deep breath. Once again, a tear had somehow escaped her eye to roll down to her chin, and she swiped it away so hard, she accidentally scraped herself with a fingernail.

"You okay?" Meddy asked quietly.

Marzana paused until she was sure she wouldn't accidentally yell again. "I really hate that you and Emilia both know something about my mom that I don't."

Meddy nodded. "I'm just thinking back to last year at Green-glass House, when Milo told that story about Violet Cross and you were so mad about it. Do you remember?"

"Of course I remember," Marzana retorted. "It was the story about the contraband maps my mom and her crew distributed around the city by disguising them as kites. That's one of the only capers she told me about herself, and I got mad because Milo got some of the details wrong."

"Well, I'll tell you what I heard; just keep in mind that I got this secondhand from my dad, who wasn't there. I might have some details wrong too. Emilia will know the truth, or at least her version will be closer to it."

"Fine. I swear I'll ask her, too. Start telling."

Meddy pulled her feet up onto her seat and wrapped her arms around her knees. "My dad worked with Mr. Cabot now and then. He was a carrier too, like this Snakebird guy. I assume that's how Emilia knew the term, that's where she heard about the Snakebird, and that's how she knew his very secret identity."

Well, that explained Emilia's *Why me?* perfectly. "Emilia asked why I'd picked her back when I first invited her to join us on this case," Marzana said. "She must've thought I only wanted to recruit her because of who her dad was."

"You guys said a carrier is an information specialist?" J.J. asked.

"Yes. Mostly they're like . . . like brokers, I guess, or fences. They buy and sell and trade information. Some are more specialized; like Emilia said, there are carriers who sell entire jobs, prepackaged, for people who have the guts to pull off a heist but not necessarily the organizational skills or the contacts to put one together themselves. Others specialize in people," Meddy explained.

"How do you specialize in people?" J.J. again. "Do they dig up dirt on folks?"

Meddy nodded. "Sometimes. Or you can hire a carrier to research a person's habits and schedules. Or, say for a certain job you needed someone with a special skill, like a code breaker or a forger who specializes in glass art or whatever: you can find a carrier to refer you and provide an introduction. Carriers come in all kinds;

Alexander Cabot was a researcher. Supposedly when he was at university he uncovered a decades-old ongoing conspiracy, and there was so much fallout in the city, so many important people implicated in it, that he had to go into hiding. Presumably that's how he wound up here."

Meddy paused to look out the window as the bus stopped again under an ornate clock suspended over the street by looping braids of old iron. It was a familiar landmark to Marzana. Sometimes she and Nialla used the position of this particular clock instead of the flip of a coin to make decisions: If the iron had pulled it closer to the bank on the south side of the street, they'd stop at Jack's Pies for pizza; if the clock was closer to the curio shop on the north side, they'd skip pizza and go straight to Peppermilk for ice cream. Meddy's eyes were wide as she stared up at the loops of curving metal, and Marzana grudgingly acknowledged that maybe she'd forgotten how strange old iron was. She heard Emilia's voice in her memory. *How have you not noticed? Don't you know where you live?* Maybe she'd failed to notice a lot.

The bus lurched forward. "My dad hired Alexander Cabot for a job not long before . . . Before. You know." *Before we died.* Meddy continued in a businesslike tone, "He actually came to the house, which was rare. Dad didn't do that; he didn't bring stuff—or people—related to work home. He made an exception for Alexander Cabot."

"Deniability," Marzana muttered.

"Yeah. For all the good it did us." Meddy glanced at her sharply. "In any case, Alexander Cabot came to us. He was really young. Like eighteen or nineteen at the time. I don't remember what they discussed. I don't know if I even paid attention. If I thought about it, I could probably figure out what job it was; there were a couple big ones right before ... Before. Anyway. After he left, I asked Dad why this guy was so special." Meddy paused again and leaned out the window as the bus rolled to a stop and wheezed its doors open. "There's less iron out there now."

J.J. glanced over his shoulder at the street. "I think we have two stops left before we're in Whipping Hyde. Five minutes or so."

"Right. So why did this guy merit a meeting at home?" Meddy asked. "Dad said he'd come from the Liberty, so it hardly made sense to meet down in the Harbors. But that was baloney; Dad optimized for safety, not convenience. When I called him on the lie, he just laughed. He said Cabot knew so much about the city and what went on in it that there was no point in trying to be sneaky with him. And here's the example he gave me."

The bus slowed again, and Meddy paused as two strangers came up the stairs and sat near the front of the upper level. Then, apparently remembering they could neither see nor hear her, she continued. "Dad told me that one day a few years back — and remember that Alexander Cabot was in his late teens when Dad was telling me this story, so at the time the incident happened, he couldn't have been much older than you are — Cabot was sitting in a café in Bayside, and he realized that two men were about to confront a young woman who didn't appear to be aware of it. Speaking of people not being aware," she said, glaring at J.J., "relax, would you? Nobody can hear me but you two. Just don't ask any awkward questions out loud."

J.J., who'd been darting concerned glances from Meddy to the backs of the two older newcomers up near the front, slouched back into his seat. "Right," he said quietly. "Forgot."

"Anyway," Meddy continued, "from a handful of other clues — things he knew were happening in the city or had happened within the last few days, and things he'd observed while just sitting there — he guessed that the young lady was a runner, and that the two men were customs. He caught her eye and waved her over as if he'd been waiting for her. The two customs agents followed and started asking questions, and Alexander Cabot, without having spoken a single word to this woman, was able to provide an alibi for the exact time she needed in order to demonstrate she couldn't have been involved in the incident in question." Meddy shook her head. "To hear Dad tell it, it was like Sherlock Holmes–level stuff—Cabot had figured out everything from who she was, to what she'd been up to, to exactly the kind of alibi she'd need to evade suspicion, and all from the tiniest clues."

"And the lady was my mom?" Marzana asked in a low voice.

Meddy nodded. "It was her first big job. She'd known there were customs agents on her, and she'd had a plan if they picked her up, but her cover would've been blown, and who knows what would've happened after that? If not for Alexander Cabot, your mother might never have become the legend she was."

"Wow," Marzana whispered. She leaned back in her seat, delighted. "Thank you." This was exactly the kind of thing she could never pry out of her mother. Honora was an easier mark, but only on days when the letters came, and even with Honora, she had to be careful not to look too eager.

"You're welcome." Meddy gave her a long look. "When you ask Emilia about this, try to remember that as awesome as her dad clearly was, he's dead now."

That killed just a bit of the joy—but only a bit of it. The knowledge was still there, like a small, precious treasure hidden in a pocket.

The bus began to slow. "This is us," J.J. said briskly, getting to his feet. Marzana followed after him, her cheeks burning. *I would have remembered to be tactful,* she told herself indignantly. *Are you sure about that?* her inner critic retorted.

They stepped down to the curb, and the bus pulled away. "How did you know?" Marzana asked Meddy. "He died long after . . . After. Right? He was alive recently enough to tell stories to Emilia. So how did you figure out so fast, when she mentioned being familiar with the cemetery and where it is, that her father was Alexander Cabot, if you couldn't have known he was dead?"

Meddy shrugged. "She looks exactly like him. I mean, *exactly.* It just took me a while to place it. He had that same way of keeping his face totally blank."

J.J., meanwhile, was busy digging the gazetteer out of his backpack. "I don't know my way around here," he explained, flipping it open to the page where they'd marked Mrs. Agravin's street. "But here's the bus stop . . . okay." He lowered the book and pointed toward the next intersection. "I think we want that left."

They walked without much conversation. J.J. navigated, a bit awkwardly, since he was using Ciro's big gazetteer; Meddy wandered around in her touristy daze; and Marzana trailed a step behind, wondering whether Casie from the Sidledywry Knot books ever felt like she was not really much of a leader after all.

Whipping Hyde was another very old part of town, and Marzana was struck immediately by the surprising number of buildings with only two stories to them. Squat buildings, even privately owned ones, almost never stayed that way in Gammerbund; yet here were entire streets whose rows of low-slung houses twisted like lizards, the neighboring lanes full of more standard Liberty structures towering up and around and even occasionally *over* them where walkways had been built between the taller buildings, as if the lower ones were nothing more than an inconvenience to be bridged.

Perhaps to help justify the hoarding of all that unused vertical space, the residents of the squat buildings had put up a handful of little green ceramic plaques to commemorate the rich history of their neighborhood. The members of the Thief Knot paused to read the first of these that they came upon, which had been nailed beside the door of a cheese shop: ON THIS SITE IN THE YEAR OF OUR LORD 1734 WAS SITUATED THE OFFICE AND STUDIO OF THE PLAGUE DOCTOR AND NOTABLE MACRAMÉ ARTIST SIMEON FRAY. Four doors down another reported: IN THIS HOUSE IN THE YEAR OF OUR LORD 1820 THE NOTED CHEMIST ILAINE HOTSON MADE SEVERAL DISCOVERIES OF GASES WHICH MAY BE USED TO SEE WONDERS. And next door, possibly, Marzana thought, related: IN THIS HOUSE IN THE YEAR OF OUR LORD 1820 FOUR GUESTS AT THE EASTER BALL OF JACINTHUS BEADLE WERE DISCOVERED AT THE REMOVAL OF MASKS TO HAVE BEEN CHANGED FOR IDENTICAL RE- PLACEMENTS OF OTHERWORLDLY ORIGIN.

J.J. guided them down narrow brick streets that led to narrower humped and cobbled lanes too old and scant to even have sidewalks. On either side, the houses got progressively older and tiltier, their façades dark with age and the glass in their green-tinged windows thick and bubbled. "Should be almost there," J.J. reported. "We're looking for Cop-Bone Way. Looks like it should be a wider passage than the one we're on."

"Like this one?" Meddy stopped dead in the street and grabbed the back of J.J.'s shirt. "Check this out." She pointed to another of those green plaques, affixed to the brick wall on their right just before the mouth of the next lane. THIS WAY WAS FOR SEVERAL DECADES THE HOME OF THE OTTOMY MARKET. HERE PHYSICIANS, SURGEONS, AND NATURAL PHILOSOPHERS OF ALL SORTS MET TO EXCHANGE GOODS, SERVICES, AND IDEAS. "Ottomy Market! Wasn't that the name of the station Milo mentioned?" she demanded, tugging J.J.'s shirt repeatedly in her excitement.

"Whoa," J.J. said, prying himself and his shirt loose. "No *way*."

"The name of the station was Ottomy Stalls," Marzana said, a little stunned. "But a market has stalls."

J.J. looked from the plaque to his map, then back up at the entrance to the lane, then all around them. "Will you look at that?" He pointed higher up on the opposite wall, where a rectangle of the same green ceramic read COP-BONE WAY. "Well, here we are, I guess. We're looking for Number Seventy-Two."

Cop-Bone Way was wider, but not by much. Like the street they'd just been on, it lacked sidewalks and was lined on both sides by low row houses, most of which sported glassy bow windows and candy-striped awnings that brought the striped canopy in Granddad del Olmo's drawing of the Ottomy Stalls façade irresistibly to Marzana's mind. Many here were faded, but all were neat and fluttering cheerfully in the cooling evening breeze, which began pushing at Marzana's back almost the second she and her friends turned into the lane and did not deign to let up for more than a second or two.

Almost every building under those flapping awnings had a little green historical marker and business hours that ended at five. *If we'd gotten here an hour earlier,* Marzana wondered, *would there actually be people around?* But Cop-Bone Way was so quiet, she couldn't quite imagine it otherwise.

They had to hunt for a bit to find a façade with an address number, and since most every shop was closed, there was no one to ask for directions. They passed a bookbindery, a law office, a dental sciences museum, and a clown museum before they spotted a discreet

#45 beside the doorknob of a pickle shop. Then they had to hike past a cartographer's studio, a shop full of religious icons, and four private residences before they found *#35*, realized they were walking the wrong way, and headed back the way they'd come.

A yarn shop . . . a junk shop . . . a café with cane chairs piled out front . . . a shop whose window was mostly obscured by the reaching and twisting black branches of the red-flowered shrub in the dusty planter below it. As they drew even with the shrubbery, Marzana smelled a papery perfume for just a second before the red flowers unfolded themselves and rose up, fluttering: a vibrating, shimmering cloud of scarlet butterflies that ascended in shifting patterns, making her think immediately of an armful of red balloons, released to find their own bobbing way up into the open air. And then they were gone.

Abruptly J.J. stopped in the middle of the cobbled road. Marzana bumped right into him, and Meddy bumped into *her,* which resulted in the ghost girl falling straight *through* both Marzana and J.J. and landing on her knees. As Meddy got back to her feet, J.J. pointed to a façade very much like the others they'd passed. "That's it," he said.

Marzana swallowed down the distinct feeling that she might vomit, which seemed to be a side effect of having a ghost fall through you, and turned to the façade. "Mrs. Agravin's house?"

Incredulous and looking a bit green himself, J.J. shook his head. "No, *the station.* This is unbelievable."

Just as it had in the blueprint and just like all the other storefronts on Cop-Bone Way, the Ottomy Stalls station had a cheerful striped awning over a big front window. The awning was older and shabbier than most of the others they'd passed, and the window was flat, not bowed, the better to paint the faded gold letters that spelled out the name of the station. But it was almost impossible to read the words against the yellowed newspaper that had been taped up inside the glass sometime long, long ago.

"Well, it's not quite unbelievable," Meddy said reasonably. "We knew it was going to be here somewhere once we found that plaque, and all these houses look just like the drawing."

"But come on," J.J. insisted. "It just happens to be on the same road as the missing teacher's house?"

"Not just the same road." Marzana pointed with a shaking finger at the window. There was a number painted there too, just as nearly invisible against the newspaper: 72.

"Seventy-Two Cop-Bone Way," she said. "That's Mrs. Agravin's address."

Marzana's missing math teacher lived above a Belowground Transit station.

"This is all starting to feel really convenient," she said uneasily, sticking her hands in her pockets and looking around. Her fingers found Ciro's phone, and she pulled it out and thumbed the camera on. "Might as well, right?"

J.J. nodded. "Good idea."

"Great, because I have no clue what we do next." Marzana glanced around, but as far as she could tell, they were still alone on the street. The windows of what had to be either 71 or 73 directly across from them were shuttered. Marzana backed up to get a more complete photo of Number 72, keeping under the shadow of the awning to stay as much out of sight as possible, and took a few pictures. J.J. crouched against the wall to her side in what seemed to be an effort to make himself as small and invisible as he could.

Meddy, meanwhile, stepped up to the window and stuck her head directly through both the glass and the yellowed newspaper, disappearing right up to her shoulders. "Pretty dark in there," she commented after she'd withdrawn. There were doors on either side of the window: one to the right that clearly led to the station, and one to the left that logically ought to lead to the apartment upstairs. A squat box with tulips printed on the sides sat on the single step below the left-hand door.

Meddy examined both entrances, then trotted across to where Marzana and J.J. waited. "There's a bell that's marked 'Eliza Agravin,'" she reported. "Shall I just go through and unlock the door and we all go in, or do you want to try ringing the bell first? Marzana, you can say you heard she was sick and you came to check on her."

"Sure, except for that." Marzana pointed at the box with the tulip decorations. "Those are probably the flowers Miss Palkowick sent on Tuesday, so I doubt anyone's going to answer if we ring the doorbell."

"How about I go in first and open the door, then?" Meddy suggested.

"Yeah, you go first. Let's do that," J.J. said. Then he had the grace to look embarrassed. "That sounded gutless. But, I mean, you can't get hurt, right?"

Meddy grinned. "It's okay, pal. You stay here and practice cards or something. Watch and learn." She patted her pockets. "You still have the reliquary, right, Marzana?"

Marzana nodded. "You gave it to me as we were leaving Marymead."

"Great. Pretty sure I'll be fine at this distance. I'll wave when the door's unlocked; then you can come right in." She jogged across Cop-Bone Way and, without pausing, jogged straight on through the front door. A moment later, it swung inward a few inches, and Meddy's hand reached out and beckoned.

Marzana and J.J. hurried over and slipped into a tiny entryway made even more crowded by a little semicircular table in the corner where any mail that came through the slot by the door would theoretically fall neatly onto a tray on top. Meddy stood next to it, eyeing what looked like several days' worth of mail that had been left to pile up, rendering the tray useless and sending a small flood of letters and circulars to the floor.

Marzana bent and poked through the pile. "There's a newspaper here from Tuesday. That was the first day she didn't show up at Marymead." She stood and faced the stairs: a single long, narrow flight lit at the top by a chandelier with frosted glass bells.

"I'll take a look," Meddy said quietly. "You stay here, just in case." She darted up, her feet eerily silent, even though they appeared to pound the steps, and vanished around the corner.

Then, barely thirty seconds later, she came flying back down the stairs. Actually *flying*. Her face was a shocked, triumphant, scared mask, and as she swooped down, she shrieked, "Police! She's there! Police! Call someone! The girl, the girl! *She's there!*"

"She is?" Heart hammering, Marzana fumbled in her pocket again for Ciro's phone and numbly punched the numbers she'd had drilled into her from the time she was barely able to walk: *Dial this in case of emergency*. "Who's up there?" she asked, shoving the phone against her ear. "Who else?"

"There's no one else," Meddy said, grabbing for J.J.'s sleeve with one hand and Marzana's with the other. "But they could come back! Come on!"

J.J. started up the stairs just as the operator at the other end of the line picked up. Marzana shook herself out of Meddy's grip. "Yes, hello? We need police to —"

The door to the street behind her burst open. Marzana flung

herself instinctively for the stairs, shouting, *"Seventy-Two Cop-Bone Way!"* into the phone as she tried to sprint up out of reach of the new invaders. Something whizzed by her face: a flash of white and red and black and gold that made her flinch low. Another flash flew by, and then another. Marzana scrambled up the stairs practically on her belly. About midway, she raised her head just enough to see that the flashes were playing cards J.J. was firing down the stairwell at their pursuers. *Throwing for damage,* she thought wildly. *He is good with those. I'll have to tell Nialla and Emilia.*

As soon as she reached the top, J.J. grabbed her arm and they darted into Mrs. Agravin's apartment. Someone — it had to be Meddy — flung the door shut and locked it. Someone else — the emergency services operator — was shouting at Marzana through Ciro's phone, which was still in her hand. She passed it to J.J. "Take over." Then she pointed to Meddy. "Find us another way out. They'll have keys." She hurried deeper into the apartment.

In the middle of the living room, a dark-haired girl was tied to a chair. It was the girl from the school photo, right down to the braces and the two long side ponytails.

"Peony!" Marzana hurried to her side and pulled away the bandanna that covered her mouth. "Are you Peony? Peony Hyde?"

"I'm Peony!" the girl sobbed as soon as the gag was off. "I'm Peony, I'm Peony!"

Meddy appeared beside the chair. "Marzana, I need you."

"I can't. We don't have time." The girl's wrists were bound behind her back and her ankles to the front legs of the chair, all with a single rope. Marzana looked at the knot just between the girl's wrists that secured the whole rig, but it wasn't one she recognized. Of course not. She was fluent in exactly three knots out of thousands. She muttered a curse and fumbled in her kit for the multi-tool.

"I need you fast," Meddy insisted. "Now. Just for a minute."

"Wait." Marzana's fingers shook. It took three tries to pry one of the tool's blades out, but finally she began sawing at the rope just below the knot. It wasn't much thicker than clothesline, but it was tricky getting a good angle with her knife. "Just focus on getting us out of here."

"I'm focusing, I'm focusing," Peony sobbed. "Just cut me loose!"

"Not you," Marzana said impatiently. "Just hold still."

"I'm *talking* about getting us out of here," Meddy insisted. "I need you to listen."

Listen. Marzana stopped cutting and looked up. It was too quiet. Where was the banging on the door? Come to think of it, how had the kidnappers not already come busting in? "Where's J.J.?" she asked.

"Who's J.J.?" Peony wiggled her wrists. "Hurry. The rope hurts!"

Marzana cut through the last strands, then folded the knife and stood up as Peony kicked loose. There were voices speaking from Mrs. Agravin's foyer. Strangely calm voices. She followed them and left Meddy to look after the sobbing Peony, completely forgetting that Peony couldn't see or hear Meddy at all.

In the foyer, J.J. was pacing by the door with his hands deep in his pockets. "Just get her," a voice was saying from the other side of it. "We'll wait; just don't do anything until you get her." The voice was muffled, female. Familiar. Very, very familiar.

"Oh, thank God," J.J. said as Marzana approached. He waved at the door with a quaking hand. "She says . . . Marzana, she says she's your *mom.*"

eighteen

NUMBER 72

HEY STOOD STARING at one another over the threshold:
Marzana on one side with J.J. pacing behind her, and her
mother and father on the landing at the top of the stairs. For
a moment, no one said anything. Then Mrs. Hakelbarend leaned
sideways to glance into the apartment beyond. "Is that Peony?" She
sounded surprised, but more than that, she sounded almost . . . what
was that tone? Almost *wary.*

"Yes," Marzana said, completely at a loss as to whether she was
about to be a hero or about to be grounded.

Her mother frowned. "Who's that with her?"

"Hey, Mrs. Hakelbarend," Meddy called. "It's Meddy. Addie.
Addie Whitcher."

Marzana's mom's eyes bugged out. She hurried past Marzana
and J.J. and into the living room without a word.

Mr. Hakelbarend spoke up. "We clearly have a lot to talk about.

But this is not the time." He looked at the cell phone in J.J.'s hand. "You guys rang the police?"

J.J. nodded. "They're still on. I just muted the call." In the living room, Marzana's mom began speaking in a low, soothing voice to Peony.

"Smart." Mr. Hakelbarend held out his hand. J.J. put the phone into it. "One of Katia del Olmo's?" he asked. Nobody bothered to answer. Marzana's father hit a button and put the phone to his ear. "Hi, who am I talking to? . . . This is Peter Hakelbarend. You'll find my name in the Q Register. Are there officers en route? Good. If you're in contact with them, tell them they want the upstairs apartment. The door is to the left of the window on the ground floor. I'll go down and keep an eye out for them. . . . Yes, I'll stay on the line." Without so much as a backward glance, he headed down the stairs to the street.

J.J. edged up close to Marzana. "What's the Q Register?"

"I have no idea," she replied through clenched teeth. "Pretty sure it's not a squash league, though."

Mrs. Hakelbarend called sharply from the living room. "Marzana!"

Marzana hurried past a nervous Meddy lingering in the short hallway to join her mother and Peony in the living room. Mrs. Hakelbarend had settled the kidnapped girl on the sofa. "Sit with her for a minute. I need to have a look around."

Oh, Mrs. Agravin! She was still unaccounted for. But did Marzana's parents even know about her? "Mom," Marzana said, "this is my math teacher's apartment. She's been out since Tuesday — she's missing. She's pretty old, Mom. She might be hurt."

"Your math teacher," Mrs. Hakelbarend repeated. Then her

expression hardened and she pointed a finger at Marzana. "You and I are going to have a *significant* conversation when we get home." She stalked out of the room. As soon as she was gone, J.J. and Meddy came cautiously in from the hall, looking like they couldn't quite figure out where to be. J.J. sat down in a tall wing chair in the corner. Meddy paced, arms folded, by the window that looked out over Cop-Bone Way.

Peony huddled on the couch. "That lady is your mom?" She held the cut rope in her hands and worried the knot between her fingers.

"Yup," Marzana replied lightly, trying to sound like she wasn't obviously in trouble.

Peony wasn't fooled. "You're in trouble, huh?"

Marzana sighed. "You know that part where Casie has the amazing escape from Ragmire and Devix only to get caught by her parents sneaking back into her house, and she has that moment when, after all the awesome stuff she manages to do, she gets grounded just like any other kid?"

Peony smiled weakly. "What?"

"In *The Sidledywry Knot*. First book." Marzana attempted a comforting smile. "You were reading that series, right?"

"Oh. Right. Yes." She rubbed her face. "It feels like so long ago." She smiled back, a little apologetically. "I'm up to the fifth book. I had forgotten about Casie."

A warm little ray of happiness curled through Marzana's heart. This was good. She might get grounded later, but for now, she was doing something worthwhile and maybe even important, comforting this lost girl. "I've only read the first one," she said, "but I think I'll keep going. Are the rest just as good?"

Peony's smile brightened, and she sat up straighter, which made her look taller, older than eleven. "Yes. Although the main character is different in the later books."

"Nell Southsea," Marzana said.

"Yes! She's awesome." Peony beamed at Marzana. "I thought you looked just like her when you came flying in."

"Aww." Well, that felt nice, at least. What would Casie Patrick, alias Nell Southsea, be doing if she were here right now? Assuming her mother had also effectively told her to sit on the sofa and not move. *Get some information.* Yes. After all, Peony wasn't only a kidnap victim; she was also a witness. But where to begin? There were so many questions. "Peony, can you tell me what happened to you?"

The girl's face drained of every ounce of cheer it had just gained. She stiffened. "I don't want to talk about it."

"Well ... can you tell me anything about the people who took you?"

Peony's mouth tightened into a line.

"Anything?" Marzana asked. "Even whether it was one person or two, or more?"

Peony clutched the rope to her chest and huddled back into Mrs. Agravin's couch cushions.

Grasping at straws, Marzana changed tack. Maybe the idea of helping someone else might shake Peony out of her withdrawal. "What about the lady who lives here? She's missing, you know." She pointed to a framed picture on the table beside the couch: Mrs. Agravin, wearing a medal around her neck and shaking hands with someone in a suit. "That's her. Has she been gone the whole time you've been here, or have you seen her?"

Peony barely glanced at the picture. "No," she whispered.

"Okay." One final try with a query she couldn't leave unasked. "Last question, I promise. Peony, did you ever hear any of them

—whoever took you, I mean—mention someone named Victor Cormorant?"

Peony said nothing. She pulled her knees up and curled herself around them. Her face disappeared under her lank hair. *Oh, no. Oh, no. I broke her.* Marzana glanced desperately across at J.J. *What do I do?* she mouthed.

J.J. hopped to his feet, picked up his backpack off the floor, and came across to kneel at the coffee table opposite Marzana and Peony. "Want to see some magic?"

"Hope you have something other than those cards you weaponized in the hallway," Meddy said drily from the window. "Kind of a pity. I bet she'd be really impressed by a perfect faro shuffle."

He shot Meddy a brief glare, but of course, the ghost girl hadn't shown herself to Peony, so she could hear none of Meddy's commentary. She looked reluctantly up from her knees. "What kind of magic?"

J.J. unzipped his backpack and took out a little black velvet pouch. "Let's see what I've got." He peeked into the pouch. "Spectator's choice. Cups or shells?"

Peony unfolded a little, interested. "What kind of shells? Seashells?"

"Walnuts." J.J. picked three brown shells from the bag, then reached in with his other hand, rooted around, and pulled out a single tiny green ball. "And a pea."

He lined up the three halves in a row and set the pea in front of them. "Here we go." He put the pea under the middle one, then moved it and the shell to its right a short distance across the table toward Marzana and Peony. Then he slid them back and did the same move with the two outside walnut halves. When all three were in a line again, he looked up at Peony. "Where's the pea?" She grinned and pointed at the middle one. J.J. nodded. "Pretty easy, right? We'll make it harder in a minute." He lifted the shell she'd pointed to.

Peony squealed. There was nothing there. J.J. looked down in consternation. "Whoops." He lifted the walnut to the left. There was the pea. "That's odd."

The girl laughed. "Let me try again." She scooted forward and leaned on her knees for a closer look.

As J.J. began moving his shells back and forth again, Mrs. Hakelbarend stepped into the doorway beside the couch. Wordlessly, she leaned against the frame, arms folded, and watched him lift the one where the pea had been to display the empty space underneath. Peony clapped in delight. He began the trick once more, varying the pattern, and Marzana glanced up at her mother, girding herself first for whatever she'd see. But Mrs. Hakelbarend wasn't looking at her. Her eyes rested, troubled, on Peony.

From somewhere outside, the *whee-ooo, whee-ooo* of a siren bounced through the alleys, getting louder little by little. "Police are coming," Meddy said from the window.

Marzana's mother straightened. "Not long now, Peony," she said. "You ready to go home?"

The girl nodded, still fidgeting nervously with the rope. "Will my mom and dad be mad?"

"Not a chance." Mrs. Hakelbarend smiled. "They're going to be so happy to have you back." Her gaze shifted to Marzana. "You guys okay for a few more minutes?"

Marzana nodded, afraid to say anything aloud. Peony's parents wouldn't be mad, but holy cow, it was obviously taking a Herculean effort for her own mother to keep her fury under control. Marzana was in for it.

Mrs. Hakelbarend departed, leaving the four kids alone again. J.J. tapped the middle shell. "Where's the pea?"

Peony hesitated, then pointed to the walnut on the left.

"Good guess." J.J. lifted it. Nothing, of course. "But wrong. Guess again." Peony pointed to the middle one. He lifted it: no pea. She pointed to the last remaining half and he lifted that one. Still nothing. Peony squealed again. J.J. scratched his chin. "That's so funny. I wonder where . . . oh." He lifted the walnut she'd pointed to in the first place and revealed not one but *two* green peas. "Guess you were right after all."

"Amazing!" Peony crowed, clapping.

"Showoff," Meddy said.

"Try it," J.J. challenged under his breath, masking the word with a short bow.

"Oh, you're so on." Meddy dropped onto the floor at his side. "Scoot over."

J.J. grinned at Peony. "You know, sometimes the shells like to try the trick without me," he said. "Want to see?"

"Without you?" Peony repeated dubiously.

"Sure. Let's see if they're in the mood." J.J. scooted over.

Unseen by Peony, Meddy took his place behind the shells. She cracked the knuckles of both hands. "Here we go." She put a finger on each of the outside shells and moved them forward, then backwards, just as J.J. had done, touching the shells as little as possible. Peony gasped, reminding Marzana that, from the girl's perspective, the shells appeared to be shifting all on their own.

Meddy moved the middle and left shells. Then the middle and the right. Then she hesitated.

"This is the part when the shells remember that there's more to this trick than just the three of them sliding around," J.J. said with a smirk.

Meddy shot him a glare. She switched the left walnut with the middle, then the middle with the right; then she switched the two on the outside. Then she switched them all again, faster. "Wow," Peony breathed. "How are you doing that?"

"How are *you* doing that?" Meddy repeated, glaring indignantly at J.J. as she brought the shells to a standstill. "You're going to get credit for this, aren't you?"

J.J. held out his hands as if to show there was nothing in either palm. "A magician never tells."

Meddy made an exasperated noise. Then she looked down at the table, frowning. J.J. grinned. He caught Marzana's eye and winked. Either Meddy couldn't remember where the peas were, or she'd realized she didn't actually know how to move them unseen. She held her hand over the walnut, closing it and opening it thoughtfully.

"Huh," J.J. said in a wondering tone. "The invisible hand . . . hesitates."

"Give me a minute!" Meddy snapped. "I can reach through the shell," she said as if talking out a problem, "but I think I need to be able to close my hand around the peas to make them both invisible to her and incorporeal enough to pass through the walnut, and I'm trying to figure out how to do that without scooping up the walnut and making that invisible, too."

Peony, meanwhile, took the shells' motionlessness as her cue. She pointed to the middle one. Marzana held her breath. The switching around would certainly have been impressive if you'd been seeing them apparently moving on their own, but it hadn't been hard to follow. Unless Marzana was much mistaken, and unless

Meddy pulled off something crazy, there were still two peas under that shell.

Meddy drummed her fingers once on the tabletop, shrugged, and reached through the shell, trying to scoop the peas into her fist. As she'd predicted, the same action caused the entire shell to vanish briefly into her hand, but only for a second. Then Meddy let go suddenly, jumping a little in surprise. She picked up the walnut shell and flicked it aside. There was nothing there. As Peony clapped, Meddy flipped the other two, one after the other. Nothing. *Nothing.*

J.J. leaned one elbow casually on the tabletop and extended a closed fist. When everyone's eyes were on it, he opened his hand to reveal two peas. Peony actually shrieked in delight, and at last she dropped the rope she'd been clutching to applaud properly.

"Okay," Meddy admitted, "that's impressive. But I get the finale." She darted out her hand, plucked the peas from J.J.'s, then leaned her head back and tossed them, one-two, so they arced up and down again into her open mouth. Where, of course, they disappeared. "Ta-daaa!" she sang with a flourish. She swallowed, then winced and grabbed at her throat. "Ugh."

"They're not real peas," J.J. said, leaning on his chin, his words mostly drowned out by Peony's rapturous clapping.

"Yes, I know that now." Meddy made a gagging noise, prodded the back of her mouth with a finger, gagged again. "Nope, they're not coming back up." She looked at J.J. "Sorry. Not sure how I'm going to get those back for you."

J.J. winced. "It's really okay." He turned a thousand-watt showman's grin on Peony. "Really. It's okay."

" 'Okay'?" she erupted. "That was so cool! When you asked if I wanted to see magic, and then you started off with that first trick,

I thought it might be lame. I mean, no offense. But then, when the shells started moving on their own . . ."

J.J.'s grin, which had begun to look a bit smug, faded a little. "Yeah. Thanks."

Meddy punched him on the arm. "Teamwork! Go, team!"

Footsteps — a lot of them — drummed up from below, the sound amplified by the narrow staircase, and a small flood of people poured into the apartment: a handful of cops, a lady in a suit carrying a doctor's bag, Marzana's mother. Mrs. Hakelbarend strode forward with the suited woman and one of the cops. "Peony, this is Lieutenant Coles. He's already been on the phone with your parents, and they're on their way. And this is Dr. Lazaride. She has some questions for you." She looked around at Marzana, J.J., and Meddy. "You thr — you guys, follow me."

Marzana slid off the couch, giving Peony's hand a quick squeeze as she got up. J.J. collected his magic supplies and returned them to his backpack, which made Marzana realize that she had no idea where she'd dropped her own bag; all she'd managed to hold on to was the toolkit purse. Meddy walked beside her as the three of them followed Mrs. Hakelbarend through the suddenly crowded apartment and down the stairs to the street, where the shadows were beginning to lengthen toward dark.

The lane was almost completely blocked by a pair of squad cars, vintage-looking buglike vehicles that had probably been chosen because of their ability to just barely squeeze through the narrow streets of Whipping Hyde. At the side of the nearest one, with Marzana's backpack hanging from his shoulder and Ciro's phone in his hand, Mr. Hakelbarend stood deep in conversation with another officer. Up and down Cop-Bone Way, doors had opened and a few of the other denizens of the street had begun to come out to investigate the commotion. They stood alone or in little clusters, talking among themselves and smoking and looking down toward the rotating red light on top of the squat cop car.

Her mom took Marzana's backpack from him. "You heading out?" Mr. Hakelbarend asked.

"Yeah. I'll drop—" Mrs. Hakelbarend glanced at J.J. "We haven't been introduced, now that I think of it. Excuse my bluntness, but who are you and where do you live?"

"J.J. Mowbry," J.J. said meekly.

"He lives a couple houses down from Nialla," Marzana put in, hoping the situation wasn't so dire that literally anything she said would only get her deeper in trouble. The look her mother shot her was not comforting.

"Okay, J.J." She took Ciro's phone from her husband, stepped closer to J.J., and lowered her voice. "I'm guessing this belongs to a friend of yours. Would you return it, please, since I gather he lives thereabouts too?"

"Yes, ma'am."

"And did I see you put a piece of cordage in your bag right before we left?"

Marzana and Meddy glanced at J.J., who frowned, confused. "Cordage?" He dropped his backpack, unzipped it, flinched, and pulled out the rope that had been used to tie Peony to the chair. "You mean this. I do some rope tricks—when I cleaned up the other trick, I must've grabbed it. I didn't mean to . . . to tamper with evidence or anything."

"Not a problem." Marzana's mother coiled the rope and turned to Meddy. "And you . . . I'm guessing you're coming with us?"

"That's the idea." Meddy's voice had an edge of challenge to it. *Must be nice to not have to worry about your dad getting called in if you get up to trouble,* Marzana thought, then almost immediately regretted it.

Her mother handed the rope off to the police. Then, as the four started down Cop-Bone Way toward the even narrower thoroughfare, a woman came hurrying toward them with a flowered suitcase swinging in one hand. Marzana recognized her immediately. Mrs. Agravin always walked like she was running late for something, even if she was just heading to the Marymead cafeteria for lunch.

"Mom." Marzana pointed, relieved. "That's her. My teacher, Mrs. Agravin."

Mrs. Hakelbarend changed course for interception and waved. "Mrs. Agravin?"

Mrs. Agravin paused, distracted. "Hello — are those police officers at *my* house?"

"Mrs. Agravin, I'm Barbara Hakelbarend." Marzana's mom grabbed the old lady's free hand, making it look like she was shaking it in greeting but probably really to make sure Mrs. Agravin stopped walking. "I think my daughter, Marzana, is a student of yours."

"Marzana?" Mrs. Agravin blinked and turned to look down at her. "Goodness, yes. Hello, dear. What are you doing here? And what are *they* doing here?" she added, nodding down at the police cars parked outside her apartment.

"Marzana tells me you've been out since Tuesday," Mrs. Hakelbarend said, still holding Mrs. Agravin's hand. "Apparently Marymead hasn't been able to get hold of you. People were worried."

That got her attention. Mrs. Agravin frowned, confused. "But it was all arranged! Before I left. Everything was arranged."

"What was arranged?"

"The trip. The notice was late, of course, but fortunately everything else was in place."

Marzana's mother nodded along, painfully patient. "What trip was this?"

"Well, the sweepstakes one. I can't remember which. I always enter them—I use sweepstakes odds as a project when we talk about statistics and probability in class. And wouldn't you know, after thirty years, I actually won something." She smiled in disbelief. "But the notification was lost in the mail, or perhaps the sweepstakes had a wrong address. So they sent someone along to the school to find me on Monday. I had already left for the day, but while the courier was in the office to double-check my home address, she mentioned the trip to Miss Palkowick, who arranged a substitute on the spot. When the courier finally found me with the notice on Monday night, she said everything had been taken care of —which was fortunate, because the cruise left on Tuesday and all I had to do was pack. It was lovely. And what are the odds? Well," she added, "of course I know exactly what the odds are. If I could just remember what sweepstakes it was, I could tell you. But it'll be in my sweepstakes file upstairs." Then her smile faded and her eyes sharpened. "But you say Marymead couldn't get hold of me. As if . . . as if they didn't know where I was."

"They didn't," Marzana said. "My friend overheard two teachers talking about it today. The person who claimed to be a courier lied to you about everything." She pointed at the flower box on the front step. "The school sent those because someone claiming to be your sister called on Monday and said you were sick. They've been trying to get hold of you ever since. I'd put money on Miss Palkowick showing up here at some point tonight to make sure you're not lying upstairs dead on the kitchen floor."

"Good Lord," Mrs. Agravin said. "This is . . . upsetting." She looked down at Mrs. Hakelbarend's hand, which was still grasping hers. "So someone at the school called the police to make sure I'm all right?"

"I'm afraid not," Mrs. Hakelbarend said. "I'm afraid the police will probably have some questions for you." She turned and waved. Marzana's father detached himself from the officer he'd been talking to and jogged toward them. Only when Mr. Hakelbarend had arrived at her side did she let go of Mrs. Agravin's hand. "Peter, this is Marzana's teacher, Mrs. Agravin. This is my husband, Peter. He's working with the police. Could you tell him what you just told me?"

"I suppose," Mrs. Agravin said uncertainly. "But I wish *you'd* tell *me* what this is all about."

"Glad to," Mr. Hakelbarend said, taking her suitcase. "Is that spot okay to sit and chat?" he asked, leading her toward a bench below the Ottomy Stalls window. "I'm afraid the police are still busy upstairs."

"Bye, Mrs. Agravin," Marzana called. "See you Monday."

Mrs. Agravin still appeared confused, but she smiled nonetheless. "Yes," she said. "See you Monday, dear."

Mrs. Hakelbarend raised her hand in a fleeting wave. She looked down at the three kids. "All right. Let's go. And while we walk, you lot are going to *talk*."

nineteen
RUM THINGS

THE BIG GRANDFATHER CLOCK in the entry hall at Hedgelock was chiming ten when Marzana, Meddy, and Mrs. Hakelbarend trudged in at last.

After leaving Mrs. Agravin's flat, their timing had been abysmal. They arrived at the bus stop just as the bus to the Ten Churches neighborhood was pulling away, and despite J.J.'s protests, Marzana's mom had insisted on waiting with him for the next one. This resulted in their missing the bus that passed closest to the Viaduct, which followed a different route and had a stop four blocks away, and having to wait twenty minutes for another. But even that bus didn't go all the way to the neighborhood on the pointless bridge, so after they'd gotten as close as public transportation would take them, Meddy and Marzana and her mom had had a twenty-minute walk to get home at last.

Honora appeared from the dining room as they entered. She took one look at the expressions on Marzana's and her mother's faces and folded her tattooed arms over her apron. "Huh. Did squash night take an unexpected turn?"

"It did," Mrs. Hakelbarend said through clenched teeth. "I could stand a pot of coffee in the study, Honora, if you're not busy." She glanced down at Meddy. "Oh, and you should know we have a guest."

Meddy huffed. "Fine." She turned toward Honora, and as before, when she'd shown herself to the members of the Thief Knot, there was nothing to indicate she'd done anything. Only Honora's reaction told Marzana that Meddy had made herself visible.

Or really, Honora's nonreaction. The steward merely tilted her head, muttered, "Well, that's a rum thing if a thing ever was," and vanished into the kitchen.

Meddy humphed again. Then she glanced back at Marzana and her mother. "I'll find somewhere else to be." She disappeared down the hall toward the parlor.

Mrs. Hakelbarend looked at Marzana. "Let's go have a talk."

Marzana sighed and followed her mother up the stairs.

In the study, Mrs. Hakelbarend dropped tiredly onto the chaise longue and rubbed her hands fiercely over her eyes. Marzana sat tentatively on the edge of the chair opposite the chaise and waited for the inevitable. "Am I grounded?" she asked at last.

Her mother looked up. "Have I ever grounded you?"

"No."

"Do I *need* to ground you?"

"No," Marzana repeated quickly.

"Good, because I don't think I have the bandwidth right now. But I'd like to know what the hell you three thought you were doing." She paused, shook a finger. "Not three. Because obviously Ciro was in on it too, hence the cell phone, and Nialla, because you two are the Bobbsey Twins. Who else? Am I missing anyone?"

"I have no idea who the Bobbsey Twins are," Marzana said, attempting dignity. "And yes, there was one other person. Emilia Cabot. She's in the Commorancy at Marymead." She watched her mother's face. "I think you maybe knew her dad."

Mrs. Hakelbarend nodded. "Alex Cabot's kid. That makes a kind of sense. Does she know everything too?"

"Pretty much."

"Okay. What is that, six of you? Good grief." She rubbed her eyes again. "I repeat: What the hell did you think you were doing?"

Marzana crossed her arms and raised her shoulders. "Same thing you were. Trying to help." Mrs. Hakelbarend made an exasperated noise. "Nothing ever happens here, Mom!" Marzana protested. "And you and Dad with your deniability thing—"

Her mother interrupted in a deadly tone. "Excuse me. I know you're not about to suggest that you got up to whatever you got up to because I didn't cut you in on a job, Marzana." She erupted into a short burst of laughter. "That's almost funny."

Marzana watched her mother warily. This was some weird conversational territory. Was she in trouble or not?

But her mother composed herself in a heartbeat, and when she spoke, it was in that very dangerous tone again. "I'm waiting."

Definitely trouble.

"I guess . . . well, I thought you and Dad weren't really focusing on whether Peony was in the Liberty or not. You were just focused on tracking down Emmett's suspects. So I thought maybe it wouldn't be bad if I looked at it from that side—if someone did bring her in, how they could have done it. And I figured maybe the Belowground. So I called Milo—"

"Ah. That's where Meddy came into it."

"Yes. I was looking for a way to get in touch with his friend who's the Belowground conductor. I never did manage to get hold of him." Marzana paused as her mother shook her head in disbelief, then plowed on, feeling a bit defensive now. That *had* been a good idea, even if she hadn't managed to follow it up. "But we had another lead. Mrs. Agravin didn't come in on Tuesday, and we got a substitute teacher whose usual school is Watermill. The one where Peony went."

Mrs. Hakelbarend sat up straighter. "Really."

"Yes. And then Meddy found out that Mrs. Agravin hadn't actually contacted the school about her absence herself, and that they hadn't been able to get hold of her. So we decided we'd just . . . check on her. And we did . . . and there she was — Peony, I mean — and there you were."

"And that's all?" Mrs. Hakelbarend prompted.

Marzana sighed and spilled. "Well, Nialla thought there might be a message hidden in the ransom note — or a message the ransom note points to — but she hasn't found one yet. Ciro's granddad designed a bunch of Belowground stops, and there might actually be a private one in Marymead. And there's a whole thing with Cormorants that we hadn't totally figured out."

"Cormorants?" Her mother leaned forward, interested. "Where'd you come across that name?"

"Everywhere," Marzana exploded. "The Marymead station — if there is one — was designed by Ezra Cormorant, who married one of the Cotgraves. His picture's up with the trustee portraits at school, along with a handful of others."

"Yes, I've seen those," her mother said. "I know the Cormorants are still trustees. But what did Ezra and the station have to do with Peony?"

"Nothing, maybe. But we noticed Ezra's name on the station blueprints because we'd seen a different Cormorant name. *Victor* Cormorant."

Mrs. Hakelbarend gave her a hard look. "You'd *seen* his name, or you heard it mentioned here at home?"

Marzana couldn't restrain herself. After all, the knot had figured this connection out fair and square, and if there was any justice, her mother would have to be just a little bit impressed. "You never said it," she pointed out. "Neither did Emmett—not when I was in the room, anyway. You used . . . his other moniker. We found Victor Cormorant's name in the substitute teacher's employee file." She decided not to mention she'd also seen it in her parents' notes.

"And you put the two names together how?"

"I looked up *snakebird* in a birding book, and the entry mentioned cormorants," Marzana said, raising her chin. One corner of her mother's mouth twitched upward, grudgingly impressed. "Emilia saw the entry and realized she knew they were the same person, I guess from her dad's work."

"All right, go back to the file. What was Cormorant's name doing in it?"

"He recommended the substitute personally, the one who's been filling in for Mrs. Agravin. Meddy says that according to the teachers, Victor was in the offices when someone called to say Mrs. A. wasn't coming in, and he recommended Mr. Otterwill there and then. And Mr. Otterwill told us—Nialla and me—that it was his great-uncle who'd gotten him the job. They're related."

"Well, that is fascinating," Mrs. Hakelbarend said, folding her arms and leaning back into her chair. "Because Victor's how your father and I wound up at Mrs. Agravin's house. Your dad had been watching the flat since late last night."

So her mother had reached out to him after all. Only the night before, Mrs. Hakelbarend had still been talking about reaching out to his granddaughter instead. And somehow he was the reason they'd wound up at Mrs. Agravin's? What was the connection there? Weirdest of all, they'd been watching the apartment *last night?* They'd left Peony in there, alone and afraid, *all night?* "Mom," Marzana asked in disbelief, "what were you waiting for?"

Her mother raised an eyebrow. "You mean when you went in like a total Leroy?"

"I — what's a Leroy?"

Her mother waved a hand. "We had a guy on the crew of the *Lancet* named Leroy. He'd just go running headlong in, whatever the situation." She paused as Honora came in with a tray bearing two pots and two mugs, along with cream and sugar. "Liked to quote Horatio Nelson and Jack Aubrey at us — 'Never mind maneuvers, just go straight at 'em' — but really I think he just had this romantic idea about how pirates ought to be."

"Leroy Jenkins," Honora muttered, pouring coffee from the bigger pot, then cider from the smaller.

"You weren't pirates, though," Marzana protested.

"Try telling that to Leroy," Honora said. "Will there be anything else, Captain?"

"Not at the moment, thank you." Honora saluted and left. "But you were asking about why we hadn't gone in after Peony yet," her mother continued as she doctored her coffee. "The answer is . . . well, there are two answers. The first is, we hadn't seen any truly suspicious activity in the house. We were watching to see if anyone came or went."

"You were just going to leave her in there?" Marzana demanded. "Alone and scared, just in case someone showed up you could capture?"

"Well, no—remember, we didn't think anyone would have risked bringing the actual hostage to the Liberty. We had no idea she was there at all. Your dad and I were watching for one of the conspirators. And by the way, there was another reason we decided watching and waiting was the best course of action: We felt that something was off. It was too easy, finding our way to that building."

"Too easy?" Marzana couldn't help but feel a little insulted. After all, she and the Knot had followed leads to the same place, and she'd been fairly proud of the information they'd tracked down to get there.

"You asked." Her mother smiled a little. "I don't know how to explain it, except that it felt like someone had left a trail of crumbs. Some of them false—we think Rob Gandreider was one of those—and some of them, like the Snakebird—Victor—moving us more directly to the next crumb. To move us to the next screen. Except . . ." She shrugged. "Except then, there was Peony in Mrs. Agravin's flat. So apparently I'm wrong. And you, my girl, were right. 'A rum thing if a thing ever was,' to quote Honora." Her face went severe again. "Don't think that means I'm not still furious. But the kid's on her way home, and that's what matters."

"Are you going to be able to find out who did it, though?"

Mrs. Hakelbarend shook her head. "Not me. Liberty police forensics will do their job. Your dad and I will talk to Emmett and his friend and give them everything we have. And everything you have, if you please. Holding nothing back."

Marzana nodded. "I promise."

Downstairs, the front doorbell buzzed. Her mother groaned. "That'll be Nick. I hope to God he's here because he got an update from your dad and not because he's got one of Emmett's suspects in tow. I don't think I have it in me to deal with anything else tonight."

She sighed and stretched. "Anyway, maybe they'll find the goons who took Peony; maybe they won't. But she's safe, and I'll just have to decide to be okay with my weird feelings about the whole thing."

She didn't sound like she'd totally made up her mind about that, though. Marzana couldn't blame her.

Honora's feet pounded up the stairs. Her face, when it appeared in the doorway, was pale. "Begging your pardon, Captain, but there's someone here to see you."

"Not Nick, then," Marzana's mother said.

"No, ma'am." Honora cleared her throat. "The gentleman downstairs asked me to give you this. Says he's sorry to visit so late. Didn't sound sorry, though," she added in an undertone as she passed Mrs. Hakelbarend a white calling card.

There was no name on the little rectangle, just a single silhouette in matte black that was heraldic in its simplicity: a bird with its wings stretched and upraised, fanlike, on either side of its long, serpentine neck.

"Speak of the devil," Marzana's mother murmured.

The Snakebird had come to call.

twenty
THE SNAKEBIRD

BOTH MARZANA AND HONORA watched Mrs. Hakelbarend as she looked thoughtfully down at the card. "He's actually downstairs?" she asked. "Alone?"

"Well," Honora said, "never having met the gentleman before, I assume it's himself. And no one with him, no."

"Show him into the living room." Marzana's mother stood and slipped the card into her pocket. "Tell him I'll be down in five minutes. Say I'm putting my daughter to bed."

"Mom," Marzana protested, "come on!"

"Thank you, Honora," Mrs. Hakelbarend said pointedly.

"Aye, aye." Honora tapped her knuckles to her forehead, and a moment later her feet went drumming down again.

Mrs. Hakelbarend turned to Marzana. "What else? Quickly."

"Come on," Marzana wheedled. "I can be useful. Let me come down."

"What *else?*" her mother repeated, patiently but urgently. "I don't have time to argue with you. What else about the Cormorants? The substitute teacher, anyplace else you saw Victor's name, anything you can think of?"

Marzana resisted the urge to stomp her foot. "The substitute's name is Brian Otterwill. He taught at Peony's school, probably knew her from Comics Club, probably was on the faculty of the camp — you know, the one with the party she was taken from that got its first week canceled. He's staying with Victor. I can't think of anything else."

"Got it." Her mother headed for the door, then paused. She glanced over Marzana's head to the fireplace. "I presume you know how to listen in on the living room from in here." Marzana, startled, began to sputter a denial. "Do it," Mrs. Hakelbarend interrupted. "Pay attention, see if there's anything that strikes you. If there's a question I need to ask and I don't ask it, if there's anything you remember that you think I need to know before he leaves, write it down and ring for Honora." She pointed to an old bellpull by the door, one of the remnants of Hedgelock Court's fancy-house days. "Understood?"

Marzana managed a nod, and her mother stalked out of the study. Not quite believing her luck, she went over to the fireplace and crouched beside the grate. She would've snooped anyway, of course, but being invited to listen in felt like a big step away from the exclusion of deniability.

Except it's not, a tiny voice of reason muttered silently in her brain. *Your mom isn't confident she had time to hear everything you know, and she can't risk missing an opportunity. As soon as this conversation's over, you'll be shut out again.*

I don't care, Marzana retorted silently. *It's a step, and for now —*

Her mother's voice in the living room below interrupted her thoughts. "Victor."

"Barbara."

The Snakebird's voice was surprising. Marzana would have expected the voice of this master intelligencer and possible master evildoer to be either deep, unctuous, and probably British-accented, like a Bond villain, or, considering he was old enough to have a great-nephew of Mr. Otterwill's age, old and brittle and venomous. It was neither. Victor Cormorant said Marzana's mother's name in an almost youthful tenor voice, and in tones that perfectly telegraphed a whole world of information: the fact that he knew Barbara wasn't her real name, that he knew perfectly well what her real name was, and that he always felt a bit silly using this false one, but what could you do, the niceties had to be observed, even if it was all a bit ridiculous, considering who he was.

So much information in a single word. So polite, and so condescending. Marzana felt herself stiffening with offense on her mom's behalf.

If Mrs. Hakelbarend was insulted, she didn't let her own voice hint at it, though Marzana was certain her mother had heard every degree of the very subtle shade Cormorant had thrown into his pronunciation of her name. "To what do I owe the personal visit?" she asked politely.

"I hear the kidnapping victim was recovered tonight. Congratulations."

"Thank you. Yes, she was."

"And she's well?"

"She seemed to be, yes, though I didn't get to speak to her much. Presumably she's on her way home by now."

"Good." With the niceties out of the way, the visitor didn't beat around the bush. "I would like to know why someone saw fit to ask the young lady if she had heard her kidnappers use my name."

"Your name," Mrs. Hakelbarend repeated, and Marzana clapped a hand over her own mouth to keep from cursing. Why hadn't it occurred to her to tell her mother she'd asked Peony that? Once the girl finally started answering questions, of course she would have mentioned to the police that she had been asked about someone named Victor Cormorant. And if the Snakebird was really the master carrier everyone said he was, he'd certainly have contacts in law enforcement. The only surprising thing was how quickly his network had reported back.

Meanwhile, Marzana's mom had barely broken stride for a second. "Why *wouldn't* they have asked her that? I told you when I called last night that your name had been mentioned by the man who reached out to *me,* on account of the information used to blackmail the officer at the jail. Anytime anyone has unlikely information in this town, someone assumes it came from the Snakebird."

"Except from what I hear"—and here again, his tone spoke volumes. *This is not merely what I have heard,* that tone said. *This is what I know.* — "the girl was not asked whether she'd heard *the Snakebird* mentioned. She was asked if she'd heard the name *Victor Cormorant.* Furthermore, it was not one of the police officers who put the question to her. It was your daughter."

Marzana thought she might vomit.

For a moment, nothing but silence filtered up through the fireplace grate. Then her mother spoke again, her voice steady as ever. "My daughter went to that apartment because it was her teacher's home: the teacher your great-nephew Brian has been subbing for over the past four days, because *you* recommended him. The scuttlebutt among the students at Marymead is that there was something not-quite-right about the teacher's absence, and my daughter's not stupid. Now," Mrs. Hakelbarend said, and there was a hint of a smile in the word, "if you're asking me how a handful of students knew that the substitute teacher had been hired on your recommendation . . . Well, as a trustee and, I presume, a very rich man, I imagine you could arrange to upgrade the locks on the school's filing cabinets."

"Fair enough," Cormorant said with a chuckle. "And I'm not a trustee, but I'll pass the suggestion on to Tasha."

"Oh, that's right," Mrs. Hakelbarend said. "I forgot Tasha is the Cotgrave trustee at Marymead these days." A very slight pause, then, "Speaking of Tasha—you know, I tried to get hold of her before I called you. I thought since this was a downhill crime and downhill is more her territory, she might have some insights. Used a couple emergency channels, in fact, but no luck. How's she doing these days?"

"Fine, I believe," Cormorant replied smoothly. "Next time I hear from her, I'll remind her that to keep . . . *luminaries* such as yourself waiting is, perhaps, bad for business." Another momentary silence, then, "On the subject of business, Violet, there is something I feel I need to say before I leave this room."

There was no condescension in the way he said her name this time. It took Marzana a full three seconds to realize with open-mouthed shock that Victor Cormorant had used her mother's true one.

"Go ahead," Mrs. Hakelbarend said evenly.

"My business is information," he said carefully, "and I have spent my lifetime cultivating sources and methods. It's rare that I find myself surprised by the effects—the outcomes—of my work. I am, I suppose, not surprised that my *nom de guerre* came up during fact-finding discussions downhill. I was, however, shocked that it would have come up in connection to this matter in any other way.

If it happened as you say, because I put Brian's name forward for a meaningless job, then . . ." His voice trailed off, and Marzana imagined Cormorant shrugging, the gesture as eloquent as his cultured voice. "But if it didn't . . ."

"I think I understand," Marzana's mom's voice said after a moment.

"Thank you."

"No need," Mrs. Hakelbarend replied briskly. "Can I do anything else for you?"

"Not a thing." They were both speaking farther from the fireplace now and closer to the door. Apparently the strange interview was over. "Anyhow, I know where to find you if anything else comes up."

Marzana shuddered a little. His voice was less distinct now as they moved out of the living room, but it was impossible not to read the hint of a threat in those words. She crouched there for another moment or two, listening, with her back against the brick and her knees drawn up to her chest. Then she scrambled to her feet and nearly broke her neck as she leaped out of the fireplace and tripped over the rug on her way to the window across the study, the one that overlooked Crossynge Lane.

Because the turret projected a short way out over the street and blocked any view of the front door, there was nothing to see for a moment. Then a man appeared on the street below. He was tall and unbent; like his voice, his posture was surprisingly youthful. He wore a pale linen suit and carried a walking stick in one hand. The other held a straw Panama hat, and he turned to glance back at Hedgelock Court as he put the hat on. Marzana slipped instinctively behind a curtain as his eyes turned upward toward the study window, as if he knew he'd spot someone there.

"That man's what my father would've called a real piece of work," Mrs. Hakelbarend's voice said from behind her, tiredly.

Marzana turned and blew out a deep breath. "I'm sorry, Mom. I did ask Peony that. I completely forgot."

Mrs. Hakelbarend waved a hand. She dropped back onto the chaise and collapsed against the high back. "You gave me what I needed to explain it. I gather Peony's answer was no, by the way?"

Marzana started to nod, then shook her head. "She wouldn't answer at all. Not that question or any other one I asked."

"And you heard everything just now? Anything new occur to you?"

"No, except you never told me what he said that sent you to Mrs. Agravin's apartment in the first place." Marzana sat in the other big chair, remembered she'd just been crouching in the fireplace, jumped up and brushed herself off, then sat again. "It sounded like he didn't actually know she'd gone missing after the first day."

"It did sound that way, didn't it?" Mrs. Hakelbarend ran her fingers over her scalp, which made her hair pop out of her braid in oddball lumps. "He might not have. He didn't point us to the apartment."

"He pointed you to the station?"

"Yes, but indirectly. I called him to inquire about the blackmail evidence Emmett had wanted to ask him about. He said he knew nothing about that, but suggested we talk to another information specialist who happened to be in the Liberty: one of Emmett's suspects, Hickson Blount, who he said had been holed up in Whipping Hyde. But Cormorant said we ought to hurry, because Hickson might be about to leave the Liberty again. Now, I doubt Blount's aware the Belowground still runs, but he probably knows where the old stations are, and we thought he might try to take one of the tunnels out of town.

So your dad went out to the Cop-Bone Alley station last night to see whether it looked like anyone had been in or out of it recently. When he got there, it was evident that the apartment above was occupied, and by someone who wasn't answering the bell. He called me, we decided to do a little watching and waiting, and you know the rest."

Footsteps on the stairs: not Honora this time, so probably Marzana's dad was home. It was always a bit of a wonder to Marzana that his footfalls were so much quieter than the steward's stomping treads. He came in, walked straight to the TV cabinet, and found the remote. Then he turned and gestured with it at the window. "Did I just pass who I think I passed out in the lane?"

"In fact, yes," Mrs. Hakelbarend replied. "Tell you about it in a minute. You're back earlier than I expected."

He dropped heavily onto the end of the chaise. "Wasn't much to do. Peony didn't want to talk, and then of course once her parents got there, they just wanted to get her straight home." He snapped his fingers, as if remembering something. "Marzana, the detective in charge wants to know, was that rope the only restraint holding Peony? There weren't, say, zip ties or anything sturdier?"

Marzana shook her head. "Just the rope."

"You're sure?"

"Positive," Marzana insisted. "I cut her loose myself."

"She'd have had some significant marks where she was tied if the kidnappers had used plastic, wouldn't she?" Mrs. Hakelbarend asked, frowning.

"She would have, and she didn't," Marzana's dad replied. "The marks were consistent with the rope from the scene. I think the cops just wanted to make sure. There's something so old-fashioned about using rope. And risky, particularly on someone with such small hands and feet. Kids are natural escapists."

He gave his daughter a dark look, and Marzana mentally girded herself for a second round of potentially catching hell. Just because the first round hadn't materialized didn't mean she was in the clear. But instead, Mr. Hakelbarend turned on the TV and focused his attention there. "Handful of reporters showed up."

Mrs. Hakelbarend's eyes narrowed. "Reporters?" Marzana's dad nodded as he changed channels. Her mom leaned back, arms folded again, and stared upward. "Well, that's odd as a three-legged duck."

"Yep."

"Why?" Marzana asked.

Her father cracked a grim, unamused smile. "Ah. Questions from the auxiliary team." Marzana flushed. "It's odd because the only way they'd have known to show up was if someone had called them and convinced them there was something newsworthy to report. Remember that the kidnapping hasn't been made public. Hadn't," he corrected himself, turning back to the TV and changing stations until the screen showed a coiffed woman in a suit standing in front of a window piled with yarn that Marzana recognized as belonging to a shop just down the road from Ottomy Stalls. "People in the Liberty guard their privacy, and they tend to err on the side of respecting other people's privacy. Yet somehow a TV station and two newspapers had representatives turn up within fifteen minutes of the cops. Basically right after you left." Mr. Hakelbarend turned the sound down low. "One of the neighbors could have rung up a newstip hotline — must have — but what made them think that anything worth reporting on was happening? A couple kids walking through the front door? Two adults going in after them? Oh. Which reminds me." He reached into his back pocket and tossed a small object to Marzana.

Miraculously, she caught it one-handed, though she almost lost some cider in the process. It was a deck of playing cards with gleaming black-and-gold backs, bound with a rubber band.

"Thought your marksman friend might like to have those back," Marzana's father said. "They look expensive. Anyway, if Mrs. Agravin had been some kind of recluse, maybe four strangers going into her flat would've been odd enough to make a neighbor call the *police*. Maybe, but I kind of doubt it — and in fact, nobody else *did* call the police; just you. But no way does four strangers going into an apartment immediately make anyone call the *press*, particularly if they didn't bother to call the cops first."

"So then it must've been the police showing up that made somebody call the hotline," Marzana guessed.

He shook his head again. "A cop car pulling up outside with a siren on usually gets people to come out for a closer look. But call the papers? Not a chance. And even if someone did call the media, the caller would've had to convince them that whatever was happening was worth reporting. And yet the press turned up within minutes of Peony being found. So either a suspicious neighbor started contacting newspapers right about when you went in the door and very rapidly convinced the press that something crazy was happening, or a person who had real knowledge of the actual incident was behind the calls."

Another rum thing, apparently. "Did any of the reporters have anything to say about it?" Marzana's mom asked.

"I heard one tell the lieutenant her newsroom got a 'vague but compelling anonymous tip.'" He frowned at the image on the TV. "That's not the Liberty."

The scene on the screen had shifted, and now a different reporter stood in front of the kind of house that Marzana had never seen in Gammerbund: a private home that was a single freestanding structure with an actual lawn of its own and crowded only by gnarled trees. And, at the moment, a lot of people: some kind of press conference was taking place. An overwrought man in his forties stood next to an equally emotional woman as she spoke into one of the dozen microphones pointed at her face.

"Those are the Hydes," Mrs. Hakelbarend said. "Coles and his people got Peony and her folks home fast."

"I bet his security detail cleared the roads between here and the Printer's Quarter," Mr. Hakelbarend said, eyes on the screen as he turned up the volume.

". . . difficult for all of us," the ashen Mrs. Hyde was saying. "We've decided to take some time away. As a f—as a family. We ask you to respect our privacy. P-Peony's privacy."

A dozen voices shouted Mr. Hyde's name. "Mr. Hyde, can you tell us," the most persistent shouted, "whether this means you're withdrawing from the mayoral race?"

Winston Hyde nodded, his face paper-white. "Yes. I'm withdrawing to spend time with . . . so that we can be together as a family, as Mariah said." He reached for his wife's hand. "We'll be leaving Nagspeake tomorrow. My campaign will make a formal announcement tonight. Thank you. That's all we have to say until then."

Several of the reporters went on shouting; a couple asking where they were going, one or two asking where Peony was and if they would be allowed to speak to her, and one loudly demanding to know who, if anyone, Winston Hyde would endorse now that he was no longer in the running. But the Hydes' security men were on the move, shepherding them toward their home and shoving reporters out of the way when they didn't move fast enough.

"Well," Mr. Hakelbarend said, killing the sound and tossing the remote on the ottoman, "I guess that's that."

"I guess so," replied Mrs. Hakelbarend.

Both comments rang a bit hollow to Marzana's ears, but she couldn't quite put her finger on the precise sentiment there. Was it annoyance? Dissatisfaction?

Over on the big table-desk, the phone rang. Mr. Hakelbarend crossed the room and picked up the receiver. "Hakelbarends." He was silent for a moment. "Tomorrow's fine. See you at eleven thirty." He hung up. "Syebuck," he said in answer to Mrs. Hakelbarend's questioning glance. "Debrief, or whatever you want to call it." He glanced toward the window. "What about Cormorant? What's your read on the situation? Was he in play?"

Marzana's mother made a face. "Honestly? This is crazy, but I truly think he was in play to the same extent that Rob was."

Mr. Hakelbarend frowned dubiously. "Never mind all the coincidences that would require — you honestly think Victor Cormorant, the Snakebird, lets himself get used as a pawn? *Ever?*"

"It's entirely likely he's never been a pawn in his entire life," Mrs. Hakelbarend acknowledged. "But I also think it's just possible there's a first time for everything, and this was his. I think he came here because he found out — and don't get me started speculating on how this happened so fast, but he found out his name got dropped when we found the girl, and he wanted to tell me specifically he wasn't behind it." She shook her head in wonder. "He came to our house himself, Peter, and with no muscle behind him. I think he was spooked."

Marzana's dad's face was a mask of disbelief. "Wow," he said, rubbing his chin. "I don't know how to process that."

His wife nodded. She stared at the flickering screen for a moment more, her elbows on her knees. "I really wish they'd all been wrong," she muttered. "I hoped." Then she got up and left the room.

Marzana's father watched her go. "Wrong about what?" Marzana asked quietly.

"Wrong about the kidnappers having come to the Liberty," Mr. Hakelbarend said, his eyes on the empty doorway. Then he glanced at Marzana. "Please don't ever pull a stunt like that again."

It felt as if her stomach had been drop-kicked by someone in steel-toed shoes. She swallowed. "Okay."

Mr. Hakelbarend gave her a long look. "You have no idea how far wrong that could have gone, have you?"

"I—"

"No," he snapped. "Stop and really think about it. Think about all the different ways that could have gone belly-up. How people could've been hurt. Do me the courtesy of taking at least sixty seconds and reflecting on how close you came to real trouble." He got to his feet. "I need to eat something."

Nialla called half an hour later.

The phone rang only once. Marzana, sitting in the window nook in her bedroom, looked up sharply. A moment later, Mrs. Hakelbarend's voice barked from the study, where she and Marzana's dad had gone with their coffee. "Marzana, Nialla's on the phone. Make it quick."

"Okay!" Marzana darted across the room. Neither she nor Nialla said anything until they heard the click of the study extension being hung up. Then, "How are you?" Nialla asked breathlessly. "Are you grounded?"

"Nope. You?"

"No. Well, I haven't precisely told my parents anything yet."

"What?"

"Mars, what would I have told them? That you got me a copy of a note and I cut up a book? All that would've done is maybe get you deeper in trouble. If your mom calls mine, I'll deal with it then." Pause. "She's probably going to call my mom, huh?"

"I don't know. She and Dad seem pretty preoccupied." Marzana chewed on the edge of her sleeve. "Have you talked to Emilia? What about the guys?" It occurred to her that, as the nominal leader of the Thief Knot, it probably should've been her job to call around to everyone, update them and make sure they were okay. "I should've done that, huh?"

Nialla made a sympathetic noise. "Don't worry about it. J.J. called me after he got home, and I figured you were catching hell, so I called Emilia."

"And J.J. talked to Ciro?"

"Yeah." Nialla paused again. "I don't think Ciro's mom will ground him, either. He loaned you a phone so you'd be safer, and you used it to call the police when things didn't seem right. How is that irresponsible?"

Put like that, it sounded perfectly reasonable, but Marzana was pretty certain none of the adults in question were going to frame what had happened in precisely that way.

"Not sure about J.J.'s folks, though," Nialla continued dubiously. "They're a little overprotective. And I never actually spoke to Emilia. She didn't answer the phone in her room, so I called the other number she gave us, the one for the common room, and I left a message with a Commorancy Kid named Hester. But *she* said she hadn't seen Emilia since dinner. She didn't sound like she thought that was particularly strange, though. I guess they're used to each other going on walkabout in the school. I can try her again later if you want."

"I should probably do it."

"Why don't you delegate it to me?" Nialla suggested. "I have nothing else to do."

"All right."

"Are we still on for tomorrow?"

That was a good question. "Yes," Marzana said after a moment's thought. "Even if all we do is debrief. Mom had an interesting visitor just after we got home . . . I guess you and Ciro didn't find any hidden messages, did you?"

Nialla's voice soured. "He doesn't think there is one."

"Well, I guess it doesn't matter now," Marzana said, trying to be comforting.

"I guess not. Whatever. See you tomorrow, Mars."

Marzana hung up the phone and walked over to the window corner. She sat and pulled her knees up to her chest. As she stared out at her view of a sliver of the Liberty of Gammerbund, glittering as it always did in the darkness, her eyes began to slide out of focus and a reflection that wasn't her own shivered into visibility.

"Are you okay?" Meddy asked.

Marzana shrugged. "I don't know."

Meddy sat cross-legged at her side and held out Marzana's pink shoelace. "Show me how to tie our knot."

Marzana took the string. "As efforts to cheer up a person go, this is pretty transparent. Also I'm pretty sure you know more knots than I do."

"Do it anyway." Meddy leaned back against the window. "It's what I've got at the moment."

twenty-one
SHELL GAMES

BY THE TIME Marzana got up on Saturday morning, her parents had already left for the city proper. Since she hadn't officially been grounded, she and Meddy trudged to the bookstore to meet with the other members of the Knot at ten as planned.

"Assuming the rest of them haven't had their social privileges revoked," she muttered to Meddy as they walked down the Viaduct stairs. "Incoming."

Meddy, walking half a pace behind as she busily tied and untied grief knots in one of Marzana's pink shoelaces, looked up just in time to sidestep a little girl heading in the opposite direction. "Meh. I think you guys are all missing a key point."

"And I think you are forgetting what it's like to have parents capable of yelling at you," Marzana retorted.

"I most certainly am not," Meddy snapped. She paused to tug the ends of her knot, unraveling it. "Well, maybe a little. But the key point is this: You didn't actually do anything wrong, you know."

"Apart from sneaking into my parents' stuff and making copies," Marzana said. "And eavesdropping. And lying, sort of. If I'm being honest."

"Okay, yes, apart from all that. But seriously. We all sat around thinking about stuff. Asking questions. Trying to make sense of things that didn't make sense. And in the end, what did we do? We went to check on an old lady who might possibly have been sick or hurt, and we found someone who needed help."

"In the course of which, we maybe did a little breaking and entering," Marzana pointed out.

"Okay, sure. But in general, I think you could categorize all the questionable stuff as bad choices rather than anything actually dangerous."

It was like talking to Nialla the night before. It all sounded so reasonable. And yet. "No adult in the world is going to see it that way."

"Maybe not. Quit beating yourself up, though. We found someone who was missing. That's a good thing."

Marzana said nothing, and after a moment, Meddy took the hint and turned her attention back to the shoelace.

I named us after a structurally unsound knot that's almost totally useless, Marzana thought bitterly. *I got caught up in the sneakiness and forgot to think about what it — what we — might actually be good for, which is next to nothing except to be not quite as good as the real thing.*

"Hey, you," Lucky said as Marzana and Meddy slipped inside the bookstore a few minutes after ten. "Expecting the study group today?"

For the second time, Marzana tensed, waiting for Lucky to recognize Meddy as the ghost girl dressed in the outlandish hat and robe from Greenglass House, but they appeared to be past that. As far as the bookseller was concerned, this was just a member of Marzana's crowd. "Yeah. You haven't seen anybody else yet, have you?"

Lucky shook her head. "You two are the first. I'll send the rest up when they get here."

Meddy decamped for a look at Lucky's role-playing-game books until the others showed up, leaving Marzana to hike up to the empty mezzanine alone. She dropped her backpack on the floor, sat in the chair at the end of the empty table, and looked down its length. What was she going to say to everyone?

The bells downstairs chimed, followed by Lucky's chipper hello. A moment later, Ciro trotted up the stairs, his backpack over one shoulder and an unopened soda in his hand. His face was . . . weird. His face was *happy*. It was *cheerful*. It was maybe even triumphant.

"What the heck are you looking so grim for?" he demanded. "Did you get grounded or something?"

"No, I didn't get grounded," Marzana said, exasperated. "My parents are furious, but—what the heck do you look so pleased for?"

"Are you kidding?" He dropped his bag and sat next to her. "What are you talking about? We did it." Ciro frowned. "Marzana. *We did it.* You see that, right? You assembled us to find this girl, and we did it. Yes, we might get in trouble, but honestly, I don't care about that. *We found a girl who'd been kidnapped.* My mom is . . . my mom had a thing or two to say, but look: Even she, in the end, only had one real gripe, which is that we didn't call in the adults sooner. She sure as anything didn't object to my giving you the phone."

Nialla had said it, Meddy had said it, and now Ciro. Why couldn't she let herself see things their way? "Maybe your parents aren't walking around looking at you like you're persona non grata, but mine are."

"Is that really the problem?" He looked at her for such a long moment that, in addition to her mounting frustration at having gotten this lecture twice already, Marzana felt herself start to blush. "How is this not how you imagined the situation might go?" he asked finally. "If we succeeded, our parents were always going to find out."

"I didn't really imagine how it would go if we succeeded," Marzana admitted. "Not after finding her." Maybe that was part of the problem: Even with her undeniable expertise in imagining a million different eventualities, Marzana hadn't imagined how her parents might react. And then, suddenly, she realized something else. "I don't know if I ever imagined we'd actually find her. I thought my parents would, long before we got anywhere close ourselves."

The day Marzana had told her about the kidnapping, Nialla had asked if the investigation Marzana was proposing was a game or not. Emilia had asked the same thing. *Of course it isn't a game,* she'd said. *Of course it's real,* she'd insisted. And yet she herself had neither imagined the most obvious outcome—that her parents would be furious—nor accepted the reality that, if the point had really been finding Peony Hyde, then getting in trouble shouldn't have mattered.

I've been treating it like a game all along.

Ciro smiled, and Marzana had the unsettling idea that he'd seen and understood every thought she'd just worked her way through. "Say it," he suggested. "We did it."

"Shut up," she muttered.

"You should try saying it. Feels good, man." He grinned. "We did it?"

"All right, all right, knock it off. Let's talk about something else. I guess you didn't find a code in the ransom note after all, huh?"

Ciro growled a little under his breath. "Not a code, but then it was never going to be that." He popped open the soda can and took a big sip. "Code's when things stand in for other words or phrases or ideas or whatever. It wasn't going to be a cipher, either—that's where you've done substitutions at the level of individual letters or numbers. *Number one* stands for *A*. *A* stands for *C*. That kind of thing. In codes and ciphers, you hide the meaning of a message using some kind of key, which you also need if you want to get the meaning out again, but the fact of there being a message is generally pretty obvious. Peony couldn't have done anything like that, first because she didn't have control over what words or phrases she had to work with, and second, because if it was obvious she was trying to send a message, the kidnappers would never have used that particular note." He rolled the can thoughtfully between his palms. "If this is anything, it's steganography: the whole fact of the message being there is hidden. But even then, how could she have hidden a message using words and a word order she couldn't choose?"

"But she had control over where she cut them from, right?"

"Yeah, that was the basis of Nialla's idea, but . . ." His voice trailed off, dissatisfied.

"You don't think there's a message to be made from the words underneath?"

He sighed. "I mean, we tried." He dug a piece of paper out of his backpack and handed it to her: NEXT AVENUE, COLD WIND CAN'T FLIES (FLY) UNDER MY AVENUE, BLUE AVENUE, COLD WIND AVENUE, UNLIKELY AVENUE, MY HOST (IS) A(N) UNLIKELY (SOMETHING), MY HOST FLIES UNDER A BLUE AVENUE.

"There are a few interesting words that seemed to have some promise," Ciro continued, looking over her shoulder and pointing. "*Avenue, host, under, unlikely, blue* . . . but it just all feels so random. We don't know if we should be trying to use all the words—I say no, but in that case, how do we know which words are important?" He stared down at the paper in disgust. "If there's a way to put these words into a message, I can't find it. I tried, Nialla tried, but nothing here makes sense, especially now that we know the message, if there is one, ought to point somehow to where you actually found her. And even if we were to hit on a version that *does* make a little sense, I'm not sure that means anything. Because this whole *idea* doesn't make sense to me."

"You don't have the key," Marzana said sympathetically. "And neither would anyone else who read the note."

"No, that's just it—we do have the key. I mean, Nialla's thought, obviously, is that the key is the book itself—the comic Peony cut the words from. Except that's not true—if Nialla's actually right, the message isn't in the ransom note at all, it's in the *book*, which means the *ransom note* is the key. But there's absolutely no way Peony could count on anyone identifying the book as the source of her message in the first place. So it's the other way around—they'd have the key but not the message, and no way to know a message even existed."

"But they *did* identify the book," Marzana argued. "And pretty much right away."

"I don't know." Ciro shook his head. "I mean, I'm accustomed to looking for what's hidden. I know that a lot of times what you think you see isn't all that's really there. But sometimes it *is* all that's there. Sometimes things are exactly what they seem to be." He leaned on the table, propping himself up on his elbows. "Nialla saw the note and immediately started thinking of *Quester's Crossroads*. I think she likes the idea that, even if it's not obvious right away, there's meaning to be found if you know how to look for it. And I like that idea too. But wanting a thing to have meaning doesn't mean it does."

He hesitated. "And I think maybe she hopes this is her thing to contribute. She wants there to be a message only she can find. I think . . . it's kind of personal for her, believing in this theory. J.J. has tricks,

Emilia's sneaky, Meddy's an amazingly useful wingman and also has all this institutional knowledge about the world the kidnappers exist in. Everybody has a 'thing' but Nialla." He made an apologetic face. "I don't know if you should tell her I said that. I could be wrong, but either way, I think it'll hurt her feelings."

It didn't escape Marzana that he hadn't mentioned any particular "thing" that was her own specialty; but then again, he hadn't bothered to mention his, either. Maybe he took their respective contributions as givens: Hidden things, and . . . leadership, maybe? She passed his notes back. "Wish I'd thought to ask her. Peony, I mean. Not that she was forthcoming about the stuff I did ask her about."

"I wish you'd asked her too. And if she had said there *was* a message hidden there, I would've loved to know how the heck she did it. Or who on earth she thought might come to her rescue, because literally no one but Nialla Giddis could have imagined the possibility." Downstairs the bells jingled again, and first J.J., then Nialla called hello to Lucky. Ciro refolded the page hurriedly and stuck it back in his backpack. "Don't tell her I said that, either."

Nialla and J.J. came up together. "I made cookies," Nialla announced, taking a foil-wrapped package from her bag. "I know some of us are feeling a bit conflicted, but I do think we have some things to celebrate."

Meddy rejoined them five minutes later. By ten fifteen, all but two of the oatmeal cookies had been eaten — those had been set aside on a napkin for Emilia, who had yet to arrive — and J.J. was attempting to entertain everyone with fancy card techniques, using the black-and-gold deck Marzana had returned to him.

"Did you ever manage to get hold of her last night?" Marzana asked Nialla as J.J. performed his sixth faro, working on restoring his deck to its original order with eight consecutive perfect shuffles.

Nialla nodded, then shook her head. "Got through to a different kid. He thought she'd gone to bed, because her door was shut and the lights were off. He said he'd leave a message for me, though. So she knows we're meeting this morning."

At ten thirty, they were still waiting for Emilia.

At ten forty, Marzana paused in pacing by the poetry shelves and glanced at her watch. "Let's give her five more minutes; then we'll call." Something was nagging at her. It wasn't Emilia's absence, though that was certainly distracting, and having to think about it was definitely making it harder to figure out what was really needling her subconscious.

J.J. got out his black velvet magic bag. He put away the cards and produced the walnut shells and some new peas. "You want to try this again?" he asked, rattling them in his palm at Meddy.

Meddy sat in the chair at the opposite end of the table from Marzana, her knees drawn up to her chest and her feet on the seat. "Sure. You first."

J.J. scowled. "There's this saying, Meddy."

"A magician never reveals his secrets? Yeah, yeah."

"No, genius, a different saying. Once is a trick, twice is a lesson."

Meddy grinned. "You worried I'm going to figure out all the hocus-pocus?"

J.J. considered. "Not really." He waved her around to join Nialla, who was lying on the bench across the table from him. Then he laid the shells out on the tabletop and set a pea in front of them. He gave Meddy an admonishing finger wag. "Don't eat it this time."

"You ate a magic pea?" Nialla inquired as she rose and scooted over to make room.

Meddy held up a pair of fingers. "Two. Fun fact: They're—and this is probably a trade secret, so keep it under your hat — not real peas."

"Well, duh, they're *magic* peas," Nialla said with a flourish in her voice. "Think you're going to grow a beanstalk in your gut now or something?"

"I mean, yeah, obviously, but I'm not getting my hopes up."

J.J. cleared his throat. "When you two are quite done." He popped the pea underneath the middle shell. "Let's do some of that fancy shell-switching you did yesterday, Meddy." Instead of simply moving shells back and forth, he switched the left and the middle, then the middle and the right, then the left and the right. "Okay, shoot."

"I see what you did there," Meddy said, frowning in concentration. "Same trick, but different pattern and different speed from yesterday."

"The pattern doesn't matter," J.J. replied. "Neither does the speed."

"You're not going to tell me the hand is quicker than the eye?" Meddy said, staring down at the shells.

"Wow, you do have a whole stock of magic clichés, don't you? No, the hand isn't quicker than the eye. Your eye just can't make sense of what it's looking at. Here's a fun fact for you: We're less likely to notice what we don't expect. Even if we actually see it. Pick."

Meddy tapped the shell on the right. And just as he had back at Mrs. Agravin's, J.J. lifted it to reveal nothing whatsoever. Then he lifted the one in the center to reveal the pea.

Meddy shook her head. "Honestly, I should just pick the one I think it's definitely *not* under, shouldn't I?"

"Try it." He moved the shells around again, faster this time, occasionally flashing a glimpse of the green pea under this one or that. After the second time he switched up the walnuts' positions, Meddy tilted her face to the ceiling. J.J. whistled as the shells stilled under his fingers. "Check you out. Don't even have to look."

"Doesn't help to look, does it?" Meddy challenged.

"Fair enough. Which is it?"

"Center again," the ghost girl hazarded, her eyes still on the ceiling. J.J. lifted the shell. Nothing. "Let me guess," she said. "Nothing."

J.J. shrugged. "Hey, what did you expect? You didn't watch."

"I thought blind guessing might actually be the better strategy."

"But it's not strategy," Nialla argued. "Even if the pea had been there, he'd have vanished it before he showed you, right, J.J.?"

He made a face. "As if I'd ever engage in such shenanigans in an honest shell game." Then he grinned. "Just kidding. There's no such thing as an honest shell game."

"You mean there's no way to guess right, even if you guess right?" Meddy demanded. "This is baloney."

"No, it's not. You have the wrong idea about what it is," J.J. said patiently. "It's not a guessing game. It's not a *game.* You can win a game, even if the odds are against you. But this is a *hustle,* and if you're the mark in a hustle, all you can do is lose. The whole thing is based on the idea that that's the only acceptable outcome."

He set the walnuts aside. Meanwhile, Ciro, who'd been leaning against one of the philosophy shelves, came over to Marzana. "Want me to try calling her?"

Marzana nodded. "If you don't mind." The nagging something was rapidly taking over every bit of her mental capacity.

Ciro reached into his pocket, then hesitated. "What's up?"

"I'm not sure."

"Worried about Emilia?"

"No. Or not really. That's not what's bothering me." Marzana suspected that Emilia, more than any of them, could take care of herself. If she wasn't there, it was because she had chosen not to be. Most likely she had found her way past the paintings in the Library and was somewhere down in the Belowground tunnels. *Okay, maybe I should be concerned about that,* Marzana thought briefly. And yet she couldn't really imagine Emilia Cabot ever getting lost, anywhere. No, this was something else. "I don't know. I can't quite work out what it is that's bugging me."

Ciro made a sympathetic face. "Is it your parents?"

Parents. "What do you mean?" Marzana asked.

"Just guessing—you clearly hate that you disappointed them somehow."

"Oh." She considered. That wasn't it. And yet . . . But no. Then she looked sharply at him. "You know . . . I think it started bugging me around the time you and I were talking about the ransom note, but I just can't . . ." She shook her head. "Never mind. Call Emilia. Lucky will let you use the store phone, I bet."

"Nah. Emilia was supposed to be here and she's not. I'm calling this an emergency, even if it's just a potential, minor one." Ciro wandered away, pulling the phone from his pocket.

At the table, J.J. took out a stack of nested silver cups and a trio of red balls. "Try this one. Similar, but not quite the same. Plus, the things to keep track of are bigger, so it has to be easier, right?"

He set the three cups in a line before Meddy and Nialla, then balanced a red ball on top of each. "This trick goes back to ancient Roman magicians. Their name for it was *acetabula et calculi.*" He lifted the ball from the cup on the right, tossed it into the air, and made it vanish as he caught it. Then he picked up the right-hand cup and revealed the ball underneath. "Goes like this."

J.J. moved the red balls around, vanishing them with elegant flourishes from under individual cups, from between stacked cups, from his palms and pockets and from midair, then lifting this or that cup again to reveal one, two, even all three balls. A single red ball placed under the center one became two balls, or all three. Red balls became green balls. Then bigger balls. Then a ball-shaped chapstick that had somehow come straight from Nialla's pocket. Then a small oval piece of plastic that turned out to be a two-stage pencil sharpener.

And all the time, the cups and the balls and whatever else turned out to be secretly in play moved in a configuration that was at once simpler than it seemed it should be and more complex than it looked, because, of course, as J.J. had explained, it wasn't the *look* of the thing that mattered. The pattern-that-wasn't-a-pattern was almost soothing. J.J.'s motions, his patter, it all had a rhythm. Rhythm with a purpose.

A purpose. The idea lodged like a splinter in her brain, and Marzana was so occupied with it, she almost missed Ciro straightening and waving, the phone to his ear. *I've got her,* he mouthed. Then he took the phone to the farthest corner of the mezzanine and began speaking in low tones.

"Be right there," Marzana replied, and he lifted a hand to show he'd heard. "He's got Emilia on the phone," Marzana reported to the others, who'd looked up from the table. "She's okay." They were all quiet for a moment, listening, but Ciro had stopped talking and there was nothing to overhear.

Meanwhile, the splinter that was the idea of *a purpose* was jabbing the same spot in her brain as the splinters that were *something to do with my parents* and *something to do with the ransom-note message.* And then, as her eye passed over the knotted shoelace Meddy had set aside so she could watch J.J.'s trick, another splinter jammed itself into the same nerve: *something about a knot.*

She forced herself to separate the four thoughts and try to examine them one at a time. What was it about her parents? Marzana paced to the window that overlooked Hellbent Street and watched the people passing below.

We felt that something was off, her mother had said. *It was too easy, finding our way to that building. . . . I don't know how to explain it, except that it felt like someone had left a trail of crumbs. Some of them false — we think Rob Gandreider was one of those — and some of them . . . moving us more directly to the next crumb.*

Her parents had spotted something, a pattern or a pattern-that-wasn't-quite-a-pattern, in the mishmash of clues that had led them to Peony. Or no, they hadn't *spotted* it, but they had certainly *sensed* it. What had it been, that thing they sensed but had not been able to articulate?

A few feet away, Ciro was quietly bringing Emilia up to speed on the events of the previous night. Marzana frowned. Something he'd said. What had it been?

The key is the book itself — the comic she cut the words from. Except Ciro had said that was wrong, backwards. So why could she not get that line out of her mind?

At the table, J.J. dropped the pencil sharpener into his backpack and took two of the cups away. "Let's try something simpler while we're waiting." He put a red ball on the top of the remaining cup. "Watch the ball. If you can tell me where it is, I'll buy you a pizza."

Meddy lifted an eyebrow. "I don't eat."

"You drive a hard bargain," J.J. said, plucking the ball from the cup. "Fine." He tossed the ball into the air. Impossibly, it appeared to vanish right when it left his fingers. "If you can tell me where it is now, I'll not only buy you a pizza, I'll eat it for you too. And I'll even give you a hint." He lifted the cup and showed the empty space beneath.

But Meddy had seen something. Her eyes glittered. "It is," she pronounced, "in your left hoodie pocket."

J.J.'s face fell. He came around the table and held out the edge of his pocket, offering it to Nialla. "Here. She won't believe me if I do it."

Nialla reached triumphantly into his pocket, frowned, and pulled out a big handful of nothing.

"Huh," J.J. said. "Weird." He reached back across the table and lifted the cup. There beneath it, smooshed into a roughly spherical lump, was the foil that had previously held Nialla's cookies.

Meddy snatched the foil. "Son of a — okay, but where's the ball, Houdini?"

J.J. coughed mildly, took the foil lump from her, and began to slowly pick it apart. At last he peeled open the middle of the crumpled foil. There, against all logic, was the red ball.

"Really?" Meddy protested. She grabbed the ball and the sheet of foil and turned both over in her hands. Then she took the cup and had a good look at that, too.

"Well, yeah." J.J. sat on the tabletop with his feet on the bench and watched her examine the props. "They're not gimmicked," he said helpfully. "They're perfectly normal."

Meddy tossed the ball into the cup and dropped it onto the table in disgust.

Ciro stepped up next to Marzana at the window and held out the phone. "She's fine. I told her what I know."

Marzana took the phone and put it to her ear. "Hey. Where are you?"

"Back at Marymead," Emilia's voice reported. "Sorry I'm not there. I found the Belowground station in the Library. I sort of lost track of time. But it's all still there, Mars. That station's totally intact. I found a map of the whole system, and I guess we're kind of done with the whole kidnapping-investigation thing, but I really think you need to see it. It's amazing. I had no idea. I think you should bring everybody here. Come in by that back route I showed you, the one that runs under the Orangery."

"Emilia—"

But the other girl went on talking right over her. "Remember that thing in *Sidledywry*, after the main lair blows up in the first book, and then later Casie—or maybe she's Nell at that point—finds the passage through the subbasement and discovers there was a whole lair within the lair? It's like that. I'm not kidding."

And then, out of nowhere, the memory of a girl's voice drowned out Emilia's uncharacteristically excited speech: *I'm up to the fifth book. I had forgotten about Casie.*

Suddenly Marzana felt certain she almost had it, that thing fluttering just out of reach, the splinter poking at her brain, the pattern her senses could almost pick out of all the noise . . .

Back at the magic show at the table, Meddy was still fuming. J.J. patted her shoulder. "You think you just have to outguess me, but really I have five ways of making you lose. More. This is just like the shell game. There is literally no way for you to win. Half the time the ball was never even on the table to begin with."

The ball was never on the table to begin with.

The key is the book itself.

Marzana grabbed the nearest shelf with her free hand to keep from losing her balance. "Marzana?"

"Hang on, Emilia. I just had an idea. Or the beginning of one.

Here's Ciro again." She shoved the phone at him and turned away, rubbing her head and thinking.

The book: You couldn't read *The Sidledywry Knot* and forget about Casie. You could maybe forget about her original name; even Nialla had done that, and that's what she'd thought Peony had meant when she'd been confused about Marzana's reference to Casie. But what Peony had really said, now that she thought about it, was *The main character is different in the later books.* Not that she was *called* something different. Peony had spoken as if she didn't actually *know* that Casie and Nell were the same person, which is a mistake you could make fairly easily if, for instance, you'd read only the most recent book. But according to Emmett Syebuck, Peony Hyde had been a big enough fan of the series for even her parents to be aware that she was in the middle of the most recent volume. Peony Hyde wouldn't have made that mistake. Couldn't have.

Following this realization, other voices, from other memories, began to speak.

We're less likely to notice what we don't expect. Even if we actually see it.

He'll see a reef knot because that's what he's expecting . . . even if the knot falls apart under his fingers like a reef knot never would.

"J.J.," Marzana interrupted. "Say that again, what you just said."

The magician looked up. "The thing about the ball?"

"You said a lot of the time the ball isn't even on the table."

"Right. Well, sure. The magician always has control of the ball or pea or whatever, but it's almost never where the audience thinks it is for more than a fraction of a second. I just make you think it is to get you to chase three empty shells around for a while. I make you look where I want you to look and see what I want you to see. The audience looks where the magician looks. Meanwhile, the pea is somewhere else, until I need to bring it back for the sake of the illusion." He grinned at Meddy and Nialla. "And here's the mark of how good this trick is: Even now that you kind of know how I'm doing it, you're still going to think you know where the pea is. And you're still going to be wrong every flipping time."

Marzana sat down at the end of the table as J.J. began to move the cups around again, proving his point. "Chase three empty shells," she repeated softly.

Shell number one: Rob Gandreider, set loose and told to lie low until the right day by someone who knew he'd run straight for his home in the Liberty.

Shell number two: Mr. Otterwill, conveniently maneuvered into a substitute-teaching gig in the Liberty only a day after one of his pupils went missing.

Shell number three: Mrs. Agravin, whose unexplained absence made room for Mr. Otterwill, and who just happened to live above a Belowground Transit station.

And then there were Emmett Syebuck and the Snakebird. Emmett, who had come to ask for help from Marzana's parents on the assumption that a criminal on the run would go straight for the safe ground of Gammerbund, and with those three shells already set into motion to make it look as if Peony, the pea, must be somewhere in the Liberty. Never mind that, as both Marzana's parents had pointed out at the time, it was almost unthinkable that anyone could smuggle an unwilling captive into the Liberty without someone knowing about it. Only the Belowground even made it look possible. But *possible* didn't mean it was definite. And the Snakebird, whose true name kept popping up in unexpected places; and who had been one more signpost pointing to the Belowground and, specifically, had pointed her parents toward the station in Whipping Hyde.

And suddenly all the other little pieces came together: Peony not knowing the real identity of the main character of her favorite series. The fact that the kidnappers had gone to the trouble to lure Mrs. Agravin away for nearly a week but hadn't bothered to construct an explanation for the full duration of her absence, which was guaranteed to eventually lead someone directly to the apartment where they'd hidden the missing girl. The fact that the specific lure they'd used was a cruise that ended before the ransom deadline, and yet they'd left Peony there to be found. If no one else managed to find the missing girl first, they'd practically scheduled Mrs. Agravin to come back and discover her tied to a chair in the middle of her living room, and they'd even arranged for the press to already be on their way when she did.

Even the fact that Peony—during the hot second she'd been sitting up straight—had looked taller and older than just eleven years. Kids came in all sizes and shapes, but when you combined that with everything else . . .

Abruptly the final splinter fell away. *The knot.*

Up in Mrs. Agravin's flat, a single rope had been used to secure the girl's wrists and ankles to the chair. One rope with a single knot, rather than four plastic ties or any other more secure system. A knot whose loose ends had been hanging right between Peony's palms when Marzana had found her; a knot that, now that she thought back on it, Peony had been fidgeting with on the sofa. The knot had been undone by the time J.J. had handed the rope over to Mrs. Hakelbarend. Would it have meant something to the police if they'd been able to see it?

"Oh, my God." Marzana leaped to her feet, glanced around, grabbed Ciro. "Sit down. Can you put Emilia on speaker or something? Everybody listen. Ciro, can you just keep an ear out for any-one coming up the steps?"

Ciro obeyed with a questioning look, placing the phone in the middle of the table, then positioning himself between the table and the stairs to the lower floor. "All clear."

"Listen," Marzana said breathlessly. "It's a *shell game.* The whole thing is a shell game. Mom was right: Something was off. But more than just off: This isn't over. Not yet."

They all stared at her. "What are you talking about?" Emilia asked, her voice crackly as it came through the cell phone's speaker. "How is it not over, other than wrapping up loose ends? You found Peony. You were there. Your *mother* was there. You found her, you talked to her—"

"Yeah, I did, and I should've known then." She told them about the momentary confusion Peony had displayed when Marzana had referenced the book she was supposedly reading. "I should've seen it, but I didn't." Marzana glanced ruefully at J.J. "And there was the rope tying her to the chair. I cut her loose, so the knot was still there, and *she picked it apart* while we were watching J.J. do the shells and peas with Meddy. But if she'd been tied up with the kind of knot you could pick apart without even paying attention, I wouldn't have had to cut the rope in the first place—I could just have untied it. Heck, if the knot was that easy, why was she even still tied up when we got there? That knot would've meant something to the police; I think it would've told them that she could've tied *herself* to that chair without any assistance from anyone else." Marzana shook her head violently. "It's like you said about your magic trick, J.J. I didn't notice it because I wasn't expecting it, even though I *saw* it. This was—*is*—a shell game."

J.J. swore. He got it, of course, because it was all a matter of misdirection. "Not a shell game," he said slowly. "It's the cups and balls. It's not just that the thing you're looking for isn't there: I let you see me putting something underneath one, I move things around . . . and *something totally different* comes out in the reveal."

Ciro clapped a hand to his mouth. "Oh." He got it too. Of course he did. Because this was all a bit of dazzle: a bit of flashy confusion to make one thing seem to be true when the reality was something else entirely, just like the dazzle his great-great-grandfather the camoufleur had painted on warships to confuse the enemy.

"It's a Hickham's Fluctuation," Meddy said quietly. "Level One Prestidigitator's exploit."

"Oh," Nialla said, her eyes popping wide. "Oh, no."

Marzana nodded. "You see it."

"*I* don't," Emilia protested. *Crackle-crackle* went the speaker. "'Something different comes out . . .'?" She made a frustrated noise. "I can just picture you guys passing significant looks around and knowing what Marzana's talking about, and I'm stuck here and I have no idea. Spell it out for me, somebody. I'm going out of my mind."

Marzana leaned over the phone on the table. "It wasn't Peony. The girl we supposedly rescued — it wasn't her. It was someone else. *Peony was never there.*"

twenty-two
COTGRAVE WALL

THE WORDS LANDED like a handful of dropped rocks.

"But how could it be someone else?" J.J. protested. "Her parents—we saw her parents on TV last night, didn't we? They would have known! They would have known the second they saw her! An impostor could have fooled us, but not them." Marzana's folder full of notes was still on the table where it had lain, forgotten, since the beginning of the meeting. J.J. grabbed it and took out the school picture of the ponytailed girl. "And this was her. *This* was the girl we saw. I'm sure of it."

"Yes, yes, I know, but . . ." Marzana got up and paced a few steps. "Just let me think a minute." She was right about this. She *knew* she was right. "Could Peony's parents have been in on it?" She pointed to the photo. "They'd have been the ones who supplied that to the police. It's just a picture of a girl in front of a plain background. It would've been easy to fake."

"Could her parents have been the kidnappers?" Emilia asked. "Maybe they needed the cash for whatever reason, and Mr. Hyde couldn't figure out how to just embezzle the campaign money on his own."

Marzana shook her head, thinking back to the man and woman she'd seen on the news the night before. "I don't think so. When I saw them on T.V., it seemed like they were just so relieved, they could barely keep it together — you know, too many feelings." She frowned for a moment, picturing Mrs. Hyde's ashen skin. Her husband's paper-white face. "Now I'm wondering if it wasn't relief, but just that they were barely able to keep the pretense up. I think what I saw was fear, and I think it was real. They were terrified. For whatever reason, they had to pretend their daughter had been returned when she hadn't been. It was an intense bit of acting, and they weren't sure they were selling it. Not to mention, if we're right, their daughter's still missing."

A strange, stunned silence settled over the assembled Thief Knot, broken only by a hiss of a sigh from Emilia on the phone.

"Okay," Nialla said. "Say it wasn't Peony you found, and for some reason her parents pretended it was. Why? What possible reason could there be for them to pretend their kidnapped daughter had been returned when she hadn't?"

Emilia's voice spoke up. "If they're not the kidnappers themselves? Maybe they were told they had to pretend it was her in order to get Real Peony back. But that suggests they knew about the fake Peony in advance."

"And what about Fake Peony?" Nialla persisted. "If you're right and the girl in Mrs. Agravin's apartment wasn't Peony, who is she? How did she get involved in this? I refuse to believe any kid would go along with a plan that involved kidnapping another kid."

"I don't think she was a kid at all," Marzana said. "She slouched the whole time to make herself look shorter. Even then, I remember thinking she looked older than eleven, but I ignored it, because it wasn't what I was expecting. She's an accomplice. That's why she wouldn't tell me anything at all when I tried to ask her questions about the people who had taken her."

Ciro spun his empty soda can on the table. "If we're right, and if the Hydes knew in advance this was going to happen—that a fake Peony would surface—then there must be a whole separate set of demands the kidnappers made for getting the real girl back. And two of those demands must've been: When the cops ask for a picture, hand over this photo of Fake Peony, and when Fake Peony shows up in person, pretend it's Real Peony."

"In which case, it was maybe never about money at all," Marzana put in. "I remember asking my mom and dad that first night whether this was really about the ransom. It seemed so weird, since the Hydes could never have raised that much in less than a week, and the whole city apparently knew it. But it makes sense if the ransom note we saw was just a front for the cops."

"Except Real Peony *did* make the ransom note," Nialla said eagerly. "We know that, right? They found her fingerprints all over it, and they matched them to prints at her school, *not* to prints provided by her parents. And no matter how much she picked up about what was really going on, from her perspective that note was real, in the sense that it was a real message going from the kidnappers to the world." She started digging through her bag, then paused to point an accusing finger at Ciro. "I *knew* we gave up on the idea of a message too fast!"

"We didn't give up on it," Ciro protested. "We stopped because Peony seemed to have been found. We can start looking again. Or maybe . . ."

"Maybe," Meddy repeated. Silence fell over the table, and one by one, the other members of the Knot looked at Marzana.

"What?" Emilia barked over the speaker, sounding totally exasperated. "I can sense the group glances happening and I'm feeling really, *really* left out."

"The adults," Nialla said. She looked up from the phone. "Your call, Marzana. We all agreed: You decide when we loop in the adults. We should tell your mom and dad, right?"

"Can I say something?" Emilia asked. "Before you call them, you should come to Marymead. Let me show you what I found. When Ciro told me the game was up, I thought it was just going to be something cool to show you. But now I'm thinking it might be more than that. If you're right, then this isn't just about the kidnapping, is it? The kidnapping is part of a bigger crime — it's about whatever the real ransom demands are, the ones we haven't seen. And if *I'm* right, you might be able to give your parents a really important clue. Come see this first."

Marzana hesitated. If there was any truth to this new hypothesis, then Real Peony was still out there, and probably they should quit messing around and call in the adults fast. But if there was an additional clue she could give her mom and dad when she made that call, then waiting just a bit longer might be worth it. "Emilia, what the heck did you find?" she asked.

"I'm not totally sure. I need to show you. Will you guys come?"

"To your school?" J.J. asked dubiously.

"Yes, to our school, where, if you recall, there's a secret, private Belowground station, which I spent all night exploring while you were sleeping, J.J.," Emilia said waspishly. "Get over here, will you? There's still a girl missing. And who's got the book of maps? Does it have a big foldout map of the whole city in it? One we can pull out?"

"I have it," J.J. said, reaching for his backpack. "I'll check." He dug out the gazetteer and riffled through it until he came to a removable folded insert. "Yeah, it does."

"Good. Bring the whole thing. I'll meet you in the courtyard in thirty minutes," Emilia said. "I'll make sure Mr. Sopwith is out of the way and the coast is clear. Marzana, Nialla, you remember the way, right?"

Westing Alley to the fire escape, through the glass museum, down to the basement, along the canal, under the Orangery, out through the shed. "Yes," Marzana said. "But what about all the locks?"

"The doors you'll use at Five Westing are always unlocked, and so is its canal door. I'll unlock the Marymead-side ones for you, and I'll prop our canal door open so you can't miss it. Then I'm taking a power nap. See you in half an hour on the dot." Emilia hung up.

Marzana punched the "end call" button on the phone and passed it to Ciro. "Well. Suddenly the day got a lot more exciting than I was expecting it to."

As they left Surroyal Books and Marzana led the Knot across Hellbent Street toward Westing Alley and the helical fire escape, three separate conversations were happening among them. J.J. and Meddy were talking magic. Nialla and Ciro were talking steganography. And then there was the imagined conversation happening in Marzana's head as she ran over the possible responses from her mother and father when they found out that she had so completely disregarded their instructions to butt out that she'd immediately reassembled her merry band to dive right back in. Would having new information, *real* information, mitigate their likely fury at all?

"Where, exactly, are we going?" Ciro asked as Marzana stopped under the fire escape.

"Up." Marzana reached for the bottom rung of the low-hanging ladder and started hauling herself up.

"Is this legal?" J.J. asked, offering his cupped hands as a boost for Nialla, who was the shortest of the group.

"It's at least intended to be used this way," Nialla said, huffing slightly as she got her feet onto the rung. "You'll see."

They ascended one after the other: Marzana, Nialla, J.J., and Ciro, with Meddy bringing up the rear. Marzana counted four floors, then stopped and peered through the window beside the fire escape. Inside, angled rays of sunlight picked out assorted bits of glowing colored glassware. "This is us," she announced. There was a single brass handle screwed into the outside of the window frame, and Marzana pulled it upward. "Careful as you climb in. Everything here's breakable."

She slipped inside, followed by Nialla. The two of them watched with satisfaction as first J.J. and then Ciro entered the kitchen. "Whoa," Ciro muttered as he swung his legs over the sill and looked from a shelf on the wall to his right, full of blue and green and purple siphons and labeled SELTZER BOTTLES OF BROOKLYN, to an elaborate setup of spiraling glass tubes and round-bellied beakers on the counter to his left. "Is this a kitchen or a lab? Whose apartment is this?" Then he gripped his stomach and keeled over as Meddy, who had been behind Ciro patiently waiting to enter the room, got fed up and stepped through him.

"Excuse me," she said, reaching down a hand to help him up.

Marzana grinned and waved a hand at their surroundings. "This is no mere apartment. Ciro, J.J., welcome to Boneash and Sodalime's Glass Museum and Radioactive Teashop. Come on."

In the main room, teacups and a plate of thick slices of lemon-iced cake had been laid out for five. Ciro looked around, confused. "Where is everybody? This place feels . . . empty. You know, apart from us." He glanced toward an arch leading to a hallway the girls hadn't explored on either of their previous visits, but that probably led to more displays of glass in what had once been bedrooms and bathrooms. "Somebody there?" he called.

Nobody answered. The boys looked down at the tea table, thoroughly confused. The girls shared a grin, thoroughly entertained.

"It's a mystery," Marzana said, remembering Emilia's non-explanation the first time they'd come through this room. She glanced at her watch. "But we have a date with Emilia. Grab a piece of cake and let's go."

Out into the hallway, then down the stairs: down and down and down, until there was nowhere to go but through the creaky metal door and into the basement. "Flashlights," Nialla announced, reaching into her bag. Marzana did the same, thankful she hadn't unpacked the little kit she'd put together on Thursday.

"I didn't bring a flashlight," J.J. whispered to Ciro.

"Me either," Ciro muttered back. "Note to self: From now on, always have flashlight."

The girls had to search the basement a bit before finding their way to the room full of washers and dryers, but only for a minute or so. The door leading to the dry canal was unlocked, just as it had been before, and one by one, the members of the Thief Knot dropped down onto 5 Westing's listing old pier.

"I just want to say," Ciro said as they started the walk to Marymead's private dock, "that I vote for the next action of the Thief

Knot — after this whole kidnapping is resolved — to be coming back here to explore. Like, how far does this tunnel go?"

"Emilia says it runs all the way under the street above it," Marzana said, squinting to read the remnants of the address on a door in the tunnel wall to her left that stood partly ajar. She was pretty sure it was too soon for them to be at Marymead, but it was better to be safe than sorry. "I don't know how far Eald Brucan Lane goes, though." *I open doors, I look through windows, I explore alleys and hallways, I assume every staircase has something interesting if I follow it up or down.* This wasn't going to be their only adventure, not if Marzana could help it. She smiled over her shoulder at Ciro. "Yeah. We should definitely explore more, as soon as we can."

The Marymead entrance was impossible to miss. Emilia had not only propped the door open with a piece of rusted pipe; she had tacked a handwritten note on loose-leaf paper to one of the pier's pilings: WELCOME TO MARYMEAD, NERDS. — E.

Marzana waited while the others followed Nialla and her light through the door and down the steps toward the waterworks, then took down the note, kicked the pipe aside, and shut the door.

"This is the plumbing under our school's greenhouse," Nialla was saying as Marzana caught up to them in the humid and perfumed dark below the Orangery. Far ahead, the flashlight beams found the ladder bolted to the wall. "And that leads up into a shed in the courtyard. That's where Emilia will be waiting."

"Speaking of which, I'm going to go ahead and see if she's there yet," Meddy said, and then she was gone.

Marzana trailed behind the others, content to let Nialla lead the way while she tried to guess at how the hidden Cotgrave Wall Station might have given Emilia a clue to the bigger mystery behind Peony Hyde's disappearance. There were too many threads that led, however tenuously, to the Cormorants. Emmett's three initial suspects and Mrs. Agravin and Mr. Otterwill all might have been cups and balls, manipulated by the unseen hand of a magician — and if her mother believed Victor Cormorant had been manipulated just like the rest of them, then Marzana was inclined to believe that was true too. But she was having a hard time seeing all those Cormorant threads as so many dead ends and nothing more.

As they got closer, Meddy's torso appeared on the ladder: upside down, as if she were leaning into the tunnel from above. The others hurried forward. "Is she there?" Marzana asked.

The ghost girl nodded. "Right outside. Hang on." She disappeared again, and a moment later the hatch in the shed floor opened and a thick shaft of greenish light plunged down. "Come on up."

When everyone was safely above, Marzana shut the hatch and stowed her flashlight. Meddy vanished through the wall and out into the courtyard; then, after the tiniest of pauses, the shed door swung open and Emilia peered inside. "Come on out, knotty companions. Quick, quick." She swung the door shut after them, dropped to one knee, and relocked the shed with tools she'd been holding at the ready. She stood, acknowledged the boys' impressed expressions with a brief bow, and picked up her satchel from the ground. "J.J., Ciro, welcome to Marymead."

"Holy cow, that was amazing," Ciro said, trying to keep the explosion of enthusiasm to a whisper and only barely managing it. "What's the tunnel? Who found the route? What the heck is up with that whole glass-museum thing?"

"The cake was warm," J.J. put in. "Oh, which reminds me." He reached into one pocket, took out a slightly squashed little slab of cake wrapped in a piece of paper towel they'd found in the museum kitchen, and offered it to Emilia. "Meddy didn't want hers. It was *warm!*" he repeated as Emilia took it. "Who makes the tea stuff? This is going to drive me crazy."

"I couldn't possibly say," Emilia replied. "It's a mystery."

"That's what *she* said," J.J. grumbled, casting a suspicious glance at Marzana.

"Marzana's smart," Emilia said airily. "That's why she's the boss." She took a bite of cake and waved a hand toward the gym doors. "Shall we?"

"Who's around that we might have to avoid?" Marzana asked as Emilia led them through the gym.

"If you're asking who's in the building other than Commorancy Kids, there are plenty," Emilia said, pausing to peek out into the locker passage and down the hallway in both directions. "Weekend cleaning crew; teachers; couple folks in the office; a couple resident adults, like the Commorancy nurse; and I think I saw the chess club arriving when I came downstairs. Fortunately, residents are allowed access to most of the school on weekends: the gym, the Library, the dining hall, all the community study areas . . ."

"Oh," Marzana said, surprised. "So we don't have to sneak?"

"Well, *un*fortunately, we're supposed to sign in visitors, which I don't propose to do, and I certainly don't want anyone following us down into the station. But don't worry, none of this is an issue." She whistled quietly.

At the end of the hallway near Marzana's own locker, a figure peered out from around the corner. A kid-sized figure, with floppy hair, holding a comic in one hand as if he'd been reading. He raised his other hand, made a fist, then made a knocking motion in the air with it.

"All clear," Emilia said. "Head for the west stairs. Try not to sound like a bunch of elephants. I'll be right behind you."

Marzana bit down several questions and led the way to the big square staircase at the west end of the entry hall, glancing at the floppy-haired boy as she passed. A Commorancy Kid, of course. Sixth-grader, she was pretty sure. His name was Monty or Murray or something. He saluted as she went by, and she saluted back. Emilia, bringing up the rear, paused to exchange a few words, then slapped him a high-five.

As they rounded the first turn in the staircase, Emilia jogged up to pass Marzana at the head of the column. When she reached the second floor, she motioned for the rest of them to hang back while she leaned around the corner. "We're clear all the way to the Library." She waved them forward. "Let's go."

Marzana followed her around the corner and jumped as she came face-to-face with the girl who must've been posted on the landing. Another sixth-grader. Ada? Allie? She grinned at Marzana, showing a mouthful of crooked teeth. "Twitchy, aren't you?"

"Just a little," Marzana admitted, a bit surprised to realize that she was. This was her own school, after all. If they got caught, what was the worst that could happen? Emilia would get a talking to for not signing them in? Still, there was no denying it: this was *exciting*. Really, properly exciting, and Marzana's nerves were abuzz. It was a feeling that seemed entirely out of place at school. "Er . . . thanks for your service," she muttered.

"Don't mention it," said Ada or Allie.

A red-headed kid sat right outside the main doors of the Library with a book on his lap. He scrambled to his feet and saluted to the Knot—to Emilia, really—as the group trouped past him.

Inside, two eighth-grade Commorancy Kids who'd been sitting at one of the long tables stood up: Barnaby, a dark-skinned boy with locs whom Marzana knew from history class, and a blond-mohawked girl called Enza whom she knew only by sight.

Marzana and the Knot followed Emilia to the table, where she slapped Enza's outstretched hand. "You realize you have cemented your own legend here, E," Enza said.

Emilia pointed to Ciro. "We have this guy to thank. His grandfather worked on the stations."

"We owe you, man." Barnaby shook Ciro's hand, then turned to Emilia. "We're all dying to get a chance to explore, but this is your show, Cabot. Stay safe. Two of us will be here on rotation until you come back."

"But if you're not back by lights-out, we're coming in after you," Enza added. She checked her watch. "It's eleven thirty now. That gives you ten and a half hours."

"Plenty," Emilia said. "We need to be back before these guys' folks start panicking, anyway."

Marzana looked up at the Library's gallery, with its paired sets of spiral stairs and intermittent heavy velvet drapes. Behind which of those curtains had Emilia found the station entrance? It wasn't immediately obvious how any of them could conceal much of anything. The wall to the east had the doors that led to the hallway and the art classroom beyond; there could be no unaccounted-for space behind the curtained paintings on that side. And the opposite wall was the west wall of the entire house. If there was any meaningful space concealed there, surely someone would have found it before now.

Emilia, meanwhile, turned to the red-haired kid who'd been standing guard at the Library door and who was now fidgeting nearby. "You have everything you need?" she asked him, looking severe. "Plenty of water, and ginger candy or licorice or whatever? We could be a long time."

"I'm ready," the boy said in a tone that suggested he was girding up for some kind of quest. "I was born ready. I'm your man. I—"

"Yeah, I get it," Emilia interrupted in a bored tone. "You'll have people here with you. But on the off chance that you find yourself alone and something goes wrong, you'll . . . ?"

"Find Barnaby or Enza," he recited. "Making sure to leave someone else at my post."

"Good. And if at any point at all you're getting tired, you're losing your voice, you have to pee, *tell* these guys you need somebody to give you a break. That's why they're here. There's no shame in asking for a break, but if you fall asleep on duty or can't keep on keeping on, the rest of the Commorancy will never let you forget it. Okay?"

"Okay," the kid replied, saluting again.

"Okey-doke." Emilia bumped fists with the two eighth-graders and turned to the Knot. "We're set. Let's go." She pointed to one of the curtained paintings on the gallery along the west wall. It was, in fact, the one beside the shelf from which Marzana had taken *Stanton's Aviary* the day before. "That's the one, right there."

"But how?" Marzana asked. "How is there room? That's the west wall of the house!"

"There's exactly enough room," Emilia muttered. "Just exactly enough."

"Hold off on that for a minute," Nialla interrupted. "Why would he potentially lose his voice?" Before Emilia could answer, the kid behind them began, in a scratchy, out-of-tune, self-conscious-but-fighting-to-power-through-it voice, to belt "We Wish You a Merry Christmas" at top volume.

"He does know it's June, right?" J.J. whispered.

"What he knows is that now that he's started singing, he can't stop until we get back," Emilia said as they crossed the Library floor.

"He's our canary for as long as we're in the station. As long as he's singing, we know the coast is clear here in the Library, and it's safe to come out again. If he's not singing when we want to come out, that means we stay hidden." She started up one of the circular stairs. "Sixth grade in the Commorancy is basically community service in the form of lookout duty." Then she stopped and felt for the bag at her side. "Crap. Hang on. Before I forget." She took out the leather folder the school historian had given her. "I brought this specifically to put it back. Not carrying it down there."

She edged past Marzana and hurried toward a shelf in the center of the south wall. "But Emilia," Marzana said, following her, "we're not actually going anywhere, are we? Why would we not come back for ten hours?"

Emilia waved a hand. "It's just a matter of safety. We're going into a space we don't know anything about. I'm fairly certain we won't get locked in, but if we do, we know we won't be stranded past ten p.m. Also," she added, crouching and shifting books to make room in the right spot for the leatherbound family tree, "it's taking a lot of restraint for the rest of the Commorancy to give us time with the station to ourselves. They're all dying to explore. So that was about fifty percent Enza and Barnaby promising to rescue us and about fifty percent Enza and Barnaby reminding me that after tonight, other people get a turn. Which is fair."

"Speaking of which, get *moving*," Enza ordered.

Barnaby dropped his head on the table. "You didn't say you had shelving to do first," he said indistinctly. "You could've given that to the canary to do."

"Two seconds," Emilia retorted.

"But the *suspense*," Enza complained.

Marzana folded her arms impatiently and eyed the trustee portrait above the bookcase as Emilia shoved the folder back into its place. Then Marzana's hands fell numbly to her sides as suddenly the Cormorant threads snapped into place, and all at once she could see the whole web.

She'd looked at this particular portrait a hundred times. It was one of the youngest of the assorted Cotgrave and Cormorant trustees, the dark-haired girl who seemed to be trying to look older than she was. The name engraved on the brass plaque at the bottom of the frame was Natasha Felice Cormorant.

Tasha.

How many times had she heard that name in the last week without really taking note of it?

Her mother, after Emmett had asked to be put in touch with the Snakebird: *Maybe I'll try his granddaughter Tasha, the one who runs the coffee shop down in Shantytown. I think I heard she's trying to make a name for herself. I've never met her . . .*

Victor Cormorant, after Mrs. Hakelbarend had suggested upgrading the locks at Marymead: *I'm not a trustee, but I'll pass the suggestion on to Tasha.*

And Marzana's mother again: *Speaking of Tasha—you know, I tried to get hold of her before I called you. I thought since this was a downhill crime and downhill is more her territory, she might have some insights. Used a couple emergency channels, in fact, but no luck. How's she doing these days?*

The recollections swirled in her brain, set to the singing kid's slightly off-key demands for figgy pudding.

"What is it?" Emilia asked. Then she followed Marzana's gaze and fell silent.

"That's Victor's granddaughter Tasha," Marzana said. "I heard my mother say she's trying to build her own reputation."

"As a carrier?"

"I think so. Mom was talking about reaching out to her for information. Tasha never returned the calls." She glanced at Emilia. "I've been trying to work out how Victor Cormorant could have been so involved in this without having been the one shifting the pieces around. But Tasha'd probably have access to pretty much all his information too, right?"

"Well, I don't have all my dad's information," Emilia said in an undertone. "You, either — but I guess we can't use ourselves for comparison." She considered. "I mean, it would seem the best way for him to invest in her career would be giving her access to what he knows, yeah. But do you really think that, in the course of using that access, she'd throw both her grandfather and her — what, her cousin, Otterwill would have to be? — under suspicion?" Emilia made a dubious face. "I can't see that."

Marzana considered. "She could afford to do that if she knew any suspicion would turn out to be all for nothing later. With the number of red herrings she put on the board, they'd just be two more. But a family member would probably be the only person who could manipulate the Snakebird himself."

"'Hey, Grandpa, Brian's going up to the Liberty for a couple days. Stop by Marymead and see if they've got work for him,'" Emilia said experimentally. "That kind of thing?"

"Right. And then of course Fake Peony would've told her I asked about Victor, which she, good, conscientious granddaughter that she is, would have reported to him right away, but probably as if she got it from a different source. That would explain how he found out about *that* so fast." Marzana thought back to her mother's comments after Cormorant's visit. "He knew he got played. He came to our house to try to convince my mom he hadn't been involved intentionally."

Emilia's eyes snapped wide. "He came to your *house?*"

Marzana rubbed her face. "Good grief, I didn't even get a chance to tell you that, so much has happened today."

"Hey, guys." Meddy trotted up to join them. "You've got folks waiting, in case you forgot." She glanced at the painting. "Oh, my God, another sourpuss." The glance became a double-take. "Guys?" Meddy said slowly. "Why is there a painting of Peony Hyde in your school?"

"What?" Marzana glanced from Meddy to the painting. "No, that's Victor Cormorant's granddaughter. We think—"

"J.J.!" Meddy called, darting back to the gallery stairs, where the other members of the Knot were trying and failing to look patient. She grabbed J.J.'s arm and dragged him over to the painting. Nialla and Ciro followed, and, with noises of exasperation, Enza and Barnaby stalked across the Library to join them as well.

Meddy shoved J.J. forward. "It's her, isn't it?"

"Her who?" J.J. asked, yanking his arm free.

"The girl we did magic for in Mrs. Agravin's apartment," Meddy said impatiently.

J.J. stared hard at the picture. "I don't see it," he said at last. "The Peony we met had braces; that girl on the wall's like twenty, and how long ago was that painted, anyway? She could be a million years old by now."

"She's not," Barnaby said. "That painting was only put up last year. She's a current trustee. Youngest ever. They made a big deal of it."

"She's Victor Cormorant's granddaughter," Marzana said again as she fumbled in her bag for the photo they'd been looking at earlier. Her heart thudded as her fingers found the picture and she held it up in the light. She felt the entire group lean in behind her to compare the face in the little photo with the one on the canvas.

Two girls. One with her dark hair coiled up on top of her head in fancy, old-fashioned whorls and the other with her dark hair parted into two long ponytails that hung over her shoulders. One wearing a red-and-gold brocade blazer and one wearing a T-shirt with a bunny on it. One with tortoiseshell glasses, one without; one with braces, one without. Or was it just one girl, a girl who had been trying hard to look older in the portrait and younger in the photo, and everything else was just costume?

"It could be the same girl," Marzana said hesitantly. "I wish she had a mole or a scar or something so we could be sure."

"We don't need one. She can change her hair and makeup and clothes and posture and stick braces on, but there's a lot she can't change." Ciro pointed at the photo. "Look at the shape of her face. Look at the shape of her ears, and her hairline and her nose." He tilted his head, his eyes flicking from one image to the other. "I didn't see her in person, but I'd bet all the Tootsie Rolls in town on that being the same girl. You said yourself you didn't think Fake Peony was a kid, Marzana. You said you thought at the time she seemed older than eleven."

"That's true." Marzana blew out a mouthful of air. "If you say it's the same girl, then I believe it." She remembered her mother's words again: *Speaking of Tasha — you know, I tried to get hold of her . . . Used a couple emergency channels, in fact, but with no luck. How's she doing these days?* Her mom might have sussed out the possibility that Tasha was involved somehow, but Marzana was absolutely certain *this* revelation would knock her parents flat.

The caroling sixth-grader took a deep breath and began singing "Happy Birthday" to someone named Mervin. Nialla spoke up. "So now what?"

That was the question. "Tasha's a carrier," Marzana said, tucking the picture back into her folder. "Emilia told us carriers sometimes package whole jobs. What if she put this caper together for someone? The fake kidnapping was part of it; now we just need to know who it was for and what the rest of the job is."

"Well, I can at least tell you something about the rest of the job." Emilia shooed them back toward the gallery stairs again. "Now we go."

"Finally," Barnaby grumbled.

The Thief Knot climbed the stairs in an awkward little train and crowded up onto the gallery. Emilia slid partway behind one of the velvet drapes, revealing the ornamentally carved gilt edge of a massive frame. "I advise you, in the words of Oz the Great and Powerful, to pay no attention to the man behind the curtain. He ain't pretty." She wedged a shoulder between the huge gold frame and the wall and wiggled in until only half of her body was visible. Marzana shivered as a soft gust of cool air slid along the floor, winding its way around her ankles like a damp, chilly cat.

The *click* that followed was deep and resonant, almost like a note played on a harp. Then, under the curtain, the frame moved sideways, like a sliding door. About a third of the hidden painting popped out from under the curtain. J.J., unable to stop himself, peeked around the hem at the rest of the picture, only to back away with a skeeved-out noise and his hands waving in a gesture of self-defense. Marzana, however, went straight for the other side of the curtain and stared into the rectangular hole that the painting had concealed. To either side of the void, the Library walls were a good two feet thick, and the velvet drapes were heavy and dark enough to block most of the room's light.

Emilia disappeared into the dark. "And Emilia said, *Let there be light!*" she intoned.

Nothing happened. In the momentary pause, the singing boy moved on to "Frère Jacques." Marzana and Nialla exchanged glances of mild concern and reached for their flashlights.

"Hang on, hang on," Emilia's voice replied. "I just hit the wrong button. *Voilà!*"

With a fizz and a flicker, the space behind the painting filled with a glow. A decidedly eerie glow. The light had an odd violet tone to it, and a translucent quality, as if already all the settled dust of the past decades was on the move again. And just as Marzana had suspected, there wasn't much back there for the violet light to illuminate. Beyond the thickness of the interrupted wall was a space about five feet deep with a wall of black brick on the far side and a tiled floor.

Emilia popped back into view and patted the satchel at her side. "Knowing that the rest of you had not anticipated this adventure, I skipped the nap — you're welcome — and took the liberty of provisioning our party while you were on your way here. Everybody in. I'll close the entrance after us."

"It opens from inside, too?" Marzana asked.

"It does. Everything's in working order, as far as I can see." Emilia made a pained face. "It kills me that this has been here the whole time and none of us knew it, but even worse is the possibility that not only has it been here but someone else has been using it all along. It's sort of a pride issue. Anyway." She held the curtain aside. "Everybody into the pool. The stairs are to the right. Mind your feet."

"Here goes nothing," Nialla said, and she crossed the threshold, followed by J.J., then Meddy, then Ciro. Marzana took a deep breath and stepped through the opening and into the dim and dusty violet light, just as the lookout down on the main floor finished singing "Frère Jacques" and launched into "Follow the Yellow Brick Road."

twenty-three

THE REVERSE OF THE MESSAGE

THEY CROWDED INTO the black-brick space between the inner and outer walls, which was lit by three sconces with glass shades cut into elaborate arrangements of white petals that instantly reminded Marzana of the glass-flower centerpiece in the Radioactive Teashop. The stairs Emilia had mentioned were marble, and they led away, down and down, between the two walls, lit here and there by more of the dusty, beautiful sconces.

It was hard to gauge the distance, because she could see at least one turning in the stairs down there where they switched back on themselves, but logic said that if this passage led to a station, it had to be at or below the level of the school's cellars, where the kitchens, the science department, and the music classrooms were. The music classrooms were soundproofed. That probably helped. In any case, they were probably about to walk at least two, maybe three, stories down.

Behind them, the sliding door that was the painting clicked again as Emilia drew it back into place. From this side, the echo turned the sound into more of a *clunk* that reverberated around them. Emilia paused, her head cocked to one side, listening. The voice singing on the other side of the wall was still just barely audible. "Perfect." She trotted to the top of the staircase. "Come on. The system map's down below. That's what I really want to show you."

They all scooted aside to allow Emilia to lead the way. Marzana looked around for Nialla and reached out for her hand. "And you said nothing ever happens around here," she whispered.

Nialla squeezed her palm. "But here we are."

"Here we are."

Down and down and down. There was an iron railing on the Library-side wall, which probably saved them from avalanching to the bottom at least three times. Those stairs were *steep*. No sound came through the thick walls. Dust swirled in the purplish-gray light.

Marzana figured they had to have dropped below ground level by the time the light beneath them began to change. Then the wall on their left ended abruptly, replaced with an iron banister. Beyond it, the space widened out by ten or fifteen feet, and the members of the Thief Knot arrived on a landing that was separated from the wide space beyond and below it by a balcony with a carved marble railing.

"Welcome to Cotgrave Wall Station," Emilia said, grasping the marble baluster and looking down.

Directly ahead of them, a massive chandelier hung from a domed mosaic ceiling decorated with flowering vines against a background of paler jade. The chandelier dripped with cobwebby green glass that had been twisted into similar botanical drapes and curves, with glowing violet bulbs cupped by white glass petals that echoed the purple-and-white-tiled blooms above.

From either side of the balcony, twin staircases curved down

—way, way down; maybe another two stories—to the station's platform below, where the marble floor was inlaid with stars and planets. "Grass overhead and stars underfoot," Meddy said in a quiet voice that nonetheless echoed through the space. "I like that. It reminds me of . . ." She shook her head. "Well, I like it."

There didn't seem to be much more to the station than what they could see from above. Marzana stared hard at the tracks as she descended to the platform, trying to decide if they looked like they'd been used recently. The steel glittered in the light from the chandelier, but she couldn't tell if it had been polished by use or merely preserved in near-perfect condition. The platform was small, only about fifteen feet deep and maybe three times as long, and there was nothing approximating a ticket booth. But then, this station had presumably been built back when Marymead had still been the Cotgrave family home: a private station, requiring neither a ticket seller nor standing room for commuting crowds.

There were two doors between the staircases. Ciro opened the one on the left and found a broom closet; the one on the right turned out to be a tiny bathroom. Between the doors, directly under the balcony, was a pair of iron-and-wood benches: old iron, from the look of it. The metal had overgrown the wooden slats of the seats and the backs as if it were a shrub rather than part of a piece of furniture, and between those benches was a marble drinking fountain in the shape of a giant blossom erupting from the wall. Above that—

"Wow," Marzana said, reaching with fingers outstretched to touch the rough mosaic surface of what appeared to be a complete map of the Belowground Transit System.

There, rendered in tiny fragments of cobalt and emerald and gold and indigo laid over a field of pale apricot in the rough shape of the Sovereign City of Nagspeake, was a branching structure like a coral, or like some sort of fanciful plant out of Dr. Seuss. Four train lines, each composed of a different color of glass, split and rejoined and parted ways again, radiating from a pewter-colored tangle near the middle. Each line was dotted along its length with small pewter circles, and beside each of these was a rectangle painted with the name of a station. Here and there, slender fingers of old iron had pierced through the map like roots protruding from the side of a riverbank. In some places, the iron fronds had punched bits of the mosaic right out, leaving glittering dust and bits of glass scattered on the floor below. In other places, the iron seemed merely to have worked its way in between the tiny tiles, and in those spots the smooth metal lay like a seam.

" 'Wow' is right." Nialla touched the map too. "Here we are. Cotgrave Wall."

"Right." Emilia dropped her satchel on the right-hand bench, dug inside, and brought out a folded piece of crinkling paper, a roll of clear tape, and a pencil. "So here's what I want to show you." She stuck the pencil through one blond braid. "Who's got the city map?"

"Me." J.J. produced the gazetteer, carefully tore the insert from the back, and unfolded it.

"'Kay. Hold it up next to the Belowground map." J.J. and Meddy stood on the left-hand bench to hold the map of Nagspeake up against the wall. Meanwhile Emilia unfolded the big semitransparent sheet she'd brought. "Tracing paper. Swiped it from one of the art studios," she explained. Then she looked critically from J.J.'s map to the mosaic on the wall. "They're about the same scale, right?"

"I think so," Marzana said. Nialla and Ciro nodded their agreement.

"Okay. So." Emilia tore off two pieces of tape and stuck them at the top corners of her paper. Then she climbed on the bench between Meddy and J.J. and taped it over the map of the city. "You guys mind just making sure these don't fall?"

"Sure," J.J. said, and Meddy nodded impatiently.

"Great. Okay." Emilia turned, took the pencil from her braid, and began tracing the outline of Nagspeake. "If we accept the Real Peony/Fake Peony theory—which, I think, is pretty much a certainty at this point—the big question is *why,* right? Not why did her parents play along with it—they want their kid back, and obviously this is what they've been told they have to do before she'll be returned." Emilia's voice ricocheted off the wall. "But if somebody went to, say, a carrier like Tasha Cormorant and said, 'I need your help to accomplish X' and that carrier put a job together, one key part of which was Peony Hyde's kidnapping, what was X?"

"If Tasha-Peony was meant to be found, the answer isn't money," Nialla observed. "The kidnapping's a steppingstone to something."

Emilia nodded and paused to point her pencil over her shoulder at Nialla. "I think the key is to look at what, so far, the kidnappers have *gotten.* And the kidnappers did get something out of this. Something big."

Ciro spoke up. "Well, there's Tasha being foisted off on the Hydes, obviously. Presumably they're stuck with her for a while. Could that be important for some reason?"

"No, no," J.J. said from the bench. "Winston Hyde quit his campaign!"

Emilia shook her head as she bent to trace the lower edge of the city. "That was my first guess too, but I think there's more to it." She finished the outline and straightened up. "This was a weird crime, and I think the answer's weirder than just money or politics. Yes, her father quit the race. But something else happened too."

Meddy, who'd been silent during all of this as she held her side of the map, spoke up at last. "They left. They took their changeling kid and they split town."

Emilia waved her pencil in the air. *"Ding-ding-ding."*

"You think this whole thing was to get them to leave Nagspeake?" Marzana asked. "Why? And do you think Tasha went with them?"

"Well, I didn't know about her when I came up with this theory," Emilia admitted. "But if she was hired as a carrier to provide a means to get the Hydes out of their house, then theoretically her part in this ends there. She doesn't have to be there for the endgame. Maybe. But let's come back to all that. Here's where I think things get weird." She pressed the tracing paper more firmly against the city map below it, so that the streets and landmarks showed through. "Okay. Here's the Printer's Quarter. Do we know where their house is?"

Marzana got her journal from her bag and flipped to her notes on the case. "Watermill Street. I think Watermill sort of dead-ends, and that's where they live."

Emilia lifted the translucent paper and leaned close to the city map. "Watermill is here," she muttered, following a line with her finger. "And here's the dead end, just past Mergenthaler Street." She dropped the paper back into place, smoothed it down so that the edges of the city she'd traced lined up again, and drew a circle around the spot. Then she peeled the tape away and jumped off the bench with her paper. "Thanks, Meddy, J.J. You guys can take a break. Ciro, can you give me a hand here? Hold one side of this." Together Emilia and Ciro took the tracing paper to the Belowground map on the wall over the fountain between the two benches, and lined it up so that the traced Nagspeake matched the tiled one. "Ta-*daaa*," Emilia sang darkly. She pressed a hand to the paper, holding it flat against the wall so that the mosaic below showed through clearly.

The circle that had been around Peony Hyde's house now perfectly ringed the pewter tangle that formed the hub of the whole Belowground network, a dot with a painted rectangular label that read PRINTER'S QUARTER/MERGENTHALER STREET.

"I don't think this was about getting Hyde to leave the campaign, and I don't think it was about getting the Hyde family to leave Nagspeake," Emilia said, lifting the tracing paper with a dramatic swoop. "I think it was about getting them to leave their *house.*"

"Peony's house is built over an old Belowground station?" Ciro asked, switching the hand he was using to hold up his side of the tracing paper so that he could lean in for a better look.

"Not just any Belowground station," Emilia corrected. "*The* Belowground station. The hub."

Marzana stepped in for a closer look of her own. Emilia was right: all four lines ran through the station on Mergenthaler Street — or had, before threads of iron had slithered in and broken up each of the colored routes on the map. She touched one tiny bit of green that had been shoved out of place and now hung by a scrap of mortar. It moved under her finger like a loose baby tooth, then fell to the ground and broke in two. "You think somewhere under the foundations of the house, there's probably still a way in?"

Emilia grinned, a triumphant flash that was there and then gone in the blink of an eye. "That's exactly what I think."

"But in that case, why bother with a kidnapping?" Meddy protested. "Why not do a little light breaking and entering and be done with it?"

"It must be completely inaccessible from above," Nialla said after a moment. "Like it's going to take work for whoever wants in to find a way through."

"Exactly," Emilia said. "I think we'll find that every part of it that used to be aboveground is totally gone — so gone that maybe not even the Hydes know it's there. Otherwise, yeah, the kidnappers could've just broken in."

"Okay," Meddy persisted, "but in that case—" She started to switch her grip on the tracing paper as Ciro had, then made a noise of impatience. "Why am I still holding this? Where's the tape?" Emilia retrieved the roll. Meddy tore off two pieces, taped her corner up, then passed the tape to Ciro so he could do the same while she used her remaining bit to secure the bottom edge. Then she pointed to the transit hub. "If this particular station is connected to everything, why not just go in from another station?"

Nialla and Ciro spoke at the same time. "The iron."

"The iron?" Meddy repeated.

"Yeah." Ciro touched one of the reddish-gray trails of metal that had pushed glass aside to encircle Mergenthaler Street. "Remember how I told you Granddad's notes talk about interference from the iron? Well, if it was interfering enough to make them eventually abandon the whole system after most if not all of it was already built, then surely it wouldn't quit interfering just because they stopped using the lines. Look at this. The station is totally cut off."

J.J.'s eyes bugged out. "You think somehow — for whatever reason — the iron poking through this map shows the actual interference pattern *throughout the city?*" He stared at the mosaic. "How would that even be possible? How could the iron here possibly . . . *know* what iron elsewhere in the city is up to?"

"I have absolutely no idea, and it sounds just as impossible to me as it does to you," Ciro admitted.

"It makes sense, though." Nialla traced the iron ring around Mergenthaler Street. "If this station actually has been cut off from the rest, it would perfectly explain why someone who needed to get into it might think the path of least resistance was to go through the house above."

"And don't forget," Marzana added, "the guy was running for mayor. And, according to Emmett, likely to win. That house was never going to be without security, not for years."

"My point exactly," Emilia said, nodding. "To get to the station, they needed to go through the house. To go through the house, they needed the Hydes gone for a significant period of time, and they needed their security detail gone too." She smiled. "And now they have both. Which means probably something is going on right here" — she tapped the circle — "and probably it's happening right now."

Marzana stepped back and folded her arms. "Okay, I'm convinced."

"So what do we do?" Ciro asked. "You want to try to call your folks right now?" He took his phone from his pocket. "You can —" He glanced down at the screen. "Never mind; I lied. You can't. No service underground, apparently."

"Wouldn't matter," Marzana said. She checked her watch: nearly twelve-thirty. "They're down in the city giving a report to Emmett and his friend. I don't know exactly where. They might have left a number with Honora. Oh, or Emmett's number might have been in my folks' notes, now that I think of it, in which case —" She stopped and scratched her head. "Here's a question. Do we think Peony's likely to be with whoever's doing the breaking in, or would they have her somewhere else?"

There was a pause; then Nialla snapped her fingers and pointed at Ciro. "Let's go. You and me. We're figuring this out right now."

She sat on the bench to the left of the fountain and the tile map, reached into her bag, and took out the photo and envelope that held her ransom-note cuttings.

"Nialla, we talked about this," Ciro said, frustrated. "There's no way there's anything hidden in that ransom note. Peony had no control over any part of that message."

Nialla shook her head doggedly. "I'm telling you, the book is the key." She yanked her copy out of her bag and dropped the envelope in the process, sending a flurry of the cutout words cascading onto the bench's seat.

"It's too complicated," Ciro insisted, collecting the fragments. "And the *book* isn't the key, the *message* is—"

"She was desperate," Nialla interrupted. "What does it matter if it's complicated, if it was the only possible communication she could send? Emilia, are you done with that paper?"

Emilia nodded and held out the roll of tape. "Want this, too?"

"She wouldn't have had time," Ciro argued, intercepting the tape as Nialla detached the tracing paper from the wall, spread it on the floor, knelt beside it, and opened her copy of *Sidledywry* to the first of the two dozen or so flagged pages. "They wouldn't have just stood there while she worked out a message to be left in a book she couldn't even count on anyone else identifying."

"It's here," Nialla said, her voice shaking a little. "It has to be. Where's my pen? I had a pen."

"It's not." Ciro set down the tape and put his hand on the book, closing it gently. "The only things she had to work with are these actual words. She couldn't have done any complicated steganography. Nialla, we need to try another tack. We need to stop wasting time. This isn't a game."

Nialla slumped. "I know it's not a game."

Ciro held out the fragments he'd collected before. "I'm sorry." And then, just as Nialla reached out to take the bits, Ciro clamped his hand closed. "'These actual words,'" he repeated, uncurling his fingers and looking down at the bits of paper.

Nialla looked from the scraps in his palm back up to his face. "Ciro?"

He stared down at the words a moment longer, then grabbed Nialla's hand and dumped them into it. "Put them in order. One more time. Every letter accurate." Nialla's face lit up.

"Guys, shouldn't we—" J.J. began.

"Shut up." Nialla shoved her glasses higher onto the bridge of her nose with one finger, took a deep breath, and began moving the fragments around on the tracing paper: turning them over, lining them up, looking at the reverse of this piece or that and comparing it to the photo, then putting it in place.

J.J. was right. They had to move on, figure out what to do next. Marzana spoke up. "Nye—"

But Nialla ignored her, just focused her energy on getting each of the zeroes in "1000000" in exactly the right spot. Ciro kept silent too. He watched Nialla's moving fingers with an almost breathless air. Emilia and Meddy stood like spectators, waiting.

"I think that's right," Nialla said at last, looking at her handiwork. She checked it once more against the note, then sat back, satisfied. "Tape." She held her hand out to Ciro, who knelt at her side and began tearing off bits and passing them to her to affix the words in place.

When they had finished, Nialla sat back. "All yours." Now *she* was breathless with expectation.

Ciro tore off two more pieces of tape and stuck them at the top corners. Then he stood, lifted the tracing paper with index fingers and thumbs, and climbed up to tape it on the wall above the right-hand bench.

He stepped back and looked at Nialla. She put a hand over her mouth. Ciro nodded, scratching his head. "You were right."

"What are we looking at?" Marzana asked impatiently.

"I'll show you." He felt his pockets, then looked around. "Who's got a flashlight?"

Marzana took hers from her kit and handed it to him. Ciro, in turn, offered it to Nialla. "You should do this."

"Thanks." Nialla pulled the bottom of the paper out just far enough so that she could stick the flashlight behind it. Then she clicked the light on. Ciro had taped the tracing paper up *backwards,* with the text of the ransom note facing the wall. One by one, they realized what they were actually looking at.

"Oh, my God," Marzana said.

J.J. swore.

Emilia swore.

"Are you *kidding?*" Meddy exploded.

"You were right," Ciro said again. "I still can't quite believe it."

Backlit by the flashlight, a new text showed through the translucent paper. It was sloppy, with the tops, bottoms, and sides of some words snipped off, and there were gaps in between words and parts where there was no text, merely bits of illustration. But it was instantly legible, and there was no mistaking it. This wasn't a case of Nialla seeing meaning because she was desperate to find it. It was a message, and it was visibly, undeniably there.

IN THE DARK WITH THE
TEA CUPS ANIM ALL NOIS E IS LOUD
BARKS HOWLS S CREAMS
SME LL IS WAT ER LIKE POOL s

"Where the heck did that come from?" J.J. demanded.

"It's the reverse of the message," Ciro said as Nialla clicked off the flashlight. "It's what's on the back of the ransom-note words. There was only one thing she could control: where she cut the words from."

"I know I argued for this," Nialla said, grabbing her backpack and taking out a stray piece of loose-leaf paper. "But somehow I'm still a bit shocked." She glanced at Ciro as she rooted around in the depths of the bag. "You were right—she couldn't count on anyone having the book. The message had to be easier to find than that. And still no one found it."

"No one but you," Ciro said, shaking his head. "I'm sorry I doubted you."

"No, you were right too. I was hunting in the wrong place. Thanks for finding the right way to look at it. Now, what the heck does this mean?" She grunted in frustration. "Seriously, who has a pen? Mine's fled the building or something. Oh, thank you." She accepted one from Emilia, plunked down on the floor again, and started copying the new message down. "She's someplace that has teacups, and all these are the animal noises she can hear, and it smells like pool water. What the heck kind of place has all that?"

Emilia blinked, frowned slightly; then her forehead furrowed in thought. "Sounds like a public pool, but you couldn't hide a kid anywhere near a public pool at the beginning of summer. Too busy."

"She said 'like pools,'" Marzana pointed out, "which implies not a pool but something like it — something she can't see but can smell."

"And the loud animal noises — what about a zoo?" J.J. suggested. "Maybe the animal sounds would drown out a kid yelling for help."

Ciro shook his head. "I feel like at a zoo, the prevailing smell wouldn't be pool chemicals. But where else would you get all those different noises in one place?"

"Maybe she's hearing coyotes or foxes or something," Marzana said. "Some animal that makes a whole range of sounds. Do they have any of those downhill?"

"I think the teacups in the dark are the key," Nialla said. "I feel like Peony must've thought the right person would read that and know exactly what she means. It must be a downhill thing, something someone who lives in the city proper would immediately know."

"Hey, Marzana?" Meddy had wandered away from the group and was standing at the edge of the platform. "Guys?" She leaned over the tracks and stared down into the tunnel. "Do you hear something, or is it just me?"

Marzana stepped away from the others and went to stand beside Meddy.

"Do you hear it?" the ghost girl asked. "It's still way out there, but . . . I think I hear a *rumble.*"

Marzana leaned out too. There was nothing to see; the tunnel was a pool of ink, fading from tones of gray to velvety-black nothingness. But was there a sound?

Ciro came to stand next to Marzana. "I think I hear it," he said hesitantly.

"Not me," J.J. said after a moment from Ciro's side.

Nialla and Emilia said nothing, just came to the edge to stand beside J.J. and listen. Nialla looked past the boys and caught Marzana's eye. *What about you?* she signaled.

Marzana hesitated. Then, abruptly, there it was. She felt it before she heard it: a just barely perceptible vibration underfoot. She crouched and put a hand on the tiled floor, then looked up at the chandelier with its blue bulbs and white petals. The sound as they, too, began to quiver was like the tinkling of glass bells.

"Yeah," Marzana said, standing. "I hear it too."

"Okay," J.J. said slowly. "Do we freak out? Do we not freak out? Run and hide, or some equivalent form of get-the-heck-out-of-here?" He glanced around. "Thoughts?"

"I think there's only one thing this can be," Meddy said, looking up as the tinkling from above began to grow into a proper rattling of glass. "In which case, I think we stay right here." A couple of the violet light bulbs flickered. "I think we just got a break."

"But how?" Emilia asked, wide-eyed. "Why? Just our being here couldn't have done it. I was here for hours before."

Marzana thought back to her conversation with Milo. "There's a call system," she remembered. *In the station by our house,* he had said, *it looks like a doorbell.* She turned to Emilia. "Maybe the button or switch or whatever you hit before you managed to turn on the lights?"

Emilia opened her mouth in a wide, soundless *Oh.* "Yeah. Yeah, maybe."

Now the sound was unmissable: a deep rumble of wheels on tracks, accompanied by a higher note that was almost like a clatter, if a clatter could somehow sound sturdy, substantial, and still remain a clatter.

And there was light: a toasty incandescent glow that was completely different from the dusty violet of the station had begun to warm the red-brick walls of the tunnel in sunset tones. Soon two gleaming slicks of brilliance poured out along the two steel tracks, turning them from dull silver to summery gold.

The glow brightened and extended its reach as the clatter and rumble approached. The members of the Thief Knot stepped back, hands reaching for hands or slipping through elbows to link arms until each one had hold of someone else.

The noise rose and rose as the glaring blaze spilled into the station and flung long shadows out onto the platform behind them. And then, with a squeal of brakes and the thudding of what must have been tons of machinery grinding to a halt, a huge bullet of wood, glass, and painted steel shot, already slowing, into Cotgrave Wall Station. Nearly blinded by the light from the massive single headlight at the train's nose, Marzana barely had time to register a dark, human-shaped form in one of the front windows before the first car tore past, flinging green sparks up from below.

With a screech of metal on metal, the train lurched to a stop. It sat there for a heartbeat or three as it settled, four cars long and tall enough to fill the tunnel it had emerged from, its greenish, many-paned windows lit from within by sconces topped by glowing frosted-glass balls. The sides of each car were paneled in deep-brown highly varnished wood, and the metal above and below was painted the red of new brick with stripes the color of goldenrod. Then there was a hiss of hydraulics, and the train leaned down until the lower edge of its doors more or less lined up with the station floor.

Marzana and her crew inched closer to one another. "We're still not getting the heck out of here?" J.J. asked in a strained voice as a set of hinged doors near the front of the train folded open. "Just making sure we're solid on not getting the heck out of here."

Before anyone could answer, a very tall man in green coveralls stepped out, his eyes hidden by a pair of leather-bound goggles. He shoved them up into his short blond hair and gave the kids a long, dubious look. "What the blazes have we got here?" he asked in an accent that marked him as very definitely not from Nagspeake.

Meddy detached herself from the rest of the Knot. "Leave this to me." She stepped forward.

The blond man pointed a long finger at her. "I know you."

"Yeah, you do. We met at Greenglass House, two years ago." Meddy smiled. "Hi, Brandon."

"Milo's friend, right?" He frowned, obviously trying to remember the details of when they'd met. "Your name's . . . Addie? Maddie?" Then his eyes bugged out as he remembered. "*Addie.* You're —but aren't you . . . ?"

"Yeah," Meddy said quickly, saving the strange man from having to pretend he hadn't been about to say *dead.* "And everybody calls me Meddy."

"Meddy. Right. I don't believe it," he said, scratching his head under the goggles. "What on earth are you doing all the way up here?"

"Oh, you know. Shenanigans." Meddy turned back to the Knot. "These are my friends. Marzana, everybody, this is Brandon Levi. He's the conductor of the Belowground."

twenty-four
THE SACRIFICE CHAPTER

T HE CONDUCTOR LOOKED at Meddy. "Almost wouldn't have recognized you without that fancy getup of yours," he said. Then he glanced at the others. "No Milo?"

"No Milo," Meddy confirmed. "He's at camp. He couldn't come up to help Marzana out, so we decided to send me. But you haven't met." She reached back and grabbed Marzana's hand. "This is Marzana. She knows the Pines and Clem and Georgie. And that's Nialla, Emilia, J.J., and Ciro."

Marzana reached back for Ciro's wrist and tugged him forward. "Ciro's how we found this place," she said. "Ciro del Olmo. His grandfather designed a bunch of the stations."

"No kidding," Brandon said. "Padraig was your grandfather?"

Ciro nodded with just a touch of awe in his expression. "Yeah. Did you know him?"

"Met him once, right about when I took over the trains from the previous conductor. About six, seven years ago, that would've been." Brandon paused. "Ailing then, I think he was."

"Probably," Ciro said quietly. "He died when I was seven."

Brandon clapped him on the shoulder. "I'd have liked to have known him better. Glad to meet you, mate." He cleared his throat, and his eyes returned to Meddy. "So why am I here now?"

Meddy turned pointedly to Marzana. "Well, technically, I think you're here because Emilia hit the wrong button," Marzana admitted. "But Milo told me about you. I called him to find out how to get hold of you."

"Well, you got me. Congratulations," Brandon said with a smile, though Marzana thought it held a trace of wariness. It made sense: That the Belowground still ran in even its minimal way wasn't supposed to be common knowledge, after all. "What can I do for you?"

"We can keep the secret," Marzana said. "I promise. But this is important. You took Emmett Syebuck to my parents earlier this week because of a kidnapping."

"You're . . ." Brandon hesitated, probably trying to figure out which name to use.

"Barbara and Peter Hakelbarend's daughter," Marzana finished for him. "Yes. And they're down in the city proper right now, talking with Emmett and whoever else is in charge of the investigation, because they think they found Peony Hyde, the girl who was taken." She took a deep breath and plunged on. "But they're wrong. And right now Peony is still out there, waiting to be found. And we think we know where she is."

Brandon put his hands on his hips. "And you need a ride . . . where?"

Where? That was the question, wasn't it? Marzana hesitated. She glanced back at the rest of the Knot, but Nialla, Ciro, J.J., and Emilia stood quietly behind her on the platform, waiting for her to answer. Marzana was in charge; she had the final say about what, when, and how they tagged in the adults. Well, this was it.

What she *should* do was ask Brandon to take them to the station closest to a police precinct in the city proper. Any one would probably do—once they were aboveground in the city, Ciro's phone would work, and she could use the contact numbers she was pretty sure she had somewhere among the photographed notes. If nobody answered, she had Emmett's name and the name of his police contact, Thad, and anybody official ought to be able to track one or the other of them down.

But on the other hand, here they were, already underground, with a train ready to go. And if they were right, the answer to everything was also underground. *Peony* might even be underground —maybe that's what the "in the dark" part of her message meant.

Plus, Marzana reasoned, Brandon was an adult. If they managed to convince him to do what she wanted, he'd have to come. There would be some form of adult supervision.

"The kidnapped girl's house is pretty close to the intersection of Mergenthaler and Watermill Streets," Marzana said. "That's where the abandoned Mergenthaler Street Station is, right? Basically right under that intersection? And there's no entrance left up above?"

Brandon nodded. "Yep. That's true enough. But if that's where you want to go, there's a bit of a complication."

Nialla spoke up. "The iron?"

Brandon tapped the side of his nose. "All eight transit tunnels in and out of Mergenthaler are cut off. That's why the city sold off the land above. There were so many breaks in the lines, so much interference, there was no getting it back."

"So the map back there is actually *accurate,* where the iron broke in and changed it?" Emilia glanced over her shoulder at the mosaic on the wall. "That can't be a coincidence."

The conductor grinned. "I wouldn't imagine it is, no."

"That's *wild*," Ciro muttered.

"Mess around in these tunnels long enough, you'll see wilder." Brandon turned back to Marzana. "So what is it you want?"

She took a deep breath. "I don't know if you saw the news last night, but Peony's father withdrew from the mayor's race and the family left town. The house is empty. We think the kidnappers wanted them out so they could get at the station from above, because they couldn't get in from any of the transit tunnels. We think that's where they are now. We want you to take us there. Peony may be with them." Given the teacups and animal sounds in Peony's message, Marzana thought that was unlikely, but certainly there was a chance. "You said there was a complication if we wanted to go there. You didn't say it was impossible. Is there another tunnel? One that isn't on the map? One that it's unlikely anyone who wasn't, well, *you* would know about?"

Brandon considered her for a moment. Then he glanced at the others, one by one, before his gaze returned to Marzana. "You say you can be trusted. And you vouch for everyone else?"

"Absolutely," Marzana said without hesitation.

The conductor looked at Meddy. "And you vouch for this girl, Whitcher?"

For a moment, Marzana was thrown by the unfamiliar name. Then she remembered that, like her own parents, Meddy had another name and another past. It felt a little like the way Victor Cormorant had used Marzana's mother's real name at the end of their interview the night before.

"I vouch for her," Meddy said.

"All right," Brandon said briskly. "Yes, there is another tunnel. Maintenance. It's not on any map I'm aware of, so I don't see how anyone but me would know about it, which makes me think your theory seems reasonable on the face of it. Only I am *absolutely not* just taking a handful of kids right in to confront a bunch of possible kidnappers," he added severely.

"Well," Marzana argued, "but you'd be there, wouldn't you? Milo said you're a fighter. We wouldn't be alone."

"The more experienced you get at fighting," Brandon said grimly, "the more you never, ever want to have to rely on it in an actual altercation with stakes any higher than bragging rights. I'm not some kind of commando."

"But there's no time," Marzana insisted. Now that she'd convinced herself this was the most logical course of action, there was no way she was backing down. "A girl's life is at stake!" That was true no matter where Peony was being held. They had to assume her life was in danger until she was safely home.

"Hang on, Mars," Nialla interrupted. "I have an idea. Ciro and I'll go back above and track down your mom and dad." She turned to Ciro. "If the contact numbers Marzana has don't work immediately, we can get your mom to help. We'll find the Hakelbarends or this Emmett guy or somebody, and we'll send them to the Hydes' house. They can meet you there," she said to Brandon, "but this way, someone gets to the house as fast as possible. You good with that?" she asked Ciro.

A quick flash of regret flickered across his face, but it was like one of Emilia's smiles: there and gone before Marzana could be totally sure of what she'd seen. He cracked his neck and nodded. "Let's do it." He turned to Emilia. "But can your friends find us a phone, so you guys can take mine? Might be good for nothing, but just in case."

"Barnaby and Enza should still be in the Library," Emilia said. "Tell them or whoever's there you need phones and privacy. They'll get you what you need."

"Great." Ciro took Marzana's hand and put the phone in it. "Here you go."

"This sounds suspiciously reasonable," Brandon said cautiously.

"Then you'll help us out?" Marzana asked.

"Here's what I'll do." Brandon patted assorted pockets on his coveralls, then extracted a pad and a stub of pencil from the one on his left leg. He jotted down a couple of lines, tore the page from the spiral binding, and passed it to Nialla. Marzana caught a glimpse of two names, followed by phone numbers.

"If you have any trouble getting hold of Marzana's folks and Emmett, call these ladies." Brandon leaned over to point to the top line with his pencil. "Georgie there is a good friend of Emmett's and might know how to find him. Clem is a good friend of hers. Hell, call them even if you don't have trouble. They'll be good backup to have, and if this doesn't turn out to be a total mare's nest, I'll feel better knowing we have backup. Tell them I told you to call, give them the rundown, and ask them if they can get to Mergenthaler and Watermill."

Nialla saluted. "Got it." She gave Marzana's hand a squeeze. "You can do this. I can't wait to hear what happens." Then she hurried to the benches, where she collected her backpack and the tracing paper with the taped ransom note.

Emilia followed her and gathered her own supplies, including the city map. "There's a latch that lets the painting slide back," she said to Nialla. "You can't miss it. But don't forget to listen before you open the panel. If the kid's singing, the coast is clear. If he's not . . .

well, use your best judgment," she finished resignedly, shoving the tape and her flashlight into her bag. "Since somebody's in danger and all." She turned and hurried through the train door, probably before she could change her mind and beg Nialla and Ciro not to give away the secret under any circumstances.

Nialla laughed. "We'll do our best not to break your new toy." Then she headed for the stairs without looking back. Ciro shot Marzana a quick, encouraging smile, then followed close on Nialla's heels.

Brandon rapped his knuckles on the metal above the open door. "All aboard who's going, then."

Meddy all but skipped inside. J.J. took a deep breath and lightly punched Marzana on the shoulder before darting through the door. But Marzana stared after the two heading up the interminable staircase as the reality of what she'd agreed to hit her all of a sudden. *Wait. Nialla isn't coming?*

"I'll be right back," she said to Brandon. Then she sprinted across to the stairs and ran up two at a time. "Nye! Wait."

Nialla and Ciro stopped a dozen steps up. "What are you doing?" Nialla demanded. "Get going!"

"I don't want you to miss anything," Marzana protested, twisting her fingers. "We started this. We *dreamed* about this!"

Nialla shook her head. "And we're still doing it." She reached for Marzana's hand. "I'm going to do my part. But . . ." She managed a pained smile. "But look. This is the place in the story where one chapter has to get sacrificed so you can move on to the next." She lowered her voice. "That guy isn't going to take you into the thick of things unless he thinks there'll be people there — adults — to handle any actual danger. It's a dead end. The adventure stops here if we don't find a way to get around that ending before it happens." Her smile deepened. "And it's not like I'm having to throw myself into some big set of gears to pull the sacrifice off. I'm not a chapter that has to get cut up. I'm just going to go make some phone calls." She patted her back pocket. "And try to make sense of Peony's message. Ciro and I can give this new information to your folks, along with everything else." Nialla managed a grin. "Honestly, by the time you poor saps get to the station, the whole thing'll probably be wrapped up and done. I'll be a hero, and you'll just be *late.*"

"But . . ." Nialla was right, but it didn't matter. This was *their* adventure. Whatever other strands they'd woven into it, Marzana and Nialla were the two ends of the knot. "But you'll miss everything," Marzana said in a small voice.

Nialla squeezed her hand, blinking hard. "Not if you promise to tell me."

Marzana nodded and squeezed back.

"You can do this," Nialla said again. "So go do it." She disentangled her hand gently, turned away, and trotted toward the balcony and the staircase that rose up from it to disappear between the walls, leaving Ciro behind with Marzana.

"Hey," he said. "You taking that there train?"

Marzana snorted and wiped her eyes. "Guess I better go."

"Yeah. So two things." He tapped the phone in her hand. "One: Use this if you need to. You may not have service, but if you do, don't hesitate. Two . . ." He bent and kissed her cheek, right where it met the corner of her mouth. Marzana stumbled backwards in pure surprise, and he grabbed her wrist to keep her from tumbling down the steps. "That's for luck," he explained quickly. "Good luck." Then he, too, rushed up, up, up the stairs and disappeared out of view at the top.

Marzana touched her cheek, then turned and ran down as fast as she could without tripping over her own suddenly very clumsy feet. "Let's go," she managed as she stepped past a silent, grinning Brandon and onto the train.

twenty-five

THE BELOWGROUND

NSIDE, THE TRAIN was all burnished brass and mahogany paneling. The seats, some upholstered in padded red leather and some made of woven cane, were separated into nooks by benches placed perpendicular to the walls. There were four vertical brass poles for standing passengers, all polished to a gleaming finish. The light from the sconces with their glass-ball shades flickered cozily, as if there were candles inside.

When Marzana, Emilia, J.J., and Meddy were safely aboard, Brandon Levi pulled a handle just inside the folding door, causing it to slide shut with a neat little snap. Then he headed to the back of the coach. "This way. Mind your step between cars."

They followed him through the middle two coaches to the last of the four. When he'd closed the door behind them, Brandon stalked to the very back — or perhaps now it was the very front — of the train. "Come on up if you want, or stay here," he said, heading for another door at the far end of the car. He unlocked it with a key that he took from his breast pocket, stepped through into the cab, and dropped into a captain's chair before a panel of controls. "But sit, anyway. Takeoff's a bit bumpy."

He began flipping switches, and the train, which had never stopped thrumming, upped its vibrations. The four members of the Knot took seats behind the cockpit, Marzana and Emilia on one side and J.J. and Meddy on the other. The train, which had been subtly listing to one side in order to line up its doors with the platform, righted itself with a little lurch. Marzana saw Brandon's arm reach up to yank twice on a wooden handle dangling between the two big front windows, and in the middle of the car, a brass bell hanging from the ceiling bonged twice, the sound repeating itself in a strange, not-quite echo: other bells, in other cars, announcing the train's imminent departure to passengers who weren't there.

And then, with a thudding forward leap that melted into acceleration, the train was off, hurtling through the inky tunnels, out of the Liberty of Gammerbund and toward the heart of the city of Nagspeake.

"All right, I'm off duty for about ten minutes." Brandon got up and leaned on the doorway of the cab, looking down at the four of them. A station flashed by outside the windows in a flurry of sooty cream-colored tiles. "Fill me in. What do we know, and what's our plan, exactly?"

A plan. Yeah, we probably need one of those, Marzana thought grimly. They gave Brandon a rapid overview of what they knew about the crime, and what they suspected. His eyes widened comically when they got to the parts about Tasha Cormorant. "Tasha?" he repeated in disbelief. "You hear things about Tasha, but I don't know that anyone takes her that seriously. I'd be shocked if she turned out to be back of all this." Then he paused, reconsidering.

"On the other hand, sometimes it's the ones not taken seriously who start thinking they have to do something drastic to change their reputations. Maybe this makes perfect sense."

Marzana folded her arms, thinking. "What about where we're going?" she asked. "Can you tell us a bit more about the layout? How does this service tunnel connect, and what's the station look like from the inside?"

"Good question. Somebody have paper?" Emilia did. She handed Brandon a yellow lined notepad from her backpack, along with her pencil. He propped the pad up against the wall and drew a circle with — Marzana counted — ten radiating spokes. Then he drew another, more irregular circle around the first. This one, however, was broken in two places: at roughly one o'clock and seven o'clock, if you imagined the circle as a clock face. He made one last line that passed through those broken places in the outer circle. "This is the service tunnel."

"How did it happen to be . . ." J.J. hesitated. ". . . not interfered with?"

"Couple of reasons," Brandon said after a moment's thought. "It runs a level below the rest, is likely the main one. The truth is, it's probably for the best that the system never got up to full functionality, because Mergenthaler Street Station alone would've been a nightmare. Everything else, all four lines, ran through the same level at Mergenthaler. The switching would've been incredibly complicated, and I suspect it would've seen crashes or near misses all the time. But the architects designed it that way because they thought back then that there would be less interference from the iron at the upper levels of the underground. It turned out not to be universally true."

"And why wouldn't the kidnappers have known about the

service tunnels?" Meddy asked. "Tasha Cormorant's ancestor was involved in the Belowground, wasn't he? His name was on the Cotgrave Wall Station plans Ciro had in his attic. Wouldn't she know about it?"

Brandon made a sort of wincing face. "Not necessarily. The Belowground was reopened years after it had been abandoned, and even if the Cormorant family was involved in the building, they weren't involved in bringing it back online. Those who were involved — my predecessor, your friend's grandfather, a few others — spent years tracking down the official paperwork related to it, especially the administrative stuff, and they hid it all. It's not very civic-minded, making that much information disappear, but they wanted the memory of it to fade as much as possible. It's still possible to find the stations, of course — you can track down the entrances if you know where to look, just as you lot did, although I do my best to make sure nobody can actually get in without my knowing about it. I'm pretty sure these days I have everything that relates to the non-public infrastructure in my possession." He made an amused face. "Except that apparently Padraig del Olmo kept a personal archive. I'd love to see that sometime."

"So we'll enter the station below the main . . . terminal, I guess?" Marzana asked as the train slid through another station without slowing. This time she caught the name tiled into the wall on the far side of the platform: CATON/INGLESIDE.

"Yes." Brandon tapped one o'clock on his diagram. "The stair to the transit level — the level where most of the passenger trains came and went — is here. Above that level is a sort of open concourse, with stairs down to all the different lines and two entrance/exits to the world upstairs. Just two: another bit of terrible planning. Here, and here." Three o'clock, and six o'clock. "This one" — six — "caved in.

The stairs leading up to the surface ran under a church, and the catacombs collapsed. Totally inaccessible. You'd have to excavate about forty feet of stone and bone. So your kidnappers can only be coming from here." He tapped three o'clock. "The stairwell and passage are intact. They'd just have to dig through the foundation of the house in the right place. Not sure how they'd have worked that out, but I suppose it's not impossible, especially with a carrier on payroll to do the research." He looked at Marzana again. "Do you know how many people we're talking about here?"

She shook her head. "I think," she said slowly, "there are probably two sets of people involved. There's the set responsible for getting the Hydes out of the house, and there's the set responsible for whatever happens now that they're gone. Of the first set, the only people we've seen actual evidence of are female. There's Tasha Cormorant, posing as Fake Peony; then the person who blackmailed the city cop by phone was female, and so was the person who called our school and told them our teacher wasn't coming in."

"Plus, remember, somebody posed as a sweepstakes representative to get the teacher out of town," Meddy said, "but I think Mrs. Agravin used the word 'she,' so all of those characters could've been played by the same person."

Marzana nodded. "Right. And if that person is Tasha Cormorant, she's presumably with the Hydes, wherever they went, still posing as their daughter and keeping an eye on them. But there's no way she'd have left Real Peony alone all this time, so there has to be at least one other adult standing guard over her somewhere, who's been with her since Sunday. That's Crew A."

"And Crew B is whoever's going into the house," Meddy finished. "But isn't it possible, since they had to sit back and wait for

Tasha to do her whole thing, that Crew B has also been guarding Peony, and maybe they'll have her with them now?"

Marzana considered, then shook her head. "I don't think she'll be there. After going to all the trouble of creating a fake daughter, they wouldn't want to risk sneaking the real one back into the Hydes' home when they broke in. If anything went wrong, the kid would be on familiar turf. She could escape. She could raise an alarm."

"So that's one person pretending to be the hostage and one person watching the real hostage," Brandon said, holding up his thumb and forefinger. "And I agree that the girl probably won't be there, though I would like to remind you that it was . . . *suggested* to me back there in the station that she might be, a suggestion that may have factored into my decision to bring you lot out on this trip." He scowled at Marzana. She blushed. Brandon rolled his eyes and continued. "So who's actually going to be doing the heavy lifting in the station? Digging through the foundation of a house would be a lot of work for one person. Any reason to think there'll be more than two?"

The Knot considered. "No idea," Marzana admitted at last. "We know nothing about them. But I think for something like this, you'd want the minimum number of people involved, wouldn't you?" Even with her limited underground education, that seemed like common sense.

"So where's the hostage if she's not there?" Brandon asked. "And explain why aren't we going straight to her, if she's in so much danger?"

"We do have a clue about where she might be," Meddy said. "She left a note. We just haven't worked out what it means yet. Nialla and Ciro will keep trying to make sense of it, and they'll give the information to Marzana's mom and dad and Emmett. But we know where the rest of the crew will be. So let's just get there, catch them, and make them talk!"

"'Catch them,' she says." Brandon snorted. "'Make them talk,' she says. Got some ghost-related strategies up your sleeve, have you?"

"Absolutely," Meddy retorted.

J.J. spoke up. "Maybe he'll understand Peony's note. He's from downhill." He, Meddy, and Emilia looked to Marzana. "Should we?"

"Try me," Brandon suggested.

"I don't remember the exact wording," Marzana said, "but it was something like, *In the dark with the teacups. Animal noises: screams, barks, and howls. Smells like pool water.* Does it make any sense to you?"

The conductor considered. "The teacup thing is a mystery to me, and the pool smell, too. But the Printer's Quarter in particular is lousy with foxes, and they do, in fact, scream, bark, and howl." He made an apologetic face. "Sorry not to be more helpful."

"It's okay," Marzana said. "After all, we still have Meddy's catch-'em-and-make-'em-talk plan."

"Right," the conductor muttered. "Right." He looked down at his watch, then over his shoulder and out at the darkness beyond the front windows. "Well, I've got a tunnel switch to manage in about three minutes; then we'll be beneath Mergenthaler about five minutes after that. So." And he turned and took his seat at the controls again, stuffing the diagram he'd drawn into one of his many pockets.

Emilia popped to her feet and leaned through the door. "Um, Mr. Levi? Where would you say we are about now?"

"Geographically?"

"Yes. Relative to the city above us."

Brandon scratched his head under the goggles. He threw a lever, and the train began to decelerate. "Ah . . . I'd say we're just about where the Slope meets Bayside."

"Thanks," Emilia said, dropping back into her seat with a contented smile. "Do you know," she said, looking around at the other three, "this is the first time I've been out of the Liberty?"

"Ever?" Marzana asked, surprised.

"Ever."

"Well, hey!" J.J. held out a palm. "That's huge." Emilia reached across the aisle and slapped it.

The train slowed to a crawl, then lurched to a stop. There was no station visible, but ahead of them, the shadowy tunnel forked. Brandon hopped up and walked through the coach. "Back in two shakes."

He opened the door between cars and climbed out and down into the tunnel. All four of the kids got to their feet to watch through the front window of the cab as the conductor stepped into the glare from the headlight, pulling on a pair of heavy gloves as he went. He hauled back on a huge lever to one side of the track, and up ahead, a set of rails that had been leading into the tunnel to the left slid with a metallic groan until they pointed into the tunnel to the right. Brandon dusted off his gloves, took a quick look over his shoulder to make sure the track was positioned the way he wanted, and returned to the train.

"Take your seats," he said as he pulled himself back into the car and shut the door again. Then they were off, accelerating into the right-hand bore.

They'd been descending for the entire trip—the Liberty was, after all, at the top of a huge hill, and the Printer's Quarter was almost all the way at the bottom—but now the train did a shorter, steeper dive, then leveled out. "We're on the maintenance level now," Brandon called back. "Just a couple more minutes."

Once the train seemed to be moving at a consistent pace, J.J. got to his feet and walked toward the far end of the car, waving for the others to follow. "What are we doing?" he asked when they were all standing together around one of the poles. "When we get there. Seriously, what's our goal?"

"I think," Marzana began, "our goal should be to figure out what they're doing there, and to delay them leaving—if we can—until the cavalry arrives. I don't know if we can make a plan for that until we see what it's like in the station, though, and how many of them there are." She glanced from J.J. to Meddy. "But I feel like a lot of this is going to fall on you guys. We're probably going to need some distracting visual stuff. Magic."

"You might be right," Meddy said.

J.J. looked at Emilia. "You brought supplies. What do we have to work with?"

Emilia began ticking things off on her fingers. "A couple more big pieces of tracing paper. Tape. A flashlight, of course. You said something about working miracles with a spool of thread on that first day, so I packed a spool of thread. Also some thin wire. A lockpick kit. A multi-tool with a knife, screwdriver, and adjustable wrench. My school ID—you can do a lot with a piece of plastic that size—a candle, some matches, a couple markers, couple pencils, some chalk. And the Official Commorancy Key Collection, not that I expect it to be good for squat down here in the real world."

"Good grief," Meddy said, impressed. "You come prepared."

Emilia shrugged. "If you want to get in and out of rooms without getting stuck in them or setting off alarms, it helps."

"And I have my basic kit," J.J. said, patting his messenger bag. "The stuff you've seen, plus an extra deck of cards. Flash paper. Some invisible thread and wax and a handful of other little goodies."

Meddy shrugged. "I have this." She reached into her pocket and produced Marzana's pink shoelace. "In case anyone's shoes come untied. And I have me, for whatever that's worth."

"It's worth a ton." Marzana peered into her backpack. "I have Meddy's reliquary, my notes and my own little kit, but that just has a flashlight and a multi-tool and a notebook and pen." Then she looked up. Suddenly she realized that, for once in her life, she knew exactly what she wanted to say. "And I have you guys. None of us — except maybe Emilia — were expecting to find ourselves here today. But here we are. And it's up to us. Meddy, can I have that shoelace back?"

She held out her hand, and Meddy put the shoelace into it. Marzana tied the fiddly, in-and-out-and-back-again thief knot.

"This morning I was feeling pretty down on myself and this whole endeavor," she said as she faired the knot. "I think that was probably pretty clear. I named us after a structurally unreliable knot that's not good for much, and that's how I was feeling. Inept. Useless. Because even though they didn't go inside first, my parents got to Mrs. A.'s apartment before we did, and they seemed to know something was off about the rescue, and I think that made it feel like not so much of a victory. And also," she admitted with a half-smile, "because I got in trouble." She held the knot up carefully between thumb and forefinger. "But just now I remembered what the lady who taught me this knot said about it. Honora said the point of a thief knot isn't whether it's reliable; the point is whether your shipmates are. So here's to us."

She closed her fist around the little twisted curl of shoelace and held it out between them. "Knot up."

"Knot up," Meddy repeated with a grin, putting her hand on top of Marzana's.

Emilia followed suit, and so did J.J. "Knot up." Then he flipped his hand over to reveal that now he, and not Marzana, held the shoelace. "Let's do this."

Marzana yanked her fist out from under the others' hands, opened it, and stared at her empty palm. "Okay, that was impressive."

"Next stop, Printer's Quarter/Mergenthaler Street!" Brandon yelled from the cab. The train began to slow. Outside, graffiti flashed by on the walls: words and drawings of fanciful creatures and strings of numbers in jewel tones darkened by time and dirt. Then the tunnel widened, and the train's headlight flashed across a shadowy platform on the right for a moment, illuminating a table, three overturned chairs, a few ragged posters on the back wall, and the upward-slanting line of a staircase. Trailing roots hung from the ceiling.

Then the shadows crept back in as the train squealed to a halt, its headlamp masked by the tunnel ahead and only the much dimmer glow of the sconces inside the cars left to illuminate the platform.

Brandon threw a final switch, and the car did its subtle lean to starboard. "Well, this is it." He got to his feet, opened a cabinet above his seat, and took out a canvas bag. "Toolkit. Just in case. Probably not good for much, but I'm not going in empty-handed." He eyed the Knot as he passed through the car and opened the folding door. "You lot are sure you want to go up there? You realize we probably can't sneak up on anyone who's already in the station. If they've made it even as far as the concourse, they'll have felt the train, even if they didn't hear it. There are no thick old stone walls here to muffle the sound, like there are at your school up there in the Liberty."

Marzana squared her shoulders. "Absolutely."

"Right." Brandon looked at her for a long moment. Then he shook his head and turned away, muttering, "This is a terrible idea," as he stepped off the train.

"Knot up," Marzana whispered to herself. Then she followed.

twenty-six
MERGENTHALER STREET

I T WASN'T ROOTS hanging down from the ceiling. It was *iron*. And it wasn't just there, on the platform. It was *everywhere*. It had wrapped around the banister of the stairs like ivy. It had altered the arrangement of the overhead lights, so that fixtures that had once been flush against the ceiling now hung at awkward angles, their electrical wiring twisted around iron armatures that had clearly not been part of the original design. It had wound its way through the steel gate that had closed off the service tunnel and platform from the upper levels of the station.

As they approached that gate, at the bottom of the stairs heading up from this platform to the transit level above, Marzana uttered a curse. In the twin beams of light from Brandon's and Emilia's flashlights, it didn't look like it could possibly open, not with all that extra metal tangled in the hinges. But the conductor was unconcerned. He merely reached into his pocket, took out a ring of keys, selected one, inserted it into the keyhole, and gave it a twist. With one gentle shove, the gate swung open without protest.

"Lights off," Brandon said. "Just in case." The staircase was wide enough for two people to walk side by side, but they went up single file in the dark, with Marzana following Brandon and the others following her, each holding the hand of the next. About a dozen steps from the top, Brandon stopped. They crouched and listened. Nothing.

Or wait.

Yes.

It was almost inaudible, but there was a noise coming from somewhere up there. Or maybe not even the noise itself but the echo of it, bouncing through the cavernous station. Not quite a thump, not quite a scrape. Marzana glanced at Brandon.

"That's coming from the concourse," he said. "I'll admit, I thought this was all a bit far-fetched, but it does sound like someone's doing their best to reopen the station."

"I can go take a look," Meddy offered. "Do some reconnaissance."

"There's another couple gates between here and there," Brandon said. "Won't cause you trouble, will they? Or the iron? Isn't there a thing about iron and ghosts?"

"Oh, yeah, there is a thing about iron and supernatural things, isn't there?" Meddy said thoughtfully. She shook her head. "I've never noticed any ill effects from it. And the gates shouldn't be a problem. We're not talking about solid doors, right? As long as my reliquary fits through some part of the gates, I can pass. And unless our kidnappers turn out to be someone I've already shown myself to at some point, I'll be perfectly invisible. Mars?"

Marzana took the reliquary vial from her pocket and held it out. "Go to it."

"Ah, Meddy." Brandon beckoned her over. "You're about to see some things, love. But no need to worry, all right? It's perfectly safe. Apart from the kidnapping bad guys, I mean."

Meddy hesitated. "What are you talking about?"

"The old iron," Brandon said. "The wild stuff. It's been at work up there."

"I know," Meddy protested. "We all know that."

Marzana gestured at the tendrils twisting and twining all around them. "That's the point, isn't it? It's how this whole situation came about."

The conductor shook his head. "Whatever you think you know about the wild iron from having seen it on the surface is nothing compared to what it is underground." He touched a warped coil of metal that projected, rootlike, from between the bricks of the wall. J.J. and Emilia edged back away from it. "Even this is nothing," Brandon said with a half-smile. "They didn't shut down this entire system because of a few small irruptions and disruptions and places where the iron decided to contribute to the décor. They shut it down because there were places where the iron ran rampant. One of those places is right above us." He clapped Meddy's shoulder. "It's nothing you need to fear, but—well. You'll see. It's perfectly safe, though."

Meddy frowned briefly, then appeared to remember that, even without Brandon's assurances of safety, she was a ghost and, as far as they all knew, past harm. "All right, back in a minute."

She darted up the stairs, taking them two at a time, and paused only a moment at the top to reach through the bars of the next gate with the hand that held the reliquary. Then she stepped through and was gone. With flashlights still off, they climbed the rest of the stairs and crouched silently behind the gate to wait for her return.

Moments passed: two or three, then two or three more. Marzana resisted the urge to look at her wrist; it was too dark to read her watch anyway. J.J. shuffled his feet. Emilia elbowed him. Marzana bit down on her tongue to keep from shushing them both. So far they had heard nothing at all from whatever was above them . . . but just in case.

At last Meddy reappeared in the dark on the other side of the gate, with an expression of shock and wonder on her face. "You weren't kidding," she said.

"Better forewarned, though, right?" Brandon asked with a grin.

"Do we need to be whispering?" Marzana asked a little impatiently.

Meddy shook her head. "I don't think so. Not yet, anyway."

J.J. and Emilia sprang backwards to make room as the ghost passed the reliquary between the bars to Marzana. "What's it like up there?" J.J. asked hesitantly.

"You'll see," she said breathlessly. "But I found the spot—the place where our baddies are trying to come through. There's a staircase to the surface that leads to nothing but a rough ceiling, only the ceiling's actively in the process of falling apart. Dust falling, clumps of mortar or cement or whatever. You can see metal mesh and bars. But I didn't see light coming in yet."

"Maybe we can get up and into some kind of strategic position before they're through," Marzana said. "Are there places to hide?"

"Oh, sure," Brandon said, selecting another key from his ring. "There were going to be a bunch of retailers on the concourse level —shops and snack bars and whatnot, plus ticket counters, a waiting area with benches and tables and stuff, lockers, you name it. The infrastructure's all still there, just . . . well, let's say it's been reconfigured."

"That's one way to put it," Meddy said grimly. "He's right, though. You'll see. We have plenty of options. I'll show you."

Brandon unlocked the gate. He and Emilia switched on their flashlights, and Marzana took hers from her kit and turned it on as well. Then they all stepped through and found themselves in the center of a platform on the transit level, the beams revealing a floor patterned with blue tiles in repeating wavy lines, broken by the occasional image of a brown water wheel. Marzana aimed her light upward and found signs marking the track tunnels to either side as RIVER LINE: COUP DE GRÂCE and RIVER LINE: INLET PALE. Here the sounds of the break-in were clearer and more insistent.

Then Emilia said, "Whoa." She swung her light to either side, along the track bed on the Inlet Pale side. "You *guys.*"

The tracks there, rather than lying flat, rose up off the ground in uneven, canted, and undulating waves, like the tracks of a roller coaster. In places they were held up from below by rough pillars of iron, and in others they were suspended from above by iron chains of bizarre and mismatched links. Marzana turned her flashlight on the Coup de Grâce side, where the track had been torn up entirely, the rails and ties used to build a curious, skeletal thing that made sense to Marzana only as some kind of sculpture.

"It gets weirder," Brandon said, waving his flashlight toward a staircase farther down the platform. "This way."

"I wish we had more light," J.J. commented. "If we knew the layout better — the rest of us, I mean —" he amended, glancing at Brandon, "this dark might be an advantage. But as it is, it doesn't help.

I don't know what I'm going to be able to do in terms of creating distractions if I can't see my surroundings."

They started up the stairs. "I can help with that," Brandon replied. "There's a control room on the concourse level. I can't bring the place up to full power — that would set off alarms at the power grid — but there's an emergency system that's powered by a generator."

"I actually think that'll work in our favor," Marzana said. "Wouldn't you be freaked out if you broke into a space that was supposed to have been deserted for decades and you found lights on?"

"They're going to freak anyway," Meddy muttered with relish. "It's nuts up there."

There was no gate at the top of these stairs, and even in the dimness, Marzana could feel that they had emerged into a large, wide-open space. The murk had a different feel to it. And the sounds of deconstruction were even more pronounced. For a moment, though, Marzana completely forgot about the kidnappers as their lights glanced over the effects of the old iron's interference in the station's concourse. The fact that they could see only glimpses and shadows made it all the more peculiar.

A big arrivals-and-departures display on one wall had been converted into a vertical metal garden, where each of the click-clacking tiles that had once flipped around and around to show a number or a letter had been repurposed as the petals of a flower on an iron stem or a succulent cupped by iron leaves. The folding padded chairs that had once been bolted to the floor in the waiting area now hung from the ceiling at uneven intervals, each suspended by chains on either side like a swing. They swayed ever so slightly, creaking gently, even though the air was perfectly still. The big circular information desk near the center of the space stood six feet off the ground, held up by a massive iron tree shape, as if the desk were part of a treehouse. Huge appendages that somehow managed to look less like branches and more like tentacles spread above it, reaching both outward and upward into the high-ceilinged darkness overhead. A big gold clock that had probably stood over the desk was now embedded in the metal trunk and peeked out like the face of an owl that had been surprised by Marzana's flashlight.

J.J. glanced at his watch. "Either this just happens to be one of the two times a day that clock'll be right, or it's keeping perfect time."

"There's a corridor over there," Meddy said. The beam of Brandon's light swung off to the left, splintering into shadows as it passed through a collection of freestanding staircases and ladders and ladderless slides that appeared to have sprouted from the floor like beanstalks and that stopped in midair, supported by and connected to nothing.

"Oy!" he snapped. "Warn me first before you grab my arm, would you?"

"Sorry." Meddy relinquished her grip.

"All right. Wait here, and I'll get some lights on." With his beam, Brandon picked out a small hallway closer by and stalked toward it, his toolkit swinging in one hand.

Emilia played her flashlight around while they waited, picking out curious pockets of ordinariness here and there: near the information desk in its tree in what had once been the central waiting area, a collection of chairs and small Formica-topped tables stood, neatly squared up to one another and apparently untouched. Here and there, yawning pits in the floor surrounded on three sides by railings marked the staircases to the various platforms on the transit level below, all of which had been kept free of obstructions, as if at any minute commuters might spill out and need clear walkways. All around the perimeter were the empty shops, like gaps in a mouth where teeth had once been. The iron seemed to have left them alone too, though wherever the ring of shops was broken up by restrooms, all the plumbing—pipes, toilets, sinks, everything—spilled out of the entrances in nonsensical and obviously-not-to-code configurations. And still the echoing yet oddly muted sound of someone methodically breaking away the ceiling somewhere out of sight continued.

We were right, Marzana thought. *I can't believe we were right.* Excitement warred with fear. She glanced at Emilia's shadowed face, and the blond girl shot back a quick, tight smile in response. Now what?

There was a strange whirring from the hallway where Brandon had gone, and then the entire space flickered once as a handful of old, hissing emergency lamps flashed to life, illuminating pockets of the concourse but leaving swaths of it still in shadow. The conductor emerged, brushing off his hands as he cut around the thicket of freestanding iron stairs and ladders to return to where the members of the Knot waited. "Better?"

"Definitely," J.J. said, looking around appraisingly. "This'll do."

Marzana glanced toward the now-illuminated corridor from which the sounds of the break-in were coming. "Let's go have a look. See how long we have before they're through. Meddy, will you take point?"

Meddy rushed ahead again, darting across the concourse and into the noisy passage. As the rest of them followed, she leaned back around the corner. "They're close."

Marzana sprinted forward, Brandon keeping up easily with his long-legged stride. The emergency lamps in the hallway glared down on a space almost completely taken up by a double-wide, divided staircase. The same water-and-mill-wheel pattern from the platform on the transit level repeated on the steps, which probably would've given a pretty—or maybe disconcerting—effect of water flowing down underfoot, except for the uneven layer of dust and grit sifting down onto it from above the very top of the stairs. The sounds were coming from a rough ceiling where presumably the staircase would have opened out onto the street level. As they watched, bigger pieces of cement began to fall, exposing more sections of wire mesh and metal bars. A thin beam of light stabbed through from above. Dust motes swirled.

Brandon put out an arm and backed them all away from the stairs as the thin beam became a wide glare. Someone above had lifted away a whole section of ceiling. With a hiss, a sparking bright dazzle flared, and a moment later, the dazzle hit the metal. "Blowtorch," Brandon muttered, herding them back into the main concourse. "No idea what they're after, have we?"

Marzana shook her head, glancing from Emilia to J.J. to Meddy. "I don't think so." Her friends shook their heads. "I guess the plan is just to see what they're up to and keep them here until Mom and Dad or Brandon's friends arrive."

"Ri-ight," Brandon said slowly, and Marzana could almost hear his thoughts: If *they arrive.* "Well, for starters, then, unless we want to be a welcoming committee, we need to find cover." He folded his arms and glanced around. "Somebody can take that information desk, if there's a way up to it," he suggested, then pointed to an alcove near a corner. "Somebody over by the lockers there? Maybe somebody over by those vending machines too?" He nodded to a different alcove just a bit farther away. "And we ought to have someone near the corridor they're going to come in from, in case your friends back in the Liberty do manage to wrangle us some backup." He pointed to the nearest empty shop. "Since that person'll be closest to the incoming baddies, I'd feel best if it was me."

After ascertaining that the trunk that supported it was, in fact, climbable, J.J. and Meddy took the information desk, pointing out that since they had no idea where the kidnappers were likely to go once they arrived, the most central place was probably the best spot from which to plan distractions.

"I'll take the lockers," Marzana said.

Emilia stuck out her tongue. "I guess I'll take the vending machines. They just seem so far away."

Clang! Something heavy and metal fell and proceeded to *thud-rattle-clank-BOOM* down the stairs. "They're through," Meddy called. "Scramble!"

Five people sprinted in four directions. Marzana ran to the alcove that held the lockers, another spot that, for whatever reason, the iron seemed to have left untouched. There was a whole assortment of lockers of various sizes, a handful of them still secured with combination locks or padlocks. Some of the metal cabinets were tall and thin like the ones at school; others were half as tall, stacked one on top of the other; some were double- or even triple-wide. *I might fit in one of those,* Marzana thought, *but then I'm stuck if anything goes wrong.*

There were three banks of lockers, and she wound up simply flattening herself against the one farthest from the corridor where the kidnappers would emerge and easing her head around the corner. In the center of the concourse, Meddy, who didn't have to worry about being seen, leaned over the counter at the information desk. She spotted Marzana and waved, then pointed into the shadows nearby, where J.J. had eased himself experimentally onto one of the broad tentacle branches. Marzana nodded, then leaned out just far enough to see the stairwell passage.

For a moment, nothing moved.

Then: footsteps. Footsteps and a voice. "This is ... unexpected." A slender figure holding a flashlight and carrying some kind of pack over one shoulder appeared, silhouetted in the light from the emergency lamps in the hallway. It — *he,* Marzana thought, though she couldn't make out the face at all — looked around the concourse. "Oh, my *God.*" He switched off his flashlight.

There was a reply from someone else, but it was unintelligible. The man stared around for a second or two more, then turned back. "Will you hurry up? The quicker we're out of here, the better."

Something thudded in the stairwell. More footsteps clattered down, and then there were two of them. Thanks to the brighter light at their backs, Marzana couldn't make out the features of either one, but she was pretty sure the second figure was also male. He was shorter and just a touch stockier than the first, and he stifled a noise of shock when he saw the iron's work in the concourse.

"What does it mean?" the second guy said, looking around in wonder.

"We knew it would be weird down here. It's the light that's concerning," the first man said. "Who's out there?" he shouted.

"Nobody here but us ghosts," Meddy called back from her post at the info counter. The two newcomers couldn't hear her, of course, but it was all Marzana could do not to erupt into nervous giggles.

"You know you're trespassing!" the tall guy called after a moment.

"That's rich, coming from —" Meddy's voice broke off. "Crap. Did he hear me? Can you hear me?" she shouted. Everybody held their breath. "He can't hear me," she said after a moment's pause.

"He's just doing that thing where you yell into an empty room, just in case. Nobody panic."

Another moment stretched, then the man who'd shouted turned to look at his companion. "I think we're alone. I bet there are motion sensors or something that tripped the backup power."

"Did they have motion sensors back when this place was built?" the stockier one asked dubiously.

"Never mind. Like I said, the quicker we're done, the better. Plus, if there *is* somebody down here, they don't want to get caught any more than we do. Here." He shrugged off his pack and shoved it into the other guy's hands. It looked practically empty. *Interesting,* Marzana thought. *They're here for something they expect to be able to carry out with them in a backpack. Something small.* He reached into his pocket and took out a piece of paper. "One fifty-two," he read. Then he looked up, glanced around, and pointed *directly at Marzana.* Or directly at the locker alcove, anyway; from where he was standing, he certainly couldn't make out the numbers.

She ducked back out of sight and glanced at the two nearest lockers. *You've got to be kidding me,* she thought desperately, staring at 150 and 151. She cursed silently. The locker they were coming for was in this aisle.

Quickly, she noted that 152 was one with a padlock on it — *Why would there be locks on any of these if the station never opened?* — then tiptoed as fast as she could toward the back of the row.

. . . Where there was nothing but wall. This aisle didn't connect with the next one over.

Her heart thudded. She could hear the approaching feet, but the concourse was so big, so open and empty, that she had no idea how close they were. Marzana bent, opened the double-width locker closest to the wall, and squeezed herself inside it. She hooked her fingers into the vents, pulled the door closed until she figured it would look shut, but stopped before it latched, in case she needed to get out fast. She held her breath.

"Marzana." She clapped both hands over her mouth, but it was only Meddy's voice, speaking through the vents. "J.J. and I are on it. Get ready to run."

"Their locker's padlocked," Marzana whispered back.

"'Kay," Meddy replied. "Emilia has lockpicks." She vanished.

The footsteps neared, then stopped. A small squeak of metal, then a clatter, as if one of the men had lifted the padlock and dropped it again. "Why couldn't he just have left us the key?" a voice griped.

"That wouldn't have been in the spirit of the thing. I still say this was supposed to be a game, not —"

"You can knock it off right now about that stuff." That was definitely the taller guy. "It's done, we're here — the picks are in the outside pocket. Hand them over."

Zzzip. Fabric noises. "You can get it open, right?"

"I think so," the other voice said, but it didn't sound particularly confident. "I've got wire cutters if we need them, but who knows how the thing is rigged? It *looks* like an ordinary padlock . . . but I didn't come this far just to ruin everything by getting impatient."

Hurry up, Marzana thought. *J.J., Meddy, whatever you're doing . . .* There was no reason to think the kidnappers would have any interest in the locker she was hidden in, so Marzana was pretty sure she was safe for the moment. But if her companions could get the two men away from the alcove somehow, maybe Emilia could do a little lockpicking herself. Thank goodness Brandon had chosen the shop all the way over near the exit stairs for his hiding place. Marzana could just imagine what the responsible adult would say if he had even an inkling of what she was considering right now. But if it worked, potentially they could trade whatever was in that locker for Peony's safe return.

"This pick isn't working," the tall kidnapper said, annoyed. "Pass me that toothy one."

"The rake?"

"Whatever it's called. Gimme."

"That's not actually how a rake works," Stocky Kidnapper said after a moment. "As I understand it."

"You want to try?" snarled his companion. "Did *you* spend the whole trip here practicing, or —"

He stopped talking abruptly, interrupted by an audible fizzle that was followed by an explosion of light so bright, the flash made it through the vents of Marzana's locker.

Here we go.

twenty-seven

PAS DE DEUX

J.J. HAD MENTIONED FLASH paper, but Marzana had pictured an effect like something you'd get from cheap fireworks, the kind you can set off on your front stoop. *This* flash paper, which had probably been deployed at very close range by a ghostly assistant, was on a whole other level.

The flare was accompanied by two muffled curses from the kidnappers, who clearly hadn't been able to close their eyes in time, along with a tiny clatter of metal that was probably the sound of Tall Guy's lockpicks falling from his hands.

"Crap, I can't see a *thing*. What *was* that? Some kind of electrical—"

"I don't know. I'm seeing stars, too. It must've been the light right over our—hey, Timmy? Look at that."

So Tall Guy was Timmy. "What do you mean, look?" he snapped. "Didn't I just say I couldn't see?"

"Blink a bunch or something. This is weird." The stocky guy's voice was moving away, as if he were walking out of the alcove and into the concourse again.

"Where are you going?" Timmy demanded, following his partner.

"Just me," Meddy's voice said a second before the door to Marzana's closed-but-not-latched locker eased open a few inches. One of Meddy's eyes winked as she reached through to drop a roll of fabric and a couple of metal sticks into Marzana's lap. The door eased shut again. Carefully, so as not to make a sound, Marzana peeked into the roll. A lockpick kit—Timmy's, presumably—and the picks he'd taken out to work on the padlock.

Meanwhile, Timmy's voice was moving away now too. "Kit, what are you looking at?" Timmy and Kit. Timmy was sounding a little desperate and a lot frustrated. "Come on, let's get this done!"

"You have to see this," Kit called back. "This is really bizarre. Is it . . . does it have something to do with the iron stuff?"

Marzana risked ever so slowly opening her locker door an inch again. Through the narrow space, she could see the backs of the two kidnappers, who'd gone to the end of the aisle of lockers and were now looking into the concourse.

Out there among the pockets of light and shadow, something was moving.

"What is that?" Timmy asked.

She caught a glimpse of it between the two men, just as Kit answered doubtfully, "I think it's a balloon." And it was: a big, almost perfectly round green balloon that bounced off the ground like a ball when it hit the floor. *A punching balloon,* Marzana thought, recalling a term she was pretty sure she hadn't used since elementary school.

She saw it only for a second or two before it moved out of view, but that was enough to show her that the balloon moved almost like a living thing. *Give me a spool of thread,* J.J. had said, *and I can do things you wouldn't believe.*

Marzana hesitated. Was this her distraction? But there was no point in climbing out — not yet, anyway, because the two thieves were still standing at the end of the aisle, blocking the way.

Meddy's face appeared in the crack. "Not yet," she said, putting a finger on Marzana's nose. "Out of sight, please. They're going to come back here after this, but just for a minute. Then it's all you and Emilia. She's waiting for my signal. Oh, and hold this for me." She took the gold reliquary vial from her pocket and passed it through the crack to Marzana. "Just in case I need a little more freedom of movement. I'd like to be able to walk through walls if I have to." Then she turned and picked up the backpack, which still lay on the floor by locker 152, where Kit had dropped it. "Now, let's see. How do I do this without the backpack disappearing?" She considered, then shrugged, carried it to right behind the two men, and drop-kicked it so that it flew between them and out of the aisle.

Kit and Timmy screamed identical screams. Marzana stifled a laugh and pulled the locker door nearly closed again just as they whirled around in panic.

"There's no one there!" Kit shrieked. "There's no one there, Timmy! No one!"

"CALM DOWN!" Timmy shouted in a voice that sounded like a bad compromise between attempting to stay calm and howling bloody murder. "WE KNEW IT WOULD BE WEIRD DOWN HERE, SO LET'S JUST GET THE DAMN LOCKER OPEN AND GET THE HELL OUT OF—" Then he lost it for real and snarled a short string of curses. "THE PICKS ARE GONE!" Timmy took a deep, gulping breath. "Kit, did you — KIT!"

"The backpack is dancing with the balloon," Kit said in a tone of terrified wonder. "*The backpack is dancing with the balloon, Timmy.* They're *dancing*. That's not the iron, right? That's something else."

"Kit!" *Thump*. Kit made a pained sound, as if Timmy had punched him to get his attention. "Kit, look at me. Don't look out there. *Look at me.* Do you have the picks?"

"No, I don't have the picks! Why would *I* have the picks? You said that was *your* thing, and now we can't get the locker open, and our backpack is *dancing with a balloon out there!*"

Timmy swore again. "The wire cutters, then. We can—" His voice fell silent. "The wire cutters are in the backpack." The curses that followed this might even have succeeded in making Honora blush. "We have to get the backpack."

"I don't know, Timmy," Kit said shakily. "The backpack looks like it's having a nice time right now with its new buddy there, and I'm not sure we should interrupt."

"We have to get out of here," Timmy gritted, "and I am not leaving without whatever's in that locker and neither are you, and I don't know where the damn lockpicks waltzed off to, so we need my wire cutters. So get moving!"

"But it's way over there," Kit protested weakly.

"Then you cut around to the left and I'll cut to the right and we'll attack from both sides. It's just a backpack, Kit." The words were confident, but his voice was shaking a little now too.

"I think it might have changed its mind about its choice of profession."

"*Move.*"

The sounds of two sets of footsteps receded: Timmy's forceful and Kit's reluctant. Marzana leaned out again, but through her little sliver of visibility, she couldn't see anyone. If one of the kidnappers was cutting around to each side of the waiting area, she figured, that probably put Emilia out of play. Should she run while she had time, aim for just getting out of her dead-end hiding place?

Even as she hesitated, Marzana discovered she'd counted out the Commorancy Kid too soon. Emilia slipped around the corner of the locker bank and darted down to her. "Hey."

"How the heck did you do that?" Marzana whispered, shoving Timmy's lockpicks into her back pocket as she climbed out.

Emilia shrugged, as if this feat of sneakery was no big thing. She took another pouch of picks from her bag. "I started moving right after Meddy came and told me about the padlock," she whispered. "Where's the one we want?"

"Here." Marzana tapped the padlock on 152. "Can you pop it?"

Emilia cupped the lock and looked it over. "Ah. Holdfast Beartrap," she said softly. "Mr. Caine uses one of these on the chemicals cabinet at Marymead." She rolled up her sleeves, selected two implements from her pick pouch, and inserted them into the keyway.

"Crap," Marzana muttered. Surely any lock a teacher would use on a cabinet full of dangerous chemicals—

Emilia popped the shackle open and glanced at Marzana's stunned face. "Don't be too impressed," she said quietly. "Beartraps are easy if you know what you're doing. The tougher-sounding the name, the weaker the lock." She glanced around dismissively. "There isn't a single one here that would take any skill to open. Not even the combination ones."

"But those guys—"

"Worse than amateurs," Emilia whispered, and stood aside. "All yours, boss."

But just as Marzana reached for the lock to pull it from the handle, Timmy's voice ricocheted through the space. "Hey! *You!*"

"Incoming!" Meddy shrieked. "Marzana, Emilia! *Get out of there!*"

Emilia scooped up her picks and her bag and darted out of the aisle. Spurred by some imp of the perverse, Marzana slammed the lock shut again before she followed. Those seconds were her undoing. At the end of the aisle, rather than flying out into the open space of the concourse, she ran smack into the tall kidnapper called Timmy.

The impact knocked the lockpicks loose from her pocket and right beneath her feet as she tried to backpedal. She went down hard, and before she could make any other move, Timmy had her by one wrist and her collar.

There was a flurry of sudden activity: to Marzana's right, Emilia struggled to yank herself loose from Kit's grip as Meddy, running in from behind him, began to whack the shorter kidnapper as hard as she could with his backpack. J.J. and Brandon were on their way too, sprinting in from where they'd been concealed. But before any of them could take another action, Timmy yanked Marzana upright and put something cold and hard against her throat. "Everybody stop. Everybody stop *right now.*"

Her heart felt like it was trying to hammer its way right out of her chest. It could only be a knife, the thing he was holding on her, because the others obeyed without a moment's hesitation.

"Move over there," Timmy said, and the pressure left Marzana's throat for a minute as he pointed toward the information desk with a short, wide utility blade. "Backpack, too. I don't know how you're doing that, but I don't want to see it move either. Everybody stand right there." To his companion he added, "Hang on to Blondie, though. Just in case, and you—" The knife blade pointed at Brandon. "Drop that wrench and kick it away." Brandon obeyed with a gritted curse.

Marzana, meanwhile, glanced at Kit, who had Emilia's wrists pinned behind her back, and realized it was the first glimpse she'd gotten of either man's face. Kit was brown-haired and fair-skinned, somewhere in his early twenties, probably. He had green eyes. And he was familiar. The thought *I've seen you before* fought its way up through the adrenaline flooding Marzana's brain. *But where?* "This has gotten so far out of hand," he fretted.

"Shut up," Timmy ordered. When Emilia had stopped struggling and Brandon, J.J., and Meddy stood together, the empty backpack dangling from Meddy's hands, Timmy kicked the lockpicks out from under his feet. "So that's where those went." He tapped the edge of the knife against Marzana's neck. "You had that lock open. I saw you shut it. Open it again."

"*I* did it," Emilia snapped. "Let her go. I'll pick it again."

"If you tell us where Peony Hyde is," Marzana added quickly. "That's all we want."

Kit's face froze with horror that would've torpedoed his attempt at playing dumb even if Marzana and her friends hadn't already known the truth. "What are you talking about?"

"Marzana," Brandon said warningly.

"What?" she retorted. "That's the deal. We know everything. You tell us where the real Peony is and we'll open your locker. Take it or leave it."

She felt rather than saw Timmy shake his head. "The time to bargain is not when somebody's got a knife on you."

"We were here waiting for you," Marzana said. "There's backup coming from above. From the Hydes' house. The only chance you have is to get out of here before they arrive. Otherwise you're trapped."

"Well, *you* didn't get here through the house," Timmy retorted, "so it seems to me that although we couldn't find it, there's another way in after all. So how about this?" He turned toward Emilia. "You open the lock, and I don't hurt your friend. Then she can show us how you all got in here, and once we're aboveground, she's free to go. As long as you stay out of the way and don't do anything to make me twitchy in the meantime."

"*She* doesn't know the way," Brandon said. "*I* do. I brought them here. Let her go and I'll gladly get you back to the surface. I know these tunnels. The kids don't. You'll be wandering the Belowground until you starve."

"*This is not a negotiation!*" Timmy screamed. He jabbed the knife at Emilia. "Get that bleeding lock open! Now!"

"Peony—" Marzana began. Timmy roared and stuck the knife up against her throat again.

"Marzana, shut up." Emilia spoke over them both in a trembling voice. "I'll do it," she repeated. "I have picks in my pocket."

Since there were picks on the ground in front of her already, Marzana suspected this was a ploy of Emilia's to try to get at something else she was carrying. Unfortunately, Timmy saw through it too. "Keep your hands where I can see them. You can use these." He kicked the roll of fabric on the floor closer to her. Kit let go of one wrist, and Emilia scooped it up, then allowed Kit—who was starting to look nauseated—to march her to the locker by her collar.

The feeling of having seen him before nagged at Marzana again, more strongly this time. The answer was there, hovering just out of reach, but between the fear and the sensation of the knife against her neck, she couldn't quite focus enough to catch it. She swallowed hard. "You're about to get what you came here for," she said. "Please tell us where Peony is. The real Peony. We know the one up in the Liberty was Tasha Cormorant in disguise."

She could just barely see Kit from the corner of her eye as he whirled around, nearly choking Emilia in the process. "How did you—"

Timmy interrupted in an icy voice. "The little girl was never in danger as long as everyone followed instructions. And everything went according to plan, right up until you all walked in here. If she doesn't make it home safely, it'll be nobody's fault but yours." He took the knife away just long enough to yank Marzana around, look her in the face, and repeat, *"Yours."* Then he frowned, and a bizarre expression flashed across his features. "You?"

And Marzana knew exactly what he meant. Because they'd met before. Earlier that week, in the dining room of Hedgelock Court.

Only he'd gone by a different name that day.

twenty-eight
THE TREASURE HUNT

MOTH FLETCHWOOD," Marzana said, bringing the name up with some difficulty. "You came to our house. Moth's short for Timothy, huh?" She turned her head just a fraction toward Kit. "And Kit's short for Christopher."

"And you're the captain's kid," Timmy/Moth replied. Then he spun her back around and put the knife in place again. "Keep at it!" he shouted at Emilia, who'd paused — or really, hadn't yet begun — picking the Beartrap.

Emilia sighed and went to work. Or pretended to, considering how fast she'd gotten it open before, because the lock didn't leap open at her touch. She was buying time.

Marzana thought fast, trying to outpace the fear that kept rising and rising. It was hard to reconcile the young man who'd come looking for her mom with the kind of person who'd harm a kid, but then again, when these two nice young men had come to Hedgelock, they'd already kidnapped — or hired someone to kidnap, but what was the difference really? — another innocent girl. There was no telling what they'd do.

Moth and Kit couldn't fight off all five of them, but — *stupid, stupid* — with Marzana a captive, they wouldn't have to. Not if Moth was really willing to hurt her. Probably right about now he was realizing that he *had* to be willing. She felt her knees begin to weaken and shake. *Don't panic. Focus.* Yes, he had to be willing, but on the other hand, he couldn't do it too early, or the others would have no reason not to rush him. If they all charged him at once, he might get a couple swipes in with that knife, but they'd be able to overcome him. Marzana eyed the increasingly sick-looking Kit and thought Little Brother wasn't going to bring much to the fight.

Still, her friends could get hurt, and by that time, of course, she'd be guaranteed to be in pretty bad shape herself. Or worse. Her knees began to knock again. *Focus. Claw down the panic and focus.* Nothing was going to happen before Emilia got that lock open. There was time. Time for something, maybe. But what? What could she do, pinned like this? She could speak; that was about all.

She could speak.

The panic that rose then was almost unbearable. *It can't all hang on me talking our way out of this,* she thought wildly. *It can't. I can't.* She had a sudden vision of herself asking Nialla the all-important question tomorrow: Did I do okay? *Well, Mars,* the imaginary Nialla replied, *you got yourself and everyone else killed. Wish I had better news for you.*

I can't do this, she thought desperately. But what else was there time for? What else could she do?

Her brain started its customary racing through possibilities: opening gambits, likely replies, worst-case scenarios — *stop thinking about worst-case scenarios* — alternate bad outcomes . . . because those were the simulations she was accustomed to running, even if it seemed like reality never did quite play out according to any of them. *There isn't time for this,* she told herself. *I don't know how to* not *do this!* her brain screamed back at her.

Seconds ticked by. She couldn't choke up, worrying about what to say. Not now. *If we get out of this alive, that means I did okay,* she told herself. *That's the metric. For once, that much, at least — knowing afterward whether I put my foot in it — will be easy.*

That's right, imaginary Nialla put in. *That's exactly right. Focus on that. You can do this. So go do it.*

The fear didn't precisely melt away, but it backed off, and Marzana found she could think again. What was in the locker? That was the point of this, after all.

Back when the Fletchwood brothers had come to her house, Marzana's mother had said their father had passed through Nagspeake fifteen years before. Christopher had asked if Tumbler might have left something behind in Nagspeake after that visit, and Moth — who had otherwise been eager to hear her mother talk about absolutely anything she was willing to divulge — had been furious. *Too late for that,* he had said, probably because by then, the job they'd hired Tasha Cormorant to undertake was already under way.

Marzana took as deep a breath as she could, considering the knife. "It's something from your father, isn't it?" she said shakily. "The thing in the locker."

"Shut up," Moth snapped.

"He left you something when he died?" Marzana persisted, putting the tiniest bit of emphasis on the word "died" and hoping the rest of the Knot was paying attention and not just freaking out about the knife at her throat. "Something that . . . that what? Told you to come look here?"

"Shut *up*."

"But you didn't mention it to my mother," Marzana persisted. "Why not? She could've helped."

"I asked," Kit spoke up. "I tried. Remember? I asked if he'd left anything behind in Nagspeake when he came back. Your mother didn't know."

Moth snorted. "She *said* she didn't know. But she made it pretty clear when she didn't reply to my letters that she didn't *care*. She sent them back unopened. The *captain* washed her hands of her crew the second that ship blew up."

"She did not!" Marzana retorted. "They were her family!"

"Well, she washed her hands of *us!*" Moth snarled. "I tried, you know. After Dad died. Yes, he left us a letter. It said he'd always meant to bring us back here. He said he'd left something special for us to find here, apologized for never making the trip with us. But that was all! Our inheritance was that and a poem, of all things. A *poem!* After that, I wrote letters to his precious captain for a year, but without a single word in reply. So we came out to see for ourselves, and what do you know but the land over this station had been sold and that damned house built and everything below it sealed up."

"So that's why he never came back with you and Kit," Marzana said, trying to make her voice sound soothing, reasonable. "He must've learned about the station being sealed up, and he didn't know about the back way in here. And Violet Cross and her crew never messed with civilians, so he wouldn't have broken in through the house above."

"It doesn't matter now!" Moth shrieked. "We'd already put this in motion when I came to your house. I just wanted to see the famous captain once. To see this person my father loved so deeply but who couldn't be bothered to so much as write back to his children."

"It was for everyone's safety," Marzana insisted, remembering what Mrs. Hakelbarend had said after Moth had left the house earlier that week. "They all agreed. Do you know what it cost my mother? Cost *everyone?* That crew loved each other."

"That's not good enough. Because those of us who loved *them* needed more." Moth's hand holding the knife was shaking a little now. Marzana tried not to think of what might happen if she made him too angry. "And here we are. What's taking so long?" he snarled at Emilia.

Emilia pointed at the lock with a pick. "You think it's so easy? You do it!"

Moth swore, but he didn't offer to try again himself.

"Your dad wouldn't want this," Marzana persisted. "What could possibly be in there that's worth this, right here?"

"Marzana," Brandon said in a warning tone, "please . . . please be careful."

"It's our inheritance," Moth spat. "And he left it here for us. He called it our treasure hunt—the treasure hunt he'd wanted to take us on but couldn't. So I'm pretty sure he *did* want this. You didn't know him. Keep your opinions to yourself."

"Timmy," Kit said miserably, still grasping Emilia's collar, "please don't."

"Would he have wanted you to kidnap someone to get it?" Marzana asked reluctantly.

"*We* didn't do that," Moth argued. "*She* did. The carrier—I hired her to empty out the house. I didn't tell her how to do it, and she didn't tell me the details."

At this, Marzana nearly laughed. "Deniability. Boy, do I know about that."

"Not another word," Moth said in a low, deadly tone.

Marzana nodded, and for a moment, there was nothing but terrified breathing and the *scritch-scratch* of Emilia's fake lockpicking.

What had her mother said about Tumbler Fletchwood? That he had been a gentle soul who loved poetry and puzzles. *He taught me everything I know about locks,* Mrs. Hakelbarend had said. *He could open anything. Absolutely anything.*

If Tumbler had known as much about locks as her mother had said, why had he put the treasure at the end of the hunt behind one that was so easy to pop? *There isn't a single one here that would take any skill to open,* Emilia had said. And who would have used them, since the station had never been opened? Where had they all come from?

Tumbler had been responsible for at least one of them, the one securing locker 152. Could he have been responsible for the others, too? That was perhaps the simplest answer. And if he had been, then the so-called treasure hunt couldn't be what Moth thought it was. If it was the kind of treasure that had to be secured and protected from anyone else finding it, surely an expert in locks would have made different choices.

"Whatever's in there," she said softly, praying that she was choosing the right words, "it's not what you think it is." *Please let me be right.*

Moth's arm stiffened even more, but he said nothing.

"When he left this for you, the station hadn't been sealed up yet. He thought all you'd have to do was find the entrance and figure out a way to get in." Marzana gestured at the banks of lockers with her chin. The blade rasped against her skin. "He went to the trouble of putting dozens of locks down here so the one meant for you wouldn't stand out. He thought it was possible other people might find it, so he gave it some super-basic camouflage. But he also used a padlock anyone with the skills could open. And you know what *that* tells me?"

"Enlighten me," Moth said through clenched teeth.

Marzana licked her lips. "Whatever's in there, it's not money or jewels or anything like that. It's not going to be a trove worth breaking laws for. Your father knew there was a chance someone else would find it, and he wasn't that worried about it, because he knew it was something only his own family would care about." She ignored the hand around her wrists that was clenching and unclenching with fury. As long as he kept the knife hand steady, that was all that mattered. "Your father wasn't a pirate, and he wasn't on a crew that smuggled just to make themselves rich. Whatever's in there, it's not an inheritance. It's a different kind of gift. I bet it's something like the book of poems he brought back from Nagspeake for your mother," she added, remembering another detail from their visit to Hedgelock Court.

Kit spoke up. "You said he used a lock that . . . that anyone—"

"Yeah. Emilia," Marzana called, "you can quit stalling. They need to see it."

Emilia sighed and gave the lock a yank. It fell open in her hand. She unthreaded it from the latch and stepped aside. "Be my guest."

Moth turned with Marzana still clutched tight and watched Kit as he let go of Emilia's collar and reached for the latch.

"Timmy?" Kit said hesitantly.

Moth Fletchwood gave a little twitch toward the locker, then seemed to remember he had to keep his eyes on Brandon and J.J. and whatever or whoever was responsible for the mysteriously floating backpack. Marzana could feel his hesitation.

"I didn't know Tumbler Fletchwood," Marzana said quietly, turning her head just a fraction to try to look Moth in the eye, "but I know who his shipmates were. So I do have a pretty good idea what kind of person he was. And . . . I know what it is to need more," she said with difficulty, wishing she could turn farther to really include Kit in the statement. "More stories, more information. To know where you came from. I think even if it's not the kind of inheritance you were expecting, whatever's in there will be something you want. You see if I'm right."

"That's all *I* ever wanted," Kit said quietly. "To know more about who Pop really was. Not this, Timmy," he said bitterly to his brother. "Not kidnapping."

"That was *her*, not us," Moth said. But his mind was clearly elsewhere. Marzana felt the knife move just slightly away from her neck as he turned to Kit and the locker. "Open it," he said to his brother.

Kit pulled up on the latch and swung the door open. He stared inside for a moment. "There's nothing here."

twenty-nine
LOCKER 152

THE BOTTOM DROPPED out of Marzana's stomach. Moth lowered the knife altogether, yanked up on her wrists even as her knees buckled, and shoved her down the aisle until they came to the open locker. Kit had been telling the truth. There was nothing there. It was completely empty.

"Somebody must've—" Kit began.

"Stop talking," Moth whispered. "Just stop."

Brandon spoke from the end of the aisle. "Let the girls go now," he said, cracking his knuckles. "You're not getting past me." J.J. stood a few paces behind him. Where was Meddy?

Moth jerked the knife back up to Marzana's neck, but he said nothing, just kept staring into the empty locker. Kit, meanwhile, kept talking, as if neither his brother nor Brandon had spoken. "I'm just saying, it's been, what? It's been *fifteen years*. Somebody could've —or maybe it was the iron! Maybe it's still here, just hanging from the ceiling somewhere—or maybe Pop never actually left anything at all!"

"*Stop.*" Moth dropped the knife from Marzana's neck momentarily and used the back of that hand to wipe sweat from his forehead. He was shaking; Marzana could feel it through the fingers that still held her wrists. Moth was losing control. This could very well go horribly wrong. Even worse than it already had gone.

What else can I do? What else can I say?

"There was a year in between," Kit said, grabbing his brother's forearm with both hands before the latter could bring the blade up to Marzana's neck again. Emilia edged herself farther out of the way, toward the dead end of the aisle. Kit didn't seem to notice. "Between the time Pop left it and the time the entrances were sealed and the house was built. Someone found it back then," he insisted. "Found their way down here and took it, whatever it was. Must have. There's no other explanation."

"Yes, there is." Moth let go of Marzana's wrists, spun her around, and slammed her back against locker 151. "You got here first. *You* took it. *What did you do with it?*"

"I didn't take it," Marzana choked. "But—but I know who we can ask. Tumbler?" she said desperately, raising her voice and hoping Meddy took the hint. "Tumbler Fletchwood? Are you out there?"

"Is this a joke?" Moth snarled.

"Tumbler?" Marzana called again. "Your sons are here. They need to know something. If you're here, we need to talk to you."

It was a Hail Mary. But, she figured, if there was one thing a ghost and a magician could maybe do, it was put together the appearance of another ghost.

Then, out of nowhere, the green balloon came bouncing past

Brandon and down the aisle toward them. Marzana glanced sharply at J.J. His face was impassive, which was maybe a pretty good indicator that he was up to something. He caught Marzana's eye and rapidly reconfigured his face to show surprise. But if he was controlling the balloon—and it had to be either him or Meddy—Marzana had no idea how.

"You're doing that," Kit said, pointing at Marzana. "Or he is," he added, swinging his hand around to point at Brandon. "You were doing it before. And the backpack, too. I don't know how, but—"

The balloon stopped bouncing midway between Brandon and J.J. at the end of the aisle as Moth, Marzana, and Kit gathered around locker 152.

"I'm here," came Meddy's voice from above the bank of lockers Marzana was still pressed against. One small hand waved overhead, just barely within her frame of vision. "Tell us what you need us to do."

Okay, Marzana thought. *I'm the magician now. And somehow I've got to tell my assistants what trick we're doing and pull the trick off at the same time.*

"Tumbler?" she said, staring at the balloon. "Is that you?"

It bounced. Not a little bounce, either. A big bounce, three feet straight up.

"Pop?" Kit asked dubiously. Moth said nothing. His face was a mask of disbelief, but he eased up on the pressure with which he had been shoving Marzana against the locker.

"Your sons came all this way to find what you left," Marzana said. "But if there was something here, it's gone now. Do you have a message for them?"

J.J. stiffened and surreptitiously touched his bag of magic supplies, which he had slung over one shoulder. Marzana nodded just a fraction. Message received: He could pull off a communication from a false ghost, but he needed a distraction.

The audience looks where the magician looks. Marzana needed a reason to make everyone's eyes look away from J.J. "I think maybe one of you should ask," she said to Moth. "He doesn't know me. You're family."

Predictably, Moth scoffed. "I'm not talking to a *balloon*," he snapped. "This is preposterous." Though he sounded less certain than before.

"I'll do it," Kit said, and before he could step forward to approach the balloon, it bounced forward to meet him. Everyone followed its motion, Marzana included. She had to sell the illusion, after all. For just a moment, as it bounced toward Kit, she linked eyes with Emilia over Kit's shoulder. Emilia, in turn, flicked her eyes past Marzana and out into the concourse. Then she gave a brief wink and the tiniest nod. Something was happening out in the station, while Kit and Moth were distracted by the balloon. Marzana was facing the wrong way to see it, but Emilia had a clear view.

Kit, meanwhile, bent to crouch before the round green balloon. "Pop? Is that you? It's me, Kit. Christopher." He looked up at his brother. "This is weird."

"It's ridiculous," Moth snapped.

The balloon bounced once and shot up off the ground until it was eye level with Moth and an inch from his nose. *Say that to my face,* it seemed to be demanding.

Moth recoiled. "What the —"

"Wait," Kit said quickly. "Pop, it's us. Kit and Timmy. We figured out where you set the treasure hunt. We came all the way from Maryland!" His voice caught for a moment. "But there's nothing in the locker, Pop."

"Did these little thieves take it?" Moth demanded, shaking Marzana. "Bounce once for yes and twice for no. If you're really there," he added, reddening a little.

"J.J.'s done," Meddy said from above. "Keep them going another minute."

The balloon bounced twice: No, the little thieves hadn't taken whatever was in the locker.

Moth snarled in fury and slammed Marzana against the locker again. She winced as her head hit metal. "I *told* you we didn't."

"And I'm supposed to take the word of a *balloon* about that?" He pointed the knife at her. "This has gone far enough."

The balloon bounced again. "Timmy, stop," Kit begged.

"Tumbler, please, tell them something," Marzana managed. "Anything. Please. They need your message."

"Stop talking to the damned balloon!"

Suddenly the streaking shape of Meddy darted between the green balloon and Kit, past Moth and Marzana. She leaped into locker 152 and pulled the door shut behind her with a bang. Everyone jumped and stared.

The balloon drifted gently over and bumped the door of 152 once. Twice. Three times.

Moth lowered his knife.

Bump. Bump.

"There's nothing in there, Pop," Kit protested. "We looked."

Bump. Bump. Bumpbumpbumpbumpbump.

Kit and Moth looked at each other. Then Kit touched the latch handle. The green balloon drifted back to give him space. He opened the door.

There, of course, was Meddy. Sitting before her on the bottom of the locker—the only thing visible to Moth and Kit—was an envelope.

"Take her." Moth shoved Marzana into Kit's hands. As he reached for the envelope, Meddy held up her hands to display—to Marzana, anyway—a matchbox and a single wooden match. She struck the match against the box and brought the flame to the edge of the envelope just as Moth picked it up.

"What the—" He tried to blow out the fire that was suddenly, inexplicably consuming the paper, but it tore through so fast that all he could do was let the burning handful drop, shaking his singed fingers.

The fire destroyed the envelope in less time than it took to reach the ground. But somehow it failed to burn away the contents. Moth bent, picked up what was left behind, and held them up: two playing cards with a pattern of gold and green balloons on the backs. The colors were different, but Marzana thought the pattern was similar to the gold-and-black cards J.J. had used as weapons in Mrs. Agravin's flat the night before.

Moth looked warily from the cards to the bobbing green sphere. "This is your message?"

The balloon bounced once.

Moth looked down at the two cards again. One by one, he turned them over. Then he shouted and flung them at Kit, who scrambled to catch them one-handed without letting go of Marzana. He failed, but the cards landed face-up on the floor, so that Kit and Marzana could see what Moth had seen. A message appeared to have been burned into the cards, both of them jokers.

You took a child
Where is she?

Moth staggered backwards and slumped against the wall of lockers as Kit let go of Marzana and collapsed to the ground, covering his face with his hands and sobbing. Emilia darted from the dead end and jumped over him as Meddy dropped out of the locker at Marzana's side, and the three of them careened toward the end of the aisle, where Brandon was already rushing in.

Moth made a halfhearted grab at them with a shaking hand, but the green balloon bounced itself up in between, and he recoiled as if it were a human with a weapon rather than a big ball of rubber and air. Brandon seized Marzana and Emilia and hauled them out of the aisle. "Go get aboveground now," he ordered, shoving them toward J.J. "Go up and call the police."

"What about you?" Marzana asked.

"Two guys with their backs to the wall, I can probably handle," Brandon said. "Even once they get themselves together, they're not going to be operating on all cylinders."

At this, Moth snarled a particularly nasty epithet at Brandon. He grabbed his brother. "Kit, we have to get out of here."

"You'll stay put," Brandon barked.

Moth straightened, flailed his way past the balloon, and ran at Brandon with a wild yell. Brandon put up one foot and planted it in Moth's midsection, easily evading the knife and kicking him down like a door. Moth fell on his backside and slid all the way back to his still-sobbing brother.

"Get moving," Brandon ordered, turning to the kids. "Go now."

"I'll stay with him," Meddy offered.

"And there's Pop," J.J. said with a wink.

"Yeah," Meddy said, giving him an odd look. "Sure."

"Would you go?" Brandon said, exasperated. *"Move."* He

squared himself up in the entrance to the aisle. "Idiots *will* keep getting up when they ought to stay down."

Marzana grabbed the straps of J.J.'s magic bag and Emilia's backpack. "Come on." The three of them ran toward the stairwell passage. "That was amazing, J.J.," she said as they ran. "The flashy envelope with the burned notes inside, the balloon? Outstanding."

"Well, I took my cues from you," he huffed, a little out of breath. "The envelope and the notes are pretty standard tricks. And the balloon was Meddy. I mean, I was up in the tree doing it when she was making Moth's backpack dance, but in the aisle, that was all her. It was too close up for my method. They'd have seen the string."

They reached the stairs and sprinted up. Moth and Kit had dug through the roof a few feet from the top of the staircase, resulting in a five-foot drop down to the steps. A rope ladder hung in the dusty light from the room above, an odd shaft of yellow in a space otherwise lit by the harsher light of the emergency lamps. Marzana grabbed the rope sides, lifted a foot onto one of the rungs, and froze. She put out a hand to stop the others, backed down two steps, and lifted a finger to her mouth.

There were voices up there.

"Our guys or theirs?" Emilia whispered.

Before Marzana could answer, someone called out. "Who's down there? Declare yourselves."

Marzana knew the voice at once. "Dad!" she shouted. "It's us!" She grabbed the bottom of the ladder again and looked up into his worried eyes.

"Marzana!" His face disappeared, replaced by a pair of feet climbing down as fast as the swaying ladder would allow. Then she was in her father's arms. "You are in so much trouble, young lady," he said into her hair, but there was no anger in his voice.

"I know." Marzana extracted one arm and pointed over her shoulder. "The kidnappers are there. Two of them, anyway. Brandon has them cornered. Is Mom here?" Her mother was already halfway down the ladder, and there was a third pair of feet up in the hole, waiting for their turn to descend. "Mom," Marzana said, not bothering to wait for her to make it down to the stairs, "it's Moth Fletchwood and his brother, Kit."

Her mother swore as she dropped the last few feet. She kissed Marzana's forehead. Then she pointed two fingers at J.J. and Emilia and ordered, "You two, stay." As Emmett Syebuck and another man who had to be his cop friend from Criminal Investigation started down the ladder one after the other, Mrs. Hakelbarend turned back to Marzana. "Show us."

Marzana nodded and led her parents, Emmett, and the cop down the stairs and across the concourse of Mergenthaler Street Station to where Brandon stood at the ready, guarding the locker bank with Meddy at his side. "Good Lord," the cop muttered as they passed the bizzare cluster of iron chutes and ladders. Emilia and J.J. pretended not to have heard the order to stay put and followed too.

"Ahoy, Brandon," Emmett called. Brandon raised a hand but kept his eyes trained down the aisle of lockers. The Fletchwood brothers sat side by side on the floor. Kit was curled over, shaking a little as if he was still crying. Moth looked up, trying to appear defiant despite it all. The hand that held his knife rested on one knee. The other hand lay on his brother's shoulder.

Between them and Brandon, the green balloon bobbed at shoulder level. But as soon as Marzana, her parents, and the two lawmen appeared, the balloon began to dart wildly this way and that, sputtering and gasping and rapidly shrinking in size as the air rushed out of it. Both Fletchwoods screamed: Kit in a bizarre mix of misery and terror, Moth in terror and rage. At last it stopped its flight and drifted down like a big green rubber feather into Marzana's outstretched hand. J.J. and Meddy broke into applause, as if clapping for an epic magic trick.

"Last chance, boys," Brandon said. "I imagine the only thing these good folks are interested in hearing from you is where you stashed your hostage."

"Oh, never mind that," Emmett said carelessly. "The girl managed to get a message out along with the ransom note, and Marzana's friends found it. When they told us where to find you all, they also told us to look for Peony someplace with chemically treated water, yipping, shrieking animals, and teacups. And there she was!" He grinned at the twin expressions of confusion on the Fletchwood brothers' faces. "Thad sent a team to the abandoned amusement park out on the city limits. The foxes were quiet, but Peony was there, in a tunnel with a bunch of retired teacup cars from the *Alice in Wonderland* ride. Can't wait to have a talk with her."

"Let us go," Moth said. He hesitated, licking his lips, and the acid began to bubble up in Marzana's stomach. He was working himself up to something, and whatever it was, even *he* didn't want to say it. "Let us go," he said at last, looking at Marzana's mother, "or I'll tell them who you really are."

Emilia and J.J. gasped. Brandon swore. Meddy groped for Marzana's palm with a hand that couldn't quite maintain its solidity. With her stomach full of boiling acid, Marzana could only manage to whisper, "No."

It was the most predictable card of all, maybe the only one left in the Fletchwoods' hands. Of course they would try to play it.

"We already know," Emmett said coldly.

"We'll tell everyone," Moth argued, his voice rising wildly.

"Everyone — *anyone*. Not a single person in Nagspeake won't know her name."

Meddy let go of Marzana's hand. "Let me talk to him. Let me tell him what happens when certain people get information like that." Her voice splintered, and she took a step forward. "Let me spell it out so he knows he'll be a murderer on top of everything else."

But Barbara Hakelbarend, by any name, was having none of it. She ignored the outbursts, pausing only to put a hand on Meddy's shoulder to draw her back toward the other members of the Knot and murmur, "Not yet." Then she faced Moth Fletchwood. "Will you, Moth?" she said quietly. "I think you won't. If there's any small piece of your father in you, you know you won't." She nodded at Kit, rocking back and forth at his brother's side. "Kit knows. Stop pretending to be what you're not."

"I'm not pretending," Moth said sourly.

Marzana's mother's mouth twitched. "*I'm* going to spell out a few things for you, and then I'm going to pretend I never heard you threaten my life, and my husband's life, and my *daughter's* life. And then you're going to go and face up to the consequences of what you did." She glanced at Emmett and the other cop. "You gentlemen will correct me if I get anything wrong, legally speaking."

Emmett looked like he wanted to tear Moth limb from limb, but he folded his arms and nodded. "Your show."

"The two of you are on the hook for breaking and entering and conspiracy," Mrs. Hakelbarend began. "But if you're smart, you can make the argument that when you hired Tasha Cormorant to arrange emptying out the house, you didn't know how she'd do it."

"We didn't!" Kit interrupted frantically, his words uneven. "She wouldn't tell us anything; she just said to be ready —"

"You should stop talking," Marzana's mother said, and Kit dropped his face back into his hands. "So you may be able to avoid kidnapping charges, and without those, Nagspeake will have a hard time extraditing you once you're back in the States."

"Back in the States?" J.J. whispered. "Why would they go to the States?"

"They're not from Nagspeake," Marzana whispered back. "They're American. From Maryland, remember?"

"American citizens," her father confirmed, nodding. "And the United States and Nagspeake have had tensions about extradition since before the Revolutionary War. You'll be deported, and you can't ever come back, but your government won't allow you to be jailed or tried in Nagspeake. I don't know what the States will do with the information about your crimes that will be sent back with you, but without a kidnapping charge . . ." He shrugged and said a little bitterly, "I don't think it'll be much."

"I don't want *any* crimes following me back," Moth argued. Kit shot him a disgusted look, and Marzana realized the older brother had said "me" rather than "us." "And you still need to bargain," Moth insisted. "There's Tasha to think about too. She won't go down quietly."

At that, the non-Fletchwood adults in the room actually laughed: chuckles of amusement from the Hakelbarends and Brandon, snorts of frustration from Emmett and his friend.

"She's not going down for this," Emmett said. "She knew before we did that the jig was up. She's gone, Moth. Slipped right out of the house where she'd been posing as the Hydes' daughter and keeping an eye on them while the family was supposedly recovering from this ordeal. Whoever she had guarding the real girl skipped out too. We found Peony untied and left with provisions. She was already following the tracks from the *Alice* ride out of the tunnel to the surface."

"No," Moth said, staggered.

Emmett shrugged at the other man's disbelief. "It took Marzana's friends six phone calls and a couple messages to track me down. Maybe one of those calls or messages happened to pass through someone on her payroll, or maybe she had a phone tapped somewhere, but her job is information, Moth. This isn't surprising."

"And even if she had been caught," Mrs. Hakelbarend said, "she wouldn't sing. She'd never work again if she did. She's already squandered some goodwill on this job throwing suspicion around the way she did. She danced right up to the line, but she won't dare actually cross it. She wants a career, and if she gives up names, she's done for."

Moth opened his mouth to argue further, but Kit cut him off. "Stop, Timmy. Just stop." He still hadn't quite managed to stop crying, and his words were like hiccups.

"Your father was a good man." Marzana's mother spoke in a voice like ice. "He would've been horrified."

Kit shook his head and began to sob again. Moth Fletchwood dropped the knife between his feet, clutched his head in his hands, and let out a single long, low moan.

thirty
VERSES

MMETT AND HIS COP FRIEND marched Moth and Kit Fletchwood back up to the surface, leaving Marzana and her parents, Brandon, Meddy, Emilia, and J.J. alone by the lockers.

"Will this cause you problems?" Meddy asked Brandon. "With
the Belowground, I mean. Keeping it secret."

Brandon shook his head, unconcerned. "I'm sure Emmett can
handle his friend. We did him a huge favor. He'll pay it back; same
with the Hydes. It's happened before. This is how the old hole-and-
corner railway stays that way."

"I can't wrap my head around it," Mrs. Hakelbarend said.
"Those boys really thought old Tumbler left them some kind of inheritance? Jewels or money or something? *Tumbler?*"

"It seems like maybe he did plant something here when he came
back through Nagspeake," Marzana said. "He described it as a treasure hunt he hadn't been able to bring them on, so they went a little
nuts — or Moth did, anyway — when there was nothing to find. It

couldn't have been valuable in the money sense — Emilia said the lock was about as easy to pick as they make them — but whatever was there must've been discovered by somebody long ago."

"Maybe, though it would also have been right in character for Tumbler to have set up some kind of elaborate wild goose chase ending in a boxful of nothing," Mrs. Hakelbarend said with a short, sad laugh. "He was a goofball. He was such a sweet goofball." The last word caught in her throat as she said it.

Marzana took her mother's hand. "I guess if somebody had found something there years ago, they probably wouldn't have gone to the trouble of locking it up again." The Beartrap Emilia had picked was lying on the ground. Marzana walked over and retrieved it. The logo engraved on the front was a growling bear. One of the locks on the old iron fence at Marymead had this same logo, only that one also had two lines of writing scratched into it, one above and one below the bear: *Bobby and Lila. February 14 — Forever.*

"Huh," Marzana said thoughtfully.

She turned the lock over, dimly aware that everyone was watching her. Ignoring the embarrassed prickles of heat this brought to her face was easier than usual. An idea was forming.

What else could I tell those kids? Mrs. Hakelbarend had asked after Moth and Kit's visit to Hedgelock Court. *Tumbler was a sweet guy. He loved poetry. He loved a good brainteaser. He was a whiz with locks. Taught me everything I know.*

The back of this Beartrap lock had been engraved too. It was much neater than the scratchy scrawls on the locks on the Marymead fence, but it, too, had clearly been done by hand, in one of those fancy, old-fashioned scripts. The letters were right-side up when the shackle was pointed down.

I'll tell you a story of wind and of water
208

Marzana covered her mouth. She glanced around at all those other locks. Maybe they hadn't been intended as camouflage after all.

Oh, Nye, I really, really wish you were here.

"Mom," she said, "I think Tumbler did leave them something. And it's still here." The other members of the Knot pushed past the adults as Marzana held up the lock.

"Two-oh-eight," J.J. read. "Another locker number?"

"I think so."

Emilia peered at the numbers surrounding them. "Must be in the next aisle."

Marzana reached into her little kit bag and pulled out the notepad and pen. "J.J., would you take this down?"

They rushed around the corner, following the numbers until they came to 208, which sported a green-enameled padlock with a fir-tree logo. Marzana flipped it upside down. Two more lines of text had been scratched through the green and into the brass below.

Of deeds great and small and a grand smuggler queen
120

J.J. squatted beside the lock to take the line down. Then Emilia picked the lock with her usual ease, and they all stared in. The locker was empty. "On to one-twenty, I guess," Emilia said.

With Marzana's parents and Brandon watching, bemused, the

four of them followed Tumbler Fletchwood's path from lock to lock. Each held a line of the larger message, along with a number that pointed them to the next one.

Each was engraved with the lettering upside down, just like the first, and each, when Emilia got it open, was revealed to be empty. "Still nothing," she observed.

They were up to the fifth lock. Marzana flipped it up so that the back faced out with the letters right-side up. "I bet that's why they're all inscribed like this. The first lock had to be easily pickable, because if you didn't take it off, you'd probably never look closely enough at it to find the words. But the lines are all written upside down so once you know they're there, you don't have to take the locks off to read them." *I'll tell you a tale of a place like a dream,* this one said.

"Maybe the locks and what they say are all there is," Meddy suggested.

There were sixteen locks, total. After the line of verse on the last one, a combination lock, the word FIN had been engraved in place of a number. "Guess that's it," Marzana said, holding the lock up so J.J. could finish writing it down. "What have we got?"

J.J. passed her the notebook. "You do the honors."

With her friends on her heels, Marzana carried it out into the slightly better light of the main room, where the grownups were waiting. "Okay. Here we go."

> "I'll tell you a story of wind and of water,
> Of deeds great and small and a grand smuggler queen,
> Of days we were heroes, of villains and hazards,
> The rivers and ocean we sailed in between.

I'll tell you a tale of a place like a dream,
Where strange things await 'round each corner and bend,
Where streets with no names lead to journeys and perils
And miraculous sights down each shadowed dead end.

We voyaged here many a magical year,
A shipful of heroes and our smuggler queen;
Now here we are, you and I, back all together
So I can share with you these places I've been.

But the best place to be and the tales I most treasure
In all my home seas, from one 'Peake to the other,
After years of adventures and exploits and wonders,
The greatest of all have been you and your brother."

She looked up. "That's it."

Her mother smiled. "Now, that sounds like Tumbler Fletch-wood." She shook her head sadly. "And those boys never knew he left this for them."

Marzana lowered the notebook. "The worst part is, I think they already had it. Moth said that along with the letter saying he was sorry he never got to take them on the treasure hunt he'd set, Tumbler left them a poem." She took the first lock from her pocket and looked at the engraved line. "They had it the whole time." She returned the lock to its latch and clicked it shut.

Emilia, who had been strolling among the lockers as she'd listened to the poem, called out from somewhere down one of the aisles. "Hey, Marzana? You won't believe this, but there's something in this one after all."

Marzana, J.J., and Meddy followed her voice back to locker

201, where the final lock had been. "Well? What?" Marzana asked, curious.

"I'm not actually sure." Emilia stood in front of the open locker, swinging the lock thoughtfully around her thumb. "See for yourself."

Inside were two tall, narrow packages. The paper wrappings were faded and yellowing, but the pattern on each was still clearly visible and unmistakably cartographic. "Wow," Marzana breathed, reaching in to bring the parcels out into the dim light. "Mom! Dad! Come look at this!"

Mr. and Mrs. Hakelbarend hurried down the aisle and peered over the heads of the kids. Her father whistled.

"I don't believe it," Mrs. Hakelbarend said. "I haven't seen one of these in ages."

Meddy watched, fascinated. "Are those what I think they are?"

Marzana's mother nodded. "Looks like it."

"Well, what are they?" J.J. asked impatiently.

"The Windrose and the Portolan," Marzana replied. "Kites. Very special kites." Her voice caught in her throat. "Kites with a story." The tale of the kites, which had been printed with maps and distributed by Violet Cross and her crew long ago in the days when any cartography not made by Deacon and Morvengarde had been contraband in Nagspeake, was one of the few stories her mother had told Marzana herself.

"And they flew like anything," Mr. Hakelbarend said, kissing Marzana's head. "Unbelievably good fliers, those kites."

Her mother grinned. "It would've been pointless if they hadn't."

Marzana clutched the parcels to her chest. Then she hesitated. "Can we take them with us?" Moth and Kit might never have them, but they were part of Tumbler's gift, and somehow she felt uncertain about taking any part of that gift away.

"You absolutely should take them," Mrs. Hakelbarend said. "I guarantee you Tumbler didn't put a pair of kites here fifteen years ago for his two young sons because he figured they'd be museum pieces. You read that poem. Why do *you* think he did it?"

"So they could all fly them together after they solved the treasure hunt," Marzana guessed, blinking away the wavering in her eyes. Tumbler Fletchwood had planned a true Nagspeake adventure for his Chesapeake-born sons, who, much like Marzana and Nialla, had probably grown up thinking nothing exciting ever happened to them.

"Kites should be flown," Mrs. Hakelbarend said. "These, especially." She laughed. "Emmett's going to go nuts when he sees them."

"Nialla and Ciro, too," Marzana said. "Can I tell them the story?" Nialla, with her obsession with manipulating paper to reveal hidden meanings, and Ciro the camoufleur? The tale behind the map kites would blow their minds.

Mrs. Hakelbarend considered. Then she smiled. "I think so."

Marzana felt herself glow. "Thank you."

"Welcome."

"All right, crew," Marzana's father said at last. "What do you think? Can we get out of here now?"

Marzana nodded. "I think we're done."

Brandon jogged away for a quick trip to the surface to have a word with Emmett, who was busy with the captives and the additional arriving police. "Peony's really okay?" Marzana asked her mother. The other members of the Knot edged closer to hear the answer.

"She's really okay," Mrs. Hakelbarend said. "And I don't know how long it would've taken for us to find her or for her to find her way home if you guys hadn't spotted that message she hid in the ransom note."

"But what about Tasha Cormorant?" Emilia asked.

Mrs. Hakelbarend gave Emilia a considering look. "She'll surface again at some point."

"My dad would never have put together any job that involved taking a kid," Emilia said defensively.

Marzana's mother put one arm around Emilia's shoulders, and Marzana, J.J., and Meddy stared as Emilia slumped into the embrace. "There are plenty of bad apples out there in the world," Mrs. Hakelbarend said quietly. "Never let that make you doubt that your dad was one of the good ones."

"All right," Brandon called as he returned. "Let's get you all home. Train's waiting."

As they walked, Marzana did something she hadn't done in a long time. She took hold of her mother's hand. Mrs. Hakelbarend looked down in some surprise. Then she squeezed Marzana's palm.

"Walk slow," Marzana whispered. Her mother obeyed. She said nothing, waiting for Marzana to put her thoughts in order.

"Mom, I feel like I understand them a little," Marzana said quietly, once there was a bit of distance between themselves and the others. "Moth and Kit, I mean. And it makes me feel . . . I don't know. Gross."

Mrs. Hakelbarend gave her a long look. "You understand why they were hurting, or you understand why they took that hurt and proceeded to set this whole mess into motion?"

"The first part," Marzana said quickly. "It's just . . . you know how I keep asking you to tell me more? About you and the old days, and who you used to be and . . . all of it? Mom, I feel like I need that.

I *need* it." Her voice rose just a bit before she managed to stop it. "I think Kit Fletchwood was feeling something like that. Maybe that's even how it started out for Moth, before he convinced himself that there was something of value here. He must've spent a ton of money and time setting all of this up, and there was really no reason to think that what Tumbler had hidden was all that valuable. This all started out with the Fletchwoods trying to find out where they came from."

"You think I should've been more forthcoming," Mrs. Hakelbarend said quietly.

"Well, yeah," Marzana said. "With *me*. Obviously. But I'm not saying it's your fault Moth did this. I'm saying I think I understand what they needed, or thought they needed, before this caper of theirs went from a game to a kidnapping . . . And it's freaking me out."

"I understand that." Her mother nodded. "Empathy is important. But making excuses — that's a whole other ball of wax. And I don't hear you making excuses for him."

Marzana shook her head emphatically. "No, and I'm not. But it feels icky that we both might have had the same frustrations and we both took them and —"

"Hold up." Mrs. Hakelbarend stopped walking. "You both have the same frustrations. Plenty of people do. Neither of you could control what I or Tumbler was willing to give — or *could* give, in his case — and I'm not going to apologize for that. I made my decisions based on the need to keep people safe, and I stand by those choices. Tumbler fell victim to a whole house being built over the only way into this place. Neither you nor Moth could control how those things made you feel. But you could both control what you did with those feelings."

She pointed back in the direction they'd come, toward the stairwell to the surface. "I'm not going to pretend they're not responsible for what Tasha Cormorant did to fulfill her contract with them; Moth and Kit are responsible for kidnapping a girl. And you . . ." Her mother tucked a wisp of hair behind Marzana's ear. "You chose to break some rules and risk your dad's and my ire — *to save that girl.* I might not think your methods were ideal, and I might hate that you and your friends put yourselves in danger, and I might even suspect that your wanting an adventure partly spurred on your involvement, but still. Rather than becoming a kidnapper — or even a smuggler or a thief, which, given your genetics, would've been my first two guesses for the most likely outcome if you ever decided to go rogue — you became a hero. You see the difference, right?"

"Yeah," Marzana said gratefully. "When you put it like that, I think I do."

"On the other hand," Mrs. Hakelbarend said grimly as they started walking again, "I think this means you take a little more after your father than me. I'm not sure how I feel about that."

They boarded the train, and Brandon started up the engine. "Next stop, Cotgrave Wall," he announced, giving the bellpull three hard yanks.

"Hey, Meddy," J.J. said, dropping into the seat next to her as the train jumped forward. "That was some wicked handling you did with that balloon. Amazing."

"Especially since those punching balloons are kind of heavy," Emilia said. "I couldn't believe the way it bobbed and floated like a regular helium balloon."

Meddy glanced from J.J. to Emilia, then looked back at J.J. for a long minute with pursed lips. "I was just going to ask how you made it deflate like that from all the way across the room."

J.J. stared at her. "I didn't do anything. Not after we stopped the balloon-and-backpack-dance thing. I definitely didn't make it deflate."

"Well, *I* didn't do it," Meddy retorted. "I was helping you set up your message on the playing cards; then I was inside that one locker waiting to start the pyrotechnics with the burning envelope. I had nothing to do with the balloon." She turned to Marzana. "You have it, right? You caught it and put it in your pocket."

Marzana produced the flattened green balloon. She handed it to J.J.

"Yeah," he said, examining it closely. "But this is just an ordinary balloon. It matches my cards because I bought them at the same magic shop, but it's not gimmicked or anything."

"I didn't do it," Meddy insisted again.

"Well, neither did I," J.J. retorted.

The two of them looked at Marzana and Emilia. Emilia put her hands up. "Not guilty."

"I had a knife to my throat, if you recall," Marzana said, lowering her voice so her parents, who were up at the front chatting with Brandon in the cab, wouldn't hear. "Innocent."

"You don't think . . ." Emilia pointed at Meddy.

"I *said* I didn't — oh." Meddy hesitated. "You don't mean me, you mean someone *like* me?"

"But you'd have known," Marzana said. "Wouldn't you?"

Meddy paused again. "I have absolutely no idea, actually."

They all looked down at the balloon. But it was just an ordinary balloon, and it had nothing to say for itself.

It felt like almost no time at all before Brandon began the process of slowing the train as it approached the station inside Marymead, and then there it was: a cave of dusty violet, lit from above by glass vines and petals that shone their light down on the floor of constellations.

The doors slid open, and before Emilia, who was closest, had even stepped all the way out onto the platform, Marzana heard a cry from the balcony above. "They're back! *They're back!*" Ciro leaned over the baluster and waved wildly.

"Hey!" Emilia shouted. "Pipe down! Voices carry!"

"Don't worry," Ciro called down. "Your canary's still at it. Or was a minute ago, anyway. The secret's safe."

Nialla burst into view on the balcony looking as if she'd just run down from the Library, paused for half a second, then plunged down the rest of the stairs. "Mars! Guys!"

Marzana pushed past Emilia and caught Nialla in a hug. "Wait until I tell you," she crowed.

"I'm going to explode!" Nialla sang, hugging her tight and dancing the two of them around. "We did it!" She held Marzana at arm's length. "We did do it, didn't we? Saved the day, caught the bad guys, found the girl?"

Marzana grinned. "We did it."

There were hugs and more hugs as Ciro trotted down the stairs and J.J., Meddy, and Marzana's parents disembarked. Ciro walked up to Marzana's side. "Good to have you back, Captain." For just a moment, his hand squeezed hers.

Marzana managed what she hoped was a nonchalant smile. She returned the squeeze; then Ciro let go, and the moment was over. "Good to be back."

"All right, all right," Emilia barked, tucking the pair of map kites under her arm so that she could wave impatiently at them all. "Can I suggest we get out of here before someone finds us? Please?"

"Why don't you all come to our house?" Mrs. Hakelbarend

suggested. She checked her watch. "It's early for dinner, but I don't particularly care. I'm starving. Brandon? What about you?"

The conductor shrugged. "Sure. If we can get out of here without having to explain ourselves to school officials for hours."

"We can manage that." Marzana turned to Emilia. "Right? Back way?"

"Back way. Follow me."

As they climbed the stairs, Marzana found herself walking between her parents, just ahead of Brandon, who brought up the rear. "This is a good crew you've got here," Mrs. Hakelbarend observed.

"Sure is," Marzana's father said. "Does it have a name?"

"You bet." Marzana grinned. "Nialla and I decided at the beginning that you need a name once you hit five members."

"And?"

"And we're the Thief Knot."

Her parents considered. "It's a good name," Mr. Hakelbarend said, nodding.

Marzana looked up at her friends as they crossed the balcony and continued climbing, their chatter and congratulations falling silent as they reached the top of the second staircase and listened for singing before they stepped out into the Library. She smiled. "I know."

Marzana's mother cleared her throat. "I was thinking, this reminds me of the time I had to put together a special group for a museum job." She looked down at Marzana. "Did I ever tell you about that one?"

"A museum job?" She could count the stories her mother had voluntarily told her on one hand, so it didn't take long to review the catalog. Her smiled widened. "I believe you have not, Mother."

Mrs. Hakelbarend put an arm around Marzana's shoulder. "Tell you on the walk home."

Acknowledgments

This book is long. You probably noticed, because you had to read the whole thing to get to this part. As a result, I have one side of one page to thank all the people who deserve thanks for this book, which is not nearly enough. So here's the most important thing: I could not have written this book without *you*. You know who you are, all of you. I love you, and I am grateful.

Nathan, Griffin, and Tess, you are my everyday support and inspiration. Thank you. I love you all, plus Ed, Maxy[N], Maz, and whoever's in Tank 2 this week. (And to Griffin especially: thank you for giving me the first two lines of "The Three Kings," and, more importantly, thank you for all your encouragement. It means so much to me. You fill my bucket every day.) Chelsea Youss, you are a sister and a saint, and I love you; ditto Sophie Groton—without you guys, I could not have done this. I owe huge thanks, as always, to Gus and the crew at Emphasis Restaurant, as well as to the folks at Coffee RX and Cocoa Grinder in Bay Ridge for giving me places to go to Get Stuff Done. My work wife Cristin Stickles whisked me away to North Carolina and gave me a place to finally finish the first draft of this book, and I can't overstate how much it meant, being able to finish this book in one of the places that gave birth to Nagspeake in the first place. Thanks also to my home away from home, McNally Jackson, and to Sarah, the Saturday crew, and every member of the growing McJ family. And, of course, last but never least, thank you to the people who made this book possible, made it special, and made sure it got to you, dear reader: to Lynne Polvino, for making my stories stronger and making me a better writer with every tale; to Jaime Zollars, for bringing Nagspeake to life yet again, as perfectly as ever; to Sharismar Rodriguez for making this book beautiful, the way she always does; and to Tina Dubois, Dana Spector, and Barry Goldblatt, for All The Other Things, including sanity.

And, most of all, to *you*, for sharing these hours with me. Roam well, friends. We will meet again.

Turn the page for a sneak peek of *The Raconteur's Commonplace Book* by Kate Milford, an enthralling mystery set in the magical world of *Greenglass House*!

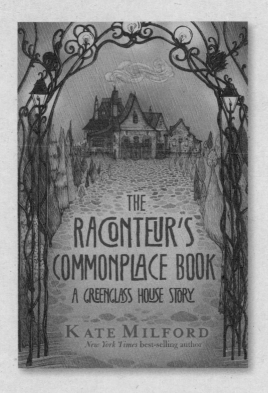

The rain hasn't stopped for a week, and the twelve guests of the Blue Vein Tavern are trapped by flooded roads and the rising Skidwrack River. Among them are a ship's captain, tattooed twins, a musician, and a young girl traveling on her own. To pass the time, they begin to tell stories—each a different type of folklore—that eventually reveal more about their own secrets than they intended.

As the rain continues to pour down—an uncanny, unnatural amount of rain—the guests begin to realize that the entire city is in danger, and not just from the flood. But they have only their stories, and one another, to save them. Will it be enough?

ONE

THE BLUE VEIN TAVERN

THE RAIN HAD NOT STOPPED for a week, and the roads that led to the inn were little better than rivers of muck. This, at least, is what Captain Frost said when he tramped indoors, coated in the yellow mud peculiar to that part of the city, before hollering for his breakfast. The rest of the guests sighed. Perhaps today, they had thought. Perhaps today, their unnatural captivity would end. But the bellowing man calling for eggs and burnt toast meant that, for another day at least, fifteen people would remain prisoners of the river Skidwrack, and the new rivers that had once been roads, and the rain.

They passed the day much as they had passed the day before, and the day before that. Eventually, Mr. Haypotten, the innkeeper, announced supper in half an hour; he apologized for the state of the meals, but without real worry. The Haypottens might run out of provisions eventually, but they had not kept this inn and tavern on the Skidwrack for a quarter of a century and more without seeing a flood or two, and they were well prepared for the whims of the river. "See that?" Mr. Haypotten would say, opening one of the windows in the lounge barroom against the cold and wet and pointing across the porch that wrapped halfway around the inn to indicate a blue step in the stairway leading down to the river. "That's where the river came back in 'fifteen. She doesn't dare come nearer than that. Water won't rise past a blue stair. Isn't that so, Captain?"

"That's so, Marcus," Captain Frost agreed today as he had every day, because Mr. Haypotten kept the captain in very good sherry. But when Mr. Haypotten left the lounge to go help his wife and the kitchen maid to finish preparing supper, the captain sang a different tune. Captain Frost's eyes were deep-lined, his face tanned to mahogany, and his hair and beard bleached to a yellowed bone color from his decades at sea. He felt himself, not inaccurately, to be somewhat expert in weather lore, and when the innkeeper was out of earshot, he muttered that he'd never heard such doss before in his life o' years at sea, and if painting a thing blue were all it took to put water in its place, then how was it every ship in the harbor wasn't sky-colored? Then he finished his very good sherry, pulled on his coat, and stomped into the hall and back out to check the weather and the roads yet again, as he did at every turn of the cracked half-hour glass he tended as religiously as if he were still aboard ship. It was never far from his elbow when he was inside the house, though it meant rearranging the place settings a bit at meals.

He left four guests behind in the lounge. Jessamy Butcher got up from her chair by the window, where she could see how very close the water was actually coming to the much-discussed blue stair, went around the bar, and found the captain's bottle of sherry. She poured herself a glass, then held the bottle up in one thin, gloved hand, offering it silently to the rest of the room. The tattooed young man named Negret declined and went back to the pages he had taken from the pockets of his tweed vest and was stacking together on the bar top: a mismatched collection of liquor labels, scraps of newsprint, wallpaper, remnants of the long, match-like twists of paper called spills that the maid kept in vases in each room for lighting the lamps and fires around the inn, and other scavenged oddments. When he had them where he wanted them, he took a sharp, round-handled awl from a roll of tools that lay open on the countertop before him and, pressing the pages flat with one palm, began to poke holes along one edge.

But his brother, Reever, nodded in response to Jessamy's offer and murmured his thanks as she reached across the bar to pass him a glass. Jessamy tried once again to decide whether or not the pale, brick-haired Colophon brothers were identical under their facial decorations. It was impossible to say. The tattoos were very similar but not quite the same, plus Negret wore his hair long and floppy, while Reever kept his short-cropped and cowlicky. And one didn't like to be rude by looking too long. Jessamy turned to the fourth person in the room. "Mr. Tesserian?"

At his table across the lounge, Al Tesserian looked up from

his half-built castle of playing cards. "Dear God, yes. No, my dear, don't bother," he said as Jessamy made a motion to come around the bar. "Be . . . right . . . there." He placed a card and got up. The other three held a collective breath — but Tesserian's castles didn't dare fall until he gave them permission, which was generally done by calling Maisie, the youngest guest, in to do the honors. Then and only then, when Maisie had pulled away a queen or gusted a sharp breath onto an ace, they toppled spectacularly, cards flying in all directions as if the laws of physics held no sway in the realm to which they truly belonged.

Tesserian accepted his glass with a bow, then returned to his architecture. He paused on his way to look at Negret's handiwork. "Binding a book?"

Negret nodded as he lifted the stack of papers and held the edge he'd perforated up to the light, checking to be sure the holes were lined up the way he wanted.

"It needs covers," Tesserian observed. He felt inside one sleeve, frowned, then took off the battered and narrow-brimmed porkpie hat he wore at all times except meals. From inside the lining, he produced a pair of aces and tossed them on the bar. "Will those do?"

Negret added the cards to his stack, one on top and one on the bottom. "Perfectly, if you can spare them."

Tesserian laughed. "An old gambler always has a couple of spare aces someplace."

Elsewhere in the inn, Petra, the guest who had been there the longest, borrowed from the maid a key to one of the countless glass cases that occupied walls and corners all around the inn so that she and Maisie could take down one of Mrs. Haypotten's music boxes, very carefully wind it, and dance for a bit.

Maisie Cerrajero was young and had been traveling alone to meet the aunt who was taking her in, with no luggage but an old ditty bag that held everything she owned. Each day someone said something along the lines of, "Won't your auntie be relieved when she gets here and sees that you're safe?" Most often that someone was Mrs. Haypotten, who had a habit of misplacing her spectacles or her ring of keys or her best little sewing scissors and was never quite sure what, other than "Thank you," she ought to say when Maisie inevitably found them for her, no matter in what unlikely place they'd been left. Flummoxed, she always came out with something like, "Won't your auntie be so happy to see what a nice, polite, helpful girl you are when she gets here, dear?"

Petra, however, never said anything like that, not even when Maisie found the dragonfly-shaped hair clip she had lost at breakfast two days before, half-hidden by the hem of one of the dining room curtains. Petra instead went for a key and a music box, because the unspoken truth was that, given the volume of rain and the slope of the hills, if Auntie had been on the roads at the wrong time, she was never coming — and Maisie was a girl, not a fool. But when that girl danced, sending her short sleek dark hair fluttering and the pleated skirt of her jumper frock swishing around her knees, her face lost its fear. And Mrs. Haypotten had an improbable collection of music boxes — forty-one that Petra and Maisie had managed to count — no two of which, as far as they could determine, played the same song.

Today, with the dragonfly back in its customary place among Petra's dark bobbed curls, they picked one from the tall cabinet in the parlor, which, like the lounge, looked out over the riverfront. The cabinet had the thick, bubble-pocked green glass that was the only sort that could be made from Nagspeake sand, and Mrs. Haypotten had told them it held some of her favorite pieces, so they took extra care. Maisie chose a music box shaped like a kite with a terrifyingly delicate-looking ceramic key. She wound it gently, the eggshell-colored winder stark against the brown of her fingers. When she set it down and lifted the lid, it took a few notes before the tune resolved itself into "Riverward." Maisie hummed along as she spun herself in a wide-armed circle, swirling her shawl behind her as she turned, making the embroidered chrysanthemums upon it float in the air.

Sullivan, the young man who'd been sitting in a chair facing the fire, his eyes glazing over as they stared up at the big antique map that hung above the mantel, shoved himself abruptly to his feet and hurried out, briefly grasping Petra's wrist in apology as he stumbled past. That was unusual enough to make Petra look after him curiously. In the seven days since he'd arrived, Petra had never seen Sullivan do anything without an almost eerie sort of grace. He was so implausibly elegant when he moved and so bloody good-looking to boot that it was hard to believe he wasn't a hallucination. Petra had had to stop herself more than once from sticking him with a pin as he crossed a room just to see if then, finally, he'd make a misstep.

But apparently all it took was "Riverward." Interesting.

The old woman in the corner, thinner even than Jessamy Butcher, rocked her chair gently in time with the song as the music box wound down. Her skin, like Maisie's and Petra's both, was dark, but ruddy here and grayish there, uneven and slightly pocked, while Maisie had the clear and perfect skin of a child and Petra the kind of faultless complexion it would've taken a motion-picture actress an hour in makeup to achieve. The lady they all called Madame Grisaille spoke little, but she hummed as she rocked, and although it wasn't a loud sound, Petra and Maisie could feel it like a thrum in their bones as they danced, as if Madame's tune flowed through her and into the very boards, the very nails in the floor, and back up through their feet, so that it could sway with them.

"Madame is a dancer," Maisie had whispered to Petra the first time she had noticed this.

"When she was younger, you think?" Petra had whispered back. This had been three days ago, one evening when they were all on their way into the dining room, where Madame was always seated first out of unspoken respect for—for what? For her age, perhaps, or for her stateliness. If watching Sullivan was like watching a mirage that was too beautiful to be real, watching Madame was like watching a queen trying badly to disguise what she was, too regal for her sham ordinariness to be believed.

"No," Maisie had replied softly. "Not just when she was

younger. Now. She's a dancer. She wants to dance when we do, but she holds herself back."

"Why would she do that?"

"I don't know." But the girl's eyes had begun to glow. "Maybe it's a secret."

"That she's a dancer is a secret?"

"No . . ." Maisie had looked thoughtfully at Madame as she followed Petra to the sideboard, where a buffet supper had been laid out and where Maisie had found a tortoiseshell button that had gone missing from Mrs. Haypotten's housedress earlier that day. "But she *has* a secret, so she doesn't dance. Because you can't dance and hide who you are."

Petra had thought that this was a very wise observation, and said so. She had also thought that if dancing showed one for who she was, Maisie danced like someone with no secrets to keep. That idea made her smile. But she hadn't wanted to make Maisie feel self-conscious, and sometimes the girl's dancing revealed as plainly as tears that she was carrying something that, when she remembered it, made her very, very sad. So Petra kept her thoughts to herself.

Today Madame Grisaille hummed along with "Riverward," and then "Gaslight," which was the tune plinked out by Maisie's favorite music box, a chrysanthemum-shaped one that nearly matched the flowers on her shawl. Then, another new thing, as if Sullivan tripping over himself hadn't been strange enough: as the sun began to set across the river and the chrysanthemum played its last, slow notes, Madame stopped rocking. She reached into the white fur hand muff she always carried with her, even indoors, and took a new music box out of it.

This one was plainer at first glance, just a round box of gold and ceramic with a scene painted on the lid. She raised one finger to her lips and began to wind it. There was something so secretive about the motion, Petra instinctively checked to be sure the parlor door was closed and that the three of them were alone.

"This one is from my room upstairs," Madame murmured in a voice gravelly with age. "I don't know that Mrs. Haypotten would be comfortable with my carrying it about, so we shall keep this between ourselves. But it plays a remarkable song."

She finished winding, held it out on one spread hand, and lifted the lid. Maisie turned her head sideways, trying to make sense of the now-upside-down painting on the lid — two people sitting at a fingerpost, perhaps? — but only for a second, because when the song began, it was everything the girl's dancer's heart could have wished for from a piece of music. It was joy and love and exquisite pain; it was danger and the thrill of adventure and the certainty of failure and the thrum of hope. It was dream and nightmare; it was flight; it was winter and summer and water and stone and metal and fire and earth, and Maisie danced as she had never imagined dancing before.

After a moment, Madame handed the music box to Petra, and at last, perhaps because it was only the three of them in the room, the old woman joined the young girl and they danced together hand in hand, and suddenly Maisie understood why Madame had refused to dance before. And she knew what the old woman's secret was, too, and she understood the knowledge for the gift it was and wrapped her arms around it, concealing it in swirling embroidered chrysanthemums as the two of them whirled together, both dancing now like people with no secrets to keep as the sunset over the river painted them in golden light, orange light, crimson light. Madame caught Petra's eye over the girl's head, and the two women smiled at each other.

Perhaps the notes found their way out through cracks in the windows, drifted on the rainy wind along the length of the porch facing the Skidwrack, and snuck back into the house through another chipped pane of glass in a different room altogether. Perhaps they had other ways of making themselves heard. Either way, beyond the hall, beyond the stairs, two people in the lounge heard the song too.

Negret Colophon, stitching an elaborate binding into his scrap-paper book, dropped his needle in surprise, then quickly picked it up again and pretended not to have heard anything. Jessamy Butcher, who had been deep in conversation with Reever Colophon a short way down the bar, was less subtle. Her head turned so quickly in the direction of the music that several joints in her neck and shoulders cracked. The popping might even have been audible had her gloved fingers not at the same moment crushed her sherry glass to fragments and powder.

Reever, who had at that moment been debating whether it was time to invite Miss Butcher to continue their conversation in a more private corner of the inn, jerked back as glass and liquor flew. Jessamy did not appear to have noticed what she had done. "Remarkable," she said in tones of quiet wonder, ignoring his stare, along with those of Negret from a few seats away and Tesserian from the table with the card castle.

"What is?" Reever asked.

"That song." Jessamy breathed out, a strange huff that wasn't quite a sigh.

Reever looked back down at the bar top between them and saw that she still clutched pieces of the glass she had destroyed. He took her hands in his and gently uncurled her fingers. One by one he removed the shards carefully from her palms, where small spots of blood had begun to seep through her pristine pink gloves. Then he held her hand for a moment when he had finished, watching her face.

She did not appear to notice any of this, and he could hear no song.

After a moment, Jessamy took her hands back and got to her feet. Self-consciously she tucked a stray bit of hair into place and smoothed it back with her palm, a gesture that left a small rose-tinted streak among the pale blond finger waves over her ear. She walked out of the lounge and across the hall, then slipped into the parlor. Petra and Madame looked over sharply, but when Jessamy closed the door behind her, they relaxed.

The song, improbably, had not yet begun to slow. "Do you want to dance too?" Maisie asked, reaching for the newcomer's hand, ignoring the blood that marked Jessamy's gloved palm like stigmata.

Jessamy spun Maisie around by the fingers that held hers,

but her feet stood firm on the floor as she shook her head. "I don't dance," she said with a smile. "But I know that song well. I tried to play it once, but it's more difficult than it sounds. I was a musician, you know. Long ago, back in another lifetime."

Musician or not, Miss Butcher is a dancer too, thought Maisie, who could always tell. *I wonder what* her *secret is.*